COLD DAY
IN JULY

COLD DAY
IN JULY

STELLA CAMERON

Wheeler Publishing • Chivers Press
Waterville, Maine USA • Bath, England

This Large Print edition is published by Wheeler Publishing, USA and by Chivers Press, England.

Published in 2002 in the U.S. by arrangement with Kensington Books, an imprint of Kensington Publishing Corp.

Published in 2003 in the U.K. by arrangement with Kensington Publishing Corp.

U.S. Hardcover 1-58724-339-3 (Romance Series)
U.K. Hardcover 0-7540-1891-1 (Windsor Large Print)

The text of this Large Print edition is unabridged.
Other aspects of the book may vary from the original edition.

Set in 16 pt. Plantin by Christina S. Huff.

Printed in the United States on permanent paper.

British Library Cataloguing-in-Publication Data available

Library of Congress Cataloging-in-Publication Data

Cameron, Stella.
    Cold day in July / Stella Cameron.
        p. cm.
    ISBN 1-58724-339-3 (lg. print : hc : alk. paper)
    1. Medical examiners (Law) — Fiction.   2. Forensic
    pathologists — Fiction.   3. Women physicians — Fiction.
    4. Louisiana — Fiction.   5. Large type books.   I. Title.
    PS3553.A4345 C65 2002
    813'.54—dc21   2002033094

For Suzanne Simmons Guntrum

ACKNOWLEDGMENTS

In a place filled with good people I met some of the best. These folks got into my story, into my quest for the details I already felt in my bones but didn't know about for sure.

Julian Savoy, an extraordinary guide, never told me he "didn't know," only that he'd "get right on that." And so he did, dedicating himself to providing me not just with tales only a true Cajun spirit could tell, but with facts, maps, and charts that decorated my office and kept me feeling I'd never left Louisiana. It was with Julian and his wife, Gerry, that I visited Breaux Bridge and learned about those dance halls that are unique to the state. Thank you, Julian and Gerry.

Connie and Al Perry, Lorna Broussard, Karin and Irvin David — and "the Ladies of Louisiana" — opened their hearts and their homes to me and gave me information far more valuable than they know! Thanks to each of you.

Thank you, Josh Perry, for your kindness.

Suzanne and John Viescas shared their knowledge of primitive art and have my gratitude.

And what would I have done without Giselle,

Bryony, and Tess McKenzie, Australian friends who taught me everything I know about poodles. Thank you, ladies.

Kate Duffy, what can I say but thank you — yet again.

Last, and most, love and thanks to Jerry Cameron, alligator man and camera-toter.

PROLOGUE

Three miles and she'd be home.

She was close enough to smell safety but not close enough to touch it. And the car didn't feel right, hadn't felt as if it were responding quite right since she'd started it. She got a sensation that she couldn't rely on the engine, and that this time it would let her down, not that she could always trust her premonitions. Her imagination often went wild in the night.

These late drives home were getting worse. Why couldn't she have been born to love darkness, the black on moonless black of the hours after midnight and before dawn? Rather than taking this suffocating back route along the bayou, which was shorter, she could start driving the better lit main street through Toussaint, then cut down Bonanza Alley to St. Cécil's and the parish house.

Only 2.4 miles and she'd be home.

The car jerked. It had been jerking since she left Pappy's Dancehall. She stepped on the pedal and it sank to the floor with no resistance.

2.3 miles.

Move, move, move. God, get me there just this one

more time and I'll light all the candles in the church.

Out of gas? The needle bounced. *I filled up last night. It's gotta be full now.* Could be more of an incline than she thought and it was throwing the gauge off. *Oh, yeah, it's those big ol' hills of Louisiana.* This was the land of the Big Flat, and people who remarked on it weren't talking about tires.

2.2 miles? Hell, no. She'd gone farther than that. *Come on. I'm bein' good now. Have been for a long time, months. Listen up, someone! I'm doin' my best to put all the bad stuff behind me. Don't punish me some more, I've been punished plenty.*

2.1 miles. Still making progress. Ah, who was she kidding? The engine had quit and she was coasting. And she was going to throw up. Sweat seeped from her back and beneath her arms. Her hair stuck to her neck and face.

The only sounds she heard were grit beneath the wheels, and live oak branches slapping against the car as it rolled to a stop on the rock-and-grass verge.

She came to a standstill with drifts of gray Spanish moss cloaking the windshield.

If she dared, she'd call the law for help, but she didn't want any special notice from Deputy Spike Devol. There wasn't anyone else she could bring out here at this time of night.

The doors were locked. Dawn wasn't too far away. Why not stay where she was until it got light? She rolled down her window an inch, and the nocturnal chorale burst inside on air that would heat up again before it ever cooled down. Katydids calling, and the staccato whine of cicadas — frogs grunting their own descants. And the bayou was there even if she couldn't see it, the nebulous surface of the water silently sucking at drenched banks. As a child she'd giggled at the sight of slick-coated nutrias sliding between marsh grasses that thrived with muddy roots. Tonight the idea of the soup made from those big white rats gagged her.

Before she'd left Toussaint to sing at Pappy's she'd stopped for gas. Could be she had a hole in the tank . . . or that someone had made a hole in the tank?

She had enemies, but they wouldn't come around to punish her now. She'd outrun them.

In the past week or so kids had been caught syphoning gas from cars and trucks around town. Damn their scaly little hides. That's what this was all about. Tomorrow night — tonight now — she'd be at Pappy's listening to everyone complain about the same thing. Two and a half miles wasn't any distance to walk, not since she'd cleaned up her act and got healthy. She knew the way well. This would be a piece of cake.

Yeah, so why can't I believe my own happy talk? Staying put until morning was the safest thing to do.

A heel could kick the glass in. Or a good sized rock could smash it — and her.

In her purse she carried a gun, a very small gun, but it could kill real well. She'd never actu-

11

ally fired the thing, but she'd been shown how. If someone crept up on the car, she'd shoot them. She would be fine where she was, and every minute that passed brought daylight closer.

There wasn't enough air. Bugs slid through the narrow opening in the window and buzzed around her head. Bugs were all the company she had out here, and they weren't going to do her more than minimal harm. *Swallow and breathe and get out . . . and walk.*

The door, as she unlocked it, ground as if muffled by a quilt. With her purse strap over her shoulder, she slid out and shut the door behind her. The pencil flashlight she had on her keys gave only a pinpoint beam of light, but even that was comforting.

Instinct — and alligator sense — made her walk in the middle of the narrow old road. Any markings had disappeared long ago. The penlight bobbled over the ground like a drunken glowworm. Faster and faster she walked until she reached a sharp bend in the road and looked back. Shapes of trees and swaying moss made an entrance to a black tunnel, and when she faced forward again, it was toward another hole filled by the night.

Just beneath her skin, flesh and nerve crawled. And even as she sweated she turned cold until her face flushed again, and her head seemed about to burst.

Something cracked. *Oh, shit.* More cracking,

splintering, the steady breaking of brittle wood — a faint whirring.

She screamed, then clamped her mouth shut and carefully withdrew the gun from her purse. Holding it in front of her, trying not to shake, she shone the penlight on the barrel. Let them see the chrome gleam and know they weren't playing games with a pushover.

Silence.

They must have seen the gun and it had scared them off. Walking on, she kept the gun in her hand and made sure it could be seen from time to time.

The sooner she got back to her room at the parish house, the sooner she could lock herself in and climb into bed. This was never going to happen to her again, she'd make sure of that. She ran until she couldn't drag another breath down her throat and had to pause.

Still quiet . . . Oh, please let her get out of this. The steady crackling started up once more. Sticks breaking, then a noisy *whump* into the brush as if someone had fallen, and a sound like breaking glass. *Footsteps.* Tears started, tears and grating sounds from her throat. Feet thudded, not on the road but in the trees along its edge. Heavy footsteps. To her right when she turned around. The light did nothing, except . . . She screamed again, and again. *There.* Something solid passed through the minuscule shaft, and that something had to be close because the light was weak and didn't reach far.

Running, pounding along, stumbling and catching her balance again, she left the road and took off through the trees. The church was no distance now. The thought cleared a cool place at the center of her panic. Her purse slid from her shoulder to her elbow, and she tried to hitch it back but couldn't. She had to have her hands free and let the purse fall. Tomorrow she'd come back for it . . . if she could.

It didn't have to be a person who moved through the flashlight beam. Lots of things moved out here.

Her legs turned formless and gave out every few steps. Her knees hit rough ground, and she righted herself only to fall headlong over a stump.

Crying didn't help. The sound of her own gasping breaths deafened her, but she scrambled on until she had to stop, to stop just for a moment. Her heart would surely explode. Her imagination had gone wild. She was alone and didn't trust her own company, that was all.

The speck of light turned brown. Soon she wouldn't even have that.

A shadow cut the weak shaft once more, and from the heavy thumps that followed, the shadow wore big shoes.

Backing away, she tripped yet again and fell to her back, completely winded.

She fought with air that didn't want to enter her lungs, and she held the gun in both hands while she squirmed to her knees and stood up. The footsteps, or whatever they were, had stopped for now.

Run to that church, girl, and don't look back till you're closin' the door. Not then, if you can stop yourself.

From the trees she finally emerged at the end of Bonanza Alley and saw the white stone church glistening in the center of the church-yard. She needed to reach the rectory but would never make it without a rest.

Everything would be fine now. Once inside St Cécil's she'd be safe. No one would follow her in there.

Walk, don't run. March along with purpose. One, two, one two. You're the one in control now. She gave a short laugh. Probably had been in control all along — and on her own. Tomorrow she'd really laugh about it.

A gate in a white wooden fence opened onto the narrow strip of graveyard in front of the church. Important folk got laid to rest on this side. The common types had to be glad of a spot out back or in an overflow several blocks away. She let the gate creak shut behind her and hurried along the path to the steps that led up to the door.

The creak she heard didn't have to be identified. The gate, opening again. She clamped a hand over her racing heart, reached the steps, and glanced over her shoulder when she got to the door. The gate was swinging shut, but she couldn't see a soul. Breeze must have taken it. Only there wasn't a breeze.

Without stopping, she went into the church and dashed, as quietly as she could, to the seats closest to the altar. Crouched there, grateful for the low-powered electric candles that burned in sconces mounted on the walls — between carved Stations of the Cross — she could lean out a little to see if anyone entered. She could also keep an eye on an exit door at the opposite side of the building. That's where she'd go if he followed her.

The church floor was of stone, and the cold felt good beneath her injured knees. She spread a hand on a brass grating in the floor and smiled at its smooth, cool surface. This was a holy place. Teenage thugs didn't want to tangle with Father Cyrus Payne, who was pastor, or his administrative assistant Madge Pollard — and least of all with Oribel Scully, who ran just about everything and wouldn't hesitate to go straight to the parents.

The door started to open. Not the front door, but the one she'd intended to use for her escape. If they wanted her badly enough, she'd never make it out by the way she'd come. *Quick, hide before they see where you are.*

Without hesitating, she scurried, hunched double, into the octagonal space at the foot of the belfry stairs. And up those stairs she went, gripping the banisters at one side and running her hand along the craggy stone wall at the other. Around and around. The parish of St. Cécil's was proud of its bells. She reached the level where red-and-white striped ropes hung, but she didn't slow down. Upward again, to a platform that ringed the tower, then up to the top of the belfry where the bells hung in a room with another gallery. This time there was a door to close, and she closed it — and turned the key in the lock.

The only way to reach her was through that locked door, and it would take one big son of a gun to break it down.

Silence was absolute this time. And it lasted. Skies beyond the open archways into the belfry hadn't begun to lighten, but there was a little cooling on what currents of air slipped in.

One thing was certain, she wouldn't be going anywhere before morning. She sat on the floor, leaned against the wall, and let her eyes drift shut. All the progress she'd made with straightening out her life hadn't been enough. She was still a mess, but tonight had shaken her back into action. This time she would really make a fresh start, move on maybe, quit singing, and get a different kind of job. One day she might even be able to look for the family she'd moved away from years ago. She wanted to show her own folks that she was someone worth loving. If she had roots, she wouldn't be alone and scared anymore.

A scrape, followed by a clink and rattle, had her on her feet and pointing the gun. The key had fallen from the keyhole to the floor. It had been pushed through from the other side — with another key, and this one turned in the lock.

Her one escape would be through the openings to the belfry . . . or she could reach beneath the bells for a rope, and slide down.

Click, click, click. The key revolved, and the door opened inch by inch until she looked into familiar eyes.

Unbelievable. This was supposed to be a joke?

She bowed her head, dropped the gun to her side, and contemplated revenge before she looked straight at the prankster. "You," she said. "You'll be the death of me."

ONE

Oribel Scully had shown him into the kitchen at the rectory. That was a friendly sort of start — or he'd take it as such. Strangers wouldn't be brought straight in here.

"Who'd you say you were?" Oribel asked.

So much for the friendly bit. "I'm Marc Girard, Miz Scully. I grew up outside of Toussaint. I'm stayin' at the old house. I'm in town to clear up a few family matters." His family had kept their distance from the town, but he'd heard his mother mention Oribel and how she ran St. Cécil's Parish.

A frown all but made Oribel's bright blue eyes sink out of sight beneath overhanging brows. "What family matters? Seems to me you Girards moved on and didn't leave nothin' behind exceptin' the half the town your pappy owns and rents out." She pulled the front of her daisy-covered shirt away from her compact body and flapped it. The blades of an overhead fan chased each other but didn't do much for the stifling heat in the room. "That what you come for, to put all those good people out of their businesses so your pappy can build something fancy and make more money — bein' you don't already have enough?"

He would be charming the way he knew how to be. A soft laugh usually took the edge off things. "Now, Miz Scully, you know the Girards wouldn't do a thing like that. We think Toussaint's just fine the way it is." It would be finer if he could have a glass of water. "Except for all the trouble we've been hearing about lately. We don't like that at all."

Probably in her mid-fifties and well cared for, Oribel had a pleasant enough face when she wasn't cross. She was cross now. "Your pappy —"

"My father's dead, ma'am. Been dead several years. Died in Florida after they moved. My mother misses him, like you'd expect. But she's one who likes to take care of herself. I deal with the bigger business matters is all."

"You don't say." Oribel's features yielded, and she waved him to a chair at the worn oak table Marc remembered from his one childhood visit. "Iced tea? It's sun tea, mind. There's some who says it's the best in all Louisiana."

"I'd be grateful," he said, but he glanced repeatedly at the door to the rest of the house. What he'd come to this town for wasn't pleasant, and he had no interest in renewing acquaintances for any reason that didn't further his task. "Smells like an apple pie in the oven. Cinnamon, too. That stove doesn't look a day older than when I last saw it, and I bet it puts out as tasty a dish as ever."

The range and stove were finished in a mottled gray, and the brand had been scrubbed to nothing readable. A spit still hung over a fireplace in an alcove next to an expanse of worn steel draining board.

"I'm not the cook, me," Oribel said with her nostrils flared. "More important things to do." A tall, frosty glass of tea appeared on the table in front of Marc. Sunlight through the windows made it glow like thin honey around ice cubes. A slice of lemon and a sprig of mint reminded him of long ago summer days in his mother's kitchen.

"Yes, ma'am. Thank you, ma'am."

"When'd you get here?"

"Just a couple of days ago."

"Where you stayin'?"

"Clouds End."

"Lordy." Oribel slapped her thighs. "I thought that place was fallen down. Ain't set eyes on it since I don't know when. Longer'n since I set eyes on you, and that's gotta be twenty years."

"Thirteen or so," Marc corrected her, not that it hurt his feelings to be forgotten in a town he'd been glad to leave behind.

"Well, you better get yourself a room at Doll and Gator's place — if you're plannin' to spend another night, that is. You don't want to be out there in whatever mess Clouds End is in."

He wouldn't tell Oribel that none of the Majestic Hotel's twelve rooms were available — to him — or that Doll Hibbs had almost expired when he walked into the place. "When will the

21

pastor get back — or is he here somewhere? I'd like a few words with him." From what Marc could gather, Father Cyrus Payne was a rock, a cool-headed man to whom much of the town turned when things got out of hand. Each time he'd mentioned the man's name it had been met with fond reverence.

"He's out. With that Madge Pollard." Disapproval hung heavy and weighted down the corners of Oribel's brightly lipsticked mouth. "Should be back by now." She put on thick glasses and looked at her watch.

Marc cleared his throat. "How's Deacon Scully, Miz Scully? The pastor must find him a real help. The load isn't so light in Toussaint these days."

"Don't know what you mean by that." She patted her close-cut gray curls. "All we got here is law-abiding folks who mind their own business but help out when they're needed."

"That's good to hear. I —"

"I expect Harold Scully's just peachy. Him and that Winifred Crane."

Marc drank some of his tea and tried to make sense of what she'd said. "Miz Crane is still president of the Altar Society?"

"She was before she ran off with my Harold. But I don't ask for no pity. The Good Lord deals with the likes of them. In time a broken heart mends." She sniffed and blinked rapidly.

"I'm sorry," Marc said.

"I've got a life to get on with. We all do. Some

of us are interested in more than rollin' around in a sweaty bed of sin."

He got a vague picture of skinny Harold Scully with his long strands of limp white hair and bobbing Adam's apple and Winifred Crane, a cheerful, pleasantly buxom lady who was older than Oribel, probably as old as Harold, who had to be sixty-five or so. The picture wouldn't expand to placing the couple in a "sweaty bed of sin."

"Well . . . I'd better wait for Father."

"She went after him, y'know. Started wearing all those short skirts and rubbing knees with him at council meetings."

"Hmm."

"Can't tell an apple by its skin."

"I suppose not." He couldn't stop his feet from twitching.

"What happened to that sister of yours?"

Marc set his glass down firmly and leaned back in his chair. If he knew the answer to the question he wouldn't be here. "Amy's busy." Wherever she was, she might be busy. Marc didn't know with any certainty where that might be, but he was growing a hunch that had the power to make him sweat. He was relieved Oribel didn't know her son-in-law, Chauncy Depew, had never stopped messing around with Amy — and he was sure she didn't or he wouldn't be sitting at this table and drinking the woman's sun tea. Chauncey was married to Oribel's only chick, Precious.

"Toussaint wasn't good enough for any of you Girards." Oribel had poured herself a glass of tea. With every sip she took her teeth clattered on the rim.

He didn't respond to her remark and stared through the windows instead. Heat rose in quivering layers of steam off the bayou, drew porous films over polished water that moved like warm lime taffy. The lawns surrounding the house were more white clover than grass, and bees hovered and dove from flower to flower. If he got closer to the panes and looked hard right he'd be able to see St. Cécil's, and any tomb that wasn't moss-covered would be glinting white like mica.

"Overstepped myself, me," Oribel said. She stood at the other end of the table and looked outside just as Marc was doing. "Been harder than I like to let on. I've said too much to you, and it wasn't called for. Holding your head up isn't always easy, if you know what I mean."

"I know what you mean," Marc said. It didn't cost much to be decent — if it was to someone who wasn't a threat.

Footsteps sounded in the passageway outside the kitchen, and a man's voice said, "Thanks, Madge. I don't know what I'd do without you. Keep a list of people asking for appointments, but tell them you'll have to call back. I want a chance to put them in some sort of order. Let me know if you hear from Jilly or Joe Gable."

The man who came into the kitchen wore

24

jeans and a dark brown check shirt with a worn collar. The shirt looked pretty good on him even if it did belong in a ragbag. When he saw Marc he said, "Good morning. Cyrus Payne," and shot out a tanned hand that was anything but soft.

"Marc Girard." He returned the hard handshake. "I'm hoping you can spare me a few private minutes."

Father Cyrus had stopped smiling. He was as tall as Marc, and that was tall. Marc doubted any priest's job would be made easier by looking like this handsome, dark-haired man.

"Don't mind me," Oribel said. "I'll be in and out, but you'll be quiet enough here." She moved a pile of books from a counter to the table and sat down. Apparently she'd decided to start out by being "in."

"How can I help you?" the priest asked.

"His family owns a lot of Toussaint," Oribel said, turning pages. "Made their money in sugar. His pappy's dead and his mama lives in Florida. Marc never did mix with people hereabouts. Hightailed it out of the area to go to school and never came back. He's here now to see about making more money out of the town. His sister wasn't any better —"

"I'm not here to do anything about our holdings in Toussaint," Marc said tightly, but he relaxed when he saw the priest shake his head slightly and smile.

"It's an honor to meet another person from

one of the old families, Mr. Girard. Let's go into my study."

"Madge is in there," Oribel piped up.

"This way," Father Payne said. "To the left, then right."

Marc went ahead of the other man along a corridor with dark wood wainscotting that rose halfway up the walls and the same dark wood on the floors. Carpet runners had probably been green and brown but were too faded for a new-comer to be sure. Photographs of happy people and places in the Quarter hung between holy pictures. Lemon-scented wax tickled the nose.

"Oribel is a good woman," Father Payne said. "She's suffered some disappointments and they've made her defensive."

"I'm not offended by her," Marc said, and lied. As a teenager chafing to run with the kids who were having the good times, he hadn't un-derstood his parents' insistence that he and Amy stay out of town other than to allow Marc to go to school there. Now he began to think he understood their reasons all too well.

"Straight ahead," Father Payne said. "It's the first door on the other side of the front door. Good view of the church — and anyone coming to the door here." He chuckled. "I like to be prepared."

Marc decided he could like Cyrus Payne. The man was open, but then he guessed a priest was supposed to be.

The hall was small, with another faded rug at

its center, this one vaguely rose-colored. Stairs on one side rose to the second floor. Someone had run amuck with wallpaper . . . above the wainscotting, ducks in flight repeated all the way to the top of the stairwell.

A high-topped sneaker, laces trailing, descended on the hall floor. Its owner would be sitting a couple of stairs from the bottom and leaning against the wall Marc couldn't yet see. A second sneaker joined the first, and a thin, brown-haired boy stepped forward. His hazel eyes passed over Marc without interest and settled on the priest. A large grin showed square teeth with a gap between the two upper middle ones, and his freckled nose wrinkled with pleasure.

"Hey there, Wally," Father Payne said and didn't sound surprised to see the boy. "Isn't this errand time for your folks?"

Wally nodded and his smile disappeared. Marc didn't recall seeing a kid look quite so worried, certainly not in quite so grown-up a way. It was hard to say how old he was, but Marc placed him around nine. Maybe ten.

Father Payne put an arm around Wally's shoulders. "This is Marc Girard. He grew up in Toussaint just like you. Do you know that big old house on the way to Breaux Bridge — the one where we went to see Cletus?"

"Clouds End," Wally said in an unexpectedly whispery voice. He lowered his eyes. "My folks said . . . They mentioned Mr. Girard was here and that he owns our hotel." He reached behind him for a heavy brown sack folded over at the top and containing something square.

"Nice to meet you," Marc said, not missing the wary way the boy held the bag tightly and sized him up. "It's my mother who owns that property. And she never gives it a thought because your parents do such a great job of running it."

The slight drop of Wally's shoulders suggested those words had taken a little tension away.

As quickly as Wally's shoulders had lowered, they rose again. He stared into Father Payne's face as if he could make himself understood without saying a word.

"Wally —"

"Father" — Wally cut the priest off — "it's, um, serious."

"Don't worry," Father Payne told him. "I've got something to attend to; then I'll come and find you outside. Okay?"

The kid's nod wasn't enthusiastic, but he left at once, letting himself out of the front door and closing it behind him.

"My buddy," Father Payne said and smiled. He walked past Marc and said, "In we go," opening the door he'd indicated. "Come and meet Madge. She tries to keep us all sane. If anyone could, she would, but she doesn't have much to work with."

Marc entered a study he'd enjoy having himself. A woman, talking on the phone, sat at a small desk that faced what was more a large, scarred cherry table than a desk.

"If this is a bad time, Father Payne —"

"Call me Cyrus, please." When Madge hung up the phone, he added, "This is Madge Pollard. I'm told she's a foreigner. She comes from Rayne."

Rayne was a town around ten miles from Toussaint. Rayne, Frog Capital of the World, as it was billed, and murals of frogs on every wall in town were intended to validate the title. "I'm surprised they let strangers like you in," he told her. "I'm Marc Girard."

She said, "I know. I've been given some great descriptions, not that I wouldn't have taken a second look all on my own and asked who you were." Her grin made sure the comment wasn't a come-on.

"Well, thank you, ma'am — I think."

Her smile was a killer. "They're gonna give me the keys to this town any day," she said, her Cajun lilt as pronounced as Marc's own. "All I gotta do is charm a couple cottonmouths out of the bayou and I'm in. I already got the basket and pipe."

"Let me know about the ceremony and I'll drop by." He liked Madge Pollard and her springy black curls, and he didn't miss the way she looked at the priest. The gentle pleasure in her dark eyes, innocuous because she kept her demeanor light, spoke volumes.

"I expect you two would like some privacy," she said, getting up and revealing a nice body, nicely covered in all the right places and discreetly showcased in a soft blue dress that clung just a little. "I'll put the phones through to the sitting room and work in there, Cyrus. Three calls so far on account of our visitor here. You are the man of the moment, Marc Girard. The town's in an uproar. There's folks don't like you."

"They don't know me. Most of them never set eyes on me."

"They're expectin' to, and they're lining up to make reconciliation with Cyrus."

"Why?" Marc asked, suspicious. "They plannin' to confess first, then take out a hit on me? Didn't think that worked."

Cyrus and Madge laughed aloud, and Madge gathered papers and left the room.

When they were on their own, Cyrus looked at a brass clock on the mantel and said, "Noon. May I offer you a beer? Lemonade? Glass of wine."

"No thanks, but don't let me stop you."

He shook his head. "Pick a seat." He chose the window seat for himself and crossed long legs. "Don't hurry. Start when you're ready."

So spoke the man of God, who listened to the woes of his flock every day. They said priests heard everything, but Marc figured what he was about to suggest to Cyrus might get his attention.

Settling himself in a swivel oak office chair with a red corduroy seat cushion, Marc followed instructions and didn't hurry. He was going to say things that would take the shine off a peaceful day. A row of *Hornblower* books in one of the bookcases that covered the wall behind the big cherry table didn't fit with his assumptions about what priests read, what they thought about. He almost smiled to see Delderfield's *God Is an Englishman.* But it was a large collection of mysteries that really surprised Marc.

He looked at Cyrus.

Cyrus looked back. He didn't smile.

The strains of a Zydeco number beat rhythmically from the next room.

"Madge loves her music."

"A lot of people do," Marc said, noncommittal. He'd begun to feel cold. This man might tell him he'd been drinking moonshine and advise him to sleep it off. "Bonnie Blue did."

Cyrus grew still. Marc realized it was hard to know if the man's eyes were blue or green, but they were fixed on his visitor's face.

"I read about it in the papers. And Cletus — he looks after Clouds End for us, but you know that — he's been filling me in on what he knows about the woman."

"Why do you care?" Cyrus said. He made as if to stand but changed his mind.

"I have a big interest in this town. On my mother's behalf. I'd be lettin' her down if I

31

didn't keep an eye on how things are. I read that you knew Miz Blue."

"Yes." Cyrus let out a long, long breath. "We gave her a room in this house. As far as we know she came from New Orleans, where something bad had happened to her. When she arrived in town she had no money to speak of and no place to go. We decided to help her. She had a job at Pappy's Dancehall over —"

"I know where it is."

"Yes, I suppose you do. Bonnie sang there. Never heard her myself, but I've been told she had a good voice."

"What do you know about her?"

Cyrus looked blank. He pushed open a window and let in a rush of humid air, and the scent of roses. "I know one of the Swamp Doggies — that's the band at Pappy's place — one of them met Bonnie in New Orleans and offered her a job with the band. Vince Fox, who plays the fiddle. He's a decent family man with a big heart. Something like that pays almost nothing, but she jumped at it because almost nothing was better than nothing at all."

"What did she look like? The only picture in the paper was taken at a distance and I couldn't make out a thing."

"Dark hair. Plenty of it. Quite long. A lot of makeup, but show business people do that."

"How old?"

The priest spread his hands. "Hard to say. She didn't make any secret about having used drugs and hitting bottom on more than one occasion. She had tracks on her arms, but she said she was clean and I believed her. Maybe she was fifty. Maybe older — or a lot younger. I was never told what they thought at autopsy."

Cyrus Payne's dispassionate references to a dead woman hit Marc like ice water. His hunches had felt real for too long now, but at this moment he was convinced his every conclusion was right, and he could hardly take in a breath.

"She kept to herself," Cyrus said. Although he looked at Marc, his eyes were distant as if he saw something else and it froze his soul. "She was here a few weeks before . . . Bonnie was Catholic. She went to the church and prayed, and lit candles.

"She told me she planned to make a new life and put the old one behind her. I didn't like the way she locked herself inside her room all day and didn't come out till it was time to go to the dance hall. She was thin. If she ate, she didn't do it here. Bonnie had something on her mind, something or someone she didn't tell me about. I had the feeling she was afraid."

Marc's fingernails dug into his wet palms. He had scores to settle in Toussaint. Settling them wouldn't be easy — or safe.

No point in circling any longer. "Bonnie Blue died mysteriously. Do you believe it was an accident? Or was she murdered?"

Reb O'Brien's unmistakable husky voice,

raised above her dog's excited barking, relieved Cyrus. Marc Girard had hit him with a broadside, and he needed a few moments to gather his wits. "Here comes exactly the woman you need to talk to," he told Marc while Reb informed Oribel that she didn't need help finding anything in the house.

Girard's expression was blank — all but his black eyes, and they were narrowed and unreadable.

"Reb's something," Cyrus told the man. "A dynamo who doesn't have much patience with small-mindedness. At least one parishioner wants her excommunicated." He laughed and went to open the door. "Apparently straight talk is a mortal sin."

Reb, with her apricot poodle Gaston, still in the chest pack she used to carry him on her motorcycle, entered the room but halted at the sight of Marc Girard. Apprehension flared in her eyes and her lips parted. Reb appeared to be in fight-or-flight mode. The look came and went quickly, but stayed long enough to let Cyrus know that these two weren't strangers.

"Reb O'Brien, meet Marc Girard. Marc Girard, meet Reb O'Brien — and Gaston the Attack Poodle. Forgive me, but would you mind if I took a few moments to check on Madge? We've got a lot going on around here today."

Marc and Reb regarded one another directly. Neither flinched — or said a word.

"Well, I'll be back," he said. He was no

coward, but he was circumspect. Let them deal with whatever was between them — including any information on Bonnie Blue — while he decided how much he ought to say to Marc.

TWO

Later, Reb thought, she would let Cyrus know what she thought of a so-called friend who left her alone with a man he assumed was a stranger to her. Cyrus had looked as if he was desperate to escape and he'd used her to do it, damn his chicken-livered soul.

Marc Girard.

He was on his feet. Marc at twenty-two, when she'd last seen him, running up a flight of stairs at Tulane and sending her a final, unfathomable smile, had been painfully impressive to her. Every move he had made that afternoon became indelible in her mind, and she could still recall how his athletic body moved inside his clothes, and feel again the shock waves stirred by any chance contact with his muscle — or skin. In his thirties he was commanding without doing a thing but standing with his thumbs hooked into the pockets of washed-out jeans, looking down at her.

He extended a hand, and she held it. He didn't say a word, but then, neither did she. His hand was that of a man who didn't spend all his time over a drawing board. Exposed by a rolled-back shirtsleeve, his big forearm flexed, and only with difficulty did she bring her eyes back to his. She caught him in a familiar downward flicker of his black lashes over dark eyes.

When she was seventeen, that intense regard had made her blush and bow her head. She wasn't blushing today, or being coy, because she was too busy absorbing her responses to renewing her acquaintance with the man the boy had grown into. With the slightest raising of his shoulders, this man moved air. He took up space as much with his presence as with his tall, powerfully made frame.

Marc Girard might have perfected a nonchalant set for his face, but his eyes gave him away. He was as uncomfortable as she was. It showed, and she took pleasure in that. A small, small pleasure.

Getting the upper hand with him had always been important to her — almost always. "Good day to you, Marc. You back to make sure Toussaint's as bad as you thought it was?"

"Some things don't change," he said.

"Get *on*. Any town changes in the number of years you've been away."

"I wasn't referring to the town."

She shook her head. "You never could take straight talk from me." Gaston wriggled and looked up at Marc with teeth bared — not a good sign.

"I understand straight talk gets you in a lot of trouble." He smiled at her, and she saw more than a shadow of the boy he'd been. "How about we sit down? Or is that too intimate?"

He wasn't as attractive as he'd been when she last saw him at Tulane. He was a whole lot more so. Back then he'd been a college senior and she a freshman who was barely seventeen and emotionally too young for campus life. Marc, a sought after man-of-note at the school, was kind to her — until she blew it.

Reb sat down in Cyrus's well-worn green recliner and scratched Gaston's tummy inside his carrier. "If I'd known you were visitin' I'd have worn my Sunday best. I don't bake cakes."

"If you'd known I was here you wouldn't have come." He sat in Cyrus's swivel chair and pushed backward until his legs were outstretched. "Does the dog always grin?"

"If you think he's grinnin', that's a good thing."

"Fashionable headpiece. He doesn't mind?"

The man had always had a sly tongue. "Gaston is safety-minded. Glad you like the brain bucket . . . helmet to you." The bucket in question was a lined steel bowl, custom fitted with straps to fasten under the dog's neck, camouflage-painted, and equipped with a lanyard to make sure it didn't fall forward over his eyes.

She took the poodle out of his carrier, removed his bucket, and slipped the pouch from her shoulders.

"This isn't easy." Marc surprised her with that. He picked up a pen from Cyrus's desk and rolled it between long fingers. "I've regretted what happened —"

"Why?" Reb forced a laugh. "We were kids. Or I was. You helped me settle when I wasn't doing a good job on my own. Forget it."

He stood the pen upright on one thigh and didn't answer her.

"That was nice of you," she told him. "To get the old times out of the way."

His black eyes made contact again, and he studied her sideways. She actually wished she weren't dressed in a too-tight T-shirt, cutoff jeans, knee and elbow pads, and a pair of black work boots with no socks visible.

"Ooh, ya-ya, it's a hot one," she said.

Marc crossed his own nicely scuffed brown boots at the ankle and folded his arms. Everything about him had matured. She looked away. She wasn't seventeen anymore, and she wasn't going to mistake nostalgia for interest in this man, other than as a male specimen worthy of study.

"It's been a long time," he said.

"Thirteen years," she said, and instantly wished she hadn't let him know she'd been counting.

"Now you're thirty." He shook his head as if he'd said she had a foot in the grave.

"Not quite thirty," she said. "But you're thirty-five. Amazin'. How is your family?"

"Mother's good. She likes Florida. My father died a few years back."

"I'm sorry to hear that. My father's dead, too. Two years."

"That's too bad. I remember the two of them playin' chess together every week."

So did she. And she remembered dogging Marc's footsteps out at Clouds End. She must have been annoying.

"You became an architect," she said. Silence with him was intolerable.

"I did. I'm in partnership in the Quarter. I'm lucky to do what I like doing. Where you practicing?"

She watched his face carefully, waiting for him to show disbelief. "Here. I took over my father's practice. That means I get paid in chickens and crawfish — which don't balance the books — but I'm happy enough."

He was good at hiding what he thought. "You don't say. At the house on Conch Street?"

"Uh huh."

There was nothing relaxed about this encounter. She wished Cyrus would come back and set her free. But then, she also wanted more time to look at Marc, to listen to him. He didn't wear a wedding ring. Heat crawled up her neck. Aw, she should let up on herself. Any single woman who still had a pulse ought to expect to respond to a sexy man.

She tapped a foot.

Marc clasped his hands behind his neck and didn't take his eyes away from her.

Gaston had sidled up to a member of his least

40

favorite species, the male human, and settled his bottom on one of those expensive brown boots. Reb prayed he wasn't planning to make his opinions known.

Her pager vibrated at her waist, and she checked the display. "Excuse me." Peggy Lalonde was two months from her due date and very nervous. Reb pulled her cell phone from the nylon pouch that hung from a cord she wore draped across her body. Peggy picked up at the first ring, and Reb listened to a list of questions. When the woman paused for breath, Reb said, "Peggy, I think I forgot to tell you you're the healthiest pregnant mom I've ever known. Keep on doing what you're doing. There's no need to cut back on any activities." Peggy rushed in with references she thought backed up a need to be very worried. This time Reb broke in. "May Lynn is a hairdresser, not an obstetrician or a midwife. If you were spotting or having a lot of premature contractions — and pain — I might suggest you rest more. Going to bed for ten weeks and having the foot of your bed put on eight-inch blocks is an outrageous suggestion. . . . That means I think May Lynn should stick with highlighting and brow-waxing and leave the practice of medicine to me. Don't give any of this another thought."

She prepared to switch off, but Peggy had a parting piece of information.

"Well," Reb responded. "If she doesn't do waxing, maybe it's time she started. Widening

41

one's horizons is good for the mind. Go take a nice walk in the park."

"This is why you went to med school, to practice in Toussaint?" Marc said when she put the phone away.

The derision was there after all. Reb balanced Gaston's bucket on her knee. "I wanted family practice. Why not in Toussaint? People get sick here just like anywhere else."

"Did you know Bonnie Blue?"

No reply came immediately to mind. What did he want with Bonnie Blue? He couldn't have known her. "Want some animal crackers?" She pulled the bag from Gaston's pack and offered them. "Sweetened with fructose. Not bad."

He cupped a hand for her to pour in a pile of crackers, and she did the same for herself. "Bonnie was a friend of yours?" she asked.

Marc shook his head and chomped one cracker after another.

"How do you know about her?" she asked.

"I still get the Toussaint paper," Marc said. "I more or less keep up. This town has had more than its share of excitement in the past few years. What with those sick murders a couple of years back — they managed to hit the news in New Orleans, too — and now this suspicious death. But I only know *of* this recent woman, not about her."

Reb felt her scalp tighten. She wanted to forget the women who had met such bizarre deaths. The law might have a man behind bars

42

for the crimes, but that didn't put her mind at rest. "I didn't know Bonnie, either," she said.

He brushed his palms together. "I guess she was a stranger passing through."

"Why so interested, then?" The crackers tasted like sand to Reb.

If Marc would move his unblinking gaze away from her, she'd feel calmer.

He shrugged and offered a crumb to Gaston, who averted his head. "How did she die?"

"She fell." And Reb's heart began to jump around. "They found her on the stone flags at the bottom of the belfry steps in the church and called me. They thought she was still breathing, but it was just breath escaping when they moved her."

Marc was permanently tanned, but she knew when a tanned man's face turned bloodless. "What killed her exactly?" he said.

"She probably fell one flight — the middle one — and got pretty banged up, then couldn't stop herself from tripping down the last stairs and breaking her neck. The coroner in Lafayette thought the same thing."

Beads of sweat stood out along Marc's hairline and above his upper lip. He swallowed repeatedly. She wouldn't have taken him for a squeamish man.

"An accident," he said.

"That was the way it looked." And that's what Reb wanted to believe. She surely did not want to connect recent events in her own life to

Bonnie's death, and if Bonnie's accident hadn't been an accident, Reb might have to do that. She shook back her hair.

"Describe her to me."

A thin woman with arms and legs twisted into abnormal positions — both arms broken. Her neck arched back as no neck was supposed to arch, and enough blood and protruding bone splinters on her face to make her anonymous. "I never really saw her before she died. She had longish dark hair. A lot of gray was covered with dye. Probably a good figure if she wasn't malnourished. Drug user — or she had been until fairly recently."

"Fits what I was told." Marc's dry, cracking voice was a puzzle. "But you never got to know her?"

"She kept to herself. Sang at Pappy's. As far as I know, no one saw her otherwise after Cyrus gave her a room here. She was a night person. Vince Fox plays the fiddle for the Swamp Doggies. Apparently he met her in the Quarter and took pity on her. Told her she could come here and they'd give her what work they could. That's all I know." Except that in her pocket Bonnie had carried a taped-together photo of a baby looking at the camera over a man's shoulder. The man was just a man, the shot taken from behind him. The baby had big, dark eyes and hair as black and curly as the man's. Reb had pored over the mangled shot. It meant something. But that was a dead woman's personal business anyway, hers and the law's, who had the photo among her scant effects. All efforts to find Bonnie's path to Toussaint had failed. No relatives had been traced, and as far as Reb knew, the case was closed — or permanently on the back burner.

"You felt sorry for her." He couldn't know he'd uncapped the pen and was doodling on a jeans leg.

"Nobody spoke up for her, Marc. She was all alone, and she died all alone, and not a soul seemed to care much — except for Cyrus and Madge, and Oribel."

"I thought doctors were supposed to be dispassionate."

"Really?" She could do whatever she had to do, but she didn't think she'd ever stop caring about people as people.

"Let's change the subject," he said. "You've still got the reddest hair I ever saw."

She was too unsettled to take pleasure in a compliment. "It needs a good cut."

"Don't do that."

Reb snapped her fingers at Gaston, who ignored her. She felt overheated again, and the heat of the day wasn't the reason.

"You were a knobby-kneed, irritating little kid, and a precocious but a pretty gorgeous teenager." He had the grace to grimace at that. "You are one fascinating woman."

"Thank you." Grace under pressure was a virtue. For once she'd control herself and avoid

45

snapping back that he was too tall, dark, handsome, and slick-tongued for his own good. She also wouldn't suggest he probably went through women like a bayonet through tofu.

"Do you remember my sister Amy?" He timed his questions for maximum impact.

"Not really. She was a lot older, wasn't she? I remember she was away at school by the time I was particularly aware of her."

"You don't know any of Amy's history in this town?"

This was awkward. "I was told she got into some trouble, but my father didn't believe in gossip, and anyway, like I said, she was another generation from me and I didn't pay much attention."

His hard jaw took on a determined thrust, and he flattened his mouth against his teeth. That memorable mouth had got him into a tight spot or two — Reb knew all about that.

"Reb, people do a lot of talking here. Even if they aren't gossips. Amy . . ." He paused. "Amy didn't have good sense, and she made bad decisions, especially about men. And men messed her up."

"I wouldn't think that was anyone's business but hers."

"Maybe not. I'd prefer not to discuss this, but is there still talk about Amy — about Chauncey Depew and Amy?"

She thought about it. "Chauncey's married to Precious. Oribel's daughter. Chauncey wouldn't risk having Precious turn on him — not that they're exactly a picture of connubial bliss. But they never have been, and there's an interdependence there. He's a lot older than she is. Precious tries to pretend her husband's something more elevated than a body shop owner. I can't figure why she's got a thing about it. He does very well. But Precious talks about his high-end specialty automobile service."

"I don't know Precious," Marc said. "I'd rather you never mentioned Chauncey and Amy to anyone."

"You can count on it." But she'd be lying if she pretended she wasn't curious.

"Can you recall how Amy looked?" Marc asked.

Reb shook her head slowly. "I don't think we ever even met officially, although I did see her a few times when I was a kid visiting Clouds End. She was always about her own business. Do you have a photo of her?" He wanted information, and he hoped to get it without revealing everything that was on his mind. The connections he seemed to be making scared her.

"Only from when she was young. Not that she's old now. Forty-five. She looks older. We were too far apart in age to be close — like two only children. But she's still my sister. She never stopped loving Depew, not since she was fourteen. He ruined her, but she wouldn't give him up."

Why was he telling her all this? "I'm sorry,

Marc. When someone you love suffers, you suffer right with them."

"Amy's been away from Toussaint for fifteen years. Depew helped her get settled in the Quarter. He didn't want her here. Not even if she was only passin' through. They had an understandin'. If she broke the rules, he'd break off the affair. You heard any of this?"

"No," she said with honesty. "Of course, I was away some years myself."

"You okay?" he asked abruptly. "You're jumpy."

"You're imagining things." She'd have to make sure her nervousness didn't show. Her plan had been to talk to Cyrus about thinking she was being followed, but this interlude with Marc had given her time to change her mind. She was overreacting.

"I still say you're jumpy," Marc said, and he leaned forward to watch her even more closely. "Did I tell you I'll be in town a while?"

He hadn't. "No." And the thought didn't do much to improve her peace of mind.

"I've got business here, and I'm probably going to need a little help from you." He bent to scratch Gaston behind the red, white, and blue bow in his topknot, and the little traitor leaned against his leg. "Reb, I think my sister came back here a couple of months ago. I think Bonnie Blue was really Amy Girard."

THREE

Madge was on the phone when Cyrus walked into the sitting room she used as her second office. She held up a hand and smiled apologetically. "Father Cyrus is looking into that," she said, waving him to the overstuffed red chair that was her own favorite. She rolled her eyes at him. "That's true, Mr. Girard's meeting with Father right now. Yes, William, I most certainly will tell you as soon as I hear something. If I hear something. Yes, but I think I can reassure you that the rumors are exaggerated."

Cyrus glanced at the common wall between his own office and Madge's and wondered how things were going with Reb and Marc. Seeing their reaction to one another, he'd had a strong sensation of being an interloper at an intimate encounter.

"No, William," Madge said, casting her eyes heavenward. "No, no, no, that is not true. Mr. Girard is not a pimp, he's an architect. . . . If that's true I just learned something. I never did hear that architect is rich-people code for pimp. There are no souls in danger because Mr. Girard is in town. . . . I think talking to your daughter that way is a bad idea, not that I think she'll take any notice. You'd have to catch Martha before you could lock her away, and that isn't going to happen." Her smile turned mischievous. "You are so right. This is a job for Father Cyrus, and I'll have him call you later." She hung up.

Cyrus frowned at Madge. He had already made himself comfortable in her chair and now he sank as deeply into the cushions as he could go.

"Now you're cross," she said to him. "I'll call William back and tell him you have to leave and won't be around today."

"You think I'd have you lie for me?" He raised his head and looked at her down his nose, attempting to be disapproving. He failed. "William, our very own custodian, I take it?"

"The same," Madge said. "He saw Marc arrive here, and he's heard there's a plan to turn The Majestic into a ritzy house of ill repute."

Even men of God could laugh at the ridiculous, and Cyrus laughed until he coughed and got tears in his eyes. "I take it he's threatening to lock up Martha to keep her safe from the forces of evil?"

Madge dabbed at her own eyes and drank from a cup of hot tea. Oribel said she wasn't normal to drink hot tea and called her a chain-tea-drinker.

A crash sounded from Cyrus's office, and he and Madge stared at the wall. Madge leaped from her chair and hurried around the desk.

"Someone's in your office," she said.

Cyrus caught her arm as she walked past him. "There certainly is someone in there. Two someones. Marc Girard and Reb, and I don't think they're comfortable with one another."

Madge backed up and sat on the edge of her desk. "Why should she be comfortable with him? He's too confident, and a whole lot too good-looking for any woman to be at ease with him. Least of all Reb. I don't remember the last time I saw her with a man. Even if she had the time, she's not relaxed with 'em unless they're sick."

"Reb might not take that as a compliment." Madge's fervor made him smile afresh. It didn't stop him from wrangling with his conscience for having left Reb with Marc.

"They both grew up around here," he told Madge. "I think they're old friends, or at least old acquaintances. As in, they may have been really close in the past."

"No," Madge said. She dropped her voice to a whisper and smiled wickedly. "Let me see. Life gets dull around here — there must be something juicy to make out of this. You think they were lovers and there was a breakup, but now Marc's come back to rekindle the affair? Do you think —" Her eyes became round, and she tiptoed toward the wall. "I need a glass to listen with. That noise in there. What if he's having his way with her? I wouldn't want to miss it, would I?" She sniggered.

Madge's sense of humor amused Cyrus. "I'm

51

sure that would be titillatin', but Marc Girard wouldn't do something like that."

"You're too trusting, Cyrus. You put a tall, strong, devastatingly good-looking, *virile* man, who is probably burning with unrequited love and sexual deprivation" — she rolled her eyes — "you put him with a beautiful, voluptuous red-head who is one smoldering bundle of frustrated desire, and what do you get?"

"You need a hobby," Cyrus told her. "Have you ever thought of writing fiction?"

"What makes you think I'm not writing something already: *Toussaint, Louisiana. Sin City on Bayou Teche. There's more than old crawfish that smell bad around here.* I've been needing fresh material."

"Maybe a husband would be a good outlet for your imagination." He knew his mistake at once. She lowered her eyes, and he heard her swallow.

"I left them in there for two reasons," he said in a hurry. "First, I do think they already know one another, and my presence wasn't going to help them deal with whatever issues they've got. Second, I had to grab an opportunity to re-group. Madge, he made a comment about Bonnie and how she loved music."

Madge paled. She pushed a hand into her thick, black curls and kept it there. "He knew Bonnie?" She had lowered her voice again.

"That's what he seemed to be letting me know. And he's got a lot to say about her, or will have when I let him. Reb arrived just as he was asking me if I thought Bonnie was murdered."

The phone rang. When Madge finally noticed, she reached behind her and switched over to the answering service.

They stared at one another until Madge broke the silence. "I've never heard anyone say he was unstable."

This was one of those times when Cyrus knew he wasn't expected to say anything. Madge liked to think aloud.

"So, if he's sane and makes a statement like that, he believes he has inside information."

She crossed her legs and bounced a foot up and down.

"He was sounding me out," Cyrus said. "Looking for my reaction. Which means he's trying to figure out how much I know."

"Just could be he was making sure you didn't know anythin' at all," Madge said.

Cyrus nodded. "And we're getting mighty irritated by our own questions, while Marc Girard is the only one who knows why he's here and what he thinks."

"Toussaint used to seem so sleepy to me," Madge said. Her brow furrowed, and she turned to glance briefly through the window at the slope down to the bayou. Willow branches hung, unmoving under the sun of a breathless afternoon. "It's not sleepy. Not anymore. It looks peaceful out there, and welcoming — but that's a disguise."

To disagree would be to lie. "There's too

53

much going on. Things we don't like, I mean."
He did wish he could reassure her. "Whatever it
takes, this little town will settle again."

"I hope it happens before anyone else dies."

So did he.

"We should do what we can to help."

Cyrus looked at her sharply and leaned forward in the chair. "What you can do to help is
be aware of what's going on around you and
keep yourself safe."

Her expression lost its sharp edge. "I thank
you for your concern," she said, "but you don't
have to worry about me. Puttin' myself in
danger isn't my thing, but I don't like sitting
around waiting for something else to happen. I
say we take this into our own hands."

"Slow down," he told her and congratulated
himself for not groaning aloud. "Anything I can
do, I will do, you know that. And I'll let you
know the minute you can help out," he added
hastily.

Madge jumped to her feet. She raised her
shoulders and rubbed her hands as if there was
something pleasant and exciting in store. "Let's
start by going over whatever we remember. All
the little details, and the big ones." She snatched
up a pad and pen. "I sure Bonnie had more possessions than they found in her room after she
died. We've got to think about that and figure
out what could have been missing. The next job
will be to find out why. Don't forget, her purse
was never found."

"You're getting ahead of yourself." The idea wasn't bad, just more than he wanted to deal with, at least while Marc and Reb were still closeted together next door. "Don't forget that the police looked into all that."

"I don't suppose we'll have any lucky finds," Madge said, but she sounded undeterred. "It's probably been destroyed, but that doesn't mean we shouldn't try again."

"You make a lot of sense," he told her, and she did. "Let's think about this before we rush into anything."

"If we remember something, it could —" She spread her hands.

"It could be a clue," Cyrus finished for her. Movement outside caught his eye. Wally plodded uphill, probably making his way in a circle around the house. "Excuse me. I forgot I promised to talk to Wally."

"What about? . . ." Madge turned her eyes significantly toward his office. "You know. Marc and Reb?"

"I'll be outside with Wally. If it sounds as if things are getting hot in there, call me." He shot her a half-serious frown and strode from the room, leaving the door open and feeling just a little guilt.

Guilt at his own irreverent sense of humor. Guilt because he'd abandoned Reb to Marc Girard. If Marc were making a move on Reb, Gaston wouldn't be a silent observer. And he hadn't teased Madge that badly. He opened the

55

front door and all but fell over Wally.

"Hey, here I am. Did you think I'd forgotten you?"

Wally shook his head. "Nah."

More guilt! "The truth's important, yes?" He waited for the nod before adding, "You know I get caught up in a lot of stuff, but you trust me to do what I say I'll do — eventually." He took the boy by a shoulder and walked him to a bench built around the thick trunk of an old oak. The next time he had a few hours off, he'd replace some rotting slats in the bench and make it bigger at the same time.

Sitting side by side, their backs against the oak, they slipped into silence. Wally wasn't a talker. He was happy whenever he could trail along with Cyrus, watching and listening and just being accepted. Attempts to talk to the Hibbses about their son, his awkwardness around other kids, his need to have others help him open up, had been met with impatience. According to Doll and Gater Hibbs, Wally was "difficult and always has been," a self-centered boy who enjoyed making them suffer.

"What is it?" Cyrus asked.

Wally gave a great sigh and plunked his bony elbows on bruised and scabby knees — legacies from skateboarding heroics and forgotten pads. He pulled an NYC baseball cap low over his eyes. "My folks are mad at me, real mad." His soft, hoarse voice troubled Cyrus, as it did Reb.

When waiting didn't bring more details, Cyrus said, "Why?" He squinted against bursts of sunlight bouncing off the front windows The grassy earth smelled warm and sweet.

"I guess I just don't turn up home too often."

Cyrus bent his head and stared at Wally until the boy looked at him from the shade of his cap bill. "What d'you mean, you don't turn up at home too often? Where are you when you're supposed to be at home?"

"Around." Wally's shoulders almost met his ears. "I didn't think they'd notice I wasn't there."

"Okay," Cyrus said. "Give me the whole story." Each time he and Wally got onto the subject of his parents, Cyrus felt the weight of watching every word. As parents, Doll and Gater weren't naturals, but they loved their boy as best they knew how.

"They're upset all the time."

"How long did you say you've been staying away from the hotel?"

"Couple of weeks."

That wasn't a time frame Cyrus had been prepared to hear. "But you've been here often enough. Where have you been sleeping?" He looked Wally's clothes over. His *Frog'N and Dawg'N Pizza* T-shirt and khaki shorts were clean.

"I sleep in my room. Don't stay there no more'n I have to, though. I hang out till their lights go off, then I go in." His hazel eyes were too bright. "In the mornin' I pick up the list off the table and do what Mama writes there. I try not to see 'em is all."

One of the things Cyrus regretted about the vows he'd taken was that they meant he'd agreed never to have children of his own. Could be he was the lucky one after all. "Okay. I'm going to let you tell it in your own time."

"Can I stay here till . . . till I've fixed something? I wouldn't get in the way."

Cyrus didn't need a chart to show him he was heading into deep water. "You haven't explained a thing yet."

Wally swallowed, but he didn't shift his eyes from Cyrus's until a pea green Volkswagen Beetle pulled onto the verge outside the fence. "Jilly," he said and didn't sound happy.

"You like Jilly," Cyrus reminded him. "We all like Jilly."

"Yep." The word was the right one, but it sounded like a habit rather than a true affirmative.

Jilly Gable who, with her half-brother Joe, operated All Tarted Up, Toussaint's Flakiest Pastry Shop, emerged from her car and left the door open wide so as not to waste the music from inside. A singer with a sawed-off voice squeezed out a version of "Jolie Blonde" as if a harmonica were stuck in his vocal chords.

"I see you, Wally Hibbs," Jilly called out. "And you are in big trouble, my friend."

"Told you," Wally said darkly, touching his brown bag beneath the bench.

"Afternoon, Jilly," Cyrus said when she drew close enough for him to see her smiling gray-green eyes. Even held back by a piece of black ribbon that was only inches from falling off, her blond-streaked brown hair reached her waist. She carried one of the bakery's rainbow-colored boxes by a string tie. "You have a delivery to make somewhere?" Cyrus asked, knowing she'd brought him something he'd enjoy.

"I do," Jilly said, arriving and sitting down on the grass, her long yellow gauze dress flowing over her body and legs. "Marzipan tartlets."

He reached for the box, but she set it on the ground behind her. "This one's cheese has really slid off his cracker now." She pointed a long finger at Wally. "If I opened up your head, I think I'd find bugs had eaten your brains."

Jilly had a way with words. "Go easy," Cyrus told her.

Wally actually smirked and rubbed the back of a hand over his eyes.

"You hungry?" Jilly asked the boy.

He said, "Nah."

"You ought to be, unless someone's feeding you somewhere — or you're stealing food. You aren't eating at home." She grimaced at Cyrus. "Your folks say you're out of control."

"They're arguin' all the time," Wally said, his husky voice even more difficult to hear. "They get madder and madder every day."

"But not with you," Jilly said. She kicked off her sandals and practiced trapping grass between her toes and tearing it up. The sun spread a glow over the coffee gold of her skin. "You're making too much out of everything."

Wally clammed up.

Cyrus considered options and figured he didn't have any. Wally had to go home, and Cyrus had better be there when he did.

"Father Cyrus." William's bottom-of-the-barrel rumble reached them while the man was still crossing Bonanza Alley from the church where the custodian's room was located out back.

"Shee-it," Jilly said and immediately followed up with, "Forgive me Father for I have sinned."

Cyrus put a fist over his grin. "Sin no more and for your penance bake cakes as well as bread for Harvest Festival."

"Hoo-mama," William grumbled, coming across the lawn. He used a large handkerchief to mop his glistening black face and bald head. "It's hot as a whore's ass on a griddle, and I ain't makin' nuthin' up. You jest gimme time to get there. I'm an old man and gettin' older ever' second in this crazy place."

"I'm going," Wally said, raising his skinny butt from the bench. Jilly eyed him, and he sat again.

"William," Cyrus said. Chastising the man for his questionable analogies would only goad him into further earthy eloquence. "Welcome, podner. You're moving too fast for a big man in weather like this. But don't give me that *old* stuff. You're as strong as an ox. Sit down." He

60

indicated the bench. "Take a load off."

"Rather stand," William said. A huge, muscular fellow, he stood six and a half feet tall and had a grin that could tease at least a glimmer of a smile out of the meanest of critters. "I ax for you to call me." He worked a red, white, and blue cell phone from the back pocket of low-riding tan jeans. His T-shirt, complete with the American flag plastered across his sweating chest, resembled a frayed and stretched Austrian blind and only paid lip service to covering his fine torso.

"You're looking good, William," Jilly said. "Keeping those brothers of yours in line?"

The man splayed a hand built like a plate-sized filet mignon over his heart. "I suffer, ma'am. I surely do suffer. How my dear departed mama came to birth those twin hellcats when she was near fifty, I cain't say. Between those two and my motherless Martha, the burden's enough to break a man's back."

Cyrus decided it would take something major, like a runaway train, to break William's back. "You do a good job with your family," he told him and meant every word. "I would have called you later."

"No reason they two cain't hear anythin' I got to say. Ever'body gotta be warned about that man."

"Marc Girard?" Jilly said, still toe-picking the lawn while she shaded her eyes to look at William.

"How'd you know, Miss Jilly?"

" 'Cause everyone in town's talking about him," Wally said, and Cyrus was almost sure he saw the start of tears. "And he's scaring my folks. Scarin' them mad. They are so mad they can't hardly talk normal at all."

"Wait a minute, Wally," Cyrus said quietly. "That's what it's all about? Doll and Gater are worried — and they don't have any need to be — but they're upset, and that's why you don't want to be at home?"

Wally shifted his eyes from place to place, avoiding looking at anyone directly. He nodded.

Cyrus saw Jilly open her mouth to speak but signaled for her to hold off. "Marc's been here only days."

"I gotta go."

"You've been staying out of the way all day for weeks," Jilly said, sitting up straight and crossing her legs under the yellow dress. "Your folks aren't even sure how long."

"I don't want to talk about it," Wally said, pulling his brown sack from beneath the bench.

Cyrus knew better than to intervene while tempers were so high.

"You'll have to talk about it," Jilly said. "They know *everything* now. You might as well face the music and get it over with."

Clutching the sack to his chest, Wally backed off. "Everything?" he said. "They found out about . . . everything? About what happened?"

"Wally," Cyrus said, but his young buddy

wasn't hanging around for more conversation. He made a run for it, and when Cyrus moved to go after him, William's hand on his shoulder changed his mind.

"Let he go, Father. You ain't gonna git anythin' out of the kid while he all riled up and scairt."

"We weren't even talking about the same thing," Jilly said. "He's got something on his mind we don't know about."

FOUR

"You know who you pushin' around, Devol?" Chauncey Depew asked, managing to swagger with another man holding a fistful of his seersucker jacket right where it pulled his shoulder blades together. "I want a telephone and a leak, in that order."

Deputy Spike Devol didn't like Chauncey, in fact he considered him the kind of lowlife who would look good floating among the water hyacinths on Bayou Teche. Spike liked a quiet life with his four-year-old daughter, Wendy, enough time for the two of them to fish and to drive into Lafayette for a movie — and for him to play a game of pickup basketball.

He'd started out his law enforcement career with big ambitions. The maverick in him had turned out to be trouble, and he was lucky to have the Toussaint job. Deputy pay was a joke, but the gas station and convenience shop his father watched over when Spike couldn't be there kept the three of them comfortable enough. For the present he'd settle for being where he was, and although he hadn't lost interest in cleaning up any scum that came his way, he'd gotten smarter about it.

"You hear me, boy?" Chauncey said, and spat tobacco juice on the pocked linoleum floor. "You hear what I'm tellin' you?"

"Now, my good friend," Spike whispered in Chauncey's ear. "We're on better terms than that. You don't need a telephone 'cause we're just fixin' to have a chat." He shoved him past two rookie deputies — the result of Toussaint's increased crime rate in the past year or so. The man and woman, both ridiculously young, huddled around the castoff television Spike had brought in. A rerun of *L.A. Confidential* had the pair lock-eyed.

"If you ain't got nothin' on me, I'm outa here, Devol. I don't chat with the law."

"That a fact? Humor me. It gets lonely in here some days. I'll send out for a late lunch."

"I don't want no lunch with you." Chauncey whined. They'd reached Spike's office, and he guided his lunch date inside with tender care, slammed the door shut with the heel of a boot, and deposited Chauncey in a green plastic lawn chair bought on special at Wal-Mart.

Depew popped to his feet.

Spike gripped a trapezius muscle over the man's right shoulder and squeezed delicately. Depew looked close to tears and sank down, whimpering at the pain. He didn't get up again.

"Hey," Spike said. "We don't need takeout. We've got doughnuts and coffee. Fresh this mornin'."

An aching shoulder took up all of Chauncey's attention. He didn't even sneer when the day-old doughnuts and lukewarm coffee were placed within his reach.

Spike closed stained roller blinds at windows that overlooked the squad room and placed himself between Chauncey and the door. "We'll start out by makin' it clear you are not under arrest and I'm not charging you with anything. I thought it was time we caught up is all."

That bought him a flat stare from Chauncey's dark eyes. The man was fifty or so, but women still found him sexy, or so Spike had been told. At the moment his face was chalky under a sallow complexion, and straight black hair, well-pomaded, fell in shiny clumps over his forehead. He was a stocky man of average height who pumped iron at the local gym, but a layer of fat softened his body. It would take more than animal grunts and a pile of iron to neutralize the quantities of food he put down.

"I'd like to leave," he said. "If my wife gets wind of me bein' here, you and me'll both wish you'd found someone else to get cozy with."

"This won't take long. I'm not even writing anythin' down — bein' we're friends. It was parking in a handicapped slot that did it."

Chauncey gaped. "What the fuck you talkin' about?"

"We try to watch our language around here, Mr. Depew. Sets a better tone."

The doughnut Chauncey grabbed sent a

66

flurry of powdered sugar all over his brown-and-white striped suit. He smacked at the sugar with one hand and stuffed the stale pastry into his mouth with the other.

"You a nervous eater?" Spike asked. Sugar sprayed in his direction.

"I ain't got nuthin' to be nervous about," Depew said. "Try mad."

"Back to the handicapped parking."

"I got a bad back. And I got a card on my rearview mirror."

"Good. I was just asking. Ila Mae Brown said you raced her for a slot outside the liquor store."

Chauncey chased his doughnut with cold coffee. "No race about it. I got there first is all."

"You drove around her to get there."

"I didn't know it was her." He wiped at full lips.

"Even when you shot her the bird?"

Chauncey found a handkerchief and mopped his sweating brow. "That woman was shoutin' at me. I could see her through her windshield, and them words wasn't so refined."

"You said you didn't know her."

"We both got a right to that spot. I was faster. I gotta look out after my back."

Spike scrunched lower in his seat. He hated the peeling pea green paint in this room, and the metal desk decorated with brilliant scratched-in wisdom. And he'd moved from disliking Depew to hating him.

"Can I go now? I got a business to run."

"Ila Mae Brown drives a special vehicle. She does everything with her hands."

Depew guffawed. "Is that so?"

"It is so. Ila May doesn't have any legs."

The pumped-up bastard took out a Swiss Army knife, found the pick, and went to work on his teeth.

"Dante Cornelius a friend of yours?"

Depew dropped his hands and looked at Spike with the toothpick sticking out between two teeth. He'd given up on mopping sweat. The air conditioning in there wasn't doing a thing, and wet rings were spreading under the arms of the seersucker jacket. The perfume du jour wasn't going to be a winner.

"I see you're overcome for the moment. Cornelius is in town. He says he knows you. Says you'll vouch for him."

Depew looked like a sick man. "I know him. He's had bad times. Might say he's misunderstood."

"I've heard hit men described that way before. Must be hard on them. He's strictly New Orleans. What's he doin' in St. Martin Parish? Said he was visitin' you, but I find that hard to believe."

Depew did a crummy job of appearing nonchalant. "He used to live around here when he was a kid. Never had no luck. His pappy was a pusher and his momma turned tricks. He gets depressed so I let him come and talk to me."

"His sheet shows he could have been involved

in taking out troublesome marks for the New Orleans family. Attempted hits, that is. Apparently his aim isn't so good. That's gotta be a drawback in his line of work. Of course, there's some who went missing and were never found, so maybe he doesn't miss every time. Maybe he's one of those people who always wins at hide, and don't seek if he plays long enough."

"I wouldn't know," Depew said. He looked still sicker. Spike hoped the guy wouldn't throw up.

"How are you and Precious getting along these days?"

"Great," Depew shouted. "Not that it's any of your goddamn business."

"Not yet it isn't. You might want to tell Cornelius to stop following Precious around. This isn't the Quarter. Guys who read newspapers while they walk get noticed, and it can be irritating if they keep bumping into people."

Depew was on his feet. "You got nothing on me — or anyone else, from what I can see. Who told you Dante was following Precious around?"

"Your wife."

FIVE

Before heading into Toussaint the following morning, Marc had left Cletus with instructions to hire a team of cleaners and get Clouds End properly opened up. The gardens were a beautiful jungle, and Cletus was also to find gardeners. The house needed extensive renovations, but Marc would deal with the contracting himself; he didn't want to overwhelm the man who had been with the Girards for forty-five years and who was spry, but elderly.

Marc drove into Toussaint and headed for Reb's place. Yesterday afternoon hadn't been a happy time. Reb had responded to another page at the rectory and headed out, terminating their discussion — if that's what it could be called. She'd been kind in the way people were kind to someone they'd decided deserved pity. The bottom line was, she didn't buy his theory about Amy having been the woman who died at St. Cécil's.

He made a turn, edged his Land Rover along Conch Street, and came to a stop at Number Four, a pretty white Victorian with galleries upstairs and down and metal railings surrounding a small but mature garden. This house, too, needed work, but a brass bell shone on the wall beside a dark green front door, and hibiscus bloomed in pots on scrubbed marble steps while a lush fern hung close to frosted glass on one side of the door. A polished plate attached to the railings still had Reb's father's name on it, but hers had been added below. He figured it was consulting-room time, so he'd take a place in the waiting room until it was his turn to see her. There were some interesting feelings attached to the thought, but he wouldn't be making anything out of them.

He rang the bell and immediately opened the front door as was known to be the routine. The waiting room was ringed with overstuffed furniture, and a large, low table overflowing with magazines took up space in the center.

Only three people sat there, staring straight ahead and listening to the loud ticking of a grandfather clock. Gaston lay on the floor outside the consulting-room door. Today his top-knot ribbon was a puff of multicolored chiffon. "Hey, Gaston," Marc said. "Go on strike till she quits dressing you like a girl."

Three pairs of eyes made his skin prickle, but he smiled all around. The patients, a man and two women, all gave him *drop-dead* stares. He didn't recognize any of them, but he'd jump on any bet that they all knew him.

The consulting-room door opened, and a man wearing a tie-dyed shirt, baggy khaki pants, and Birkenstocks came out with a small boy under each arm. "Thanks, doc," he called back. "Home to bed for you two." Both of the children coughed and wiped pudgy hands across their noses.

Marc held his breath and waited for the germ gang to leave.

The next patient, one of the women, spent only ten minutes with Reb and left smiling. The second woman bustled in, and he heard her laughing even with the door closed. She was still laughing when she walked out. Reb must have turned into a comedienne.

Shuffling, the last patient went into the office and closed the door. He emerged forty-five minutes later, grumbling about doctors who were still wet behind the ears and announcing that Reb was wrong, he wasn't any better, and he shouldn't be sent back to work.

His turn, Marc thought, and approached Gaston and the door feeling like a schoolboy. For a man who had a reputation for being hard-nosed and completely sure of himself, the sensation was irritating. But yesterday's meeting with Reb had shaken him up — badly. He hadn't been prepared to see her at all, and if he had been, he wouldn't have expected the woman she'd become. This time around he might have an even worse time walking away than he had years ago. The only thing that had changed about his attraction to her was that it had grown more intense. The number of hours he'd spent awake and . . . and however you described swinging between something that felt like longing that actually involved his mind and hard-ons that didn't feel like anything but the real thing. They were the real thing.

He tapped the door, and Reb said, "Come," so he entered with Gaston at his heels. Reb saw the dog before she looked at Marc and said, "Out, sir, you don't belong in here and you know it." Then she saw her "patient," and clapped her mouth shut. From the look in her eyes, he wasn't the only one unsure of how to behave.

"I'm the last," he said. "You had a light morning?"

"It was busy earlier. It's first come, first served. Everyone tries to get here first. Sit down, please." She indicated the chair that faced her desk and pulled a new folder from a drawer. She opened this and slid a few sheets of paper over metal clips. "What seems to be the matter?"

Laughing wouldn't be polite. Mark sat down. "It's complicated, but I don't think you'll need to take notes."

She set down her pen and frowned — and her green eyes certainly were troubled. "Why didn't you say you were ill yesterday? I'd have seen you at once, you know that."

Marc felt guilty. "I know you would, cher. I'm not ill." The instant he used the automatic endearment he knew his mistake, but it had come naturally and he couldn't take it back.

Reb propped her elbows on the desk and steepled her fingers. Her hair was pulled on top of her head and smoothed as best as it ever could be. The bones in her face were fine, and the hair seemed almost too heavy. She was taller than average, and well-covered. A standard-issue white coat with a stethoscope hanging out of a pocket didn't seem to belong on her. He couldn't get past thinking of her as a teenager. He'd better get past it fast. They had grown-up business together.

An unpleasant idea struck him. "Did you get married?"

Her fine eyebrows rose. "No. What would make you ask that?"

"Natural. Some guy should have wooed you up the aisle by now." He must remind himself to avoid this line of interrogation in future. "I'm not married either."

She laughed and settled her wide mouth in a wicked grin. "I think you've lost your touch, Marc. A desperate woman might make something out of all that."

He didn't feel like grinning, but watching her mouth was a real pleasure, even if it wasn't comfortable. "But you're not desperate, so I'm safe." Recalling a certain kiss on the campus at Tulane was easy. She had kissed him, but he could have stopped her. He hadn't. Reb might never have kissed anyone before that, but she'd shown promise. Oh, yes, indeed — a lot of promise. That promise must have turned into some realized dreams by now, not that he liked thinking about her kissing other men, or . . .

Damn it all, they were as good as strangers and he was feeling possessive.

"Motorcycles aren't safe."

Her expression turned speculative. She pulled the stethoscope from her pocket and pushed it into a drawer.

"People get hurt on them every day."

"That's true," Reb said. She took off her coat and hung it on a hook. The consulting room looked exactly as it had in her father's time. Dark wood, glass-fronted cabinets where instruments were spread. An examining table along a wall with a curtained changing cubicle at its foot.

A neat, green cotton blouse and tan pants had replaced yesterday's hillbilly biker duds. Not that Reb hadn't looked good in cutoffs and a tight T-shirt. He could have passed on the boots.

He was here to carry out serious business. Diversions weren't part of the plan, particularly diversions that might not want to remain casual.

"Do you wear a helmet when you ride?"

That got him a withering look. "Yes. Thanks for your concern. I've ridden for years. It's an economical form of transportation, and I like it."

"Right. None of my business anyway."

"What you suggested yesterday shocked me,

Marc. Made me do some thinking. First, I know you're wrong. But I can understand you coming to Toussaint to look for your sister. I wish I could help, but I can't. If you think of something I can do, ask. I make a good sounding board, too."

For the first time in days the tension in his chest relaxed. "Thanks, Reb. Something tells me I'll be taking you up on the offer. I don't seem to have many friends in Toussaint. In fact, I don't seem to have any."

"You're not looking in the right places. You already met the best man I've ever known. Cyrus will be your friend. Just call. Madge Pollard is special — she'd do whatever she could to help, and for all her prickly pokes, Oribel is always ready to champion the underdog."

It didn't take much to grate on his nerves these days. "Underdog isn't something I do so well, Reb. Any more than you would."

She came around the desk and stood in front of him until he looked up at her. "You and I have that in common and it isn't good. We're too tough to be relaxing company. That doesn't give us badges of honor — it's sad. I'm trying to loosen up. Of course, I'd never give you advice on anything you might want t'do. Does Amy live in New Orleans?"

Dr. O'Brien distracted him. The light makeup she wore suited her, especially the pale, shiny lipstick. When she was a little kid, he used to take her swimming in the pool at Clouds End, and he remembered her laughing like a manic imp. Would she like him to tow her around in that blue water now — with the sun on her face, and body?

"Marc?" she said, and he realized they'd been studying one another equally closely. He smiled and felt warm in all the best places.

"Amy doesn't seem to live anywhere anymore, but she did live in the Quarter last I knew."

"When's the last time you saw her?" She sat on the front of her desk and swung her legs. Her waist was slim and her stomach flat, but her breasts were more than handfuls, and her hips curved just the way he liked. She'd fit very nicely on his knees.

He cleared his throat. "I haven't seen Amy in a couple of months. That's not unusual, but she used to call every other week or so. She's only called once since I saw her last, and that was right after we had lunch that last time."

"Funny you don't run into each other more often when you live in the same city."

"We frequent different places, with different people and on different schedules."

"Too bad."

"Yeah." But it was the way Amy had wanted it, and in the end he'd wanted it, too.

"Surely she's more likely to move on some-where other than Toussaint." She took hold of a pendant that hung at the vee of her blouse collar, and he glanced up, realizing she'd caught him looking at her breasts.

Fortunately his blushing days were over. "That would be logical, but Amy isn't logical about a lot of things. She shared a flat with a medium. Had for a year or more, but the woman would never have contacted me. I called, looking for Amy. The medium said she hadn't seen her since the beginning of May. Almost two months."

Reb frowned. "But this person hadn't tried to find out where your sister was?"

"No." This had to be couched so he didn't sound crazy. "She said she didn't because she knew where she was. She was *in touch* with Amy."

"As in Amy was dead and communicating from the other side?"

"We didn't get too specific on that. The gist of everything said was that Amy had been seeing a man all the time she was in New Orleans. Not at the flat, but at some place they rented for when they were together."

"Are you talking about Chauncey Depew?"

"She never cared for anyone else. He was her first and only love, starting from before she turned fourteen. He was twenty-one."

Reb wrinkled her nose with distaste. "But he can't have kept that up since he married Precious. She's not much more than half his age — and she's too high-maintenance. I doubt he gets to make a move she doesn't know about."

"Amy told me it was all over after the marriage, but her friend told me Depew even man-

78

aged to get into town from his honeymoon in Orange Beach."

"But that was a long time ago, Marc."

He shrugged and gripped the arms of the chair. "I'm telling you what I was told myself. Evidently they kept seeing each other until Depew finally got scared his wife would find out — she must hold the purse strings — and called everything off. By my figuring that's when Amy went missing."

"That must have been a powerful relationship. To last so long under the circumstances."

You're thinking Amy's probably a mess by now, and you're right. Depew isn't the type to hang around has-beens. Marc hadn't had the heart to ask Amy if she had something on Depew that kept him around.

With her hands in her pockets, Reb got up. She went to a file cabinet and riffled through folders. She pulled one out and opened it, rapidly scanned pages, then replaced what she'd read and closed the drawer.

"What is it?" Marc asked.

She looked at him as if she'd forgotten his presence. "Excuse me. I was just making sure I hadn't forgotten something from one of my morning patients."

Like hell. She was a lousy liar, but he couldn't press her to breach patient confidentiality.

"What do you want from me?" Reb asked suddenly.

Her tone caught him off guard. "I'd have

thought that was pretty obvious. I want your help."

"With what? You've come up with some theory, but from what I understand, you don't have a thing to back it up. Did you report her missing?"

"You're angry with me," he said, and struggled not to return the favor.

"You always were used to getting your own way. You asked, and people ran to give you what you wanted. No attachments, no personal involvements, just ask and you received. Well, I've got troubles of my own, and I'm not going to try making any points with you. And for the record, I don't like being put in a position where I'm supposed to feel responsible for you."

He got to his feet. "What troubles?"

She opened her mouth and kept it that way.

"I asked a simple question, Reb. You said you've got troubles and I asked what they are. If something's wrong, I want to know."

Drawing a short breath, she said, "Thanks for the concern, but I'm hardly your problem. I doubt if you've given me a thought in a lot of years. It was just a figure of speech anyway. Everyone has troubles of some kind."

"Okay, I'll accept that, but I don't want you to feel responsible for me," he said quietly, although he was glad to be on his feet and looking down at her. "This isn't even a 'for old times sake' deal. You happen to be a doctor, the doctor who was the first to examine whoever fell down those belfry stairs. I'm not asking for personal favors, just information."

Reb's face stung. Her belly felt tight and her legs weak. When she took a step it was jerky. When she'd been a little kid following him around at Cloud's End, he'd laughed at her regularly and shooed her away, but he'd never turned mean or put her down. He wasn't mean now, but he knew how to dole out a cutting put-down.

"I didn't mean to sound rude," he said, and she wished she didn't like him being so much taller and bigger than she was. He ran a hand through his short curly hair. "I didn't always get my way, Reb. There's a lot you don't know about me, a lot you don't need to know. If I seemed self-involved when I was younger it was because I needed to be to save myself. It would have been easier to do what was expected of me, but I believe I'd have died in a way if I had."

"I think I understand," she said, recalling what her father had said about Ira Girard's determination to have his son go into the business, and Ira's furious disappointment when Marc had refused. "Go see the deputy. Spike Devol. Misfit around here but conscientious — and straight. People trust him, even if he can be a loose cannon. There could be things you ought to know, but I don't want to be accountable for choosing which ones and maybe dragging this out for you."

"I'd rather talk to you than some deputy. You

were there. Maybe if we talk you'll remember some detail that'll help."

Talking with Marc Girard wasn't without appeal, but once again he was applying pressure. "I don't think it will," she told him. "And I've got house calls to make."

"*House calls?* Doctors don't make house calls —"

"This doctor does. We've got an aging population, and I believe they should get what they're used to when they're ill."

"You're brushing me off." Two large hands took her by the shoulders and held her as if she might run away. "Don't do that to me just because I messed up all those years ago."

The curse of the pale-skinned redhead was that they could really blush. Reb's face throbbed. "This is ridiculous," she told him. "If you weren't upset you'd never behave like this. You didn't mess up anything. I did. You were the one who figured out how to smooth things over, and I thank you for that. Let's not bring it up again."

"Because it embarrasses you?" he said, dropping his hands. "I'll say this much and no more. You were the sweetest thing, and I . . . I liked you for your spontaneity. I never tried to make you understand the way things had to be — at least for a while. I left you thinking you'd done something wrong while I protected myself. Well, the joke was on me because I was the one who lost out. It's in the past, but I wanted to tell you.

"Look, if I asked you," he continued, "would you consider coming out to Clouds End with me? Early evenin' maybe? I'll feed you and see if I can't figure out a way to talk about the things you might be able to help me with — as the doctor who was there."

Any defenses she might have thought she had against him had taken a hike. "As far as I'm concerned, the woman I examined was one Bonnie Blue."

"But her relatives didn't show up to claim her, right?"

She didn't know how he'd found that out. "No, they didn't."

"Please come for dinner. You can bring him." He pointed at Gaston, who had climbed up to stretch out on her desk. His bulbous brown eyes moved back and forth between Reb and Marc as if there were a tennis match underway.

The pager at Reb's waist rang, and she checked the readout. Immediately she snatched up the phone and punched in numbers. With a hand over the mouthpiece, she whispered, "Peggy Lalonde. First time mom-to-be." She put a single finger to her lips, signaling for silence. "Hey, Peggy, what's up?" She walked back and forth by her desk. "You've got two months to go and you're doing beautifully — yes — yes, that's normal. There's a whole lot of stretching going on and you're feeling that. No! No, absolutely not — it is *not* abnormal. Get a glass of tea and put your feet up for an hour.

Nap if you feel like it. You do too much . . . *No!* I am not trying to take your mind off something serious. Peggy, I'll get over to see you this afternoon, okay? Good. Later then." She hung up.

"You're unbelievable," Marc told her. "No wonder they love you in this town."

"How would you know if I'm loved here?"

"You've got to be. You're a pushover." A dangerous glint in her eyes changed his mind about pursuing the topic. "You're exactly as I'd expect you to be. Completely involved and caring. That's wonderful."

She smiled a little, and he breathed easier.

"The house is being cleaned up. It's a mess. But the gardens are still something. Come tonight? Please?"

"I hate to see a man beg," she said and didn't care if she wasn't original. "Okay, I'll be there." But he'd raised some doubts for her, and they didn't make her more secure about ignoring recent events. If anything he suggested was true, someone might have a motive for trying to scare her, to think seeing her dead would be a good idea, in fact. She needed help but didn't want to cause a panic in Toussaint.

SIX

Some might say trading three years of unpaid medical bills and a player piano for a fourteen-year-old motorcycle didn't show good business sense, particularly when Reb had been told the player piano was a valuable antique — after the trade.

Reb arrived outside her house on her pride and joy, her Ultra Classic, fully loaded except for the AM/FM cassette Ozaire Dupre had insisted tipped the deal too far in Reb's favor. After all, out of respect for her occupation, he'd left the CB and intercom, and the chrome-trimmed Tourpack so she could carry supplies.

She mounted the sidewalk, noticed Oribel Scully's bicycle leaned against the fence, and the yellow Jag that had to belong to Precious Depew, and braced herself. She drove through the front gates. Then she saw Precious Depew and Oribel seated on the steps to the house. Glowing in the neon orange workout clothes she wore to Toussaint's tiny health club, Oribel clasped a showy bouquet of flowers.

Oribel bearing gifts? Now that was a scary thought.

"You're gonna break your head riding that thing," Oribel called. "A lady — a *doctor*, cruisin' around town on an ugly brown motorcycle with all that flashy stuff on it. Not dignified at all."

Reb thought her chocolate brown wheels were the most beautiful conveyance she'd ever seen. "Excuse me while I put this in the garage." She wheeled the cycle around the house to a single, separate garage at the end of a gravel pathway and placed it carefully in the middle of the floor. Then she hung her helmet over a handlebar and removed her gloves.

When she returned to the front of the house, Oribel and Precious had risen from their perches and were standing expectantly at the door. Reb could have groaned with frustration. She didn't want visitors. She wanted to take a long, bubbly bath, listen to some music, and get ready for Marc to come and pick her up.

As if this were going to be a date. Hah! All work and no play was making this girl dull and fanciful.

"Okay, ladies. Which one of you is sick?" If Precious, who had visited Reb the previous week, wanted her health mentioned in front of Oribel, she'd bring it up. "Clinic was over hours ago, but of course I'll take care of you."

"You always were somethin' special," dark-haired, gold-skinned, and voluptuously petite Precious said. Even in impossibly high heels, she didn't come much past Reb's shoulders.

"Kind, that's what you are. I don't think you ever turned a soul away no matter who they were. We all know half your patients don't have insurance — or any money."

Precious was spoiled, but she had a sweet side, and when she smiled her expression was ingenuous. Her light brown eyes shone. A pretty thing. Reb thought about Marc's revelations and wondered why women fell for Chauncey Depew.

"That's a nice thing to say," Reb said, still wishing her visitors would leave. "Let me open the door and we'll go right through to the consulting room." *And then they'd go away again — quickly.*

"Will you listen to her, Mama?" Precious Depew said. "I think that's just plain sad. A nice woman who doesn't think anyone would want to visit just because they like her company. It's been too long since we came by, sugar. Besides, Mama and me is parched. We need some of that good iced tea you make."

Reb's iced tea came from a mix, and she couldn't recall ever serving any to Oribel and Precious. But she said, "You've got it. Come on in."

They followed her straight into the kitchen, where Gaston slept in his favorite spot — in a puddle of sun on the chipped enamel draining board.

Oribel tutted at the sight of him. Reb lifted his nose and kissed it, and said, "How come I don't get a better greeting than that." She frowned a little. It wasn't like Gaston not to rush to the door to greet her. He must be miffed — probably with the company.

Grateful she'd mixed up a jug of tea earlier, Reb filled three glasses and waved toward the back porch. "It's nice out there." Oribel showed no inclination to set down her flowers and carried them with her as she went.

Seated in facing gliders, they drank in silence. Reb's daylilies crowded together, their colors alternately garish or delicate in the sunshine. They grew in wide, irregular beds near the porch, and their scent was sweet and heavy.

"Nice bouquet," Reb said of the cellophane-wrapped explosion of color Oribel held. "Would you like to put them in water — just till you leave?"

"Oh," Oribel said, looking not at Reb but at Precious. "Silly me, I forgot. They were delivered before you arrived, so I took them for you." She held the flowers out.

Reb accepted them. Floral gifts weren't something she was accustomed to receiving. The greetings envelope parted company with the staple that had held it to the cellophane and fell to the shabby wooden floor of the porch. Reb retrieved it, feeling certain the bent card had already been read. When she glanced from Oribel to Precious, Oribel looked truculent and held her lips tightly pursed while Precious shifted her curvaceous bottom on the glider and wouldn't meet Reb's eyes.

Peach roses, sprays of cream orchids, and fragrant freesias. Reb excused herself and went inside to put the flowers in water. And she read the card quickly. *Hi Reb: Looking forward to dinner. Pick you up at 6:30. Thought we'd drop by Pappy's later and see if I've forgotten how to dance. Marc.*

The mention of Pappy's took the shine off getting the kind of bouquet any woman melted over. Not that she minded visiting the dance hall on very rare occasions. Early in an evening, people brought their children to eat and dance. It was later that the atmosphere changed. But there was only one reason Marc wanted to go there, and it had nothing to do with dancing. He wanted to look around the place where Bonnie Blue had sung — where he was convinced his sister had sung and spent the last hours of her life. He was wrong, but she was deeply sad for his sense of loss.

She pocketed the card and rejoined the other women.

Oribel sniffed suddenly and turned her face away.

"Mama," Precious said. No matter how often she pulled at her short yellow skirt it didn't get any closer to her knees. "Oh, Mama, what is it? Reb, Mama's cryin'. She never cries."

Reb picked up Oribel's glass of tea and gave it to her. "Take a few sips and tell us what's the matter. It isn't like you, getting upset like this."

Oribel fumbled in a pocket of her orange

pants and found a tissue to wipe her eyes. "I'm gettin' silly in my old age, but I worry about you young girls. Maybe you've forgotten what happened here not so long ago, but I haven't, and I'm not talkin' about poor, dear Bonnie."

"Don't, Mama," Precious whispered, her own eyes moistening. "That's all over, thank goodness. I don't want to talk about it. And you're not gettin' silly, you're sharper than anyone I know."

Reb hadn't forgotten the killings that had terrorized Toussaint for months until a victim got away from the murderer and picked him out of a lineup. Or so the story went. Pepper Leach, the least likely murderer Reb had ever met, was in jail for the attempted crime, but although there was a lot of suspicion, and the town had convicted him, no physical evidence had tied him to the first two killings, and he'd been judged innocent on both counts. How she wished she could be sure Precious was right and the horror of it was behind them.

"I don't know what this town is comin' to," Oribel said, sounding choked. "Used to be a person could go anywhere, anytime, and not worry about a thing. Now you just don't know."

"What made you think about this?" Reb said. "Bonnie?"

"Oh, Bonnie wasn't anythin' like them others, God rest her sweet soul." She sniffed again and hugely, and Reb thought how hard it must have been on the woman to arrive at St. Cécil's early

90

in the morning to clean the sacristy, and walk right in on Bonnie's body.

"Tell us what we can do," Reb said, patting Oribel's clenched hand.

Oribel made a choking sound. Never good at keeping still, she stood up and marched to the edge of the porch where she bounced on the toes of her sneakers. "You can stay away from that Marc Girard for a start. There." She looked defiant. "Those Girards never do anything unless they want something. I came to warn you about him, and since I'm here, I might as well speak my mind. Those people kept their distance from folks they considered beneath them, and that was just about everyone in Toussaint. When that Marc was growin' up he was the kind of boy who was too smart for his own boots. Couldn't run around with the other kids because his pappy wouldn't have stood for it, but he was good at going behind his pappy's back and showin' them ways to get into trouble. Instigator, that's what he was. And his family thought he was a saint. He made a play for Precious, y'know." She breathed in deliberately, expanding her lungs and expelling the air in long streams.

"Now Mama," Precious said, smoothing the sides of her hair, which was wound into a puffy pleat at the back of her head. There was a ringlet in front of each ear.

"Don't you 'now mama' me. That pervert put his hands down the front of your cheerleadin' top and don't you deny it. You came home crying about it."

Precious wiggled a little. "Boys will be boys," she said. "And that was a very long time ago."

As Precious's doctor, Reb knew that the cantaloupe-sized breasts that thrust from the woman's chest wall were in good part man-made adornments and from a crop not more than ten years old.

"I don't care," Oribel said, "I'm worried about you Reb. Agreein' to go out for dinner with that man. Goodness knows what he's got in mind."

Precious sniggered. Reb congratulated herself on her control in not telling them what she thought about those who read private messages.

"Father Cyrus would never forgive me if I didn't tell him what's goin' on," Oribel said. "I'll have to get back to the parish house."

"You will not talk about my business," Reb said, growing annoyed. "There's no need. I've known Marc just about all my life. He used to put up with me following him around when I was a little kid."

Oribel raised her chin and looked Reb over. "Well, you ain't no little kid now, and when that man looks at you he's got hot eyes."

"Hot eyes?" Reb shook her head. "You need to get out more. You've never even seen us together."

"I saw the way he watched you when you left

Father's house yesterday. That's why I had to come, to warn you. But now I can see he's movin' in fast and there's no time to waste."

"You're making more out of the card you shouldn't have read than is actually there."

Once more Oribel sniffed. Then she burst into tears and returned to the glider. She would not be consoled. Precious flapped ineffectually around her, waving a hand like a fan.

"You think I'm too old to know what men are like," Oribel said. "Well, you're wrong. I know better than anyone. Oh, why did that man have to show up here after all this time and take after you, Reb? What can he want?"

Precious sniggered some more. "He wants what they all want. I never met a man who wasn't horny."

"No!" Reb said, appalled. "He's looking for his sister."

"His sister," Oribel said, her tears drying. "Why, that doesn't make any sense. She was gone from here years ago."

Standing up and tugging at her skirt again, Precious looked disbelieving. "Is that what he told you? That's a line I don't think I ever heard before. I never set eyes on that sister of his, or I don't remember if I did. But I've heard about her. A lush who slept around."

Reb couldn't bear all this. "Please don't talk like that. You've said you didn't know her. Why malign a stranger?" Chauncey Depew's adultery with Amy was never directly mentioned.

"There's got to be another reason why he's here and runnin' around after you," Precious said.

"I examined Bonnie after her accident," Reb said.

That brought a fresh gale of tears from Oribel, who trembled and rocked on the glider.

"I'm sorry," Reb said, wishing she hadn't come home. "Of course, you found Bonnie. That's never going to be easy for you to think about."

"Never did believe in cell phones," Oribel said. "But I got me one now. I didn't want to leave that girl there alone but I had to. Why Father had that newfangled phone put in the . . . It doesn't matter anymore; I had to go for help. I ran all the way to get Father Cyrus. I didn't want to wake him up, but there wasn't a choice." She hiccuped and her shoulders shook. "Like I told you when you got there, I thought she was still alive — even though she was all broken up," she ended on a whisper.

"You turned her over," Reb said gently. "You heard trapped air escaping from her lungs, that's all. She was already dead, so you did everything you could."

Precious had grown still and quiet. When Reb looked at her, she said, "What does Bonnie have to do with Marc Girard being here?"

She had, Reb realized, spoken carelessly. Now she might as well tell it straight because everyone in town was likely to find out anyway.

"Amy Girard — Marc's sister — dropped out of sight a couple of months ago. He thinks she came here. He thinks she was the woman who died in the church."

"My heavens." Precious sat down. Mother and daughter stared at one another. "Why, that's the craziest thing I ever heard."

Oribel shook her head over and over again. Every hint of color had left her face.

"You asked what was on Marc's mind, and I told you. Better to give it to you straight."

"Yes." Oribel nodded mechanically. "I hope the restaurant y'all are goin' to for dinner is somewhere a lot of people go."

"We're not going to a restaurant. Marc's taking me out to Clouds End to eat. Cletus will be there, so —"

"Out to that old place?" Oribel's voice rose. "Why, it's halfway to Breaux Bridge and in the middle of nowhere, and that Cletus is a hundred if he's a day, and deaf. What good would he be if that man decided to ravish you?"

"And Pappy's place is no place for a lady," Precious added.

An urge to laugh was very inconvenient for Reb. Precious was no stranger to Pappy's, or so gossip said.

"Taking you there shows no respect," Oribel said. "And a man can't be trusted if he shows no respect."

"You know what's next door to Pappy's," Precious said, obviously enjoying herself. "The Lay

95

By. Three hours for fifteen dollars. Very convenient for a man who wants inside a woman's pants."

Reb snorted, and sat down to laugh.

"That is the most disgustin' thing I ever heard," Oribel said. "And you laugh, my girl? Book learning's all very well, but you're too unworldly for your own good. You make sure he sticks to undressing you with his eyes. I got to talk to Father Cyrus right away."

"We've all been to Pappy's," Reb said. "Maybe Marc Girard's the one who should look out for his honor. I've been feeling a bit — well, you know, *frisky* lately."

"That's it." Oribel stood up. "Come along, Precious. This girl doesn't have a living soul to look after her or care for her. I knew and respected her pappy. In his memory I've got to do the best I can for her. Father Cyrus will know what's best."

Precious followed her mother's footsteps to the front door, but she looked back at Reb and wiggled her eyebrows. Reb smiled and was grateful to hear the door slam behind them.

She gathered the glasses and carried them into the kitchen. There was plenty of time to get ready, but she wanted to enjoy it. For once she'd pretend she was like other single women and about to spend a romantic evening with a man she was mad about.

Pursing her lips, she rinsed the glasses and put them in the dishwasher. Marc Girard had the power to move her — maybe too much.

Gaston whined.

"Okay, buddy, enough sulking. Hey, you didn't eat your food. C'mon, do it now. You're looking after the house tonight." She'd already decided not to take him to Clouds End.

The dog sighed, and his brows drew up and together in the middle to make a tragic picture. He'd curled himself around his food dish, but Reb could see he hadn't touched it.

"Sometimes you are just too cranky for your own good," she told him. "Oh, don't look so sad. You're a sweetie pie and I love you." She knelt down and scooped some of the wet food onto her finger to feed him — something he liked a lot.

"Ouch." She drew back and snatched up the dish. Blood ran from a cut on her forefinger. With a spoon from the sink she stabbed at the chicken and rice. "Oh my Lord." Pieces of broken glass crunched beneath the bowl of the spoon.

Reb turned on cold water and ran it over her finger. She grabbed a paper towel to staunch the flow of blood and picked up Gaston to examine his mouth. There was no sign of a wound, but she'd check him over anyway.

She hadn't broken any glass. No shards were on the floor or in the sink — just in Gaston's bowl. But something must be broken. She'd been too involved with Oribel and Precious to notice before, but the latch had been popped off on a sash window she always kept locked. The window had been opened and left that way. White cotton curtains ruffled in the breeze.

Feeling sick, Reb went closer and picked the latch off the floor. Someone had slipped a sharp implement between the upper and lower windows and pried off the metal lever.

Getting in had been just that easy. She knew, because she'd done it often enough herself when she'd forgotten her keys.

SEVEN

If he told Reb she smelled like the wild roses at Clouds End . . . she'd laugh herself sick.

Once out of Toussaint, Marc got on 31, drove four miles north, and cut off before reaching St. Martinsville. When he'd arrived a few days earlier he'd expected things to feel unfamiliar, but he'd driven to the old place just like he'd never been away.

"Sorry, Reb," he said, breaking a long silence. "Would you rather I rolled up the windows and used the air conditioning? That's what happens when you spend a lot of time alone — you forget not everyone likes things the way you do."

"Don't change anything," she said. Her hair was wound up in the professional do again, and he decided he liked it. "I'm fond of this time of evenin' when the sun's low and it feels like a cool sauna instead of a real hot one."

He grinned and reached to close the windows.

Reb put a hand on his forearm. "I never did learn to leave off the little dig," she said. "I mean it. I'd rather have the windows open."

She withdrew her hand just as quickly as she'd

touched him, but the sensation remained. Well, damn, he did believe he was developing an inconvenient interest in the doctor — again.

"You don't seem relaxed," he told her. "Is that because of me?"

"I'm not a good passenger," she said. "I like to be in control."

Marc glanced at her again, and she shrugged at him. He'd never forgotten how her green eyes could open wide and make him smile. He smiled at her now, and she wrinkled her nose at him the way she used to when she was a kid, only neither of them were kids anymore. They'd both do well not to forget it was the small, teasing things that could get a man and woman into trouble — if sex between them was a bad idea.

Well now, he mused, time to lock up the old testosterone and think pure thoughts.

He hadn't made any comment when she put her dog into the back seat, but he'd taken it as a reminder that their being together was almost strictly business. Anyway, he had more or less invited the toothy critter to come. "How about Gaston? Is he a nervous passenger, too?"

"Not if I'm driving. Forgive me for bringing him. I was going to leave him at home, but he's been alone most of the day and he won't be a bother."

Only a desperate man took heart at a comment like that. "I like animals." Maybe she hadn't brought the poodle along for protection — or because the evening meant nothing to her.

"I know you do." She settled her head against the rest, closed her eyes and let hot wind through the window toss loosening strands of curling hair. "I remember Buzz. Took me ages to figure out you called him that because he was a Ridgeback and the fur on his spine stood up like a buzz cut."

"Good dog," he said. "I remember him, too."

She wasn't relaxed at all. Her eyes moved beneath their lids, and her teeth were so tightly clamped together, muscles flexed in her cheeks.

"Is something wrong?" he asked, then wished he hadn't.

"Nothing."

"I'm not going to lie," he told her. "I intend to ask you questions about the woman you call Bonnie Blue, but I also hope we can have an enjoyable evening. It'll be fun to look at Clouds End with you after so long."

She jerked to sit up straight. "It's all about you, isn't it? It always was."

"Where did that come from?" He raised an eyebrow at her. The overgrown entrance to Clouds End was just ahead.

"Forget it."

"Okay." The sign for the house was barely visible beneath a tangle of berry bushes. Grass sprouted in tall clumps through cracks in the paved drive that needed resurfacing.

Reb crossed her arms and sighed loudly.

"It's a mess, isn't it," he said. "It depressed me when I first drove in, too."

"Unbelievable," she said. "Why would I be depressed because Clouds End isn't in the kind of gorgeous shape it used to be when y'all lived here? I shouldn't have come. I've got too much on my mind. Too much personal stuff, my stuff, not yours, Marc."

The driveway was a mile long and lined with live oaks, his father's favorites. Marc arrived in front of the house frowning, and searching for whatever he ought to say.

"Let's discuss this," he told her, suddenly inspired. Women wanted to talk. She'd decided he was selfish. He'd talk until she realized she was wrong. "You know what's on my mind. That's not fair. It gives you the advantage. Tell me what's going on for you."

"Nothing," she said again and sat with her head bowed and her hands pressed together between her knees.

So maybe she was different from other women.

Marc turned off the engine and slowly applied the emergency brake. She wore a wide-necked, sleeveless gray dress with a full skirt and a narrow matching belt. Her pager decorated one side. He didn't remember ever seeing her other than plainly dressed. Rebecca O'Brien, who had refused to answer to anything but Reb for as long as he remembered, didn't need finery to make her unforgettable.

He got out and went around to open her door.

Reb looked into his face, and her expression stopped him. He stared back at her. "There is something," he said. "Come out here and tell me what it is. Better yet, I'll get you inside the house and give you a drink — then you tell me." He offered her a hand and she held it while she twisted sideways in her seat and hopped to the ground.

Before she could call the dog, Marc reached in and picked him up.

"Oh, don't," Reb said. "I don't think he'd bite, but I don't want to find out."

Eye to eye with Gaston, Marc knew he was being sized up. The animal bared his teeth in what might have been a smile. Marc put him down before the dog could prove him wrong.

"Shall we go in?" he asked Reb. She surveyed the lush but ruined grounds, including tennis courts with rambling roses cascading from the wire fencing. Vines scaled massive Ionic columns at the entrance to the house. "Reb?" He held her elbow.

Steps rose to a terrace that stretched the width of the central wing. Two stories of windows flanked substantial front doors. A second and third wing, one on either side, were recessed. Dormer windows in the attics were opaque with filth. The basement had no windows at the front of the house. The steps had been brushed clean. A crew had labored on the inside of the house all day, but they would have weeks of work ahead of them.

"It's still very beautiful," Reb said. "What does Cletus do with himself out here? You're lucky he's so spry — amazing, really. It'll be good to see him."

"He was tired from all the activity around here today," Marc said. "He doesn't do much but live in rooms off the kitchens just so there's someone here. He wouldn't want to be anywhere else now, so he'll stay as long as he wants to. His daughter came over this afternoon and took him to Lafayette to spend the night."

The speculative flicker in her eyes surprised him. So, she wasn't completely unaware of him as a man — or of being alone with him. He'd grin, only she might catch him.

He unlocked the front doors and pushed them wide. Reb walked onto dark wooden floors — something else that needed work. She stood with her back to him, taking in peeling wallpaper and peeling paint. Rolled and wrapped carpets were stacked to one side of the staircase. The way Reb patted a thigh must be a habit. When she glanced down, then back at him, he realized she'd expected the dog to be at her side. Gaston sat beside his left foot, but when Marc bent to scratch his head another of the maybe-smiles appeared and Marc changed his mind.

"You used to like the conservatory," he said. "It's a bit surreal now but still kind of special. I thought we could have drinks out there. There's an ice chest. Try not to be wowed by all the ultra-modern comforts. I'm campin' out."

"I'd forgotten how much I miss this place." She started toward the open doorway into the dilapidated chaos of what had been his mother's pride and joy, the dining room.

"Good thing the furniture was draped," he told her, indicating fallen ceiling plaster scattered in chunks on the table that could easily seat twenty-four. "The roof is a priority. Damp made its way through the walls and between floors."

"Your father and mine played their chess in there," Reb said, leaving the dining room for a small drawing room and pointing toward what had been his father's study, a handsome space opening off the drawing room.

The certainty with which she marched through the house amused him, and lifted his spirits. It was good to share a special place with someone who had also made good memories there.

This was likely to be the calmest time he spent with her tonight, perhaps ever, so he might as well enjoy himself.

She reached the conservatory that had been built for his grandfather by an Englishman for whom limits didn't exist.

The frame of the soaring space was of copper. Years of grime had built up on the windows until they'd become more like shades to hide the gardens outside than clear glass, with a border of stained-glass grapevines intended to turn each view into a picture for those inside.

"There's still a pool house," he told Reb. "Another major repair project, but the shell's there and it's solid. The pool is as good as new. It's being cleaned and should be ready for test runs in a day or two."

"Oh, Marc," Reb said, raising her hands and turning a circle on chipped and cracked marble tile. "It's so wonderful. Nothing can take that completely away. But it makes me sad to see it like this. Thank goodness you came when you did — before it got too late for some things to be repaired rather than rebuilt. They wouldn't have been the same."

He watched her without responding.

"The palms." She dropped her head back and pointed to where the graying crowns of palm trees extended through panes they'd forced out of the stained-glass roof. "Oh, Marc!" Hurrying closer, she looked at him with very serious eyes. "You're getting this place ready to sell, aren't you? Why didn't I think of that?"

Why hadn't it struck him that Clouds End might matter to her? He didn't need any explanations for why her reactions pleased him. Not a good sign. But also not one he had to be concerned about, since he planned to be back in New Orleans before long.

What would he do with the place? Leaping in to fix it had been reflexive, but would he ever use it? He studied Reb, thought about her here — with him — when he could pay visits. Oh, yeah, the pictures that crossed his mind were pretty, but he thought they might shock her.

"I'm not selling it. It isn't mine to sell

anyway." Not strictly true, since his mother had already deeded it to him in something close to a fit of temper. The house was his responsibility now. Giving it to him had been a challenge. He knew what it had meant to his father, and it was in his hands to decide whether to keep it in Ira Girard's family or sell it to strangers.

Reb smiled her relief. "It's none of my business. I haven't even given the place more than a few thoughts over the years, but I like knowing it's here and that it belongs to your family. Sounds silly, I know."

"No." No, no. He wasn't sure she could say anything he'd find silly. "What would you like to drink? Dinner's interesting. You still like desserts, I hope."

She rolled her eyes. "They are my waterloo. I try not to eat even a bite of them or I can't stop."

"Good. If necessary I'll slip you a bite when you aren't looking just to get you going. We've got dessert and dessert, and then there's dessert, and maybe . . . dessert?"

"What do you mean?"

"Life's short, eat dessert first," he said, and winced.

"You should look embarrassed," Reb told him. "You never used to fall back on clichés — you didn't need them." She closed her mouth, blushed a pretty shade of pink, and turned away to study orchids that continued to bloom in profusion together with bird-of-paradise, ginger, and proteas.

"When we were at Tulane, you mean?" he asked and didn't even feel guilty for bringing up what had been a period of sweet agony for him.

"I don't know what I meant."

Sure she did. What she obviously hadn't known at the time was how much it had cost him not to take what she had offered. By now she knew all about raging male hormones, but at seventeen she hadn't been worldly.

"Come and see what we've got." If he decided he wanted to pursue her, and he might, there would be time enough to see what happened if he got her riled up just the right way at the right time.

For a moment she behaved as if she wasn't going to respond to the lure of the sweet things he knew she loved, but she put her hands behind her back and approached until she could look beneath each of three silver covers he'd had polished. "Took me most of the day to make these," he said.

He earned himself an unexpected dig in the ribs. Then Reb was too busy examining raspberry-almond torte, mango cheesecake, lemon chiffon pie, crystallized pears in caramel sauce, and fanciful marzipan shapes tucked into chocolate nests to show any remorse for poking him.

"You didn't have to get all these," she said.

"Nope. And I didn't. They were brought here from Toussaint. Whoever thought it was a good idea to rename The Pastry Place, All Tarted Up?"

Reb sputtered. "Flakiest Pastry in Toussaint? The Gables, I guess. I heard Jilly and Joe got tired of the old name and decided the place needed a new image. They've got a booming business there, and Jilly's so efficient I think the only thing Joe does is the books — and of course he likes to hang around and talk if he's in the mood. He's pretty busy with his other business. He's a lawyer."

"I didn't know that," Marc said. He'd met Joe and liked him. "Maybe I'll get in touch with him if I need representation right in town."

Reb examined the pastries from several angles. "That's Girard property, too, isn't it? The bakery and shop. Were they supposed to ask permission before they changed the name?"

"Of course they weren't supposed to ask first. But I think the name stinks."

She sucked air through her teeth and lowered a finger and thumb, like a pair of pincers, over an apricot in a meringue cup fluted with whipped cream. Once it was in her mouth and her eyes were squeezed shut in ecstasy, she mumbled, "I think it's funny. And this is almost worth what it's doing to my hips."

Marc picked up one of the miniature mango cheesecakes but said, "From where I'm looking, your hips are perfect," before putting the very sweet mouthful away. Reb didn't say a word, but he got a long, warning look. She ought to remember that he'd always been excited by a challenge.

109

He opened the promised ice chest. This was one he'd found abandoned in a parking lot after a concert on the campus at Tulane. Its silver sides were dented, but the words painted in red, one word on each panel, were still clear. "Horniest Toads in Louisiana."

"White wine, pink wine, champagne, or something mixed. Name your poison."

"Nice ice chest."

"That wasn't on the list, but thanks."

"I'll have champagne."

He popped a cork and poured it into two heavily cut flutes with fragile stems. "I saw your Father Cyrus in All Tarted Up. Had an odd kid with him. The kid was hanging around the parish house, too."

"He's not *my* Father Cyrus. He is my friend. Was it a boy around ten?"

"Uh huh. He had something in a brown bag, and Cyrus was ticking him off by not letting him take it out in the shop."

Reb's fingers hovered over the dishes again. "Wally Hibbs. Doll and Gator Hibbs's boy. That would have been Nolan in the bag."

"I'm almost afraid to ask," Marc said.

"Wally's tarantula. He takes it everywhere in a plastic box — and part of everywhere is following Cyrus whenever he gets the chance. Cyrus insists he cover the spider in front of anyone who might be disturbed by it. Wally isn't odd, just a loner and too old for his years."

"The priest wasn't pleased with him. I could

tell that much." Marc clinked his glass against hers and said, "To old times."

"To Clouds End," Reb responded, not meeting his eyes.

"I thought I'd buy you dinner at Pappy's, but I didn't want to short you on the good stuff. They aren't famous for desserts."

Gaston, who had been poking his way through the plantings, came within feet of them and lifted his head to sniff the air. With no warning he whipped his simply clipped body from a flower bed to the top of the ice chest and halfway onto the trolley Marc had brought in to bear the goodies. One cover was askew, and the animal snooted it aside to take a petit four in his teeth.

"Gaston," Reb cried. "Drop it. Now. I said, drop it." She put down her champagne and ran at the dog, who promptly streaked away with the cake still in his mouth.

Marc began to laugh and Reb turned on him. "It's not funny. I don't know that there aren't pieces of glass in those things. Come here, boy." She set down her champagne and captured Gaston as he swallowed the last of his stolen treat and licked his lips.

"Shouldn't have laughed," Marc said, disturbed by her remark. "He might get sick."

"He won't get sick," she said, clutching the dog to her chest. "He . . ." Her voice trailed away, and she sat down hard on a blue-tiled bench. "I'm sorry. I shouldn't have come. You

111

must think I've lost my mind."

"Reb . . ."

"I overreacted. It's been . . . This hasn't been a good day. If you wouldn't mind taking me home, we'll make an appointment for you to come and talk in my office."

"I would mind." He offered her the champagne she'd hardly touched, and when she didn't take it, held it in front of her face until she did. "I invited you out for the evenin' and you accepted. Something's eating you, and if it's the prospect of talkin' about the woman who died, then you've got a lot more complicated feelings about it than you've indicated."

She drank the champagne down and coughed. "You, you, you," she said and sounded furious. "There you go again. Someone else doesn't feel so hot and it has to be because of you. Well, it isn't, Marc Girard."

"Then open up and tell me what it is."

"It's none of your business."

"I'm a good listener, and I'll help if I can."

She stood up, still cradling Gaston in one arm, and replaced each dish cover firmly. The pager grabbed her attention, and she quickly located her cell phone in her purse. "Hi, Peggy. Everything okay? Did you rest like I told you to?"

For some time Reb only listened. He admired how much she cared for her patients, but she took it too far.

"I'll write all that down when I'm back in my

112

office. Now listen; *then* I want you to lie down and get some sleep. No, no argument, or I'll have to call George at the mill and have him go home to you."

She listened again.

"Well, do as I tell you, then, Peggy. I won't let anything happen to you. Yes, I heard what's bothering you, and no, it is not necessary for you to make special emergency plans in case it snows when it's time for you to deliver. I think we're going to be okay there. Can you trust me on this? I know you're glad I'm here for you, and I'm not going anywhere."

The call ended and she put the phone away without comment. He guessed that was his cue to keep his mouth shut about doctor-patient business.

"Reb, like I said, I listen real well."

"I don't need help."

"I think you do. And I think you're just as pig-headed as you were when you were a kid, only now you're a doctor and you think that makes it okay to be a pain in the ass. You don't need help? Fine, but I do, and I'm not giving up till I get it."

"Some things don't change," she said, and he saw how she shivered. "You're still pushing me around and deciding what I have to do, what I have to accept. Just like you always did. Any decision involving you and me was always made by you."

He wasn't touching that. "I have a responsibility to my family. I take those things seriously."

"I don't have a family," she told him. "I only have me and Gaston, and today someone tried to kill him to make a point with me." She paused with her mouth open, then turned away from him.

"Reb?"

She shook her head.

Marc gripped her arm and spun her to face him. "I'm not giving an inch until you explain what you just said. Are you serious? Someone did that?"

"No. I don't know why I said it." When she brought her lips together they trembled. She was upset, but she was also one angry woman.

"Don't treat me like an idiot. Of course you know why you said it. Now tell me about it, or we're going to get real tired of standing in this conservatory."

"That's a new twist." Her voice rose. "I know you're overbearing and opinionated; I didn't know you'd turned violent."

"Violent? That's rich." He laughed but was far from amused. "I'm holding your arm, so now I'm violent?"

"You're threatening me. If I don't do what you want, you won't let me leave. Don't you think I'm going through enough?" Her breasts rose and fell with each breath. "You let me go right now. I'll find my own way home."

"Reb, I want —"

"*Just let me go.* I don't care what you want.

114

When are you going to get that through your thick head?"

"Dammit!" Blood hammered at his temples, and he pulled her close. "You're bein' weird and scarin' me to death. Either you're frightened, or sick. Which is it?"

She let Gaston jump from her arms and amazed Marc by taking a swing at him with an open hand. He caught it before she could slap him.

For seconds she stared up at him, her eyes unblinking and her lips parted. When she started to slump, he gathered her against him.

She clung there, drove her fingers into his arms. "This isn't your problem."

So there was a real problem, not that he'd needed her confirmation on top of what he was seeing here. "Whatever's going on with you *is* my problem because I'm making it so. We're far from strangers. We're old friends, good friends, with unfinished business." When had his timing turned so lousy?

Reb shuddered. She looked over her shoulder at the dust-covered windows, and overhead, as if she might be attacked through the broken panes there. The great breath she took was obviously meant to calm her. She took another and another and let her hands go limp on his muscles.

"You are fearful, cher. Terrified. Are you in danger?"

Her body tensed again, and she pushed against his chest. From somewhere close by came a thump followed by a series of small clunks. Reb's eyes filled with tears, but he wouldn't let her shrug away from him.

"Just more plaster coming down," he told her.

"Okay," she said quietly. "You want me to tell you something you can't do a thing about. You can't let a person have her own dignity and make sure she isn't imaginin' things before she starts shooting her mouth off, so I'll give you your way, of course."

"Are you imaginin' things?" he said, growing agitated again. "Is some nonexistent threat turning you into a jumpy woman afraid of her shadow — and dreaming up a few shadows maybe?"

"That is so like you to laugh at my concerns."

Pushing with both fists, she really struggled to get away from him. If he let her go he was sure she'd fly out of the house and he'd be chasing her until she got too tired to run anymore. "Settle down, Reb. Let's get some tea."

"I don't want any *tea*. Okay, this is the way it is. The killings you mentioned yesterday, the ones that happened a couple of years back. I got involved — professionally — because I was the first doctor on each scene. Afterward I was threatened. If I didn't say certain things — tell lies — I'd die too. Then it was all over, just like that." She passed a hand across her mouth. "A man was arrested and convicted of attacking another woman. He wasn't found guilty of the murders, but everyone around here believes he did them. I didn't get any more warnings after that, so I thought it had gone away."

"Shh," Marc said. "It's okay. Everything's okay now. You're overworked is all, and dealing with what happened in that belfry shook you up. I'm not going to make things hard for you, cher. Simple questions are all I've got. This other thing you're talkin' about is in the past. Forget it."

"It's *not* in the past. It's come back. And dealing with Bonnie made me sad, not shaken up." She was dry-eyed again, but colorless.

"You think you —"

"I don't think, I know. You don't. It's started again. They're after me. I'm being followed, and this afternoon they showed how easy it'll be to get at me . . . when I'm alone."

She closed her eyes, and terror passed over her face like pain. "It's just been little things I noticed that made me suspect I was being watched. I hoped I was wrong. Now I know I wasn't."

Marc laced his fingers around her neck and supported her head. And when her eyes started to open again, he kissed her.

EIGHT

No way was the bitch he'd married going to hold him up and squeeze him dry. No sir. Chauncey Depew checked himself over in the bathroom mirror and slicked his hair back one more time.

She'd put him off for days, since the deputy pulled him in, but tonight was showdown time. He'd remind Precious that regardless of what she thought she could hold over his head, he was bigger, stronger, and smarter than she was.

"Down, Big Boy," he muttered, smiling at himself. The thought of teaching Precious a lesson had brought the big boy to attention.

He heard the bedroom door close and turned so he could see his dear wife in the mirror, but she wouldn't see him until she got a lot closer. She walked in, pausing between steps to kick off the fuck-me heels she favored. If she knew he was watching her, she'd probably keep the shoes on because she liked what they did for her legs.

At her dressing table, she took a brush, and hung her head upside down while she worked on her black hair till it was straight and gleaming. When she threw it back, her face was flushed. She unbuttoned her blouse and took it off, then untied a wraparound skirt that would make a better belt. Music burst from the CD player she kept on the dressing table, and she hummed and wiggled to the beat.

Her black bra fastened between her breasts. She unhooked the clip and let the thing hang from her shoulders while she kept on dancing. She played with her nipples, watched her tweaking fingers with her tongue between her teeth.

Chauncey pressed a hand over his zipper. His dick pressed back.

She stripped without missing a beat. That's when she fluttered the fingers of one hand at him and he realized she'd known he was watching. A show for him? How sweet. Too bad she'd used her naked body to punish him for so long, and too bad he hadn't figured out a way to make her pay for the torture without jeopardizing the nice little fortune she represented.

He moved around the door and leaned on the jamb. He didn't wave. From what he could tell, not a soul but himself and Precious knew that her mother didn't live on social security and the droppings from whatever she did at St. Cécil's. She liked fooling people. Oribel Scully was no fool herself. She'd inherited, and made the right moves to turn what she got into major money. He got regular updates on how much she was worth. It was all going to Precious, and the two women made sure Chauncey didn't forget it.

Let them enjoy the power. Once Oribel was gone, Precious — who didn't believe in divorce — would add her windfall to the nice heap he'd built. And she wouldn't have her devil mother to tell her how to handle her husband.

"You're lookin' lovely, you," he told Precious. Why not try some sweet talk first. It had been a long time since he'd offered her much more than silence — which she seemed to enjoy well enough.

Precious put one hand flat on her belly and rolled her hips.

"Oh, baby" — he spoke low, the way that made most women feel like warm taffy — "I do believe you're a natural belly dancer. Let's us get you some of those scarves and pants what you can see through. Some strings of coins to jingle. I'll help with the lessons, me. Hell, I'll give you the lessons. I don't forget how much you like my hip action."

She kept on dancing. Mrs. Depew didn't need any bra. "I wouldn't want you coverin' up those boobs — not even with somethin' I could see through." The nipples turned up. Nothing moved much since the operation, but he did love the way those things felt. "With what they cost — although I always told you that you didn't need a thing extra to turn me on — but for what we paid, you gotta make sure they appreciated."

"Oh, sugar," she said. "They're appreciated."

She lived to rile him. Chauncey pulled his

T-shirt over his head and made sure his hair still looked good.

"Why did you take that off," Precious said, and stood still with her hands on her hips.

"Too hot," he told her, and winked. "In more ways than one."

"At your age you look better with the shirt on," she said, staring pointedly at his stomach.

She never missed a chance to remind him about the sixteen years that separated them.

"That so?" he said. "Maybe the same goes for you, but you parade around in front of me like that every chance you get. And we both know why you do it, don't we?"

"Do we?" she said.

He wouldn't make her day by pleading even one more time for her to stop punishing him for what she considered his sins. If he wanted to, he could force himself on her, but he was too smart for her, he knew that was what she wanted — one more story to add to her list of imaginary grievances. Well, mostly imaginary. Women were like that, they exaggerated. "Hell, you ain't given me none in two months and you want to make sure I know what I'm missin'. Well I do, but you gotta make up your own mind 'bout things like that. I love you and I'll wait as long as it takes."

She rolled her eyes and strolled from the room. Chauncey followed her downstairs and into the kitchen, where she poured herself a tall gin and tonic. Rolling the glass against her brow, she trailed into the all white living room. He closed the white shutters over the windows while Precious arranged herself on a shiny damask couch. White was, she liked to say, her color because it showed off her tawny skin and dark hair.

That was *it*. Now she'd learn he wasn't taking any more shit from her. "What you doin' talkin' to Devol? I think you interferin' in my business. That never was part of the deal and never will be. Get out of my way, woman, and stay out. And I better never find out you've got friendly enough with that big, brainless nothing to say things that would take us both down. You never trust the law, Precious baby. Even when they admirin' you assets and tellin' you they on your side."

"I have no idea what you're talking about. Deputy Spike's a friend of mine. If you've got a problem with that you'll have to live with it. You aren't in a position to point any fingers."

He laughed but his throat was dry. "What you been sayin' to him?"

Her light brown eyes were so innocent he almost believed them. "I'm not sayin' anything you need to worry about, Chauncey. A girl has to find company where she can. Be grateful I've chosen an upright citizen as a friend. At least he respects me and doesn't try to get inside my pants."

"What would you do if he tried?"

She giggled and raised her shoulders. "Why,

I'd give 'em to him, sugar, and tell him to put 'em on. But it's nothing like that. Honest. All we do is talk."

Sweat on his back turned cold, and his skin crawled. Somewhere in the room a horsefly buzzed loud enough to drive a man mad, but Chauncey couldn't see the critter. "Why'd you tell Devol I was havin' you followed?"

"You are." A long, long swallow of gin moved her throat. "And you're scarin' me, so I had to say somethin' to buy a little insurance. Life insurance."

"Damn you." He ran his fingers through his hair. "You know I wouldn't do nothin' to you. I love you. You ain't put out diddly for me in weeks, but have I touched you?"

"You know better." With one knee drawn up, she rested the opposite ankle there and turned her foot in circles. "I told you a long time ago that if you cheated on me again, you was never gettin' inside this body again. And you went right ahead and did it anyway. You went back to sleeping around because you can't help yourself, Chauncey Depew. You're like a cock in the henhouse. How is Big Boy these days, anyway?"

Every way she could think of turning him on more, she did it. Right now it was with crude talk and a view of those heavenly gates. "This big boy's more than ready to go whenever you say the word," he told her. "Always has been, remember? I wouldn't try to make you, Precious.

But you sure are makin' it hard on a man."

"You've got that nasty man from New Orleans creepin' around after me. Then you have him in this house watchin' those movies I don't like as if there wasn't a thing goin' on with the two of you. He's someone bad, isn't he? He never speaks to me, just watches me. If he really is your friend you ought to tell him how you feel about him lookin' down my blouse every chance he gets. And he shows up everywhere, followin' me, and either he wants me to know he's there or he's real bad at his job."

Chauncey sat down where he had a good view of her and spread his legs, not that he could do much to make himself comfortable. "I'll speak to him."

"You're scared," Precious said. "You could have plenty to be scared about if you push me too far. And in case you got ideas about having Dante deal with that, don't, because I've taken precautions. There's letters in several safe places to be opened when I die."

"Damn you, woman." Fear shortened his breath. "I wouldn't do nothin' to you. I told you that over and over. Why you punishing me?"

"I knew you sniffed around that woman again. There's others got to know if they think about it hard enough. Someone must have seen you watchin' her, followin' her around. They just got to have their memories jogged. It's the little things that give you away."

His eyes stung. "When you mess with me, you

do something dangerous, sugar," he told her, deliberately whispering because she hated it. "Take yourself out of what I'm doin' and you won't have a thing to worry about."

"I can't do that."

"Allow me to decide what's best for both of us, and *stay* away from Devol's office."

Precious turned on her side and balanced the glass on a hip. "No one's linking you to that woman's death — yet. They think the Rubber Killer's back. They think what happened to May Lynn didn't have anything to do with the other things. May Lynn never was too strong in the thinkin' department anyway. Also, from the evidence at the time, whoever killed those two women covered his face, and May Lynn insisted she saw Leach's face. I think the gossip is right. There was two different men. One was a murderer — a psycho — and the other was Leach, who didn't want nothin' but May Lynn's body. The guy's sexy. Lookin' the way she does, I think she should have grabbed a rare opportunity and enjoyed herself."

Chauncey didn't care about May Lynn. He turned cold. "What you sayin'? Why they thinkin' about any killer? She wasn't murdered, that Bonnie Blue."

"How do you know that?"

"The docs said so," he told her. He really started to sweat. "She fell and broke herself up." He swallowed and said, "And she wasn't raped like those others. You gotta give me what I want,

125

Precious. You never should have taken what was mine in the first place."

Chauncy wouldn't be on the receiving end of any favors, not if she could help it. "We're getting to that," she said, her eyes narrowed. "How do you know the law isn't doin' what it does a lot these days: not makin' the real evidence public. They like to make sure no one gets too much information and figures out a way to muddy things up while the cops are still workin'. For all you know, she could have been murdered."

He got up and stood beside her. From her position she'd get a real good idea of what little chance she'd have if he did turn on her. "What happened at St. Cécil's wasn't nothin' to do with me. Why you makin' all these suggestions?"

"I'm not suggestin' a thing, just having a discussion."

The temptation to take her by the throat was dangerous. Violence wasn't his thing, but any man could be pushed. "Drop it. Where is the place — your place you're keepin' so damn secret?"

"I said I'm gettin' to that. In a way. Every woman ought to have somewhere she can call her own. Makes her feel like her own person. I like that. But I'm not givin' a thing away that I don't want to give away — and until I decide I'm feelin' like sharin'. So call off your little snoop because there isn't any way he's going to

126

catch me with my guard down. I won't lead him anywhere that interests you, Chauncey. And in case you haven't figured it out. That boy's got fuckin' on his mind. He watches those movies and gets all worked up, then he looks at me and he doesn't have to say what he wants."

"Give it up." She had to. He couldn't live under this much stress. It bothered his stomach.

"You know Marc Girard's here?"

"Who . . . Girard? No, I fuckin' didn't know."

"You do now. He's lookin' for his sister. Yeah, he loves his sister Amy and intends to make sure she gets treated with respect."

"What you do with them little pills for my stomach?"

"Your pills, for your stomach? Why, I wouldn't know, but I guess they're wherever you put them."

His gut burned and acid rose in his throat. "What do Girard's concerns have to do with me?"

Precious stood up so suddenly, he flinched and stepped backward. She kept on coming and stood close enough for him to smell gin on her breath and to feel the heat of her body. He recovered and held his ground.

She kept her eyes on his. "Marc Girard doesn't think there ever was a Bonnie Blue. He thinks the woman who died was his sister Amy."

Chauncey swallowed a mouthful of acid.

Precious layered herself against him with her

arms draped around his waist. She rubbed her breasts back and forth on his chest. He felt too sick to enjoy the moment.

"Don't you have something to say?"

"Maybe," he said, but knew his attempt to sound cool didn't come off. "What would make Girard think a thing like that?"

"Descriptions fit."

"Yeah? But it wasn't Amy."

"You know that. I know that. We're it."

She scared him. She'd forgotten one or two people who belonged on her list of people who already knew too much about the body. Her experience with things like this was nil, and there was so much at stake, she could put them both behind bars. "Tell me what you're thinking," he said, as reasonably as he could. "You haven't forgotten that none of this must go anywhere but between the two of us?"

"Of course I know that."

"You can't tell your mother."

Her mouth dropped open, then she laughed as if amazed. "I may be difficult on occasion, but I'm not mad. We'd both better hope she doesn't find out or she'll turn us in. No way is my mother going to cover for criminals, even if they are her kin."

"We aren't criminals. Sometimes you just have to look out after your own interests."

"I'm not arguing that now. This is all your fault, but if you get out of it, it'll be because I help you."

"Help me, then." The whining note in his voice didn't embarrass him. "Quit stringin' me along. Tell me what you're thinkin'."

"I've got something you think is yours. I say it's mine because it messed up my marriage before it ever had a chance. Your fault. You made a damn-fool wild move and stashed Amy Girard in *this* house. She came to talk to you because she's sick crazy about you, and you turned the bitch into a prisoner. And you thought I'd just go along with it? Well I didn't, and now *I'm* the one playin' nursemaid to the woman my husband screwed before and during our marriage. He was still screwing her until a couple of months ago, for cryin' out loud. What do you think I'm made of, ice?"

"I've told you I'm sorry a million times. You shouldn't have interfered. I'd have dealt with her and sent her on her way by now."

"Quit whining. The fact is that your whore can never be set free. Amy Girard would ruin every damn thing we've worked for. And Mama would give everythin' she's got to the Church."

"Don't say that woman's name aloud. Someone could walk in."

"Not unless they've got keys, and if that greasy pet creep of yours does have keys —"

"He doesn't." Chauncey's mind wouldn't settle on one thing. No matter what spin Precious put on this, they were done for. There was no way out.

"We're gonna be just fine," she said. "Know what Mama heard Marc Girard say to Reb?"

"What?"

"The Gambles aren't certain about Girard, and Doll and Gator wish he'd wake up and find out he croaked in the night. They say he's just like his mean ol' daddy — always wantin' his own way and not givin' up until he gets it."

"I don't give a shit about any of the small-timers. Just tell me what Girard said to Reb?"

She clasped her hands behind her neck and arched her back. "He's goin' to get that body exhumed. He won't pay no mind to how a decent burial put that poor Bonnie at rest finally. Out of that grave he'll have her dragged, so he can look her over."

"Oh my God, no," Chauncey said. He fell back into the chair. "That's horrible."

"Of course. Terrible." Precious grinned while she said it. "No one knows where Amy is at the moment, and they don't ever have to know."

Chauncey's eyes stung and he blinked. "I don't follow you." Girard knew about him and Amy. He could already be watching the house. He was probably out there now. Chauncey covered his face. He was going to have to run and leave almost everything behind.

"Damn it, Chauncey. Concentrate. You're going to stop lettin' your dick lead you around. You're going to let me make all the decisions from now on. Girard thinks it's Amy in that casket. Why not give him what he wants?"

She would never lose the power to shock him. "Bonnie's in there," he said.

"She doesn't have to be."

Chauncey stared at her. How right she was.

Precious bent over him, and he couldn't even get interested in an eyeful of her boobs only inches from his nose. "I see you're starting to understand me," she said, and sat astride his thighs while she undid his pants. "We just gotta make sure that when the paperwork's done and that grave's opened, it *is* Amy they find. We're gettin' a gift. The perfect murder. The perfect way to make everything right again. First you prepare the restin' place."

"You want —"

Warm air moved by the overhead fan hit his exposed body.

"I want you to get rid of an unwanted guest of the parish."

That's what he thought. "I need to concentrate, baby." He pushed halfheartedly at her fingers. "That means you're going to have to forget playin' around for now."

"This?" She flapped him back and forth. "Don't read anythin' into this. I'm just checkin' it out."

He did, Chauncey decided, hate her.

"All our troubles are about to be over, big man."

"I think you've forgotten one or two points. Like a body that's been . . . Bonnie Blue's body's in different condition from Amy's."

She let her head fall back and laughed aloud. "It is now. I wasn't suggestin' you were gonna bury Amy alive."

"Damn you." He pried her fingers loose. "If Amy had been dead two or three weeks it'd still be obvious the timing wasn't right."

Her grin disappeared. She slid down to kneel on the floor, bent over to take him in her mouth, and bit down so suddenly he yelled. But she didn't bite hard enough to hurt, only to make sure she had his undivided attention. "All you have to think about now is making sure there's a nice empty restin' place waitin' for your friend. The minute you give me the word things are clear there, we'll go to the next step. Givin' her the same injuries as Bonnie won't be a problem. Then there's ways to make sure no one gets any ideas about someone playing who's-got-the-real-body. My daddy wasn't in the funeral business for nothin'. Never could understand why he gave it up to be a deacon. But he taught me plenty.

"You better get started. I got to go take care of things." She snorted. "That woman actually thinks I'm a saint. She thinks I've saved her from you and I'm gonna find a way to take her someplace where you can't get to her.

"Guess that's kinda what I am gonna do — unless we turn up another guest who needs the bed more than she does." She mounted him and put a hand over his mouth to contain his cry. "Could be we're gonna need more than one space, but you could always stack 'em."

NINE

"Apologizing for kissing a woman isn't a great idea."

"Excuse me?" Marc said loudly.

Reb framed her mouth with her hands to make herself heard over the Swamp Doggies performing "Toussaint Nights" — with a lot of help on the lyrics from Pappy's patrons. "I wish you'd drop the subject. I'm sorry you're sorry you kissed me." But she surely was not sorry he had.

The song ended, and she was convinced her last few words must have been heard by everyone in the smoky, low-ceilinged dance-and-eats hall.

Marc leaned across the table. "You needed comforting, cher. And I didn't want you to really start cryin'."

She rolled her eyes.

"No, no." He held one of her hands, and she would not give satisfaction to the curious by pulling it away. "Reb, kissing you was worth the effort —"

She'd laugh if she didn't want to let him suffer and stumble his way through his own discomfort.

"I don't mean it was an effort," he said, and his unforgettable eyes were deeply sincere. "I wanted to comfort you."

"And keep me quiet."

"That, too."

She did laugh then, and she enjoyed the indistinct reddening along his cheekbones. Gaston, whom she'd smuggled in and put beneath the table, shifted between Reb's ankles, and she prayed he wouldn't decide to bark.

Trying to smother his own smile, Marc bent over her hand, turned it palm up. Reb didn't have to look around to know they had their own gallery of listeners. Toussaint had suffered its share of bad news in recent years, but in general, not enough happened day to day to satisfy busy minds. Reb was aware that she and Marc must make an interesting spectacle for the locals.

"I liked kissing you," Marc said without looking up. His nose was as straight as ever and up close, his eyebrows were as dark and flaring, his hair as curly and blue-black, but the smile lines at the corners of his eyes and beside his mouth were deeper. The kiss they were both thinking about had stunned her. If necessary she would remind Marc that they'd both clung, weak-kneed, to each other afterward.

She got a sideways glance and the faintest of grins from him. "You smell nice, cher, and you taste nice. And you feel nice, too."

When she'd recovered enough, she said, "The set's over. Keep your voice down."

"I am. You make the mistake of thinking everyone's interested in your business."

"You, Mr. Girard, have a mean tongue."

"Thank you."

"I wasn't talking about . . . ooh, you have not changed. You still think you're God's good gift to women."

"Do I?" The look he gave her from beneath his brows turned her heart. There had always been something poignant in Marc. It didn't show often, but it did now, and Reb's resolve not to get close to him wobbled. Not that he was in Toussaint because of her, or that he would stay a moment longer than it took to get what he'd come for.

She smiled at him and sat straighter. "I could have insisted on you driving me home rather than coming here," she told him.

"Yes, you could. But you didn't want to."

"Marc —"

"Sorry. That wasn't cute. I'll rephrase it. I was relieved when you didn't ask me to take you home."

She must not forget that he'd been a master of charm all his life. On the other hand, that charm had matured into something really . . . charming. "Thank you, Marc."

"I don't want you to be afraid," he said. "We will not be passive about what has been happening to you. The law must become involved. And I know many people. Some of them could prove very helpful if we need them."

"I've been thinking about what I told you." The idea of "helpful people" unnerved her. She didn't want to explore exactly what he might mean by that. "I think I've been too sensitive. All that happened before has made me touchy. What I intend to do is calm down and stop looking for goblins."

With a long forefinger, he traced the lines on her palm, and tapped the finger on which she'd used a dressing. "Because you are touchy, you imagined glass in Gaston's food?"

He would never allow her to be less than honest with herself. "If I want to put everything behind me and start over, is that so bad? I will improve security in Conch Street, but I will not continue to expect someone to jump out and grab me. And for all I know, the glass was in the bowl when I poured Gaston's food in."

"You don't lie well."

She couldn't meet his eyes. "I'm trying to mean what I say."

"I can't allow you to take these risks."

"You won't be able to stop me from doing anything I want to do . . . *Cyrus?* What's Cyrus doing here?"

Marc followed the direction of her gaze to where Cyrus stood at the bar talking to Spike Devol. "A priest can't have a drink?"

"That's Spike Devol he's with. Deputy Sheriff. Spike never comes in here, either — unless there's trouble or he's lookin' for someone. Spike was already here. I saw him talking to the man wearing a suit." No one wore a suit to Pappy's. "I think Cyrus just got here."

"I'd forgotten how important it is for everyone to know everyone else's business in Toussaint."

She ignored the remark. "I think I've seen the other man, but I'm not sure where. He definitely doesn't come from around here."

Reb couldn't feel Gaston anymore. She tapped her toes left and right, but he wasn't there.

"Relax," Marc said. "Gaston's okay."

When had her reactions become so transparent?

He pushed the plates that had held his jambalaya and Reb's chicken gumbo away from the edge of the table and peered down at the dog. "Hey, boy," Marc said, leaning back in his chair to get a better look. "I love it when you smile at me that way. He's fine, he's sitting on my feet." He sat up and scooted his chair in again but not without Reb noting how cautiously he did so.

"Gaston doesn't usually bite," Reb told him. "Just keep still and you'll be okay."

Marc steepled his fingers beneath his chin and turned his face up to the beamed wooden ceiling where thumbtacked business cards, the deeply yellowed layers from years gone by visible in spots, added a designer touch to the decor.

Let him be irritated with her, Reb decided.

Her pager alerted her, and she muttered an apology to Marc before returning a call to Ozaire Dupre. Ozaire had been talking to William at the church and wanted to warn Reb to stay away from "that bad man." "Thanks, Ozaire," she said. "I'm doing very well. How's your ear? No more pain?"

Marc's expression was difficult to read, but she'd take a bet that he was chalking another one up to her being too soft and too available to her patients.

Ozaire wasn't to be put off so easily. His ear was just fine, had been for two months. Had she heard what William heard about that Marc Girard?

"I heard what was said," she told him. "That isn't true, Ozaire. Please do your best to stop the rumor."

He was just warming to his topic when Reb had to say, "I want to talk to you about this, I really do, but I'm eating dinner with a friend." She drummed her fingers on the table. "Just a friend. Bye."

"You must give your cell number to anyone who asks for it," Marc said. He set his teeth.

"They need to be able to reach me."

"For medical reasons maybe — but only maybe. To chat and ask you personal questions? I don't think so."

Reb deliberately looked away, first at dancers on the floor, then toward the bar. "I've never seen Cyrus here . . . Oribel must have told him we were coming." Why would she ever think the woman might not carry out her threats? "She said she was going to."

"Does it make any difference if he's here?"

Reb drank some of her water. "It does to me."

Marc fixed his attention on her face. "Why?"

"We're friends." Not that it was any business of Marc's. "We have been since Cyrus came here. He's interesting, and good company."

"Why would Oribel think she had to share your business with the priest? For that matter, why did you tell her?"

"Are you practicin' to be some woman's overbearin' husband —" Reb poked a forefinger into a paper placemat where a map of the area suggested that Pappy's Dancehall covered more geography than Lafayette. "That wasn't a smart thing to say," she said.

"Could have been. I could be plannin' on being overbearing."

Just not a husband. Marc Girard wasn't husband material any more than she was wife material. "I didn't share any information. You did. She was visitin' me and saw your note on the flowers."

"Read my note, you mean? Wasn't it in an envelope?"

Reb glanced at Cyrus and wondered if he was ever aware of how he caught the attention of every woman who saw him. Female faces turned toward him. Those that weren't trying not to stare too hard at Marc. The ladies at Pappy's were getting a double treat this evening: Marc and Cyrus. And Spike Devol wasn't hard on the eyes.

139

"Did Oribel take my note out —"

"Yes. This is a very small town, and sometimes people forget about little things like respecting privacy. I don't think Oribel thinks you're honorable." She smiled at him. "Or maybe she thinks you're not to be trusted with my honor."

"And maybe she's right."

Reb looked at him sharply and actually caught something other than the expected teasing grin. Marc stared back at her, and he was very reflective — reflective enough to send the message that he could be interested in more than kissing her.

"Cyrus keeps looking at me," she said, and swallowed. "The poor man takes his responsibilities very seriously."

A waitress brought them two more glasses of house red wine — the only kind available at Pappy's — and cleared the plates. Once she'd left Marc said, "Cyrus isn't responsible for you, is he?" and Reb heard a little edge in his voice.

"Only as a priest and my friend," she told him. "And I think he likes to watch out for me because I'm pretty much on my own. He's like that."

Marc picked up his wine and said, "Too bad he wasn't available to look out for Amy."

"Marc . . . I'm sorry. Sheesh, I'm really sorry. You're here because you're looking for your sister and I'm not being as tuned in as I should be."

"You've got a lot going on yourself."

"Not so much that I can be excused for being

140

thoughtless. I'm not supposed to be that way at all."

He sought and held her hand again. "We'll get around to Amy. *I'll* get to her. What you can do to help me, I know you will. But I'll need to go elsewhere — and ask a lot of questions — to get what I want."

"You're wrong about it being Amy, not Bonnie, who fell down those stairs," Reb said, and threaded her fingers between his. "If it *had* been Amy and she'd asked Cyrus for help, he'd have given it, though. He gave Bonnie help by letting her stay at his house rent-free."

The neon-lighted jukebox burst forth, and Elvis filled in for the band with "Blue Suede Shoes." Carmen, the bouncer at Pappy's, kept the old machine chained to a section of concrete road divider he'd "borrowed" — on account of the jukebox being a valuable temptation.

"Why would Cyrus take in a stranger?"

Sometimes men could be so single-minded they became totally obtuse about everything else. "I think taking in strangers could go with the job, Marc."

"He wasn't here before Amy left." He rubbed the tips of his fingers across the inside of her wrist. "He wouldn't know her."

"What do you really want to get out of what you're doing?" she asked him. "Do you *want* Amy to be the one who died?"

She knew her mistake as soon as his hold on her hand became rigid.

"I'm sorry. Of course you don't want it to have been Amy, but you really believe it was, and you aren't going to be persuaded otherwise."

"I'd love to be persuaded otherwise. But I don't think it's going to happen."

Reb saw a group come into Pappy's and relegated Cyrus and Spike to the back of her mind. She silently pressed fingers into Marc's hand.

He swallowed the mouthful of wine he'd just taken. "What now?"

"Just tell me I can hope you won't lose your temper with anyone this evening."

He blinked and managed to make his eyes look innocent — and he pressed his right hand over his heart. "Moi? Why, I'm the most mild-mannered man you'll ever meet."

"Just promise."

"I promise not to throw the first punch."

"*Marc*. Trouble, or at least irritating people, are heading this way. You may not care about your reputation, but I care about mine. There won't be any punches at all, no nastiness of any kind."

"Who is it? Tell me, or I'll have to turn around and look, and whoever it is will know you're talking to me about them."

"You have a really nasty streak. It's Doll and Gator Hibbs and Jilly and Joe Gable. Jilly and Joe are wonderful, and I don't know how they stand the Hibbses. Maybe the Gables are the only ones who see the good side of those two."

Marc made motions with his head as if he were oiling the vertebrae in his neck. "I know

142

what you're trying to do," Reb said. "*Don't* turn around, Marc. They're still making their way over here. Slowly, because everyone in the place is as surprised to see them here as I am — and from the looks on people's faces, they're asking questions."

Marc gave her hand a familiar squeeze and wiped all expression from his features. "You don't have a thing to worry about with me, cher. Whatever you want from me, you get. As long as no one pushes me too far."

The innocent expression cracked a little, and Reb couldn't help smiling at him.

Doll Hibbs led the advance. Of medium height and build, she combed her fine brown hair back into a long, straight ponytail. Pale gray eyes, anxiously rounded, gave entirely the wrong impression of Ms. Hibbs. Reb was well-acquainted with the woman's sharp tongue, persecution complex, and obsession with her own health.

Doll pretended not to see Reb and sat at the next table — which wasn't the only vacant table at Pappy's. Gator balanced his round rump on the chair beside her, pushed his Achafalaya Gold Casino baseball cap to the back of his bald head, and wiped his sweating face with a paper napkin from the table.

Marc cupped his jaw with one hand and rolled his eyes at Reb, but he didn't look toward their newly arrived neighbors, so she decided to forgive him.

Not speaking to the Hibbses was ridiculous,

but handsome, black-haired and blue-eyed Joe Gable and his half-sister Jilly reached the space between the two tables and immediately stopped to say hi.

"Well," Jilly said, "if you aren't a dark horse, Doctor Reb. How long you been hiding this tall, dark heartthrob?" Jilly's mother, her father's second wife, had been the child of a part black mother and a white father, and the result was Jilly's marvelous honey-colored skin, her startling light hazel eyes, and long brown hair with natural blond highlights.

Joe stood at his half-sister's shoulder and shook his head in the fondest way. "Hello, doc," he said, but offered his hand to Marc. "Joe Gable, Marc. We were told you were in town. Pleased to meet you."

"Likewise." Marc nodded at Joe. "I spoke to one of your staff this morning. Thanks for getting the pastries to Clouds End. They were great, right, Reb?"

Let the whole town know we were together there, why don't you? She raised her glass to the Gables and said, "The best."

"He doesn't get any credit," Jilly said, elbowing her outrageously good-looking Cajun brother. "He does the books, *when he's got time,* and criticizes. The rest of the time, he's the lawyer. Is it true you two knew each other when you were kids?"

Reb almost groaned. "Our parents were friends."

Joe winked at Marc and said, "Amazing what differences a few years can make to the kind of friendships we have, hm?"

"Amazing," Marc agreed and flashed Joe a boy-to-boy grin that gave Reb an urge to stomp on his feet under the table.

"Well." Joe was still smiling and now raised his fine black brows. He had the kind of thick, curling eyelashes a lot of women would kill for. "Our Reb isn't the easygoing piece of custard pie she'd like you to think. Tamale pie would be closer, if you know what I mean."

Speechless, Reb could only shake her head repeatedly.

"Jilly?" Doll Gater called from the next table, even though it was so close there was no need to shout. "We want to order."

"Coming," Jilly said, frowning at her visibly aggravated brother and pulling him toward the Hibbses. "Maybe we can visit some more later."

Cyrus came their way carrying a glass. "What an interesting evening," he said when he reached the table. "We seem to have half the population of Toussaint here, and I don't think some of them ever came through the doors before."

Reb held back from saying that Cyrus was hardly a regular.

"Sit down," Reb said to him. "Unless you want me to leap up and ask you to dance."

Cyrus sat beside Marc. "Is the doctor giving you a hard time, too, Marc?"

"We're friends from way back," Marc said.

"I gathered that." Cyrus put his glass of beer on the table. "Good friends, I hope." He smiled, but Reb could tell he wasn't happy.

"Our fathers played chess together," she said. Something wasn't sitting right with Cyrus. He'd made fists on the table and his knuckles were white. He seemed . . . uncomfortable, as if he couldn't decide how to behave.

"Reb was a little tyke when I first knew her," Marc said. "Pushy already, though."

"Then you knew each other at Tulane."

"Uh uh," Marc said, and his lips had thinned. "Only for a while. I was a senior when she arrived. It was good to have her there, though. She was always a good listener."

Amazingly, Cyrus leaned in front of Marc so that Reb couldn't see either man's face. "So that's the only reason you're hanging around her — so that she'll listen to you?"

Reb held her breath. That comment was as close to something unnecessarily confrontational as she'd heard from him. She was grateful Marc had taken his hand away from hers. She was also grateful when Cyrus turned toward her again.

"Now you mention it," Marc said tightly, "Havin' Reb care about what's happenin' to me does make me feel a whole lot better."

Oh great, the local priest and a man most of Toussaint thought was a plague, getting all riled up over the town's lady doctor. "I'm a lucky one," Reb said. "I have wonderful friends. I'm grateful."

Cyrus and Marc cast flat stares at one another. She wasn't helping things around here.

"Well," Doll Hibbs said loudly. "Whatever next? A man of God frequenting a place like this."

Cyrus smiled benevolently at Doll, then at each person sitting at her table. "I'm changing my ways. What's good enough for my flock is good enough for me. I can't have all of you out here drinking and dancing and socializing and be too remote to join you, now can I?"

Marc's cheeks were blown up with air. He craned his neck to look toward the windows. Heavy droplets of rain sparkled in the reflected lights from inside Pappy's. Thunder rolled in the distance.

"What're the rules on exhumation, Father?" Doll asked.

Reb felt as if water traveled beneath the skin on her legs. She dared not look at anyone.

"Why would you ask a thing like that?" Cyrus said.

"You can't expect people not to overhear things when they're said real loud in the parish house" — she angled her head toward Marc — "by this one. We heard he wanted to take that poor thing, Bonnie Blue, out of her resting place. No matter. We know you won't have nothing to do with that."

"Hush," Reb said, pulling her chair close to their table. "You know better than to start rumors on hearsay. "You're going to upset people with talk like that."

Doll looked around with relish. "If there's something wrong going on in this town, the people have a right to know." She leaned past Reb. "We know these two were at Tulane together, don't we, Gator? Reckon there's more to that than meets the eye. And there's plenty of theories. Come back to make an honest woman of her, have you, Mr. Girard?"

This would be a perfect moment for the floor to open up and swallow her, Reb decided. She shunted her chair back to their own table.

The Doggies resumed their places, and dancers took to the floor once more, surefooted in the almost elegant patterns they'd been taught by parents and grandparents.

The atmosphere at the table was heavy. Spike Devol appeared, skirting the dance floor on his way toward them. He carried his Stetson. Blond, blue-eyed, his appealing face tanned and showing his mother's Scandinavian roots, Spike advanced their way. His regulation shirt, with its precisely ironed-in creases, fitted broad shoulders, a good chest, and flat stomach like a coat of khaki paint. If his somber manner hadn't made Reb uneasy, she might have come to like him a lot. Regardless, she was glad to smile at him now and wave him toward the seat beside her. Rather than smile back, he frowned. A girl popped from her seat near Pappy's eighteen-foot-long stuffed and varnished alligator and stopped Spike. She stood on her toes to whisper in his ear — probably asking him to dance. Spike shook his head but did manage a smile this time.

"Good evenin'," he said to Reb, very formal. "I will sit, thank you."

"Everything okay?" Cyrus asked him, and when Spike gave a slight nod and a confidential glance passed between them, Reb only just stopped herself from asking what was going on.

"Trouble?" Marc asked. He shook hands with Spike and said, "I'm Marc Girard. Clouds End belongs to my family. I'm staying out there while I get some business attended to in Toussaint. The house and grounds need a lot of work, too. Somethin' goin' on here tonight?"

"Spike Devol," the deputy said. Spike had a reputation for being tough when he needed to be. "There's nothing to be concerned about. I'm surprised to see you here, doctor."

"Reb," she told him, not for the first time. "Look around you. People bring their children here to eat and they all dance. There's nothing wrong with Pappy's."

"There is when it gets later," Spike said. "I avoid speaking about police business, but there are things going on down here that aren't obvious. It would be better if you got along home before too long."

Marc hooked both elbows over the back of his chair and tilted his head as if waiting for an explanation of Spike's announcement.

"This is ridiculous," Reb said and didn't care if she did look and sound annoyed. "What do you and Cyrus think you're doing? I'm not here on my own. You're being insultin'. To me and to Marc."

Color rose along Spike Devol's cheekbones. He swiveled sideways in his chair and made as if to touch her arm, but his fingers remained suspended, inches from her skin. He cleared his throat. When he finally managed to meet her eyes, his absolute misery softened Reb. "Forget it," she told him. "The man you were talking to at the bar — wearing a black suit — who is he?"

Spike looked toward the bar and so did Reb. The man had left.

Cyrus said, "Dante Cornelius. Visiting from New Orleans. Oribel told me he's a friend of Chauncey's."

Gator Hibbs, sidling up beside Cyrus, doused any discussion. Gator settled his head to one side. He had no neck, and his jowl rested directly on his meaty collarbone. "The wife wants me to have a word with you," he said, sniffing and hitching up his wide jeans. Almost free of lines, his smooth, ruddy face didn't increase any impression of wisdom or wit. "Y'know how it is. These women worry. It's about Wally. You're letting him hang around too much."

Cyrus thought for a long time. He bent his head forward, and the top of his black, thick curly hair glinted. Reb didn't recall seeing him with a beard shadow before, but he had one now, and he looked tired — and maybe a little mad.

"See," Gator said, "the boy stays away as long as he thinks we're up. Then he sneaks in to sleep, and sneaks out again before we see him.

"If you didn't let him make a nuisance of himself at St. Cécil's, he'd come home. No respect. That's what we get, no respect."

Reb caught Jilly's apologetic expression and nodded at her.

"You're right," Cyrus said, and not for the first time Reb wondered just how much it cost him to be perpetually reasonable and gentle. "Call Madge in the morning and we'll make an appointment to get together and talk this through." He deliberately turned his back to the other table.

"Maybe we should speak about this Dante Cornelius alone, Father," Spike said, squared off to the table once more.

Cyrus appeared surprised, but said, "Surely."

Reb saw Marc's eyes turn hard and his lips pull back in a grimace, and she got to her feet. "Dance with me, Marc," she said standing beside him. "Let's see if we remember how." Without waiting for a response, she walked to the floor and by the time she turned, a smile tacked to her face, Marc was approaching with an equally phony smile on show.

TEN

"One-two-three, one-two-three," she said as he drew near enough to take her hands. "I think we can still do a killer Cajun two-step. How about you?"

His features softened. "I don't think I trust myself to say the right thing — on any subject — right now." He spun her to wrap one of his arms across her shoulders and clasp her hand. His other hand he placed over hers at her waist, and they swept into the circle of couples, revolving together and around the others. The band members were on their feet, with Vincent Fox plying the bow across his fiddle like a man who didn't have enough time for all the notes he had to play. The accordion whined, and the banjo player picked and scraped his strings. The rhythm set every foot in the place stamping.

Reb looked up at Marc, and this time her grin was genuine. All around them colorful dresses whirled. Her own soft gray skirt floated and wrapped itself first one way, then the other around her body.

"Does Cyrus talk about the death?" Marc

asked. "He must have been there afterward."

"Yes."

He raised her hand above her head and twirled her, and held her tightly at his side afterwards. His thumb and fingers spread over her waist. He was warm. "What was his reaction?"

Reb made as if to stop dancing, but Marc kept her moving. "Humor me, cher, okay? I've got a lot of catching up to do before I know what everyone else knows around here."

"Everyone else *doesn't* know."

He landed her against his chest and held her close. Instantly they were dancing their own intimate, swaying form of the number. Marc bent her backward, low over his arm, followed her down, and brought her up so fused to him she could feel the buttons on his shirt — and other things.

"We have real style together," he told her. "Remind me to tell you more about what I want to do with Clouds End."

Reb looked straight ahead where hair showed at the open neck of his shirt and mumbled agreement.

"So, everyone doesn't know what's going on, hmm? Must be some deep stuff a few of you are trying to keep under the rug."

"No such thing, Marc Girard. What's gotten into you?"

"When we've got more time, I'll explain that in detail. Every time there's mention of the woman who died in St. Cécil's, Cyrus looks like a man in a lot of pain. Just wondered what that's all about."

She shouldn't have expected Marc to be less observant than she'd known him to be. "I think he feels responsible."

"For a woman's death."

"No, dammit!"

He kissed the side of her neck, took the lobe of her ear between his teeth.

"Stop that right now," she told him.

"Now you know it's all part of the dance."

"You're incorrigible. *Stop* it. I don't want to have to make a scene."

"Of course you don't. And you won't. Mmm, you are the softest, sexiest morsel I ever came across."

She closed her eyes because she couldn't keep them open. "*You* are shameless and manipulative. And you're incorrigible. I want to sit down."

"And risk havin' me argue with your champions?"

"Marc —"

"Why does Cyrus feel responsible? All he did was give a destitute woman a place to sleep."

"He knew the other two," she told him and snapped her teeth together.

"The ones who were murdered?"

"Drop it." She pressed her face into his shoulder. This was the worst possible direction in which to lead him.

Up and down her back he smoothed his hands, up and down. And he hummed to the

music — close to her ear. He danced beautifully. Letting him make all the moves was easy
to do.

"Our table neighbors must think they've got
what they came for," he said.

"Looks like it." Reb observed the Hibbses and
the Gables talking together as they made their
way out. "We won't have heard the last from
them."

Marc grunted. "What about the woman who
didn't die, the one who took the murderer off
the streets? Did Cyrus know her, too?"

"May Lynn? Of course. Everyone knows May
Lynn."

"You know what I mean. Did he know her in
some special way, the way he knew the three
dead women?"

"I'm not answering any more of your questions. If you're goin' where you may be goin',
you're sick. You don't know Cyrus, or you
wouldn't even think anythin' so horrible. He's
the priest. People go to him for reconciliation.
His only connection with those women was that
— their confidences."

She stopped dancing. "Oh, Marc! I left
Gaston over there. He'll be on the dance floor
next."

He released her and followed her back to the
table where Cyrus and Spike still sat. Behind relaxed body positions, both of them gave off an
air of discomfort.

"Don't we make the pair?" Marc said, putting

a hand around her waist again. "She was about eight when she nagged me into teaching her to dance and I agreed so she'd leave me alone." He laughed, and tucked strands of her hair behind her ears. "You were a nice little girl, and I liked teaching you."

And that's what he'd always been able to do — turn on the charm just when a person was ready to let fly at him, and charm them into submission. The worm.

Gaston, his topknot bow — gray to match Reb's dress — listing badly to one side, sat on Cyrus's lap and ate fries out of a red checkered paper bowl. "He was hungry," Cyrus said, sounding defensive. "I could tell by the way he looked at me."

"No such thing," Reb said. "You just know if you feed him he'll be your best friend — until the food's gone. He's not supposed to be in here, let alone eating off the table."

"The waitress felt sorry for him — him looking so scrawny — and went back to ask Pappy if it was okay. He said . . . well, he said anything I decided was okay was okay with him."

"Peachy," Marc commented, holding Reb's chair until she sat, then sliding back into his own. "Are we talkin' about the same Pappy who owned this place years ago?"

"Yes," Spike said. "A lot older from what I've been told, and he doesn't move as fast anymore, but the same man. He doesn't like people, that's why he keeps to himself in the back room."

"Countin' the money he makes from the people he doesn't like, I suppose." Marc's expression had returned to its pre-dance belligerence.

This time it was Spike who broke the ice. "I'd say you've got that about right. The more he makes, the more he retreats, but he's got a good heart."

"A good man," Cyrus agreed.

Reb couldn't miss how Cyrus took every opportunity to study Marc — and that he didn't look too pleased with what he saw. She glanced at Spike and thought, as she had before, that he was too quiet. He needed to meet just the right woman to bring him out of his shell, and she'd have to be something special.

"Were you called to the church after the death?" Marc said.

Spike hesitated only a moment before answering, "I was."

"And you thought it was an accident?"

"I don't make decisions about the cause of death in those circumstances. But it looked like an accident to me, and that's what it turned out to be — a terrible accident. I think she was knocked out before much of the damage was done, though."

"Really?" Marc's posture, the way he held himself so still, cut Reb. "How could you know that? Why isn't it just as likely she was conscious until she landed on that stone floor?"

"She may have been," Spike said. "But the steps and walls are also stone, and she hit a lot of them."

"Stop it," Reb said.

Marc wasn't stopping. "What do you know about what brought the woman here? You all say she was a stranger, a singer who showed up in Toussaint with no money."

"Vincent Fox met her in New Orleans," Spike said and inclined his head toward the band. "He's the fiddler. He met her casually in a club and felt sorry for her so he brought her back to sing with the Doggies. There wasn't much money in that, but it would have put her on her feet eventually."

"Bonnie Blue," Marc said, apparently to himself. When he added, "How did you establish her identity?" it wasn't for his own benefit.

Another glance passed between Cyrus and Spike.

"I know she ran out of gas and must have decided to walk home," Marc continued. "Only for some reason she decided to go to the church in the early hours of the morning instead. And climb up to the belfry."

Cyrus pushed his glass away. "Don't you think I've asked myself why she did that? I keep on asking myself. She was a Catholic and de-vout —"

"Well," Spike said, and shrugged.

"It isn't our place to judge others," Cyrus said. "I'm not just supposed to say that, I want to.

Whatever Bonnie had been through before coming here, she was working to make her life simple, and the Church was part of that for her."

"You didn't say how you confirmed her identity," Marc said, and the stillness had left him. He gestured with his hands and leaned toward the other men. "Did she have something other than a driver's license? A checkbook maybe? With an address on it. Well, there would be an address on the license, but the checks would be more likely to have the most recent one. Why couldn't you locate her next of kin?"

"What's your interest in Bonnie?" Spike said. Reb felt him bristle and assume his all-business role. "These aren't matters I can discuss with just anybody."

Marc made fists on the table. "You don't have to discuss them. I'll just tell you the answers. What you don't want to say is that when you tried to trace Bonnie Blue you couldn't find anything. The I.D. she had was phony, right? Where are her things now? What does it take for me to get permission to look at them?"

"It helps if you can stay calm," Cyrus said.

"I asked how I can see her things."

"She had about nothing," Cyrus said. Gaston had finished his fries and turned to gaze into his benefactor's face. "A few clothes in her room. An old suitcase. Makeup —"

"And in her wallet? What did she carry around with her? An address book? Everyone has an address book."

159

"Hush, Marc," Reb said. "This isn't the place."

"It's as good a place as any. All I'm asking for are some simple answers."

Spike swiped the sweat from the side of his glass of Coke and seemed poised between answering and telling Marc what he could do with his interrogations. He answered without looking at the other man, "Bonnie's wallet is missing. All her personal papers, whatever they were, are missing. Or we can't find 'em. But she did have a license. I saw it because — well, I saw it."

"And she had a wallet," Cyrus said. "She opened it in front of me."

Marc's hands came down flat on the table, and Gaston did a one-eighty in midair. He forgot himself entirely and leaped on the table, planting all four legs apart and assuming his "Come on, come on, you want trouble? Come and get it" face. His whiskers wiggled and his lip curled.

"Dammit," Marc said. "Can't you control that animal, Reb? He just wiped out my train of thought."

Lightning crackled directly overhead and zipped away like strings of firecrackers, casting flickering light on the green water of the bayou. The next clap of thunder was huge, and rain beat the tin roof like fine drumsticks on a bunch of bongos.

"Gaston took the wind out of your sails, you mean," Reb muttered.

Marc knew not to persist. "Bonnie had a wallet, a license, and other things? You never found them, but you buried her."

"The law allows us to do that with an unclaimed body — in thirty days. It was done with respect and good people in attendance. We continue to look for next of kin, but I don't think we're going to find any now."

"Maybe you aren't looking hard enough," Marc said in a low voice.

Reb exchanged glances with Cyrus. They were helpless to stop Marc from digging himself in even deeper.

A young female deputy was making her way to the table. Sturdy, with long, straw-colored hair scraped into a rubber band at the nape of her neck, she appeared nervous. "Sir," she said when she stood beside Spike. "A word, please?"

If Spike was irritated at the interruption, he hid it well and excused himself.

"Saved by the bell," Marc said.

"You are an angry man," Cyrus told him.

Reb closed her eyes and waited for Marc's reaction, but he said, "You're right," even though it was through his teeth. "Deputy Devol and I will speak again. You knew all three women who have been killed in Toussaint in the past two years."

"Bonnie's death was an accident, remember?" Reb said rapidly.

"The question's the same, Father."

"Yes," Cyrus responded, and his piercing eyes met Marc's gaze squarely.

"That's obviously bothering you."

That blue-green stare shifted to Reb, and she cringed. "I explained —"

"No need to say anything," Cyrus told her. "Marc will get to his point."

The priest's cool voice didn't appear to encourage Marc to back off. "Why were you so upset about the three deaths?"

Cyrus brought his lips together in a line. The storm had completely lost control. Runoff sluiced down the roof and poured in illuminated sheets from the gutters. A wind had risen, and it drove blasts of rain into the windows like bullets from automatic weapons.

"I have normal, human feelings," Cyrus told him. "Three women with a lot of life ahead of them — a lot of work they wanted to do spiritually — and with their place in the world — cut down before their time."

"Were you their confessor?"

If disappearance had been an option, Reb would have grabbed it. She couldn't believe Marc's bald approach.

"Yes," Cyrus said. "I was."

"Do you still do that in the box, or is it all in a cozy room these days? Do these women come to visit you at your house? I'd think that would be nicer. More relaxed."

"Face-to-face reconciliation is commonplace. Many people prefer it."

"Do you?" Marc asked. "With some of your parishioners."

"I prefer what they prefer. Whatever makes them more comfortable makes me more comfortable."

"Don't you have any opinions or preferences of your own?"

This was between the two of them, Reb decided. She had no right to intervene. But her time would come to tell Marc Girard what she thought of him.

Cyrus turned toward Marc, crossed his arms, and took an uncomfortably long time to say what Reb could see him getting ready to say. "I have a lot of opinions and preferences of my own. Some might say I'm a very opinionated man. Could be that growing up with parents who only wanted me to say "yes" to whatever they wanted of me taught me to think before I speak. Any child of Bitsy and Neville Payne — who was my adoptive father — learned what was expected of them. Ask my sister Celina. But maybe that wasn't such bad training. There's not too much wrong with thinking before you open your mouth."

Reb had a crazy desire to cheer and tell Cyrus he'd made a good point.

"Did *Bonnie* tell you anything that might help catch her killer?"

"Marc!" Reb put her hands down on his and gripped them hard. "Bonnie had an accident. She wasn't killed."

"Do you believe that, Father?" Marc asked.

Cyrus looked away.

"Is it hard, being a priest, and being a man alone with women who confide their deepest secrets in you? Of course, maybe you aren't still a man in the way I mean. I don't mean . . . you know what I mean."

"I'm still sexual, if that's what you mean," Cyrus said, his face pale. He wasn't offended, Reb saw that, but he was shaken.

"So you want to make love to women?"

Reb studied each of these unforgettable men in turn, and rested her forehead on the table. She couldn't believe what she'd just heard.

"I struggle with a normal sex drive," Cyrus said, very softly. "Is that what you want to hear?"

"Oh, hell," Marc responded. "I don't know what I want, but I just stepped way over the line. Forgive me, please. I couldn't do what you do, even if I wanted to. But I'm going to give this to you straight. No frills. There wasn't any Bonnie Blue. I'm convinced of that, and more convinced now I know there isn't any identification. The woman who died was my sister, Amy Girard, and I'm not relaxin' or leavin' this town until I find out exactly what happened to her."

Lifting her head, Reb looked at Cyrus, at the shock he registered. Marc's eyes were softened with emotion, but every other line in his face was rigid. "I want that body exhumed," he said through his teeth. "Tomorrow I'll start the wheels in motion. I'll speak to your buddy the deputy and get him on board. I want to put my sister to rest where she belongs — with her family — and to find out what made her come here after all that happened to her before. I want to know every person she spoke with, anyone she spent time with, and I'll work on that. But I want to . . . see Amy."

Marc's voice broke up, and tears sprang into Reb's eyes without warning. She didn't stop to think before getting up and going to put her arms around him. He held her and whispered, "I'm a pig, and you should hate me."

"I don't," she whispered back. "I hurt for you."

"Excuse me, Father." It was Spike Devol, who rotated his Stetson by its brim and gave off waves of discomfort. "There's been a 911 call from St. Cécil's."

ELEVEN

He must not, Cyrus thought, resent his ancient Chevy Impala station wagon, or the fact that blown shocks had the dark red monster floating and rocking its way toward Toussaint. So what if there was a sound like glass grinding in the transmission — he'd lived with that for months, and tonight the rain belting against the car partially covered the noise. What did make him angry was watching the blurred taillights of Spike Devol's vehicle (together with his flashing lights) and Marc Girard's Range Rover, *and* Jilly Gable's pea green Beetle grow fainter in front of him.

And he didn't like it that Spike had refused to expand on the emergency call other than to say an aid car had been sent for.

He punched in the auto-dial on his cell phone — again — and again got a busy signal. Sweat ran past his temples and stung his eyes. The air conditioning was selective at best, and the inside of the wagon felt like a steam room. What if Madge had stopped in, as she often did, to put in extra hours?

Cyrus gave the Impala more gas — which

only seemed to confuse the engine. His reward was a hiccuping reaction that added serial jolts to the float-and-rock motion. Water fanned a plume over the hood.

So he wouldn't get there with the others. They'd make sure Madge was taken care of . . . he didn't *know* something had happened to Madge.

She was the best assistant he could imagine finding, and she was as good a friend as he ever expected to have. Madge kept his life running smoothly, endeared herself to the most difficult parishioners, kept Oribel as in-line as anyone could, and made sure Lil Dupre, Ozaire Dupre's wife and cook-housekeeper, at the rectory, had as few reasons as possible to go into a sulk. And Madge alone laughed at Cyrus's jokes.

If she was all right, he'd find the money to give her a raise. He should have arranged it at least a year ago. He might not be the most observant man about such things, but although she invariably looked lovely, she had few clothes. And her car wasn't much better than his — which was a bad idea for a woman driving around alone.

What if . . . Bonnie had been alone and driving at night.

He tried to phone again, and got a busy signal again.

No lights of any kind shone on the road ahead anymore.

He peeled off and took the back road, the one Bonnie had taken. Through breaks in the trees he saw the sluggish waters of the bayou gleam beneath strands of lights that shone from a dock. The surface wallowed more than flowed. Cypress trees stood with their feet underwater and their silhouettes grotesque, like thickened and posing skeletons. Cyrus rolled the window down an inch and breathed in the scents that pleased him, faint, impenetrable green odors from the bayou; soft, mossy mold; dust mixed with overdue rain; and drenched pine.

Another bend in the road took him to a place where the bell tower on St. Cécil's shone white above the trees. He blinked and swallowed an acid rush. Since Bonnie's death, the reaction had plagued him each time he looked at the belfry, or heard the bells.

Poor little Madge. If she was okay, he'd forbid her to drive over from Rayne at night.

He steered a loose right turn onto Bonanza Alley. Flashing lights were everywhere, and he could hear raised voices from the area in front of his house. Evidently whatever was going on warranted backing up Toussaint's lone firetruck with support from neighboring communities. That, or the parish was having a slow night.

At least the activity wasn't around the church as it had been last time.

Emergency vehicles blocked the entrance to the driveway. Breathing harshly, Cyrus left the car and ran through sloppy gravel and mud toward the house.

Shrieking horrified him.

"I am calm, me," a female voice announced before breaking into loud sobs.

"Now, now, Lil," an unidentifiable male said. "I don't blame you for being upset, but this isn't helping anything."

"Not — natural," Lil Dupre said. "My heart will never be the same. Capering hoodlums. But they weren't from this world. I saw the horns, and their teeth, me. Red teeth. Blood, I tell you." She moaned. "Oh, what's happenin' in Toussaint? Makes a body glad to put her head down in Crowly at night, I can tell you."

Cyrus collided with Marc, who stood by watching Reb. She was bent over Lil, who was stretched out on a gurney beneath a tarp canopy while a medic took vital signs. "Madge," Cyrus said. "Where is she? Have you seen her?"

Marc's expression was indistinct in darkness constantly sliced by revolving colored lights, but Cyrus saw enough to catch a curious glint in the man's eyes. "We just got here," he said. "All I know is that Lil Dupre thinks she's having a heart attack and there are people swarming all over the place."

"Who's in charge? Spike, I suppose."

"He's inside the house," Marc said. "They all are."

"I'm going in," Cyrus said, but first he checked out the cars present, and saw what he'd hoped wouldn't be there: Madge's battleship gray Pontiac. The gray was an undercoat for a new paint job that had never happened.

"What is it?" Marc said, his voice coming to Cyrus distantly. "Cyrus, you look sick. Let me help you."

Cyrus turned to him once more and managed a smile. "I need a priestly refresher course. Acceptance of God's will doesn't come as easily as it used to. Help me find out who's where in there."

They squelched hurriedly toward the house, pausing only long enough for Cyrus to smile down at Lil and pat her hand. She said, "Oh, Father Cyrus," and he nodded reassuringly.

Marc had placed a hand on Reb's back, but he didn't attempt to interrupt her.

"Come on, if you're coming," Cyrus said to him and walked through the open front door. As far as he could tell, rather than all over the house, the activity centered around the ground-floor rooms at the back, and he took off, bouncing off a deputy in conversation with a fireman. Cyrus was beyond putting names to faces.

The throng had gathered in the kitchen and crowded in front of the steamed-up windows. Sleeves had made swathes across the glass. Warm dampness hung in the air. Cyrus thought he heard a laugh, and the rage he felt shocked him.

He couldn't see her.

The others made a semicircle on one side of the kitchen table. "Get out of my way." The words burst from him, and men turned their heads as he elbowed a path through them.

He heard Marc say, "We're coming through," behind him.

Madge's bright eyes met his past a brawny shoulder, and she smiled. She *smiled*. "Madge?" he said. "Are you okay? Madge?"

She reached him and said, "Fine. But you don't look so good, Cyrus."

"Thank God," he said and drew her into a bear hug. "You scared me."

Gently, she eased away but smiled softly at him. "I think we've all been scared, but it's okay. Lil saw what she saw and just about collapsed. Don't blame her."

He deliberately shook his head and grimaced. "What now? I'm permanently on edge." His behavior confused him. His feelings confused him. But why wouldn't a man be concerned for a good friend? In the future he'd be more careful about his reactions.

"Father Cyrus?" Wally Hibbs dashed at him and stood on his toes until Cyrus brought his ear to the boy's mouth. "They found me here. My folks."

Cyrus responded quietly. "What are you doing here at this time of night?"

"I came 'cause of the sirens. I was scared somethin' was wrong with you."

"Okay, okay." This child needed him, now. Past Wally's shoulder he saw Doll and Gator hovering, casting accusing stares at their priest. The Gables stood at a short distance, looking uncomfortable.

"Just one thing," Wally said urgently. "If they ask about my bike, please don't say anything."

There wasn't time to tell Wally that Cyrus didn't know anything about the bike before Doll and Gator descended. Doll pulled her son against her and glared at Cyrus. "You're alienating our boy from us," she said on a hiss. "That's going to stop, right, Gator?"

Her husband coughed and didn't manage a word.

"You're coming home now. Jilly will drive us — you'll have to pick up your bike tomorrow."

Wally took off, half-dragging his mother with him. His father and the Gables followed, but Jilly popped to Cyrus and said, "This is nothing to do with you. You're good to Wally. But it might be for the best if you persuaded him to patch things up with Doll and Gator."

Cyrus was grateful for the hubbub that drowned out most distinct conversation. Madge said, "Let it go for now. Let's follow Marc."

Marc had opened the door from the kitchen into the yard, and he disappeared outside.

Cyrus made to follow him, and Madge said, "I hope your nerves are ready for this. Maybe you're not ready to go out there yet."

"Make sure everyone gets something to drink before they leave," he said, and went outside.

Instead of following orders, Madge was right behind him. "They haven't done anything to earn drinks," she said. "It's you I feel sorry for.

172

You're the one who'll need a drink, and iced tea won't do it."

His stomach crunched one more time before he reached Marc's side and froze.

"Lil stopped by a while ago and went into the kitchen," Madge said. "I was in the office, but she was alone back there." She indicated the windows.

"Ooh, ya-ya," Marc said and folded his arms. The rain had eased, but the gathered party, hair plastered to heads, licked water from their lips and wiped at their eyes.

Cyrus couldn't find his voice, or couldn't make it work.

Ranged on the lawn where it would be visible to all who came or went from St. Cécil's was a six-foot-tall bronze sculpture resembling a two-dimensional line of paper-doll cutouts. And Lil hadn't been wrong. They struck prancing poses, and their jagged teeth, open in jack-o'-lantern rictus were indeed red — painted that way. The horns Lil spoke of adorned three of the five heads but were most likely intended to depict flipping ponytails.

Reb joined them and muttered, "Oh dear."

Temporarily placed spotlights illuminated the work of art.

Madge held Cyrus's arm and said, "There's a plaque. I didn't notice it before."

They went closer and crouched to read: "Joy! Primitive form by Jonas Running High. Gift to St. Cécil's from a grateful parishioner." This cheery message was set in the top of a partially sunken concrete base.

"Will you look at that." William, together with a swelling crowd of Toussaint's residents, had ventured closer. "They's little letters, them. Humble. Just like you always tellin' we to be, Father."

The "humble" letters announced: ORIBEL SCULLY.

Cyrus and Madge looked at each other, and when he could speak, Cyrus croaked, "They're fu . . ." The sound of his own voice astounded him. "They're ugly. Pagan."

"They're the Fuglies," Reb sputtered.

Marc added, "Cyrus is right, they're fucking ugly."

TWELVE

After they'd left the rectory, Marc realized that what had happened there wasn't all funny. "I'll see you inside," he said to Reb as they arrived in Conch Street.

She held a sleeping Gaston on her lap. "I appreciate the thought," she said. "There's no need."

"I'd appreciate a thought from you," he told her. "How am I supposed to get any sleep if I'm not sure you're safe?"

"I've been keeping myself safe for a long time," she said, gathering the dog in her arms. "I mean, thank you, but I'm not your concern. Not that I think there's anything to be concerned about."

"Okay. We'll revisit that."

"Great." She reached for the handle.

"In about five minutes," he told her. "Or as soon as you give me your impression of what we saw tonight."

Reb kept her fingers on the car door handle and looked at him over her shoulder. He could only see her eyes and the upper half of her face.

"Well?" he said.

"I don't know what you're really asking, but that thing shouldn't have been set on the lawn — in concrete — without Cyrus being consulted. It's inappropriate, and the money could have been spent on things that are really needed. But Cyrus has got a dilemma, because he won't want to hurt Oribel's feelings when she's probably gone into debt to give something special to the parish."

In his business, Marc dealt with art enough to know that the primitive piece was probably worth a goodly sum. "In the end he'll have to do what the majority of his parishioners want. Oribel should have sought advice first. Putting the thing where it is and pulling off a surprise like that couldn't have been easy. The concrete isn't completely set, but it's close. That isn't what I was talking about, though, Reb. Cyrus and Madge have . . . they have feelings for one another." He waited for her to get mad.

"I know that," Reb said, and her expression was worried. "They make me sad because nothing will ever come of it."

"How can you be so sure?"

"You don't get it, do you?" she said, her brows pulled together. "A committed priest, which Cyrus is, doesn't turn his back on his vocation — on his vows. And Madge won't allow herself to be more than his friend. I doubt if Cyrus is fully aware of how he feels."

"Crazy," he said. Also not something he could do anything about even if he wanted to. "One more quick topic, then we'll go in."

Reb shook her head and looked weary.

"Bear with me. Tell me about the first two murders."

"A quick topic?" She settled Gaston on her lap once more, pulled her heels onto the seat and wrapped her skirts around her legs. More of her damp hair fell to her shoulders than remained pulled on top of her head. "It's complicated. Or bizarre would be a better description. And I don't know why you want to know."

"Of course I do," he said. "I've got to look for any similarities between those deaths and Amy's."

"The coroner did the autopsies." Reb rested her forehead on her knees and said, "But I read the reports, and there were absolutely no similarities between Bonnie's accident and the two murders. Nothing, Marc. Not a single thing except all three women ended up dead."

He couldn't tell if she really didn't believe Amy had been the one to die, or if she wouldn't consider the possibility. "Isn't it possible some of the common elements were missed?"

"No." She shook her head. "My opinions were way down the list anyway, but the murders were carbon copies. The third death was different. If you're really interested in the macabre, you can get more information from public records."

He took the wide neck of her dress between finger and thumb and ran them back and forth over the silky stuff. Her skin was cool. "I want you to tell me," he said. "The closer to the chest I hold my cards, the better."

"I don't get it. What makes you think you'll feel better if you get to go through all that terrible stuff?" The clinical distance left her voice. "I wish you wouldn't. It won't help, but it'll hurt. Hard as we try, most of us are changed by each tragedy we deal with. My prayer is that Amy will get in touch with you."

How soft she was. He shifted his fingers a little lower and tensed for her to slap him away, but she didn't. Instead she rested her head back and closed her eyes.

"Tell me about it — please," he asked her quietly and kept on stroking her. He sensed her mood matched his — she wanted to explore how they would be together — but he didn't kid himself that she'd be amused if he started now.

"Around here they were called the Rubber Killer Murders," she said, and he heard her swallow.

He almost laughed. "You're kidding."

"I'm not much of a kidder."

Faint moonlight gleamed along her profile, and down the outline of her arched neck. He had never touched her — not really touched her. It would have been so easy when they were at Tulane. She had even offered a clumsy invitation for him to spend the night with her. At least he'd had the sense, and the decency, to stay away from her after that.

"Both women talked about feeling watched." She swallowed again, and his own spine tensed. "So did May Lynn. In each case they'd gone so far as to report being frightened."

And now Reb was being watched — and she was frightened.

"The first one, Carla Jennings, hadn't been back in Toussaint long. She'd been in New York. She wanted a serious acting career, but she ran into problems. Got in with the wrong people. There was a baby involved, but she didn't bring the child here."

So far nothing sounded similar to Amy's background.

"Louise Simmonds died about two months after Carla. Two and a half. She'd always lived in Toussaint. Her family blamed her for her own divorce, and she was needy, lonely. She'd married while she was in high school and never worked. A sad woman."

Not a thing to link any of the deaths as far as Marc could see. "What about May Lynn?"

"Her last name is Charpentier. She's got a beauty shop on the west side of town. A boyfriend came on the scene last year. They're going to be married, and she seems very happy. But she was pretty much alone before. She involved herself with the church choir and 4H projects with kids. I like her, but I'm not sure she isn't holding back valuable information."

He played with her hair. Through the slightly open windows of the Range Rover came the sound of earth absorbing water, and the frogs were at full throat. "What makes you think she's got information?"

"Just a feeling." She rolled her face toward him. "A lot of details about the murders aren't common knowledge. It's pretty much routine for the police to keep important aspects quiet. They don't want to tip the criminal's hand or set off copycats."

Marc craved kissing her again. How right were those who said a man's head and his sex drive rarely made one another's acquaintance. "But the guy involved in the first three is behind bars."

Reb's discomfort showed. She sat up and braced her weight on her arms. "Cyrus knows what I think. So does Madge. We keep trying to figure out what to do. We don't have a clue to offer the law. We have filed our concerns, but that's all they are, concerns. We don't believe the man who got put in jail had anything to do with the two killings. Nothing was proved. But Pepper Leach is behind bars for the incident with May Lynn, and everyone — almost everyone — seems happy to condemn him for the deaths because that means they can pretend to feel safe."

She had his entire attention. "You didn't mention this before."

"You've been here a few days. You and I haven't seen each other, or spoken in years. Why would I spill all this the moment I saw you?"

"You think this *Rubber Killer* is still on the loose?"

She nodded. "Yes. And I think he's aware that I do. Which means I'm dangerous to his freedom — or he believes I am. I'm a long way from being a danger, although I intend to get there."

"Telling you to keep your nose out of it won't do any good. I will tell you I'm involved now. You and I are going to be good at three-legged races, cher."

"Marc, you mean well, but you aren't my father, husband, or brother. I don't have any of those. If it turns out you have a good idea, throw it in the pot, friend. That's the best any one of us can do."

"If you and Cyrus came up with this — and Madge — why isn't the law crawling all over? A man's in prison and y'all think he shouldn't be there? That's wild."

"I didn't say I'm sure he shouldn't be in prison, only that I don't think he's the killer. I've already said too much," Reb told him, but she smiled and wrinkled her nose. "Habit, I'm thinking. We aren't ignoring what's going on. And I don't know what the Sheriff's Department is thinking. Spike Devol isn't about to tell me. My take is that Pepper's keeping quiet in return for something I haven't been told about."

"He should be free."

"If he's free, R.K. knows his cover has gone away. We don't want to set him off again."

"R.K. Why Rubber Killer?" He almost dreaded the answer.

"He never touched them with any part of his body, not directly. From what the medical examiner and forensics could determine, the murderer probably wore the equivalent of a wetsuit — and used a condom. DNA testing was out. The victims were hit over the head and about the face many times with a blunt object, raped and strangled — and hit some more."

Her clinical recitation, almost devoid of emotion, reminded him forcefully that she wasn't the teenager he'd sweated over and dreamed about at Tulane. "But the Charpentier woman saw him and got away."

"Exactly. And hard to swallow maybe? If you went to the trouble to completely cover yourself, wouldn't you cover your face, too?"

He thought about it. "Yes."

"She insisted she saw his face when she managed to twist away, then she picked a man out of a lineup. They never found any of his paraphernalia. But Pepper didn't put up a fight. He's a painter who was starting to make a little headway. Quiet. His behavior from the time the law knocked on his door amazes me."

Only one thing yelled at Marc. If Reb was right, the murderer was still out there, and he was following her around. "Could someone else know what you think?"

"Cyrus and Madge, of course, but anything's possible. As I keep saying, this is a small place.

The condom was talked about by the police, but not the really weird part of the sexual assaults. Damage was done to the victims. I've seen that kind of thing in women who try to abort. Usually the result of inserting foreign bodies into the vagina. I'm not the only one who believes just raping wasn't enough for him, he wanted to punish and punish, and he used other things to accomplish that. And the investigation is still wide open, you can bet on that."

"Reb —"

"I absolutely should not be telling you about this. For some reason you still feel like the one I confided in when I was a kid. It feels safe to talk to you. I hope I'm not wrong."

Since when had it taken so little to make him feel so good? "I would never hurt you, Reb. Never. Anything you say to me might as well be told to a dead man."

"Don't!" Her left hand slid behind his neck and she held on to his hair. "Just don't say things like that, okay?"

Marc smiled at her and moved his face closer to hers. "Okay." Some joker knew she was on the right track and wanted to shut her up. The second kiss of the night was coming. A second kiss tended to mean there would be more.

Leaning over her, he touched their lips together, keeping it light but making sure the tip of his tongue let her know this kiss didn't fall in the brotherly classification.

Reb held still, but her mouth responded to

183

his, and he felt her breath shorten. Still no resistance when he opened their mouths wider and got less subtle with his tongue. She seemed to settle down, turn dreamy. The heel of his left hand, settling beneath her breast, earned him light panting. Reb tasted even better than when he'd kissed her at Clouds End. Soft weight on his thumb tightened his belly and he had to stop himself from stroking her nipple. *Not too fast.* Any moment now she'd remember she'd been mad at him for thirteen years and push him away.

Gaston, shoving his curly, bony little head between Marc's arm and Reb's chest was more togetherness than any sexy interlude could endure. But Marc kept right on kissing Reb, even when the two of them made a Gaston sandwich and the mangy nuisance took to licking their faces.

"I don't want to stop," Marc said, groaning, and settling his face beside Reb's head on the rest. "I love your dog, but —"

"He's right. Our timing's bad. It always was."

"It's not going to keep on being bad."

She pushed hair away from her face. "There isn't going to be a future for us. Extraordinary circumstances are throwing us together. They'll pass, and you'll move on. You need to go home, and I need to sleep. I've got early clinic in the morning."

And he had to go into New Orleans in the morning. Business was waiting. But that didn't

184

mean he wouldn't stay up all night if Reb was the one making sure he didn't get any sleep.

A rumbling sound reminded him of Gaston. The dog's "grin" glistened, and that was a growl Marc heard.

"Okay, okay, let's get you settled." He got out of the vehicle and went around the hood, but Reb was on the sidewalk by the time he reached her side. He was grateful the rain had eased off. "Please let me take you inside. I'll look around and make sure everything's shut tight."

He sensed how much she'd like to refuse, but she walked quickly to the front door instead and let them in.

Within fifteen minutes he'd been all over the house and found nothing unusual — with the exception of the broken catch on the kitchen window. He used a wedge between the upper and lower sashes and felt satisfied it couldn't be budged from outside.

"Look, Reb. I don't have anyone waiting for me." He'd rarely had anyone waiting for him. That had been his decision. "Let me use a spare bedroom just in case."

They stood inside the door to the old Victorian house where antiseptic scents reached out from Reb's consulting room. She appeared to be considering his offer.

"I could leave from here in the morning and run into New Orleans. My partner's complaining that I'm neglecting business. I'll be back again by the evening."

Too much time went by before she let out a slow breath and said, "I don't think that's a good idea, but thanks for the offer."

THIRTEEN

If she'd agreed to have Marc spend the night, regardless of where he slept, by nine in the morning everyone for miles around would believe they were having an affair. Why suffer all the advice that would follow when she hadn't had a good enough time to deserve it?

Reb giggled while she shot the bolt on the front door and put on the chain. The house was too quiet and too big, but it wouldn't seem that way once the natural fear had passed. There were reasons to be afraid, but admitting them wouldn't help.

"Up to bed we go," she told Gaston, and he bounded ahead of her. By the time she got to her room, he'd be settled on her quilt.

She hadn't made many changes since her father died. Somehow she found solace in being among his things, the things she'd grown up with. However, worn leather chairs, tufted ottomans, and a lot of brass could use some updating. Book-laden shelves covered so many of the walls, who knew what color they'd ever been. Halfway up the first flight of stairs she paused to look down into her father's study, her study now. It opened off the hall, and she could almost convince herself she smelled the faint odor of pipe tobacco.

Reb moved on. The only bad thing about having had a wonderful father was that he'd had to die and leave her with a giant gap in her heart.

Going to bed held no appeal. She sat on the stairs.

If Marc were with her . . . Yes, if he were with her, the night would become that seductively mysterious thing she usually pretended she didn't need — a time and place for intimacy, for two bodies entwined and reaching for more and more. The air was close, humid; they would grow damp together and bind themselves in twisted sheets.

They would make love, and from what little experience she'd had with Mr. Girard, that would be no insipid kind of loving. He would be heavy, but agile, and he'd know how to please her. Sharp pleasure surprised her now, a reminder of what a clever man like Marc could give her. Congestion, all sexual and demanding, throbbed between her legs.

Did she really want it with him, or had he only reawakened a need.

She wanted him, had wanted him since she first began to discover the difference between males and females and why those differences could be so good.

Reb stood and went on up the stairs. Marc

had wanted to stay, and she had no doubt he'd have ended the night in her bed — if he didn't start it there. The choice had been hers.

The decision had been the right one.

She tensed the muscles in her belly. It could be time for Dr. O'Brien to stop doing the right things.

A shower made her feel better once it was over. While she'd stood beneath the steaming water and spread soap over her skin, she'd been able to think only of Marc performing that little job for her.

She was becoming a case.

Reb was certain he would have been real efficient with the lotion she liked to smooth on.

A cool cotton nightgown felt wonderful. When she'd combed through her wet hair and left it to air-dry, she applied a dab of perfume, then felt silly because there was no one to smell it but her.

She opened the bathroom door and jumped. A tearing sound reached her and kept on going for several seconds. Thuds, objects hitting a hard surface, followed.

Reb drew back. Locking herself in the bathroom might buy time for her to attract attention from the window. Outside was a sheer drop, and she didn't kid herself that she wouldn't do a lot of damage if she jumped.

The noise stopped as abruptly as it had started.

Gaston wasn't barking. Reb's heart neared a

normal rhythm once more. Her pooch wasn't the world's greatest noisemaker, for which she was grateful, but if there was an intruder in the house he'd be raising the alarm.

Opening the bathroom door again took courage, but Reb managed to do it. Nothing appeared to be amiss in the bedroom. Neither was Gaston evident. She frowned and called, "Gaston!" He frequently decided to pop downstairs for a snack at night, and she had no doubt that's where he was now.

The dress she'd worn was fine and could be used another time before it went to the cleaners. She swept it up and went to the walk-in closet. "Oh no, not that, darn it." The light was off in there, but she could see clothes piled in a jumbled heap on the floor and garments on hangers hanging at a crazy angle from the rod behind the door. That rod had pulled out once before and was supposed to be fixed for life.

Pushing the closet door wide open, Reb climbed over piles of soft debris and reached for the light pull. One of these days she'd actually get around to having a better, brighter lighting fixture put in. Purses and upended boxes of photographs lay in a tangle. The number of sweaters spread around reminded her of how badly she needed to give things away.

Another creak stopped her. She began to turn around, just in time to see another shelf pulling away from its screws into the wall. That was the high shelf where she kept gifts she bought in advance, boxes, and paper for wrapping. Vases and ornaments she hadn't had the heart to throw away were also pushed up there. All of it slid toward her, and she threw up her hands to shelter her face and head.

The light went out again. Something barreled into her with enough force to drive her to the ground among her clothes. She felt weight, and smoothness, and she felt mortally sick. A hand that smelled of latex forced her head back and poked fingers into her eyes.

Reb screamed, and she fought. She managed to turn onto her knees.

A rounded, hard thing connected with the side of her head, and she slid forward. The fittings from the wall seemed to break entirely free and cascade over her, and her head was hit again. . . . Reb tasted bile, and the edges of her mind leaked darkness.

FOURTEEN

"Any particular reason why you were driving around Dr. O'Brien's block, Mr. Girard?" Spike Devol asked. "Around and around, from what I can gather." He'd come in response to Marc's call — placed after he'd made sure no uninvited guests remained in the house.

Reb had refused to see another doctor, or to lie down. She sat in the kitchen with one hand wrapped around the mug of hot tea Marc had made for her and the other holding an ice pack to her head. He had appreciated her in a thin white cotton nightgown, but he'd made sure a wraparound robe was added before the deputy arrived.

"You may not believe in premonitions, Spike; I do. I dropped Reb off, and I couldn't just drive home and rest easy. I took a couple of turns around the block. Three. And on the third pass the front door was wide open."

"Dr. O'Brien said she opened the door herself."

Marc looked at her and had an urge to hit some heads himself. "I know, but don't ask me how she dragged herself down here to do it."

"I didn't completely lose consciousness," she said. "I was groggy, but I wanted to find Gaston, only Marc found me first." Her wan face moved him. Every few minutes she called the dog.

"You should be checked over," Spike Devol said.

"I've got a couple of bumps on my head. They're nothing. I'm more shocked than anything. Please, can this wait while I look for Gaston?"

"If you won't allow me to take you to emergency, I must advise you to stay where you are," Spike said. "I'll call in some help. We'll find your dog."

Marc decided he was older than Spike. Maybe not by much, but despite his apparent ease in his job, Spike surely wasn't comfortable around women. That didn't have to be anything to do with his age. Could be they just made him nervous. Smart man. He liked Reb, Marc could feel that, but not exactly what "like" meant in this case.

Her eyes filled with tears. "I'll go search for him," Marc said hurriedly. Reb never used to be the crying type. "Spike will look after you for me."

She sniffed, and smiled at him. Spike showed no reaction at all — and that said everything about how much he didn't want Marc looking good to Reb, or assuming responsibility for her.

Marc didn't get a chance to ride off on his

white horse. One mostly apricot poodle trotted into the kitchen and leaped on his mistress's lap as if she wouldn't notice he looked as if he'd rolled in dust bunnies.

If she did notice that dust, it didn't stop her from hugging the critter until he squealed. "Where have you been, Gaston O'Brien?" she said, kissing his dirty face over and over. "You have scared your mama half to death."

Marc glanced at Spike, who looked at the floor, but not without a faint smile.

"You've been in the attic, you naughty dog," Reb crooned to the animal. "That door's supposed to be kept closed." Gaston turned his wet black nose toward Marc, who could have sworn the dog sneered at him.

"Ever thought you might prefer a dog's life?" he said to Spike in a neutral tone.

Spike grinned at that and raised one blond eyebrow. "I don't like to interrupt the reunion," he said, "but we've got to get serious here. From what I gather, you think someone hid in your closet and hit you over the head when you entered."

"She doesn't think," Marc said. "She knows. I went up to the attic, Reb. I didn't see anything, but I could have left the door open."

"I hadn't realized you were with her during the event," Spike said.

"I wasn't," Marc said, and let the sarcasm go.

The deputy pulled out a second chair. He sat beside Reb and set his notebook on the worn maple tabletop. "So, you dropped Dr. O'Brien off and —"

"I'm sick and tired of asking you to call me by my first name," Reb said. A spot of red appeared on each cheek. "You remember for an hour or so, then go back to treating me like a traffic stop. We've known each other as long as you've been in Toussaint, and I don't take it as a mark of respect that you call me doctor. You sound prissy. So *don't* do it again if you want me to speak to you at all. And the same goes for Marc. You know his first name. Darn it, Spike, we aren't strangers. We . . ." She closed her mouth and the two red spots spread.

Spike shifted in his chair and his gunbelt creaked. He cleared his throat and said, "No offense meant."

"None taken," Marc told him. Reb worried him. She wasn't herself, and he figured she was even more shaken up than he'd thought.

"I'll be proud to call you by your given name," Spike said to Reb, so earnest that Marc felt uncomfortable. "Now, Marc dropped you off and —"

"I didn't just drop her off. I did say that, but I meant I brought her home. I checked around the house to make sure everything looked okay before I left."

Spike's very blue stare nailed Marc. "Why did you think there might be something wrong?"

"I apologize, Spike," Reb said, as if she'd just come to her senses. "I was rude."

"You couldn't be rude," Spike told her. "You're having a bad time. I was asking Marc why he checked the house over before he left."

"Because I told him about the glass in Gaston's food," she said.

Explaining the incident gave the deputy a reason to scribble rapidly in his notebook. He wasn't pleased that he hadn't been called at the time.

"You think an intruder came in through this window?" he said, getting up to look at it with his hands behind his back. The pull that had broken off was on the sill. "Did that land there, or did someone move it?"

"I picked it up," Reb said.

Stupid was a weak word for the way Marc felt. He took a long look at the ivy-print wallpaper. "The wedge to keep it shut was my idea," he said.

"Uh huh. But neither of you thought it might be a good idea to call us in? This town doesn't show on a lot of maps. That means we don't have a hifalutin' police department standing by, and we surely don't have a lot of the fancy stuff, but we're keeping a pretty clean town, and we even know how to lift fingerprints."

"I should have called," Reb said quickly. "It was scary, but . . . well, I felt silly about making a fuss. For all I knew, glass broke in the dishwasher and got in the bowl."

"You wash the dog's bowl in the dishwasher?" Spike said.

Reb frowned at him. "Of course. I hope you do the same for your dog."

"I don't have a dog."

"Too bad," Reb said. "It would be good for you and Wendy — maybe for your daddy, too."

If an already reserved expression could close down, Spike's did. The idea of a Mrs. Devol hadn't crossed Marc's mind.

"Anyway," Reb said, "I've locked myself out before and managed to open that window to get in. I don't even know for sure it was shut before. Although the latch was on the floor . . . I guess it could have fallen off on its own. See why I didn't call?"

"Nope."

"Could we get back to what happened tonight?" Marc said. He didn't want to witness Reb falling apart before his eyes.

"I'd like you to show me the closet," Spike said. He got up and held Reb's chair.

She set Gaston down on waxed green-and-white linoleum tiles. "I didn't touch anything," she said.

"Let's go," Spike told her, leading the way into the hall. "We'll see if we can put this one to bed."

Marc crossed his arms and followed them up the stairs. He wasn't sure how he felt about the direction Spike's questions seemed to be taking.

In Reb's bedroom the deputy said, "Now tell me exactly what happened after Marc left. Try not to leave anything out."

Marc hadn't heard all the details yet — other

than how someone had pushed her down and hit her with something hard.

Sitting on an old cedar chest at the bottom of a mahogany bed with tall spindles at each corner, Reb spoke of taking a shower. Marc chewed a lip and tuned out that thought. The decor in the room was strictly Early American quilt-and-ruffles — not at all what he would have expected of Reb. But he figured this had probably been her room, and very much the same since she was a kid and cared for by her protective widowed father.

When he heard mention of a tearing noise, he looked toward the closet. The door was partly open, and it was dark inside.

"You could tell some of the fittings had broken?" Spike said. "So things shifted in there?"

"One of the rods had swung away from the wall. It's a mess. Clothes all over the floor, and the things I kept on the shelves above fell, too."

"So you went in to look at the damage?"

A teddy bear, worn smooth, sat on a wicker chair beside the bed. Perhaps she still slept with him at night. What a waste.

"I went in to hang up my dress," Reb said. "I didn't know the noise I heard was the rod till then. Another shelf started to tip, and I covered my head. That's when I was pushed to the floor. The light went out. A hand covered my face, but I managed to turn over. He shoved down on top of me, and then I was hit on the head — twice."

Spike wrote and Marc waited, watching Reb.

She rubbed the space where she'd drawn her brows together.

"Let's check this out," Spike said, tucking his notebook back into the breast pocket of his shirt. He opened the closet door wider, pushing against the rubble on the floor, and reached for the light pull. It didn't work. His flashlight showed the bulb was broken. "It's a mess in here, all right." Spike dug around in the closet, checked behind the clothes left hanging.

Reb looked forlorn. Her hair had been wet when Marc found her at the front door, but it had mostly dried and now stuck out in a tangle of red curls.

"More of the stuff in here will break away if it isn't braced," Spike said. "Best get some of the weight off as soon as you can." He bent over, then turned around with a pottery vase in one hand. In the other he held a coconut carved into a monkey head.

He walked out of the closet and set both pieces on the bed. "Like you said — things came off that shelf," he said, looking at the toes of his polished black shoes. "One of them could have broken the lightbulb."

"Could have," Reb said. She tightened the belt on her robe and sat straighter.

Spike cleared his throat, took out his notebook again, then returned it to his pocket. "You don't know whether or not your kitchen window was opened from the outside, by someone else?"

"Not for certain."

"Can you show me Gaston's dish?"

Reb stared straight ahead, not looking at either of them. "I washed it again. Reflex."

"You didn't save the glass?"

She pressed her lips together and shook her head.

"Don't feel bad," Spike said, but watched Reb intently. "Each person reacts differently to these things."

"And I did everything wrong," Reb said.

"Those clothes in there — when they were all hanging on the rod they must have been pretty heavy. If they swung farther out with you there — well, they could be heavy enough to make you stumble over the stuff on the floor and fall."

She didn't answer him.

"D'you think one of those" — he indicated the vase and the coconut shell — "maybe both, or something else that's in there could have come down on your head?"

Marc couldn't keep his mouth shut any longer. "What are you suggesting?"

"You went through the house before you left and didn't find anyone," Spike said. "And you didn't pass someone in latex gloves on your way in again."

"Yeah," Marc said, seeing the deputy's points but wishing he could rip his head off for not taking Reb seriously.

Spike puffed up his cheeks and let the air out slowly. "Are we all agreed that if someone had intended to kill you they could have done so?"

"He thinks I dreamed it all up." The corners of Reb's mouth turned down. "You don't believe there was any intruder, Spike. I should probably be insulted, but it would take too much energy."

Undeterred, Spike said, "With all that's happened in this town — and all you've seen, Reb — you're entitled to imagine a few things."

Marc looked from Spike to Reb and almost laughed. Spike Boy had missed some basic warning signs around here. The lady was about to blow.

"All that's happened in this town you keep so clean?" she said. "I suppose that could be enough to make some people unbalanced, but I'm not one of them. There are two possible reasons why I'm not dead in there. First, this was another warning and intended to scare me silent. Second, he was spooked by something, something he heard, and got away before he could be caught. It's getting late. You need your beauty sleep, and I've got an early clinic."

Marc smiled at her, reassuringly he hoped, "Reb —"

"Thanks for coming," she told him. "I'd appreciate it if the two of you could see yourselves out."

FIFTEEN

The instant Reb heard the front door close behind Marc and Spike, she wasn't happy to be on her own. This time Marc hadn't made any attempt to stay with her, not that he would in front of Spike — who thought she was a hysterical female.

Grimly, she walked through the house once more, checking each room downstairs and up.

Admitting, even to herself, that Spike could be right was out of the question. No, she hadn't imagined that shove, or the hand over her face in the darkness. She shuddered at the memory. She didn't know how someone had got in and out unseen, but she was sure they had.

From here on she'd go it alone. Guns frightened her, but she'd get pepper spray, or Mace, and carry it at all times, and she'd compile her own list of clues. She had a flitting daydream of marching into Spike's office with however many criminals might be involved. They'd be completely under her power, their arms tied behind their backs, duct tape over their mouths, and she'd hand them over while Spike, and Marc, watched — amazed.

Maybe she was hysterical. . . .

If she decided it was a good idea after all, she'd talk to Cyrus. He was logical, he didn't think she was a moron, and he and Madge were no more satisfied that Pepper Leach was a killer than Reb was.

Back in her bedroom, she didn't close the door. Better to be able to hear any unusual movement in the house.

Gaston's rear stuck out from beneath the bed. Thick clumps of dust still clung to him. "Come out, you naughty boy," she said.

The only thing that moved was his bottom — and his wagging tail. Reb got on her knees and lifted the bedskirt. "You know you don't eat up here," she told him, capturing him in one arm. "Disgusting. What do you have there?"

She pulled him out and looked into his face. Blinking slowly, he stared back, his head on one side while he allowed his body to sag as heavily as possible. A long, pink tongue passed around his lips and she peered closer. Crumbs of pastry and of meat clung to his mustache. If she didn't know better, she'd think he'd been eating a meat pie, only she never had such things in the house.

No remnants were to be found beneath the bed.

Sitting on the floor with her legs crossed, she began to pick the fluff out of Gaston's coat. His gray topknot bow hung by a thread. She undid and retied it as best she could. "There," she told the miscreant, "you don't deserve the attention, but you look better."

The only place the dog could have found that kind of dust was in the attic. Such a prospect didn't thrill her, but she decided to go up there and see what her buddy had got into. After all, Marc had looked there and hadn't found a bogeyman.

A door at the end of the upstairs hallway opened onto a steep, narrow-stepped staircase. She carried Gaston as she climbed the stairs and slipped the light on at the top. She searched around and swallowed. Her father had preferred that she not come up here. Trunks and boxes lined the attic walls, which were covered with rose-sprigged paper so faded the flowers were brown on a yellowed background.

Reb's mother had liked coming up here, or so her father had told her. She'd made it her hideaway. A seat had been built beneath a dormer window where dusty chintz curtains hung. Charlotte O'Brien used to sit on the velvet-covered seat cushions to read. Her books remained in three low bookcases visible behind trunks. Her father hadn't wanted Reb to look in the trunks. Once she'd resented that — until she'd been mature enough to know he'd never stopped loving his wife and that all he had of their life together must be there. Now she could look at whatever she pleased, yet she continued to hesitate.

With a wild wiggle, Gaston shot free of her

arms and landed on a room-sized braided rug with enough of a scrabble to raise clouds of dirt.

Reb sneezed and closed her tearing eyes. She would find the time to clean up here herself.

Gaston disappeared behind a pile of boxes, and a snuffling noise issued forth. "Gaston. Out of there," Reb said, barely above a whisper. The attic had brought a kind of reverence upon her for as long as she could remember. "*Now.* Gaston, if I have to —"

He appeared, a piece of clear foodwrap in his teeth. At Reb's feet he dropped to his tummy, held the wrap down with both front paws and licked hard enough to drag his mangled prize from the floor with each swipe.

Stroking him with one hand, Reb took the wrap away and turned it so that she could read the sticker that remained on one side. All Tarted Up. Sausage Roll. And the date was today's, yesterday's now that it was past midnight.

Reb's heart beat too fast. The food had come from the bakery in the middle of Toussaint yesterday. The only way it could have gotten into the house was if someone else had brought it in.

Gaston hadn't been barking when Reb had left the shower and walked into that closet. "You're not easy," she said to the dog, "but you can be bought, you traitor." And that's how the intruder had dealt with the poodle. He had used food to lure him up to the attic. The creep must have hidden outside until Marc left. Reb picked

Gaston up and squeezed him till he yelped. At least he hadn't been killed.

Alone used to feel so comfortable.

Reb didn't like it so much anymore.

That hand over her face had been encased in a latex glove. She used them every day and knew what she'd felt and smelled. Two women had been murdered in Toussaint by someone who had worn them, too, or so it was believed. Gloves and some sort of rubber suit, or a wetsuit, they'd decided. How long had it taken her to feel normal enough to go downstairs after the attack? The front door had been closed when she got there, but that didn't mean the intruder hadn't got out that way, although it was more likely he left from the back of the house where he had the best chance of getting away unnoticed.

As Spike had pointed out, the man most likely hadn't intended to kill her. This had been one more scare tactic. He'd carried it out really well.

Killing Gaston hadn't been part of the plan either, or he'd have done that, too. And a dog known to be very protective of her but who didn't raise an alarm made a great case for Reb having imagined the whole episode — because she was so jumpy.

She turned off the attic light and made her way to the bedroom. At each creak and sound of settling in the old house, she jumped. Her skin felt too small.

In the morning the closet would have to be

fixed — or she'd try to get it fixed. The trouble with living in a tiny place like Toussaint was that there wasn't any competition. Things moved like molasses, and so did people, including those who ran their daddy's and granddaddy's repair businesses. She'd be lucky if she could get the work done in a week or so. If necessary she'd try to find someone out of Lafayette.

Something snapped.

With Gaston still in her arms, Reb sat on the chest at the end of her bed. Her scalp prickled and her mouth dried out.

Sounds crowded her ears. Pops and creaks, even the soughing branch of a persimmon tree against the windows jolted her. She looked at the phone. Marc would be home soon. She could call him.

No, she absolutely could not call him. No matter how she'd reacted to him, they didn't have that kind of relationship.

Calling him to thank him for taking her out would be okay.

Tomorrow would be soon enough for that, and they both knew it — if there was any need to call at all.

Darn it, she would make noise of her own and scare away her own fears.

Whistling, trotting downstairs, she started toward the kitchen . . . and stopped, cold all over, almost feeling a draft on her back. Slowly she turned around.

The light, usually on all night outside the front door, was off. A trailing fern in a hanging basket softly swept the green pebbled glass panel at one side of the door.

A shadow, perhaps a shoulder and an arm, showed against the lower portion of that glass. Why hadn't she already bought the pepper spray. Moving quickly and quietly, she went into the kitchen and, without turning on a light, found a carving knife.

Reb returned to the hall, slipping along with her back to a wall, Gaston in one arm, the knife in the opposite hand. She was good with knives, maybe not carving knives, but blades and using them didn't bother her.

The clock in the surgery socked out its hollow, brassy bong and she almost dropped both dog and knife. Her hands sweated, and she wiped each one awkwardly.

Flitting through the gloom, she went into the patients' waiting room and rose to her tiptoes to approach the bay window. No way was she calling anyone out on another false alarm. She edged behind a heavy curtain and managed a one-eyed peer through lace curtains — and had the sensation she'd just swallowed her own heart.

A man sat on the top step, his back against the front door. She dared another peek, and quickly drew back again.

Walking quickly and quietly, she went to the door, realized that since she hadn't been there when Marc and Spike left, the bolt wasn't on and neither was the chain. Reb yanked on the handle.

The man with his shoulder pressed to the door, fell backward, flat backward. He scrambled to get up, but flopped down again when he came eye-to-blade with the carving knife.

"Look," he said, holding up both palms.

Reb didn't wait for whatever he had to say. With her weapon she made small circles an inch from his nose. "I used to think I'd like to be a plastic surgeon," she said. "Maybe I still would. I could start by getting rid of your ears. You'd appreciate a narrower head for sneaking in and out of places. Women like scars, y'know. How about something flashy about here?" She rested the knife on the side of his neck. "What'll it be, Marc? Ears, throat, or . . . anything else we might come up with?"

SIXTEEN

He thought, Marc decided, that Reb O'Brien was the cutest serious woman he'd ever met. Telling her so at this moment might not be wise. "Look," he repeated for the third time, knowing her reaction would probably be the same as on the first two attempts to communicate.

"I'm not ready to listen to your excuses."

Right again, Girard. Not that being right would make her wooden floors any easier on his back. The knife he could so easily take away continued to dangle a few inches above his nose.

"Reb, I've got a confession to make." The pesky poodle poked his nose in Marc's ear.

"Save it."

She stood with her feet braced apart. Her silhouette was fuzzy inside the flimsy cotton gown and robe, but not too fuzzy for a man with any imagination. He adjusted his position on the floor without any positive effect on his discomfort.

"Reb —"

"I said *save* it."

"I can't. I need to use the bathroom."

"Hold it. It's good to practice bladder control."

He sighed and decided something so terrifying, he turned his head to avoid choking. *He loved her.* And not only because he wanted them to be naked together. That was asinine. He and Reb had only shared one kiss years ago. Okay, one kiss and a lot of time together when he didn't think of much other than how much he wanted her. But that and the couple of days and kisses they'd shared since he'd returned to Toussaint didn't add up to a reason to . . . Nothing was normal anymore, that's what all this was about.

"Do you really need to use the bathroom, Marc?"

"No. I wanted to confess that I think you're really something. In fact, I could become very attached to you." Complimentary, but not overly effusive. Just the right note. So why was she staring at him like that?

"You worm," she said through her teeth. "You lowlife. I'm not a wide-eyed seventeen-year-old anymore. You can't sweep me off my feet, or distract me with a few wild lies."

But he had distracted her. He captured the knife-toting wrist and lunged upward at the same time. The knife clattered to the floor. Marc threw Reb over a shoulder, kicked the front door shut, and threw the deadbolt.

"How does this go, you idiot?" she said, her voice jarring with his every move. "Tarzan subdues Jane with brute force and she loves it? What happens now? The tree house? Are you going to gather fruit? What?"

Gaston yipped about his ankles. "Call him off, Reb. If he bites me . . . I think dogs that bite have to be shot."

"Shot?"

"Put down." He carried her into what he remembered as her father's study and switched on the first lamp he came to. The dog ran ahead and made his way, via a swivel leather chair, onto a handsome desk. There he stood: grinning.

"Enough of this," Reb said.

He dropped her to a couch and sat close beside her. "Escape is impossible," he told her. "Don't try. What's gotten into you? You opened the front door when you were all alone in here."

"Why were you hiding outside?"

"I wasn't hiding. I was keeping watch."

"Why?" The lamp didn't give much light, but it was enough for Marc to see Reb clearly.

"The deadbolt wasn't on. Neither was the chain."

She made to get up, but he plunked her down again. "Being manhandled isn't a turn-on to me," she said. "How would you know about the locks?"

"Think about it."

"Maybe I put them on after you left."

"Uh uh. Spike got in his car and took off first. I started to leave but doubled back. You were walking all over the house. I could tell by the way the lights went on and off, but you didn't bolt the door. That was stupid, Reb. You still aren't thinking like an intelligent woman who knows she's being threatened."

She shrugged his hands away. "I didn't think you believed me."

"Spike made good points, but he doesn't know you as well as I do. And I do still know you. You aren't an alarmist. You're level-headed. How well would you do as the primary medico in this town if you weren't? I know some of what you've been through, but you aren't falling apart."

Her eyes glittered. "If I were a man, that wouldn't surprise you."

"Maybe you're right. Maybe I need you to teach me how strong women can be."

She didn't answer him. He ought to be glad because he didn't seem to be able to stop his mouth from running away.

If he told her she was sexy when she got mad, she was likely to kick him out, and he'd deserve it. He said, "Spike and I let ourselves out, re-member? You can't put deadbolts on from the outside. All I intended was to wait until I heard you lock up, then be on my way."

Her light, freckled skin in that white gown and robe, her scrubbed face and startlingly red hair hypnotized him. When she was angry, Reb O'Brien's green eyes were a sight no man was likely to overlook.

"You don't frighten me, y'know," she told him. "You can get as close as you like, and stare as hard as you can, I'm not intimidated. You never have been able to make me feel small, and you tried hard enough in the past."

He wasn't ready to face uncomfortable history. "If you were intimidated more often, Reb, you might be less annoying."

She caught at the neck of his shirt and held on. "I'm a gentle woman. I spend my life looking after people, but you bring out the worst in me. You incite me, just the way you always did." She had more than shirt in those strong fingers and her hair-removal technique wouldn't become popular.

"Taking a man by the throat isn't what I'd call gentle." He sucked air through his teeth. "People don't get into situations like this if they don't care about each other."

She whipped her hand away and thought about that. Marc added, "How did you know there was someone outside?"

"I saw your shoulder through the glass."

"But you didn't think the smartest thing would be to call for help?"

"Call who?" Her fingers slackened against his chest. "You? Or Spike, who doesn't believe a word I say, any more than you do?"

He didn't want to fight with her, oh no, he surely didn't want to fight. "Yes, cher, that's exactly what I had in mind."

She took hold of his shirt and chest hair again.

"Why didn't you just go home? Why did you stick around here waiting for another opportunity to insult me?"

"Gimme a break. So I say the wrong things sometimes. I didn't mean you were an idiot with too much imagination, I just meant you should have called for help if you thought something was wrong."

Reb leaned toward him and Marc lost his battle to keep his eyes on her face. Her breasts were only a couple of inches from his chest. Erect nipples pressed against cotton.

"Reb," he said, too aware of his heavy breathing, and of another painful heaviness he'd like to take care of. "I didn't want to go home."

"I knew it was you outside. I went to the waiting room and looked out of the window. I saw you there. That's why I opened the door. It had nothing to do with my being an idiot."

He smiled and she flushed, irritation turning the corners of her sweet mouth down.

"I won't make you pay for that remark. Did you hear me say I stuck around because I didn't want to go home. I didn't want to leave you."

Her expression softened, and she started to straighten away from him. "You were always decent, even if you did, and do, hide it under all that prickly skin."

"I believe you're sure someone attacked you."

She put the back of her right hand on his cheek and smoothed it. "I didn't go into it a lot, but it was so bad when I knew someone was following me the first time."

When she touched him, even lightly, and probably as she would an old friend, his body turned unbearably hard — in the most bearable way. Her hand rubbing his face wasn't enough. He wanted to make love with her.

"Marc? What are you thinking?"

Maybe she should find that out — with a little help from him.

He checked Gaston's whereabouts while he said, "You're sure someone's following you again. Is that what you mean?" The dog was still on the desk but now held a pen in his teeth.

"Someone is. I should have gone back to Cyrus like I promised I would — he's very analytical. I'd started to explain to him but chickened out. You know how it is when you start to hear yourself explaining something and it sounds stupid to you."

What he felt was new. Fear that gnawed at his gut caught him off guard. "Please don't hold anything back from me," he told her. He was thinking about Amy, visualizing her all twisted up on those stone tiles. "Something's very wrong in this town." If it cost him his last breath, he'd find out what it was.

"Yes," she said quietly. "I've already said I don't think that man was ever caught. And I think he's back. Marc, I'm trying to be cool with this, but he thinks he needs to shut me up — I'm sure of it. It must mean he thinks I could give the police some damning evidence against him."

Gaston dropped the pen to the floor and yawned. Sometimes his eyes closed and he wobbled until he jerked awake again, and snorted. He gave the impression of having bags under his eyes.

"Reb, what's happened to make you so sure you're being followed? Apart from what happened tonight? And if you are right, why you?"

"I already told you about the first —"

"I'm asking about since Pepper Leach was put away," he told her.

"You do believe what I've told you?"

"I believe you, and I want to help you. And I want us to help each other."

He saw her make up her mind to talk. "When I made the mistake of leaving my cycle out one night, something heavy was used on the wheels, and the tires were slashed. That happened two weeks ago. Fortunately one of my patients insisted on fixing it for me. I feel eyes on me, and get the impression someone's been watching me. Then I see something move — bushes mostly — and I know whoever's doing these things is close by but has moved on. It's happening a lot. And now all this." She spread her arms to indicate the house. "This was meant to be a horrible, frightening warning. Whoever did it intended to scare me into taking some sort of action — so that he could know how I'd react. If he'd wanted me to die in that closet, he could easily have killed me.

"Then there was poor Gaston. What kind of person attempts to kill a helpless little dog?"

Marc glanced at the dog, who had stretched out on his back, with all four legs sticking up in the air, and who was snoring and chomping in his sleep.

"He likes to sleep that way sometimes," Reb commented. "Marc, do you think someone broke in to put glass in Gaston's food?"

"I surely do. And I believe he came through the window."

Her great, relieved sigh exhilarated him. He was in a bad way with Reb. Marc didn't want to look very far into the future. Too much could happen in too short a time, and it didn't all have to be good.

"It wouldn't be human if you weren't scared about being alone with all this."

She looked into his eyes, and, not for the first time, Marc was certain Reb knew something useful about Amy's death. She might have no knowledge of what it was, but it was there and waiting for the right circumstances to trigger its revelation. He told her, "You aren't on your own now. You're with me. This man isn't brave; this is a coward who attacks women. I'm taking you back to Clouds End with me where I can make sure you aren't vulnerable."

Where he could make sure she wasn't vulnerable? Reb looked for signs that he was joking. His serious, fabulous face showed he really didn't know just how vulnerable she was, to say nothing of what might happen to her resolve if she was staying in his home. "I have to be strong," she told him. "People expect it of me."

"You know I can't let you stay here alone, don't you?" he asked. "You and Gaston will be with me until I'm certain there's no more danger."

He didn't know what he said. "You're very kind, but I must remain in town in case I'm needed. My patients rely on me to be here for them. It's a rare night when I'm not called out."

"I noticed. They take advantage of you." He mouthed, *Sorry,* and said, "You can be called out at my place and I'll drive you where you have to go."

"Too far. It would take too long to get where I had to go. But thanks."

"So you usually go on that motorbike? Even in the middle of the night?"

"Yes."

"Not anymore, you don't. Next time a thug decides to rearrange your wheels, you could be riding them."

"This is a waste of time. I'm very grateful for your concern, even if it does come from left field. I'm careful — I look after myself."

He got up, and pulled her to her feet. "You are a gutsy woman, brave, and sometimes you're an ass."

Marc had never been one to sugarcoat his feelings, but he could be going a little far this time.

"Hear me?" He held her hands firmly. "All this wait-and-see, and trying to tell yourself this will all go away if you just carry on business as usual — it's irrational."

"You don't know that," she told him and wished she weren't wearing something so flimsy. She felt exposed. "We can all find trouble if we look for it. What's wrong with the idea of not looking for it."

"You and I don't have to look for it, it already found us — or am I imagining things?" His steady gaze made her want to look elsewhere.

"It went away before," she said, and could have kicked herself for sounding so simplistic. "And there's something else: what if the flurry around me now is meant to divert attention from what's really happening? I could be a decoy."

"You could be right," he said. "I hope you are. But if this guy really is your rubber killer, he's reminding you what he's capable of and how easy it would be to get to you."

To Reb's disgust, she trembled, and when she tried to hold herself rigid, her teeth chattered loud enough for her to hear them.

"What can he want from me? There haven't been any notes — just a steady campaign to scare me."

"Damn it all," Marc said suddenly. "No one is going to do this to you, not without going through me. From now on, until this is over, the shadow you see on the wall will be mine."

She took his hands to her lips and kissed his knuckles, each one, carefully. Turning his palms up, she brushed her lips against first one, then the other. Then Reb let him go and turned to walk away.

Before she'd taken her first step, Marc caught her about the waist and planted her in front of him again. When they were growing up he had seemed so big and strong. Then, at Tulane, she'd seen that he wasn't only tall, broad, and physically powerful — he was also handsome in a way that turned heads. Now, in his thirties, she would describe him as imposing, a virile man in every way. And his looks had only become more striking. She'd already seen how the heads still turned.

He was staring into her face, but she wouldn't look back.

"You think you can kiss my hands like that and walk away without a word?" he said.

"There isn't anything to say," Reb told him. "The last person I expected to see back in Toussaint was you. Sometimes you have a way of making me like you so much. Your loyalty shakes me. It makes me feel close to you."

He took a step backward, and they both heard something crunch under a heel. Marc grimaced and picked up Reb's flattened pen. "Sorry about that." He offered it to her, but she wrinkled her nose and put her hands behind her back.

"Trouble brought me here." The pen missed

the wastepaper basket. "*Damn,* I'm losing my touch. Your trouble makes what I intend to do more difficult."

"I'm sure it does," Reb told him. "You never expected to see me at all, let alone discover I'm involved in what you came for."

He pulled her closer and gathered her hair at the nape of her neck. "You could say that. But I'm managing to adjust — and like it.

"Finding Amy and establishing that she is who I say she is will be the simplest part. Tracking down her killer will be hell. When this town senses an outside threat to one of its people, it turns inward on itself. Loyalty is a good thing, but if it's not reasoned through, it can be dangerous. My family is already disliked in Toussaint, and most of the people who live in the town won't believe I'm not here to interfere in their lives."

"They'll get over it. I'm planting positive seeds wherever I can. But you can't walk around telling your theory about what happened at St. Cécil's to anyone who will listen."

"Try me." He stroked her sides with his fingertips, and she felt like telling him he had a week or so to stop.

"I don't want to try you," she told him. "How many people already know what happened at Pappy's when we were there? Every word will be spread all over. Just this once, would you humor me and be careful, please?"

He looked downward and said, "The only

good part of all this is that we met again."

Reb flushed, and not entirely because he was staring at her breasts. Could she believe the things he said — about the two of them? When she'd first seen him at Cyrus's house, her heart had thumped so hard she'd wanted to sit down where she was. And each time they'd been together since his return she'd felt the same shock. Yet she didn't want him to go away again. If he told her right now that he'd decided he wanted nothing further to do with the town, or with her, and that he'd decided not to continue his search for his sister, Reb wasn't sure just how long it would take for her to get over him.

"Did you hear what I said?" he asked.

She crossed the robe more firmly around her and made much of tying the sash into a bow.

"Damn it, Reb."

"Don't swear. I heard what you said. Thank you, Marc."

"Thank you, hm? Like, thank you, but don't expect me to change my opinion of you? Is that it?"

"It's not the way you make it sound." If Gaston rolled on his side he might fall off the desk. "Excuse me," she said and went to the dog. She lifted him and put him in a comfy chair. He wiggled a little, but didn't wake up.

"A dog's life, huh?" Marc said. "Would you consider taking in a second one. He's house-broken and follows commands most of the time.

Of course, we wouldn't be signing any long-term contracts. Thirty days' notice of the intent to sever relations — on either side — should do it." He'd followed her and stood behind her while she looked down at Gaston. "My requirements can easily be spelled out. Food is good. Walking in a park is great. I'd prefer it if you waived the bit about going outside to relieve myself. Your neighbors might complain."

Reb crossed her arms tightly and kept her back to him. "Just how big would this dog be?" He was making a joke out of this, so why did his "thirty days' notice" tighten her throat?

A single finger, slowly running the length of her spine, caused her eyes to close.

"Pretty big," Marc said, and his voice sounded different. "About six foot two standing on his hind legs. Probably a hundred eighty-five pounds. And if you rub his belly and kiss his nose, he'll follow you anywhere."

He put an arm around her waist and eased her to lean against him.

He bent to settle his face against her neck. His breath shifted her hair, and she felt the roughness of his beard on her skin.

"Marc," Reb said softly. "I'm not going to lie and say I don't want this, but we don't have a past together. We won't have a future, either. Even mentioning one is ridiculous. You'll do whatever you came to Toussaint to do, then you'll go back to New Orleans and keep on designing beautiful buildings."

"I can work well wherever I am. My plans are up in the air."

In other words, he might or might not be around long, and the risk of both hurting and embarrassing herself shouldn't get in the way of his need — no matter how temporary. Marc needed a woman, and she was convenient. He liked her, she knew that. She was also a challenge to him, and Marc Girard had a history of wanting whatever seemed out of reach.

He spun her around and kissed her jaw as if he hadn't heard a word she'd told him. Lightly enough to singe her nerves, Marc stroked her from jaw to decolletage — and let his hand rest there.

She pushed the fingers of her left hand through his hair. It sprang into place again as her touch passed.

"We're both involved in the same struggle," he said and crossed his arms behind her back. "The people who are after you will have my name on their list by now. Doesn't it make sense for us to stick together?"

She couldn't pretend she wouldn't enjoy having someone close to rely on, or that the only person she truly wanted with her wasn't Marc. But neither could she accept his offer. It would be easy to do, but some of her reasons for not doing so wouldn't be understood by Marc. She lived in a little town where she was relied upon not just to treat ills but to be an available listener. Now would be a bad time to jump into bed with a man so many of the locals distrusted. Not that anytime in the foreseeable future would be a good time.

"I'm not trying to rush sex with you," Marc said, and Reb chuckled.

"You're laughing at me," he said, sounding aggrieved. He eased away from her — the minutest distance — and settled a strong but gentle hand at either side of her face.

He was going to kiss her. Or he would if she didn't stop him.

"Reb." Marc placed his cheek against hers. She heard him swallow, and breathe none too steadily. "Can we work together on this?"

Her very physical responses to him disturbed Reb. If it were possible to blush inside one's head and body, she'd be sure that's what was happening to her now. And the region of her heart ached. There were other sensations that were one hundred percent sexual. She burned with wanting Marc.

He watched his own fingers in her hair. "Did you ever get close to being married, Reb?"

"No. I've had boyfriends. One or two of them . . . well . . . The past needs to stay where it is — past. We move on, or we do if we're healthy."

"Maybe I'm not healthy," he told her with a naughty-boy grin. "I have a past, and no matter what you say, you're a part of it. For that I'm grateful. I'm not saying I've lived like a monk, just that things never turned out for a long-term commitment. Probably my fault." He held close, and she wanted to respond, but any step she took now could turn her life into a maze, not that it didn't already seem too complicated.

Reb had never knowingly hurt someone, but if Marc meant even part of what he'd said to her, she'd have to put distance between them. Her life was in Toussaint, but Marc would never live here again. There was no point in starting something.

"We don't have important memories together."

His lips parted, and she was pretty sure she wouldn't like what he intended to say. "We could start changing that." Only the dimpled smile saved the comment from sounding oily. "Maybe we started already. There's no way to see the future, but it's likely to come just the same. When it does, even you won't be able to say there's nothing between us that's worth remembering."

Reb plucked at his shirtsleeves. He concentrated on her mouth and began closing the gap between them. The tanned skin on his face drew tight over sharp bones. His dark eyes gleamed.

"Are we going to help each other?" she asked.

"Only seems sensible to me, cher."

"Me, too. I think. But that means we can't be too close — unless we've got somethin' urgent to share, or somethin' interesting relating to what we hope to do. Sex and business don't mix."

"The hell they don't," Marc said, and startled Reb by rubbing the tip of a forefinger back and forth over her lips. "Relax," he said. "We're not doin' anything more than keeping each other company on a lonely night." *Company* had a whole heap of meanings.

SEVENTEEN

Wind picked up and turned into a manic noise-maker. Just that suddenly, the windows rattled in their frames and a whistling set up through the trees.

Marc caught the flicker of Reb's eyes as her attention switched from him to the weather, and bought him a few seconds to regroup. He was almost sure she was going to ask him to go home.

"You need to get home."

He saw a new career ahead of him: Marc Girard, Clairvoyant.

"I don't want to go." Some risks were worth taking. "But if you really don't want me with you, just say the word."

She said, "That's not fair."

Marc kissed the corners of her mouth, slowly. Reb squeezed her eyes shut and he parted her lips with his tongue. He ran a fleeting path just inside and felt a subtle change in her. She was responding to him.

Marc nibbled her bottom lip and sucked lightly. The already dim room grew darker, didn't it? Changing the angle of his face, he opened both of their mouths wide. He reached, and she met him. The moment was wild, then desperate. For an instant he paused, his mouth almost relaxed on hers, catching his breath, but she didn't allow him more than that moment.

He lost track of how long they'd been kissing. However long, he wasn't ready for it to be over.

Raising his head, Marc looked down at her. "Want to stop?" he asked.

"No," she told him, and she sounded certain.

"What then?"

"Surprise me," she said and wrinkled her nose. "My stomach just flipped. That was a stupid thing to tell you."

"I kind of liked it," he said, leaning to openly size up her body. "Maybe that's because I'm a man."

Reb laughed aloud.

"Laugh away, cher." With one smooth motion, he untied her robe and pushed it from her shoulders and arms. "There are differences between the male and female mind."

Reb choked and asked, "Is there a punchline to these revelations?" She folded her arms over her breasts.

"There is."

She plucked at the neck of her nightgown. Suddenly the signals she sent weren't so clear.

"What's wrong?" Marc asked. "You look as if you aren't sure whether to enjoy the moment, or flatten me."

"I couldn't flatten you," she said. "That's one

of those differences you mentioned. And given what we know about the minds of men, it's very unfair. Also, it's uncomfortable to be wearing nothing but a nightie while you're fully dressed."

He frowned, then said, "I guess I can see that," and pulled off his shirt. "Better?"

"Very nice," Reb said with enough feeling to show she meant each word. She giggled.

He threw out his hands. "I look so bad you gotta laugh at me? How good is that for a guy's ego?"

"Don't mind me," Reb told him. "I had a fleeting vision of you working on a building site and deciding to take off your shirt."

He stared at her and said, "I don't get it."

Reb held him just above the elbows. "Loosen up. There was a guy on a TV commercial with a killer body, and when he took off his shirt, women who could see him from some windows clawed past each other and pretty much drooled over him. He had a nice body, but in a competition you'd win hands down."

"Uh huh." He raised his eyebrows and rested one palm against his chest. "Thank you, I guess."

He smiled. He'd never seen himself in the alpha wolf role, but he wouldn't mind if she read, *Come with me, I've decided to make your day,* in that smile.

"What?" Reb said. "Why are you grinning at me like that."

He'd have to work on his mouth signals. "I spoke with my partner today. Guess what he wanted to know?"

Reb kept her gaze in the region of his collarbones. "When you're going back to New Orleans to take care of business?"

"I'm taking care of business from here. I can do that for as long as I please. If I need to be in New Orleans, you know that's easy. I'll give you one more chance to guess what Len asked me."

He could almost hear her searching for a comeback before she said, "Nope, Marc. Can't think of anything."

He shifted his hands to her sides and brushed slowly up and down — and ran his thumbs over the sides of her breasts at each opportunity. And his control tilted. He wanted them both naked, which could mean his timing was dangerous.

"You're not going to get it," he told her. "I'll put you out of your misery. Len wanted to know if I'm bored." The way she quickly bowed her head, covering a smile, cinched his tension another notch. "He doesn't know the real reason I came here; he also doesn't know about you. A man could never be bored if he was with you."

Her expression turned quizzical.

"Reb, you once made me a great offer, remember? Given your age at the time, and our family connections, it seemed a lousy idea. But I wanted to accept. You know what I'm talking about?"

"I was an infatuated, immature teenager.

Thinking about it still makes my skin crawl."

"You were so sweet," Marc said. "You don't know how badly I wanted to come to you, I would have if I could have been sure I'd do all the right things. What about that offer now, Reb? Was there a statute of limitations on it?"

"Well, well," she said, "I do believe you just said you want to have sex with me. I live a quiet life. I surely can't remember the last time I was propositioned like this — so directly. Give me a minute and names will come to me."

"Did you sleep with all of them?"

"Why, Marc, I do believe you sound annoyed that I've had a life of my own. You haven't been pining for me — you've been too busy. You could have written to help me through. Being nice is cheap, but worth everything sometimes."

Her tone stung as much as her words. "I was wrong," he said. "I didn't know what to write. More pain was something I wanted to avoid — for both of us. I managed to convince myself that the best thing was to leave it alone."

"Probably right," she said and stepped out of his reach. "I think we can help each other, but that doesn't mean we experiment just to see if we've been missing a lot of good sex. We live very different lives, and they please us. Let's accept that."

"I'm still asking the question, Reb. Straight up. Will you let me accept your offer now?" His skin turned up the heat, but the real burn was inside his body.

"Now?" she asked quietly.

"If you're willing. That's one of those basic differences I mentioned. The ones between men and women. A generalization, but from experience I know men are goal oriented. I'm male, but I'm different from all the rest. They only made one like me. I live for foreplay, get off on kissing and cuddling, and . . . exploring every little inch, every little feeling. My favorite occupation is to lie in front of a December fire with a woman who turns me on with her head as well as her body. Hours — I could spend hours doing just that."

Reb saw no sign that he was joking, but he had to be. He looked serious. She had been breathing through her open mouth. She shut it and straightened up. Let him see whatever he could through the nightie — she wasn't above throwing a rope to a drowning man. *Frustrated* was the word that came to mind.

"I'm talking too much," he said. "Chalk it up to too much work and not enough play, for a long, long time. May I touch you, Reb? If you don't like it, stop me."

"You've been touching me." But she knew what he meant, and he wouldn't hurt her, of that she was certain. "And for the record, it's July, not December."

"July is as fine a month as December," he said. "One more time. Are you telling me yes or no? Say no and I'll try never to broach the subject again."

"You aren't the only curious one around here. Yes, Marc. I want to know just how far I've come from those days of mad infatuation."

Most men would take a direct hit to the ego if a woman said what she'd just said. Reb waited for Marc to discover he had to leave.

"You always did have an analytical mind. I'll take what you just said as an invitation, or at least an agreement to humor me."

Pressing her against him, he eased the back of the nightie up enough to get his hands underneath. He gripped her hips and lifted her, stood her on an ottoman, used long, caressing sweeps from the backs of her knees to her bottom. He didn't attempt to remove her white lace panties, opting instead to slip both of his hands inside. Sometimes he lingered where he could hold a cheek in each hand and drive her wild with a touch so light, if she didn't tingle with each new motion, she might think he hadn't touched her at all.

He rotated her on the ottoman so she looked over his shoulder at their reflection in an old gilt-framed mirror.

Reb looked into a face she scarcely recognized as her own. She leaned her cheek against Marc's ear and watched her hands as she stroked his shoulders and back.

With one foot planted on the ottoman, Marc parted her legs and sat her astride his thigh.

He ran his hands up the fronts of her legs this time, and settled his thumbs on one of the places she couldn't ignore. Startled, knowing how easily she could give him whatever he wanted, she moved his hands away.

"You don't like that, cher?"

"I like it a lot — too much. And I feel this is nothing more than the two of us satisfying our appetites."

"I don't belong to anyone, Reb. Neither do you. I believe we're going to spend a lot of time together making that past we talked about. And if you allow me to be very direct — feel free to slap me here — I'm going to admit that I never forgot you. Time and again I almost came looking for you, but I was afraid I'd find out you were already married and I didn't think I could take that. Then, when I did come, I was too preoccupied to think about the two of us. Now I can handle it all — I want to make love to you."

"You do not mince words," she said. "Maybe I like that."

While she stared silently into the mirror, watching muscle ripple in his back, intensely aware of his thigh between her legs, she tried to weigh the dangers of giving in to him. They were obvious. Wanting him enough to be able to forget potential disaster was reckless.

Softly, his fingertips flitted around her ribcage from back to front and he cupped his hands beneath her breasts. Reb put her arms behind her and braced herself on his knee. And she let her eyes close.

Marc's mouth, seeking her nipples through

her nightie, popped her eyes wide open again. Marc supported her breasts as if he were weighing them. His teeth and tongue soaked the gown, turned the fabric transparent.

"Marc." She wished she didn't need to talk, not now. "Marc, listen to me."

He paused long enough to nod.

"Slow down," she told him. "This is going too fast."

Instantly, Marc raised his head and looked at her. "Thirteen years doesn't seem too fast to me," he said, breathing heavily. "I'm sorry. It's the male, goal-oriented thing, but that's no excuse."

Reb said, "We don't need excuses. I'm as ready for this as you are, but I don't want to get hurt." She could have said, 'again' but stopped herself. "So I'm doing the sensible thing and standing back a bit. Neither of us is interested in a long-term commitment. We don't need to spell out the ground rules, but we can start by getting to know each other better."

Women, Marc decided, were weird. He could have sworn she was ready for him. He'd felt how wet she was and the fact that she'd moved herself on his leg as if she couldn't get enough of him. But she could have a point about rushing the sex. On the other hand, how did a guy deal with being told the lady wasn't interested in anything more than a fling — at the pace she dictated? Praise be he hadn't announced his real feelings for her. He'd have been the one hurt —

not that he wasn't already — and afterward he'd be the fool.

"How about it, Marc?"

"Sure. From here on, you call the shots. That way we'll both know we're on safe ground."

She leaned forward and wrapped her arms around his neck. Into his ear she whispered, "Bullshit."

He frowned and asked, "What did you just say?" A direct view down the front of her nightie didn't do a thing to cool him down.

"I said, bullshit. As in, you sound petulant because you don't like a woman setting the pace in a relationship. You're going to let me set the ground rules? Garbage. Let's see how long you last without losing your temper."

She swung herself from his knee and stood behind him to massage his neck and back. Between strokes, and frequent applications of evil little knuckles, she kissed him. And she took nips at his ears.

Pushing one of her legs between his, she threaded her arms around his waist and brushed her breasts back and forth on his back. Marc closed his eyes tightly and gritted his teeth. The lady was either a natural, or she'd learned some sophisticated methods for driving a man nuts.

"Does that feel nice?" she asked, and when he trusted himself to speak at all, he said, "So nice."

"I've always thought it was a good idea for the

woman to take the initiative sometimes. Why should men be responsible for all the moves?"

She undid his belt and unzipped his fly.

"Couldn't agree with you more, cher," he told her. Her fingertips slipped through the opening on his undershorts. Given the mental workover she'd already accomplished, she didn't have to do much to free his straining penis. She held it, stroked it, made small circles over the end with the flat of a palm.

Ecstasy or death must surely follow — fast.

"So this pace is okay with you?" he said.

"Very okay."

"Good, just wanted to be sure."

"Is it okay with you?"

"Oh yes." If he told her he was close to disgracing himself all over the ottoman, she'd probably recoil, and he surely didn't want that. He'd prefer to have this unexpected turn of events continue.

Asking her "what's next?" might not be too cool.

"Will it be okay if I sleep on the couch?" he said.

Reb held still with both of her hands on his penis. He wished she would let go — as long as nothing was to be done about his condition tonight — let go and suggest they both get some sleep.

"I went about this all wrong," he told her. "For some reason, in my mind, we haven't been parted for a bunch of years. I feel as if we were never separated. Being with you feels so natural."

"If it's meant to be, we'll be okay with the wait. As long as we're both satisfied with working on the way we are when we're together."

"You're right," he told her, and was glad she couldn't see inside his fevered mind.

She moved away from him and pulled a cotton throw from a chair. "I think it's easier to talk if you're comfortable."

She sat, cross-legged, on the rug and swung the throw around her shoulders.

Only one thing would relax him, and it didn't look as if he was going to get it. "Are you cold?" he said, taking a place beside her.

"Not really, but creating the illusion comforts me."

Well son-of-a-gun, making her feel good was his job now. She'd been the one to decide they should go slowly, but she hadn't mentioned that "slow" meant "stop," or pretty near.

She leaned on him and patted his back. "Being here with you, just the way we are, is perfect. Forgive me for getting a bit pushy just now."

He didn't trust himself to look at her. "You weren't pushy, you were very, very nice. I've ruined your evening and put you out big time."

"Not a bit of it."

Not a bit was right on as far as she was concerned, Marc thought, she'd lost her nerve at the last moment, and he was the one who'd been put out, big time.

"You don't need to stay here with me, y'know.

Nothing bad's going to happen this evening."

"If I leave, you leave with me. You don't want to do that, so I'll stretch out in here. Is it okay if I use a cushion from one of the chairs? And maybe you could point me in the direction of a blanket."

He put a pillow on the floor for his head and sat there.

"You said you'd sleep on the couch." Reb had stood up but made no effort to leave.

"I like sleeping on the floor. Probably reminds me of my Boy Scout days. How about that blanket?" he asked, smiling at her. "I promise I won't beg you for anything else."

Without a word, or a sign that she'd heard what he said, she pulled the nightgown off and let it fall.

Marc knew his mouth was open but thought he might suffocate if he closed it.

Reb knelt beside him and pushed him until he lay flat. The pillows weren't needed, at least not in the immediate future.

She straddled his belly and sat there, staring at him as if she were trying to read his mind.

Reb stretched out on top of him, and put her hand under his head. The sensation of having her breasts pressed to his naked chest obliterated any thoughts he might have had. She looked into his face and he looked back.

"Are you here for the company, or did you have something else in mind?"

"I can't do it, Marc."

His heart plummeted into his loafers, only he wasn't wearing shoes.

Reb said, "I can't keep up an act and pretend I'm too cool to be turned on. I am turned on. But don't humor me. If you don't want to have sex with me now, I'll understand."

"I'm confused," Marc said. "Didn't you just say we had to take things slower?"

"I changed my mind. Women do that. Men don't because the possibility of rejection frightens the pants off them. But I'm being rash, throwing myself at you like this — although, well, I've never done anything like this before — nothing exactly like it — and it excites me. I enjoy a little danger now and again."

She sat on his . . . She sat on a part of him that was now crying "foul," but his head was rejoicing. She would get to make the first moves — most of the time.

"I hope I haven't ruined any chance of a friendship with you. I like you so much." She smiled, but it didn't come from the heart.

She made to leave him, but he caught her by the waist and plopped her down again.

"You grew into such a gracious woman," he said, swallowing his laughter.

She kissed his mouth so abruptly, so hard, he expected to see blood when next he saw himself in a mirror.

Her tongue was inside his mouth. She ran her hands over him. When she planted her elbows near his ears and started to play with his hair, he knew the slowing-down proposition wasn't going to work.

She rocked back and forth, planting kisses at will, and her breasts swayed close enough to his mouth that he fought with himself against holding her still while he availed himself of a heaven-sent opportunity.

His patience ran out, just like that — gone. He flicked his tongue across a nipple as she swayed forward, and repeated the process when she returned to her haunches.

There she sat for an interminable pause. Reb stared at his eyes, and he almost lost his battle for dominance — equality would be good enough — by looking away.

As abruptly as she'd stopped moving, she started again. This time he realized her face was very pink and there was a feverish light in her green eyes.

She positioned her breasts no more than an inch away from Marc's face. He had only to raise his chin and he'd score a hit with his tongue every time.

Reb was on all fours, her lace-clad bottom thrust into the air — waiting. She reared back, shaking her head. "You're driving me crazy," she said. "I can't keep on like this. May I?" She pointed to his belt and Marc nodded while he set up an incantation inside his mind: *Take sex or leave it. No big deal. I don't even like it, but I'll humor the woman. Shit, protection. How long have I been carrying the same rubber in my wallet? Does latex perish? Nah, of course it doesn't.*

Reb had pushed her bottom low on his thighs. She was hard at work, and any second now Marc's readiness for an upcoming engagement would be standing to attention and demanding satisfaction.

"Lift your hips," Reb said, and when he did so, she shimmied his pants and underwear down to his knees.

At first Reb just stared, her lips pushed out as if she'd like to whistle. She bent over him to get a closer look, and said, "Oh my" in a tone guaranteed to make a man question the adequacy of his utensils.

Reb leaned forward until her breasts actually clothed his most tender parts.

Gosh darn it, she couldn't be heaping adoration on him, or doing some of the other noble rituals intended as tributes to a man's virility. Hell no, she probably thought that if she warmed him up he might grow.

Contorting her body, Reb contrived to remove her panties. "Don't let me fall over," she said.

Nonchalance was the only way to save one's ego in these situations. He pulled her down beside him and started kissing every inch of naked skin he could reach, which was a lot of skin at the moment.

When he reached the apex of her legs, he pulled her legs apart, to make room for his face and tongue. He hesitated and said, "Sorry. I'm getting carried away, and you don't like it when I do that."

"If I ever said that, I was lying," Reb said, with no sign of discomfort. "You said I get to call the shots. I don't want you to feel emasculated, so you go first."

"You're beautiful," he said, surprising himself. "By the time you started at Tulane, you'd grown into the prettiest thing I'd ever seen. But you, cher, have become a woman no man could fail to stare at."

She pulled her hair to the top of her head, with interesting results. He tried not to ogle, but he was only human.

"Reb, your breasts are the stuff of wet dreams." *Oh, god!* "I mean they're fabulous, and I could be a happy man just looking at you the way you are right now."

Promptly, she pulled her arms down and crossed them over her chest. "You're beautiful, Marc Girard, the most handsome man I've ever seen. And you're pretty good on the inside, too, from what I hear. Is the floor too hard? We can continue this conversation in my bed if you like."

Time to really take command, Marc thought. He lifted and swung her to lie on her side, facing him, with the firelight playing over her face and body.

"I get the first move?" He knew how he could break down any remaining inhibitions.

Reb had nodded. He rose to one elbow and

looked her over, took great pleasure in observing the little signs that she was learning to enjoy herself with him, but she wasn't as uninhibited as she'd like him to believe.

"Got it," he said softly before kissing her full on the lips. She kissed him back, her naked breasts forgotten while she held his shoulders, and she seemed determined to crawl right inside his skin.

They were both breathing hard when Marc took his kisses on the road. He pressed his mouth to her jaw, her neck and arms, stomach and thighs. And all the time she reached for him — to no avail, because he might be a big man but he was also swift, and determined. He was a man who didn't have to have a woman in his life all the time. The hunt was the biggie, especially when he got close to running his quarry to earth. He could wait as long as it took to see Reb across the breakfast table — his table.

For a man who prided himself on dealing in absolutes, he must have had a frontal lobotomy in his sleep, and he'd lost control over speech.

The first round was his? Great, this should take the frost off the pumpkin.

Holding her carefully, he maneuvered her to sit astride his chest and then the guiding was gentle, but guaranteed to take him where he wanted to be.

"Marc?" The uncertainty in her voice was no put-on.

A little tug and she was kneeling. Marc rocked

her forward and she stopped herself from falling on him by planting her hands, one on either side of his head.

Her breasts swayed a little and he took pleasure — a whole lot of pleasure — in watching them. He couldn't make out what she crooned to him, but figured if he gave his all to whatever he did, then they should both be in heaven. Marc was ready for that kind of heaven.

Marc smiled inside. Reb wasn't talking anymore, and he was sure she held her breath. "Relax," he told her and clasped her hips. He pulled her just close enough to make it easy for him to reach between her legs with his tongue.

First Reb stiffened, but then she leaned backward to give him all the help she could.

She climaxed almost instantly. With her eyes closed, she trembled, and tears coursed her cheeks.

"I've upset you," he told her, but Reb shook her head and smiled through the tears. She said, "You've made me feel wonderful," and showed him just how wonderful by kissing him until he felt suffocation was a possibility. And what a way to go. He'd make sure he came back from the dead to do it all over again.

"Reb," he said when she took a breath break.

"Oh, of course," she said, not allowing him to finish his thought. "What am I thinkin' about? Just me, I guess. That's not like me. I want to give you as much pleasure as you've given me."

Crawling backward rapidly, she reached her

target. Marc propped himself on his elbows and watched her. At least, he watched her red hair drape his belly, the movement of her head, and he felt too much. Too much, but he wouldn't change a thing.

"Reb," he said before decision-making time ran out. "You must be getting rug burns on your knees, cher."

She paused and mumbled, "And you're gettin' them on your tush." She laughed, actually laughed, and went back to her task.

"I want to make love to you for what's left of the night," he told her. "And do it in a place where we can pass out between sessions."

She let him slip free of her lips again and said, "Sounds clinical." The tips of her breasts, being deliberately drawn back and forth over his engorged penis, undid him — if there'd been anything still done up before.

"Maybe we should go to bed after all."

"As soon as I've finished here," Reb told him, and he had to laugh at her less than romantic turn of phrase.

He stopped laughing and fell back onto the floor. Faster and faster she moved over him. Pressure built, a pressure that constricted his belly and butt, and tightened him into rocks elsewhere. His head ached, the best headache he'd ever had. His hips refused to quit chasing her lips each time she withdrew a little.

"Go with it," she told him when she stopped to breathe.

He heard the noise he made, but it came from a distance, as if it wasn't connected to him. He clawed the rug with his fingertips, and he reached for Reb.

She stopped moving. Just stopped!

"Reb, you can't do this to me. Please."

"Come on," she told him, and he'd never heard her sound desperate before, not this desperate. She leaped to her feet and tried to haul him up, but he ignored the hand she offered and got up on his own.

Gaston had started barking.

"Grab your clothes," Reb said, while gathering her own.

The front door slammed. "Someone just left," Marc whispered. "God, has he or she been here the whole time?"

"In here," Reb ordered, swinging open a bookshelf that worked like a revolving door. There was a dark space beyond. "Quickly. We've got to get dressed and try to look normal."

"For someone who just left —"

"For someone who just used a key to open the front door and came in."

"Hi, Reb, where are you? I've been sent —"

The bookshelf slid silently back into place.

"Now dress," Reb whispered. "Fast."

Stale air with a hint of mold thrown in turned Marc's stomach. "Who is it?"

"Cyrus. He keeps a key to the house. We have to be out of here, fully dressed, and with some great excuse, by the time he checks my study.

Otherwise he'll call in Spike and go over every inch of the house. In the end Cyrus would remember me showing him this space and open it. If he does, and we're still in it . . . If it happens, I'll close my eyes and play dead. And if you say I'm alive, I'll deny it."

EIGHTEEN

Cyrus went into Reb's reception room and stood in the dark — and felt like a complete fool. Holy . . . Toledo, he was long past old enough to figure out what he'd walked into.

The house was pretty dark, but a line of light shone beneath the closed door to Reb's study. She hadn't responded to his knock. And she wasn't answering his shouts, although Gaston was coming through loud and clear.

And Marc Girard's vehicle was parked out front.

Why hadn't he taken one look at the Range Rover and rung the doorbell. A knock on a door, made out of so-called consideration, wasn't necessarily heard, not everywhere in a house, not if there was a lot going on in there.

Television could cover ordinary sounds.

Pursing his lips, he managed a loud, but tuneless whistle. He used to be an accomplished whistler but hadn't had much reason to practice for years. "I'll wait in the kitchen," he announced loudly. A click came from somewhere close. Cyrus peered toward Reb's consulting room. The door was open, but it was dark inside. Old houses were creaky places, and people blessed with excellent hearing didn't miss a pop or scritch.

He thought he heard another sound, a thud this time, and inside Reb's study. What if she was in trouble? Gaston's bark had subsided to an intermittent grumble. The dog wouldn't settle down if something had happened to his boss.

There wasn't a television in Reb's study. If a television was playing at 4 Conch Street, the sound was off.

Thuds didn't always mean trouble . . . depending on the situation in progress. He'd been around Spike too much lately. Activity would be a better word.

Damn it all, why had he let himself into Reb's house at this time of night — morning?

Cyrus wanted out. But he couldn't just go away — he'd really embarrass her then.

"Yes, I'll do that," he all but yelled. "Wait in the kitchen, that's what I'll do. No, I'll sit on the stairs; that way I can say 'hi' the minute she comes in and I won't shock her."

Another subtle click.

If he was into being nervous, he'd be one jumpy man now. A swift trip into the consulting room, where he turned on the lights, showed nothing unusual.

Sitting on the stairs was a dumb idea. They — or Reb — would never come out if he was there. He closed his eyes and flirted with the idea of pretending to fall asleep in a chair right here in the waiting room. They'd find him and he'd "wake up," apparently groggy. They could use that as a cover. . . .

They were all going to be humiliated, and they might as well get it over with. It wasn't as if they weren't adults, or as if anything new to him was in progress — was *happening* — on the other side of the study door.

"Reb!"

She could be asleep in there — really asleep.

With Girard's transportation out front?

He stomped through to the kitchen, opened the refrigerator door, slammed it shut, rattled glasses on a shelf, opened the freezer and shook the ice drawer, scooped out cubes with the glass, noticed the blender, dumped the cubes in and turned it on.

It had been said he ought to be singing in the Quarter. "Didn't He Ramble" was one of his favorite numbers. Madge suggested it was the "ashes to ashes" bit that appealed to him.

Cyrus poured his ice slushy into the glass and raised his voice in song. Where his gravelly, right-on-key, N'awlins-nights belt had come from, he didn't know. Not a soul in the family — that he was aware of — could carry a tune in a balloon.

Barking, Gaston hurtled into the kitchen and skidded to a halt with the aid of his front claws. When he saw Cyrus, he snapped his jaws shut.

Close behind came Reb.

She wore nightclothes and looked as if she'd

spent an hour or so in a tumble dryer. Pretty, but really mussed.

The old dictates clicked in, and he averted his face. Must not encourage carnal thoughts by looking upon a provocatively dressed woman.

"Hi, Cyrus," Reb said, in a high, surprised schoolgirl voice he'd never heard her use before. "When did you arrive? I didn't hear a thing until Gaston barked."

A future line for reconciliation just got one penitent longer. "I was starting to think you weren't here." *And one longer.* Gaston hadn't quit kicking up a ruckus since Cyrus approached the house.

"Yesterday was one of the most tiring I've ever had," Reb said with her eyes on the almost totally liquefied glass of ice. "You don't even know what happened when I got back here last night —"

"Sure you do, don't you, Cyrus?" Marc, his shirt inside out, joined them. "Spike told you all about it. You're a good friend to Reb, letting the law send you over here at this hour."

The man was good-looking. Rugged would be a word women would use. And he was mad. "Spike takes his responsibilities very seriously."

Marc shoved his hands in his pockets, kept one eye on Reb, and said, "He takes *himself* very seriously. And he doesn't like the idea of Reb being here with me. You're his patsy. You're supposed to make sure I'm not spending time with Reb. Spike Devol is frustrated, and he wants to make sure no one else is having a good . . . Forget it."

The reason for Marc's irritation was pretty evident *before* he wandered into the murky, male area of frustration. Even if he didn't say "sexually frustrated," that's what he meant. Strange how men never saw the irony in getting heated on the subject around an expert who had signed on for lifelong abstinence.

"Spike would have checked back on Reb himself, but he needed to get home to Wendy."

Marc muttered to himself, and Reb patted his arm. "What Cyrus says about Spike is true. He feels as accountable to this little town as I do."

"Who the fuck is this *Wendy* you people use to excuse his interference? His wife? If so, how come he doesn't behave as if he's got a woman he really wants to get home to?"

Cyrus hid a smile and emptied his glass into Reb's old but scrubbed-to-a-shine sink. He guessed Marc was wishing he could suck that outburst back.

"Wendy is Spike's daughter," Reb said, and a heavy frost had formed in the kitchen. "A man can't have any kind of life on a sheriff's salary. He has a gas station — last thing you see on the way out of town to the south."

"First thing on the way in from the south," Cyrus commented.

"Thank you, Cyrus," Reb said. "There's a convenience store there, too, and they carry a bit of everything. Spike's dad, Homer, holds down the fort, and looks after Wendy. She's four. Spike's wife took off with a bodybuilder. End of that story."

Cyrus chanced facing them again, just in time to catch Marc's glance at Reb's hand on his sleeve, and to see his realization that his shirt was inside out. He showed no awkwardness, just exasperation.

"Man after my own heart," Cyrus said. You had to help a fellow out when things weren't going so well for him. "I've worn shirts on both sides before washing them. Bachelors have to conserve their energy for more important things."

The hush that followed was heavy stuff. He was a diplomatic man, Cyrus thought, everyone said so. *So why did every other word he said sound suggestive.*

He was too touchy. They wouldn't have noticed a thing.

"Nice going," Marc said. "Let me know about your next night out with the boys, I'll tag along."

"That's enough," Reb said. "Thank you for coming, Cyrus. When you speak to Spike, let him know I'm okay."

"I put my shirt on wrong." Now Marc was belligerent. "Is that a sin? If anyone would know, you would."

Cyrus felt the smallest twinge of guilt, but he grinned. "That's one that seems to have slipped my mind. When I get back I'll look it up." He'd give the guy points for chutzpa. "I didn't expect you to be . . . I hoped to get to you with a question later, but I'd be grateful to do it now. A call came in at the rectory. Right after I finally thought the commotion was over and I could catch my breath. Do you know a woman who calls herself *Oiseau de Nuit?*"

"Night bird? No," Marc said promptly. "Sounds like a hooker."

Reb's "Marc!" was predictable.

"He's heard the term before." Marc Girard was a last-word kind of guy. Cyrus could handle it, but he'd spent enough time listening to wife-parishioners on the topic to know what women thought about the syndrome. Reb's flared nostrils didn't bode well for her old buddy.

"She called me from New Orleans," Cyrus said. "She'd heard something about a pending exhumation in Toussaint and wanted to warn me of the terrible things that would follow if it happened."

"Great," Marc said. "How the hell would this bird woman find out? Who is she?"

"It's so late," Reb said. "We're all tired. Why not go after this in the morning?"

"It's already morning," Marc said in a more reasonable tone. "Did she fill in any of the gaps, Cyrus?"

Cyrus shuffled his feet. "I think she's a medium, or she could be a medium. She talked about the other side, and hearing from the other side."

Marc was unnaturally still. He looked haunted,

his eyes black and bottomless. "Did she mention a name? Like my sister Amy's?"

"No."

"How about a return phone number?"

Cyrus hadn't been able to get any answers from the woman. "Nothing."

"It has to be Amy's roommate in New Orleans. She talked about communicating with Amy and I knew she didn't mean by e-mail." He shielded his eyes. "I think she's got contacts she isn't talking about. How else would she get her information."

"She's probably harmless," Reb told him. "Some of those people are sad. The only way they feel important is by putting on an act and frightening others."

"It shouldn't be difficult to isolate the people who know about the possible exhumation," Cyrus said. "Then it's a matter of following the trails to this woman. And I think she has a need to play this out, so she'll make contact again."

Reb shook her head at him. "I wouldn't be surprised if everyone in Toussaint knows about it — and I don't see why you're so sure she'll call you again."

"She said she'd be coming here, with help, to stop the, er —" He cleared his throat. "I think she mentioned the forces of evil."

Reb said, "Just what we need. Let's go sit down where we can be comfortable. I'm not sure if it's too early or too late to offer drinks, but I'll do it anyway." She glanced up at Marc, and the smile he gave her was gentle, and to Cyrus, out of character. It made the man more likable, and squeezed Cyrus's heart, just a little.

They trooped along the hall toward Reb's study. Rather than lead the way in, she pulled up short and closed the door. "The best brandy is in my consulting-room desk. And the chairs in the waiting room are the newest furniture in the house. They are *really* comfy."

The procession moved in that direction, with Cyrus scolding himself for wishing he could see inside the study. He'd definitely interrupted a . . . tryst? Was that what they called such a meeting? Or was it an interlude? Why look for euphemisms? They'd probably been making love.

He prayed hard for control over his wayward thoughts — all the way to the waiting room. Reb told the truth. The chairs were easy on the body. She went into her office and called out, "I don't know one brandy from another, but I think this is good."

There was the click again. Faint, subtle, but something out of place. Cyrus frowned toward Marc without expecting any response. Marc's eyes were screwed up, and he leaned his head to one side.

"Whatever it is, bring it on," he said to Reb.

And there was a click.

"I'll be damned," Marc said, getting to his feet. "Are you hearing what I'm hearing?"

Cyrus was grateful for a corroborator. "If I'm

hearing what we both think we're hearing, there's been an amateur night around here."

He led the way into the consulting room, meeting Reb as she made to rejoin them. "Listen to this," he said and held his tongue. Right on cue, the sound came again. "Did you hear it?" Once more he was rewarded.

"I think so," Reb said, turning toward the examining table. "From over there."

Marc dropped to his haunches and peered under the table. Then he reached in and apparently tore something away.

"Here's our culprit," he said, and held out a voice-activated tape recorder sporting ragged pieces of duct tape.

NINETEEN

These days Scully's Mortuary Parlor belonged to a tall, thin Italian whose black sideburns and moustache — some said he never took off his bowler hat — were the source of speculation around town. Did he, or did he not apply black boot polish to them? They were very black, and very shiny, and Luigi, as he insisted upon being called, had bone white skin resembling the surface of uncooked pastry twists.

Unlike the case in Harold Scully's time, the mortuary parlor no longer had sufficient black umbrellas for other than the deceased's immediate family. As on the four preceding afternoons, rain streamed to earth without pause, and the large, uninvited gathering huddled beneath motley clusters of parasols and umbrellas.

When Cyrus, quite casually, let it be known that this was not to be a funeral, since a funeral had already taken place for the deceased, and that it would be a private affair, the populace had become incensed. The result of his announcement had been the arrival of "mourners" from miles around who swelled the crowd to such proportions that it overflowed the graveyard at St. Cécil's, even though many people were to be seen encamped on tombs, eating their picnics and singing mournful songs between mouthfuls.

Dressed in their best mustard-colored suits, orange shirts, and purple ties — mourning clothes being too expensive to hire — the Swamp Doggies stood on the front steps to the church and played with vigor "for Bonnie, God rest her tortured soul."

Numb and disconnected, Marc stood with Reb, Spike, and a somber collection of official types present to make sure all was accomplished with as much pomp and suspicion as possible. An awning had been erected over the simple tomb donated by the members of St. Cécil's and a barricade erected to keep onlookers well back.

Since the interrupted night at Reb's house, Marc had barely seen her. The tape recorder had been handed over to Spike, who had yet to make any comment on its discovery. Cyrus, with Luigi a respectful foot or so distant, waited near the foot of the tomb, and he wasn't trying to hide his unhappiness at the proceedings. For the first time, Marc looked at the priest in his collar and long black cassock and saw him as other than merely a man.

This was an unbearable occasion, and he was more glad than he should have been to have Reb's hand tucked beneath his arm. The slab was in the process of being removed by men whose muscles shone and steamed in the humid atmosphere.

A thump on his shoulder startled him. Spike stood behind him and said, "You doin' okay? Tell me you want this graveyard cleared and I'll call in the volunteers and get it done. They're all here, so they'll be easy to reach."

"I don't know how I'm doing," Marc told him.

"You're a tolerant man. This has got to be a hellish experience."

"Awful," Reb said and squeezed Marc's arm. He appreciated their restraint in not trying to insist the body they were about to disturb wasn't Amy's.

"Leave all of them," Marc said, indicating the gathering. "They don't mean any disrespect. Anyway, why mess with tradition. Maybe Amy would like it. She surely didn't get much attention while she was living."

"However you want it is the way it's goin' to be," Spike said. Marc decided that to give the man his due, he seemed sincere.

Those shiny muscles bulged in straining backs, and the slab atop the tomb moved an inch or so.

Moans started out nearby and swelled as they passed backward through the crowd. A rhythmic swaying began. Some of the older folks bore parasols with long fringes, and they waved them back and forth. Vincent Fox and the Swamp Doggies burst forth with "Dem bones, Dem bones, Dem, Dry bones." The assembly quickly gave up its unearthly wail to join their voices with awesome enthusiasm.

Marc shook his head slightly and marveled at so much natural inappropriateness in one place. Maybe he'd laugh about this one day.

The slab moved again.

And dem bones kept right on drying out.

Marc turned his face down to Reb's, and she put her arms around him in a gesture that let the world know she set her own rules. She hugged his waist and rested a cheek against his dark suit jacket.

The officials put their black hats together to confer, then returned their wary eyes to the slow task of opening the tomb.

Marc held Reb tight. "You've been hard to reach," he said.

"Lots of sickness," she told him. "You haven't been far from my mind."

"I'm not going to fall apart here, am I?" He detested public displays. "If I show any sign of making a fool of myself, kick my ankle."

"Sure," she said, still holding him. "Then I'll see what I can do to make you too mad to be upset."

"You do that," he said and kissed the top of her head. To hell with what people thought.

Grumbling set up from the direction of the gate to Bonanza Alley. Marc narrowed his eyes but could only make out a parting and immediate closing of ranks.

"Now what?" Spike said.

Cyrus joined them and stared toward the commotion. "Marc," he said. "You could still call this off."

"I know, but I won't. How am I supposed to make peace with my life until I can put my sister to rest properly?"

Cyrus didn't respond.

A small procession arrived at the barricaded area. Oribel and Wally, who pushed his bike with Nolan's soggy brown bag in a basket behind the seat, led the way. Jilly and Joe were there, and the Hibbses, and, bringing up the rear, a small woman all but hidden inside layers of jet-beaded, satin-bound black chiffon.

"Shit," Marc said. "Our night bird? What d'you think, Cyrus?"

"I think this had better not get any more out of hand than it already is."

The woman in black capered about on the other side of the fence, leaping in some sort of formless dance that needed a whole lot of elbow, knee, and bare-foot action.

Swathed in a black nylon poncho and wearing black Wellington boots, with what looked like a hollowed-out crow perched on her head, Oribel forced aside the man who tried to stop her from entering the enclosure. She waved Wally inside — with his bike — and cast disapproving looks at the Gables and the Hibbses when they followed.

She marched Wally to Cyrus. "Tell Father right now," she ordered the boy. "If you forget anything, I'll help you." There were small bets, and some not so small bets, around town that Cyrus was still looking for a way to confront Oribel and get rid of the Fuglies, as the rusted sculpture outside the rectory was widely called.

Madge, who had been keeping an eye on William in case he threw one of his enraged fits about strangers "messin' " with his graveyard, hurried to stand with Cyrus. "Oribel, dear," she said quietly. "As you know, this is a very somber day —"

"I don't need you to tell me what kind of day it is, Madge Pollard. I been in this town since you were in diapers. This is a somber day, and it's goin' to get more somber with things they way they are."

Cyrus put a hand on Wally's neck and smiled at him. "Is there something that can't wait?"

"Well . . ." Wally checked Oribel's expression and continued, "I kept tryin' t'tell you what I was afraid of. I couldn't go home much on account of bein' scared what Mama and Daddy would say. They think I'm irresponsible and lazy, see."

"We don't think it," Doll said, "we know it. And we don't appreciate strangers interferin' in our business. Particular in front of all Toussaint and whoever all the rest of these folks are. Embarrassin', I'd call it."

"Speak up," Oribel said, her mouth a straight line. "The bike?"

"It went missin'," Wally said with tears in his voice. "I leave it in the shed William doesn't use much. He said I could."

"I know that," Cyrus said, leaning to see what progress was being made on the tomb. "It's a good place to keep it safe."

"It's been gone," Wally said, sniffing. "For weeks."

"And for weeks this boy has been trying to keep it from Doll and Gator because they're such unreasonable cusses."

"Oh, Oribel," Jilly Gable said, her hazel eyes glittering. "Let's not argue at such a time. We could just rejoice that Wally has his bike back and let it go."

"Good idea," Spike chimed in. "We won't go far wrong if we listen to Jilly."

Temporarily distracted, Marc looked from Jilly, with her striking coloring, to Spike Devol. The deputy sheriff stared at Jilly's café au lait complexion and light hair, at her startling hazel eyes, and the interest Marc saw there was anything but casual.

"Has that bike been gone, son?" Gator said. The man rarely spoke at all.

"Yes, Daddy."

"And you didn't want to be around us in case we found out you'd been irresponsible and whupped you for it?"

"Yes, Daddy."

"Don't you shame us in front of everyone," Doll hissed. "You know we don't whup you."

"Only sometimes," Joe Gable said helpfully. He showed no sign of thinking any of this was funny. "You're right, though, Doll. This isn't the time or place. The dead deserve the respect of the living."

"You're a wise one," Oribel told him. "I'm only goin' to say this much, then I'll lead us in a song. Wally's bike went missing — for weeks. I know, because he confided in me when it happened. I didn't know he was runnin' around like a gypsy or I'd have made him go home, but he's a good boy who doesn't get his due.

"He come to me again today, just 'cause he needed an honest listener. I took him out and we did one more search around, and this here bike was back where Wally left it, and shinin' clean like new. Not a speck of dust on it or a lick of mud even in the tires. I'm thinking someone *borrowed* it, then found religion and brought it back. That person's got to be rooted out. We gotta make this town a safe place for God-fearin' people again."

A collective sigh went up.

The tomb was open.

He could still change his mind, Marc thought. He'd believed he was strong enough to deal with whatever had to be done to prove it was Amy and not Bonnie Blue lying inside that cold stone. Now he wasn't so sure.

Reb laced the fingers of one hand through his. "You can do this," she said as if she read his mind. "We'll do it together. I was told they'll remove the casket and take it to Lafayette to be opened."

"It's indecent," he said. "I hate the idea of strangers staring at her when she's helpless."

"We'll be with her. And Cyrus, and anyone else you want to ask. She won't be without friends."

If he could speak again, he'd thank her. The burning constriction in his throat and chest made that impossible.

To his horror, another chorus of "Dem Bones" started. Cyrus went to Vince Fox and spoke in his ear. The band shuffled close for a powwow, and "Just a Closer Walk With Thee" was quickly picked up. Hands rose and waved.

The night-bird lady had ceased to hold Marc's attention until now. She joined in the hymn, and he found himself wondering exactly what her angle was.

Without warning, those working over the tomb stood back, their heads bowed. Spike, Cyrus, and the men from Lafayette walked to look inside the stone resting place. Marc heard the word *open* and felt sick.

A small sound from Reb reminded him that he was holding her fingers between his — and crunching them to pulp. "Sorry," he murmured, and carried her hand to his lips. He kissed her elegant fingers and held her palm against his cheek. "Okay. I can do this. You don't have to come."

"Oh yes I do."

They walked together to stand on the low wooden frame erected around the foot of the pinkish tomb. Reb pushed a hand beneath his arm and around his waist, and he held her shoulder while they slowly bent over.

"Dear God," Cyrus said. "Help us all."

Oribel stepped up beside Cyrus, with Madge at his other side.

"No," Oribel shrieked. "No, no, no." And with that she fell backward onto the wet grass and appeared to pass out.

Madge cried quietly while, one by one, those inside the barricade ignored the rules set down, stepped over or around Oribel, and moved forward to see the horrifying sight.

"The casket done gone," William said. "This the work of the devil, this."

Marc stumbled from the step and turned blindly away. He became vaguely aware that he was embraced by Spike Devol.

Wild, unrestrained laughter rang out. "L'Oiseau de Nuit tell the truth. This the devil's work am here. She been taken away. Ain't nobody here."

TWENTY

Precious Depew scurried along, keeping close to the shops on one side of what passed for Toussaint's town square. A triangle of grass with a wide, old oak bowing over statues of small angels and small animals was the central feature in a short but wide rectangle of shops and business. The statues, some very old, kept guard over a burial place for beloved animals. People said the plastic flamingos, ducks and gnomes were in poor taste, to say nothing of Santa, his sleigh and his reindeer — all illuminated — perched in the oak and ready for Christmas.

The very sight of Santa visiting those little animals brought a tear to Precious's eye, and when the sun shone on them, she thought that the pinks, blues, and greens, the touches of yellow and orange in the plastic decorations blended in nicely with the color-washed buildings that faced them.

The rain was a real pain. It made her hair frizz, even though she held Chauncey's red-and-yellow golf umbrella. Chauncey didn't play golf, but he reckoned keeping his expensive gear in the back of his Lexus SUV lent just the right tone.

She passed All Tarted Up and Boudreaux's Sundries and Connie and Lorna's Eye For Books before she felt the presence she'd known would arrive before she got too much farther on her route.

At the corner stood Doll and Gator's Majestic Hotel with its lime green facade and eastern-looking dome on a round tower on one side. The dome was painted lilac and crisscrossed with a gold diamond pattern. In pots flanking the open double front doors, Doll's sunflower whirligigs moved sluggishly, slowed down by the rain despite a determined wind. Precious slowed down, too, and stopped, removing the clackity-clack of her high heels from what noises there were on a Sunday morning.

The scuffing footsteps behind her were slower to halt. She turned around and stared baldly at a man with a newspaper held before his face. A wet newspaper that slowly bent in half to reveal Dante Cornelius, his black hair plastered to his forehead. Water dripped from his chin, and his black suit and shirt, together with his black tie, hung in folds around his thin body.

She waved at him and smiled — and turned away without waiting to see his reaction. Damn that Chauncey to hell. A woman couldn't step out of a Sunday without her husband sending a spy after her. Of course, after Friday's *exhumation,* he was more anxious than ever to find her secret home away from home. He had a bed to fill, although how he thought he'd carry that off now, Precious had no idea. Even her own plans needed some rearrangement. Wouldn't do to have extra bodies floating around.

Her temper snapped. She went back and caught Dante by the hand. "Come with me. We need to get you dry before you catch your death in this weather."

His fingers closed, almost trustingly, around hers, and he allowed her to pull him along. The sodden paper trailed from his other hand to drag on the sidewalk.

Precious took a sly peek at his face. He was good-looking in a narrow, wiry way. If she didn't know his reputation for professional blunders, the bulge inside his jacket might not make her jumpy. After all, Chauncey needed her alive. But it was the knowledge of Dante's blunders that set her nerves on edge.

"Didn't see you at the funeral on Friday," she said conversationally, homing in on her car parked out back of the sheriff's offices.

"Where you going, Miz Chauncey?" Dante said at last. He tried to drag her to a stop. "You fuckin' mad or somethin? You tryin to get me killed by your husband, or what passes for the law in these parts? Chauncey warned me not to let anyone see me followin' you."

"You aren't following me, sugar. I'm holding your hand and takin' you with me." And she didn't give a cottonmouth's ass about the length of Dante's life.

"Shee-it," Dante said with feeling.

Precious smiled and hurried him to her Jag sports model. Silver, with dark tinted windows and a license plate that marked her as the owner, the car was her pride and joy.

"Get in," she told Dante, pressing her key pad. When he stood there staring at her, she looked toward Spike's window and said, "Better wave to the law, Dante."

Instantly he lowered himself into the passenger seat, put on dark glasses, and pressed himself as low as he could. Precious joined him, gunned the engine, and screeched out of the parking lot, spewing grit from beneath the tires as she went.

She drove south and out of town. The trees and occasional rows of shotgun houses blurred together as she passed them with Dante squirming beside her. Precious was a natural behind the wheel. Fearlessness helped. She found a crossing over the Teche and headed for Spanish Lake.

"I don't get this." Dante dug his fingers into his knees and peered through the steamy windshield at the narrow track lined by drenched willows with branches that occasionally brushed the top of the car.

Precious knew the spot she was looking for and took so sharp a left that her passenger, who evidently thought seat belts were for wusses, fell sideways against her.

She took another left down a lane you'd never find if you didn't know it was there, and spun to a stop against a fallen cypress log that already sprouted green shoots.

"What you doin' this for?" Dante asked. He ducked his head to see through the windows on all sides. "Where are we? Chauncey finds out about this, I'm a dead man."

"You worry too much. He's not going to find out. Take off your clothes."

Dante slammed himself against his door and hunched his shoulders. The look in his eyes was that of a hunted animal.

Precious pulled up her skirt and put the car keys inside her panties.

"Shee-it." Dante had a stunted vocabulary.

"Chauncey trusts you a lot, doesn't he?" she asked. "He tells me so."

"Yeah. He trusts me because he can. I owe him, and he deserves my loyalty. Quit messin' around and drive back to town."

She managed, with almost no effort, to burst into tears.

"Hey." Now Dante was alarmed. "Quit that, will ya?"

"I . . . can't," she sobbed out. "I love Chauncey, but he's an important, busy man and he doesn't have any energy left over for me. He . . . hasn't made . . . love to me in weeks. Dante, I'm so lonely."

He shifted in his seat.

Precious worked off her short, belted coat and tossed it in the back of the car. She wore a thin, purple mohair top that crisscrossed her breasts and tied at her side. Above her matching skirt, her midriff was bare. She fluffed up her hair and checked her makeup in the driver's mirror.

"I want you to be honest with me. Am I ugly?"

He made a noise that had no distinct meaning.

"Am I, Dante? Look at me and tell me." She leaned toward him over the stick shift and braced her weight between the seats.

Dante kept his eyes lowered. "You're a beautiful woman, Miz Chauncey. If he ain't givin' you much attention it's because of what you said. He's pretty strung out now."

"I'm hot-blooded," she told him. "And when I don't get any satisfaction, I'm not reliable. I can't help myself. Pretty soon the opportunity for a little fun, and relief, presents itself, and I lose my head. You wouldn't want me to do that to Chauncey?"

"I would not. But there ain't much I can do about it."

She rocked forward on her arms until she could nudge Dante's face up and close in for a full, wet, tongue-thrusting kiss. He resisted, for about ten seconds.

Panting, Precious let her head fall back. "I knew you were a passionate man. Think of it this way. You're doing it for the man you most admire, to make sure his wife doesn't spread herself around in dangerous places." With her mouth still moist and open, she looked at his crotch and said, "I like a man who stands ready to sacrifice himself for the good of another."

Dante came for her with fire in those dark eyes. He dug her breasts free of the purple mohair and held them like oversized doorknobs which he turned and pulled.

Finesse wasn't the man's forte. But despite the discomfort, she was turned on. How Chauncey would hate knowing about this. She hadn't planned to do more than ring Dante's chimes, but why take your hand out of the cookie jar minus a cookie?

She pulled the top undone and opened it wide, then transferred her weight behind her. Precious had felt eaten alive before, but so far this guy had the biggest appetite she'd encountered. She was going to be bruised, but what the hell.

He took one of her hands to his zipper and molded her around him. "Okay, big boy," she said, and opened up his pants. "I guess you're loaded and ready to go."

No clever words of seduction came her way.

"I gotta have it now," he said, ripping his belt undone and pushing his pants and shorts down to his ankles. He didn't seem to notice that his pole was framed by the two sides of his soggy jacket and shirt.

Precious said, "Oh, Dante," and actually felt something close to passion. He had plenty to play with, and she buzzed in all the right places.

Kneeling on his seat, he yanked her by the

waistband of her skirt, fumbled beneath to rub his fingers hard between her legs. He yelped. "Ouch. Damn it." He pulled out her car keys and threw them on the floor.

Dante was like a kid in a candy store. He didn't know what to fill his mouth with first. He tried to stand her up until he realized it was impossible. Finally he tore off her panties and pulled her legs across the drive shaft, only to discover the gear shift was right where he wanted to be.

Precious yelled, "Careful," and he managed to hike the second thigh free.

At last, with her head under the steering column, and one knee hooked over the back of the seat, Dante took her with the delicacy of a jackhammer. From her angle, she could see his skinny ass pumping up and down and managed to swallow her laughter on account of really admiring the only part of him that wasn't undernourished.

One second, two, three, four, "You're taking me all the way to heaven, baby," she squealed, and that's what happened, she flew on that boy's efforts. "You may never know how much I needed that," she said, panting. "Good stuff shouldn't be over so quickly. We'll just have to do it again real soon."

Dante's response was to shiver and return to his door-handle action. She caught him by the sleeves and hauled herself up to a sitting position again. Playfully slapping his hands away, she pulled her sweater around her and squeezed her legs together. "Look at the time. Where did it go? Oh, Dante, we gotta get back before Chauncey suspects something."

He turned chalky white and nodded.

"Be a good boy and get out of the car while I get myself together here. I can't do it with you so near. I'll forget what I'm supposed to be doin'."

Her coy smile brought a man-of-the-world curl of the lip from him. He winked and got out of the car.

Precious gave him sixty seconds to feel like a stud. Then she drove away, and she didn't need to hear him to know he was cursing as he leaped from the Jag's path.

TWENTY-ONE

The wine Cyrus had apologized for tasted good to Reb. Not that she had either a "nose" or a "palate" in that direction.

"How long do you suppose Cyrus will be gone?" Marc stood in the middle of the black and bronze carpet in Cyrus's second-floor sitting room.

"Hard to be sure." She didn't like Marc's hollow-eyed, distant look, although she couldn't expect the events of only two days earlier to have left him unscathed. "He wouldn't have left if he hadn't thought it was important. Ozaire Dupre's mad enough to be threatening."

"What could he do?"

"Spread lies if he doesn't get what he wants. He says bird woman's the sign he's been expecting. Evil — like Oribel's sculpture."

"That capering thing's growing on me." Marc swayed as if to some music she couldn't hear. "Hey, we found out we dance well together, huh?"

Reb rolled her eyes and pulled her feet beneath her on Cyrus's beloved dark green leather couch. "Ozaire is into barter." She wouldn't reveal how he'd fleeced her on the bike transaction. "He gives this or that. And what he wants is always worth more than he's prepared to give up."

Marc finished his wine, looking down at her while he drank. "So he'll keep the devil worship stuff to himself in exchange for what?"

"I don't know all the specifics. Something to do with higher wages for Lil, and Ozaire getting to sell fish outside the church after Mass every Sunday."

She didn't blame Marc for laughing. "Cyrus told me last night that Ozaire was making things up so folks will start asking questions about what's going on in this house."

"Nothing is," Marc said, then smiled cynically. "Apart from me. But, of course, that's what's got a feather up the guy's . . . I'm the reason Dupre and the rest of them are all riled up. Is Oiseau still actually in town?"

"Oh, yes. One more person who's looking for a fast buck. She's got a room from — are you ready? — Chauncy Depew. It's no more than a cubicle in one of his warehouses. She's going to do night watchman duties in return for living rent-free.

"In the few days she's been here she's worked up quite a trade for readings. I saw May Lynn Charpentier sneaking away. She took one look at me and ran."

"Geez," Marc said. "And they think I'm trouble, that I've brought trouble to their quiet town. I guess they're right, only not in the way they seem fixed on, and not like some of the crazies who fit into Toussaint like oiled screws."

"Your mother owns a lot of this town," Reb pointed out. "By default, that means *you* own it. These people still haven't got a reason to be reassured you mean them and their businesses no harm. They barely get by. A rent hike would take some of them out altogether."

"Damn it all." He thrust out his jaw. "If they want to keep things smooth with me, they could try treating me with some respect. I don't mean they have to grovel, just behave like regular people. I swear it's as if they're baiting me into making their lives difficult."

She avoided the temptation to go to him. "Are they managing to do that?"

Marc gave her his narrow-eyed stare. "What do you think?"

"I think I should give you a physical. You don't look so good."

"Really?" His new grin was purely lascivious. "Now that sounds worth being sick for. He indicated Cyrus's afghan-draped sofa. "I'll stretch out there. I don't need to put on a gown, do I? I'm not shy if you aren't."

"I bet Cyrus would like walking in on that scene," she told him.

Marc gave a brief shake of the head. "I doubt we could do anything to shock him. I've about had it, Reb. At night I'm jumping out of my skin. I sweat, then get real cold and have to take a hot shower. That's when I'm not taking a cold shower."

He looked at her pointedly, and she averted her eyes.

"Do you like this room?" she asked and felt ridiculous.

"As a matter of fact, I do. It's lived in, but it's comfortable. Cyrus has a good sound system, funny to have no TV, though. Did you notice all the kids' books on the bottom shelves?"

"Oh yes. He does family counseling up here and believes in putting everyone at ease. He also loves children."

"What a waste."

"Hm?"

He wandered to look down on a basket of baby toys. "He'll never have kids of his own, that's what I meant. Too bad."

"He has hundreds of children of his own — children of all ages." In truth, Reb agreed with Marc, but she was honor bound not to say so.

"I guess."

It was dark outside, and branches hit the windows. She got up and drew the brown velvet drapes. "Some of these chilly days and nights must be breaking records for July."

"Maybe it's not so cold. It could just feel that way because of what's happening."

She strolled back, pausing every few steps to sip the red wine. "Either way, everything seems strange."

"Does having me in Toussaint seem strange?"

"You're fishing." And she couldn't bear looking at him after a question like that. She cleared her throat. "I'm glad you're here." She was also panicking, just a little, at the prospect of his leaving again.

Abruptly, Marc put down his glass and left the room.

Reb stared after him, her stomach doing flips and goose bumps shooting over her skin. Whatever he'd wanted her to say, she'd apparently chosen the wrong thing.

Minutes passed and he didn't return.

The corridor outside the room ran the width of the house with bedrooms to the right and to the left of the staircase. This room was a converted bedroom.

Reb poked her head into the corridor. Marc was nowhere to be seen, and she couldn't hear him. She went to the top of the stairs and looked down. Again, no sight or sound of Marc.

He wouldn't just walk out without a word.

A door opened at the far end of the corridor, and he looked out, looked at her. He waved, and beckoned to her. He held a finger to his lips.

Frowning, Reb tiptoed quickly toward him. "What are you *doing?*" she whispered. "What will Cyrus think if he gets back and finds us poking around his house?"

"His car's still gone," Marc told her when she arrived on the threshold of a small bedroom. "I'm keeping an eye open at the window. This was Amy's room."

She thought *Bonnie's room,* entered and looked around. "How do you know?"

"There's nothing here but sympathy cards. They aren't written to anyone specific, but they're all sorry Bonnie died. Makes sense Oribel might put them in here."

Reb nodded. "She puts on a good act, but she's sentimental."

"I thought we might check around . . . just a bit." Marc sounded unsure of himself, as if he wanted her approval. "There's nothing happening, Reb. Not a word about finding, or having a lead on the . . . on Amy's body. And Spike's still refusing to discuss the tape recorder."

"Be patient," she told him, knowing it wasn't what he wanted to hear. "It's only been two days."

The single bed was made up with a clean blue chenille bedspread on top. Nothing personal was to be seen anywhere.

Marc opened the closet. "Empty." He moved on to drawers and even looked under the bed and passed his hands under the mattress. "I guess there wouldn't be anything." He sat back on his heels and looked at Reb.

She snatched up a card and pretended to read. Her decision to pretend they'd never almost made love wasn't working. She couldn't get it out of her mind, and each time she saw Marc she was back in her study — with him.

"How are you doing, Reb?"

"Fine," she said and heard her own sharpness. "You?"

"Sometimes I think I can't keep on going — not without feeling you in my arms again."

"That's not fair." She blinked rapidly before looking at him. Her eyes stung, and her throat let her know what denying him was costing her.

"I don't mean to be unfair," he said, his voice very low. "But I'm only telling you what's true. I want you."

"Stop it."

"I want you. All of you. I want you with me all the time, waking and sleeping. I don't want to try to sleep again without knowing you'll be there when I wake up."

"Marc." The battle to hold back tears was about to be lost. "You have feelings. I have feelings. Neither of us has a right to expect to get our own way all the time."

"How about some of the time. Like now."

She blushed until her body glowed.

"Okay, okay, later, then."

"We'd better get back before Cyrus does." And before she did something outrageously stupid.

"I told you he's not here yet. I'll hear him when he comes." He stood up slowly and let his hands hang at his sides. "Will you help me get them to let me see Amy's effects?"

Each time he opened his mouth he threw her another curve. "Why?" She didn't tell him those few things belonged to Bonnie Blue.

"Because I might find something useful, something that means nothing to anyone but me."

Reb thought about it. The few feet between them were too much, but if she didn't want a disaster on her hands, she'd better widen it. "I don't know. I'll have to think about it. You don't have a right to see them. That means strings would have to be pulled."

"I don't care if it's only been a couple of days, something must have happened. I don't get why they aren't telling me anything."

This was so hard. "You can't prove there's a reason for you to be informed," she told him.

The instant she opened the door he was at her side, ushering her into the corridor. They walked side by side until Marc put a hand at her waist and excused himself to use a bathroom that stood open.

When the door closed, Reb couldn't seem to move on. The house pressed in around her. She was lonely and a little scared, and the only one who stirred passion — a feeling that she was truly alive — was close to her but might as well be miles away. If he wanted her help, she'd give it. Spike could get at Bonnie's possessions.

The bathroom door opened again. A candle had been lighted on the tile counter, and gold shadows leaped over pale walls.

Marc leaned on the doorjamb. "I didn't think I heard you walk on," he said.

"I didn't," she said, redundantly. "I mean, I

didn't want to somehow. I guess I thought I'd wait for you."

"Are you starting to feel you like having me around?"

She took a breath and held it before saying, "What makes you ask that?"

"I thought you might feel the way I do. I like having you around."

"We're in a pickle," she told him. "Damned if we do and damned if we don't."

Marc laughed shortly. "That's one way to put it." He shot an arm around her waist, swung her into the bathroom, and locked the door.

She tried to reach the door handle at once, but he made it impossible. "Let me go, Marc. We're in the rectory. Cyrus isn't a fool. He knew what we'd been doing when he came to my place last week. Under the circumstances there was nothing he could say about it, but if we're indiscreet in his house, he can have a lot to say."

"He won't," Marc told her softly, staring at her mouth. "Cyrus's a priest. He's also a man, and I think he likes to see other people happy."

"We don't belong together."

"Who says so?"

"Good sense does. We have nothing in common. We don't want any of the same things. And I've only just begun explaining."

He caught her hair in handfuls, one on either side of her head, and turned her face up to his. She had never been so thoroughly kissed. She had also never heard singing sounds at such a moment, or felt as if she were underwater, floating around and around, guided by a relentless force from which she wanted no escape.

"We've got unfinished business," he said. "I've walked around with the evidence of that for days."

"You can't have." Reb deliberately kept her eyes on his.

He unbuttoned her shirt. "Want to bet? No bra? Oh, yeah." He dispensed with the shirt by feel and tugged her against him. "I love the feel of you."

Her breasts received his entire attention. His eyes closed and his breathing grew heavy. He held on to her with his teeth and lips while he shed his own sweater, then layered her against him.

Reb saw colors and pressed her eyes shut. She touched him intimately and he cried out as if in pain. When she touched him again, he held her hand there, and she didn't need explanations for his discomfort.

Her body grew moist and she ached, an ache that only one act, with one man, would relieve.

Marc walked her against the counter and thudded his hips into her pelvis. She met him, and held him with both hands between his braced legs. "I want you," she murmured.

"Yes, yes."

The room felt like a sauna. Beads of sweat popped on her forehead. They fumbled with each other's clothes, their fingers clumsy in such haste.

She didn't look at him when he reached into his back pocket and took out his wallet. But she didn't waste the opportunity to push his pants down while his hands were behind his back.

They panted, so loudly, she thought, that surely they'd be heard all over the house. Reb didn't care. Every inch of her skin felt raw and ready.

Marc ripped her pantyhose and mouthed *Sorry.*

She kissed him and let him get rid of her skirt and panties.

Her belly met him and he was so hard she was consumed by her own need. "Now," she told him, standing on her toes to make his access easier.

Marc ignored her efforts and lifted her. He wrapped her legs around his waist, and she felt wild. He all but threw her free, caught her, and drove himself into her again, and again.

The force of their joining caused him to step backward — and to stumble over the pants that were still around his ankles.

"Ah, hell, sweetheart," he said through his teeth, flinging wide an arm that didn't stop him from thudding to sit on the edge of the bath-tub.

"Shhh," Reb crooned to him. She planted her feet inside the tub. "See, we hardly missed a beat."

At that he laughed. "Great choice of words. I may never be the same when you're finished with me."

She made all the action and kissed him to silence every time he protested. "My turn," she said. "My way."

Tomorrow she might be sore. Today she didn't give a damn.

Tension swelled between her legs and inside her belly. Her breasts felt as if they pulsed. She held the edge of the tub to get more purchase and overbalanced backward. Marc caught her around the shoulders, but couldn't keep his rear on its narrow perch. Amid a chorus of "ouch" and "oh, no" and "hold on to me," they landed in the bottom of the tub — miraculously still joined together.

"Wound-check later," Marc said, breathing harshly and using his heels to keep his hips coming at Reb.

They clung together, and cried out at the point of no return. Holding Reb's face in the crook of his neck and speaking streams of incoherent satisfaction and affection, Marc fell to his back.

He squirmed, and straightened her on top of him, and continued to kiss any part of her he could reach. Reb tried to hold his face still, but he was too strong.

"I've dreamed of this," he told her.

"You're mad."

His chest shook with silent laughter. "Then

you're mad too, unless you can say you didn't like it."

These were the feelings she'd only heard about. "I do like it."

"I'm so glad to hear you say that, cher, but we'd better get out of this tub and make ourselves respectable. Cyrus will be back, and we need to talk to him — before I carry you away again. We've got to be where we can give our entire attention to doin' all the things we need to do."

"Mm." Reb wanted to sleep on his chest, but she shifted, and Marc reached behind him to find a handhold and push them up.

He didn't let go of the faucet in time. He did make real solid contact with the shower controls.

TWENTY-TWO

At the exit for Lydia and Patoutville, Precious left Highway 90 and headed directly south. She had made the switch from the Jaguar to a Honda Civic she paid to keep in a barn on some old man's property deep in a swampy cypress grove. They'd had the arrangement for over a year, and she hadn't set eyes on him since they'd struck their deal. Each time she came, she left an envelope containing new twenties on an up-turned crate outside the door to his cabin. When she returned, the money was gone. A good arrangement.

Her own place was built on stilts, a single story with a gallery on all sides. Close to Cypremort, so she had some view out to the Gulf, but on this muggy gray day — in the aftermath of so much rain — she would see little through a frame of trees filled with sullen mist.

The same shed that protected her rowboat had room for the Honda. She made the switch and set off on the short crossing to the tin-roofed cabin. Not twenty-five yards from the boat, the surface of the sludgy water parted and a gator's weed-draped jaws smoothly knifed ahead of its humped and glassy eyes. The place smelled like a hundred years of mildew cut with sweetgum pitch.

Nothing changed around here. Precious liked it that way.

She tied up at a piling and climbed a vertical ladder twice, carrying one oar to the short boardwalk each time. Once they were stashed and locked away with a combination padlock, Precious let herself into the cabin. There were supplies in the boat, but she'd get them once she'd checked things out here.

The place smelled bad. She'd have to open up the windows and get some fresh air inside.

Scraping and rattling sounds from the bathroom grated on her nerves. Her plans had gotten more difficult to pull off, but she was still determined to make them work.

Before the exhumation, everything had seemed smooth. But *bam,* from left field Chauncey the fuck-up had jumped the gun and gone into action without even warning her. No way was he supposed to empty that tomb without letting her know first. It had to mean he thought he was still in charge and had come up with a new plan. The fact that he hadn't let a word of it slip made her jumpy.

She wanted explanations, and she'd intended to get the information she needed out of Dante, but things had gotten out of hand. She smiled at the thought. He'd never have the guts to tell

Chauncey what they'd done together, and she'd bought enough time to lose Dante — and gain a beautiful little gift she intended to use if and when the time was right. After all, a poor, helpless little woman like her couldn't force a strong man like Dante to do a thing. She had been wronged.

Precious took her gun from her purse, stashed it in the waistband of the jeans she'd changed into, and threw the purse on a bamboo chair.

Taking a deep breath and making sure her denim shirt covered the weapon, she opened the bathroom door.

Sagging shades were drawn over the windows at Chauncey Depew's "office" in the middle of the lot at his body shop.

"Don't do this, Sheriff Devol," Dante Cornelius said. He squeezed out each word. From the black hair that fell from the top of his head straight down on all sides, to his mangled black suit and shoes so caked with mud who knew what color they used to be, he was one miserable-looking bastard. "Please," he said, clasping his hands in front of him.

"Calm down," Spike told him. "You were lost. Now you're found, and I'm takin' you home to your best buddy."

"I wanna go to a hotel."

"Which hotel would that be?"

The man's eyes darted around. "The, er, Lay By. It's out by —"

"I know where it is. You got a reservation for tonight?"

"No . . . Yes, I got a standing reservation."

"Wow," Spike said. "You live a rich life. Must be hard slumming it with Chauncey. Unfortunately I have it on record that you live with Depew. Got it from the man himself, and the last time I talked to you, you were glad to agree."

Spike drove around the hut and parked facing out of the lot. He'd had no reason to handcuff Dante, useful as that would have been. In such situations, a man had to improvise, and he couldn't be sure Dante wouldn't run if he got a chance. He grabbed his guest's left hand, unlocked the doors on his cruiser, and dragged Dante across the two front seats and out of the vehicle.

"What d'you do that for?" Dante said, all righteous and outraged. "You was afraid to let me out of my own door, right? You thought I wouldn't stick around. I got rights. Police brutality, that's what that was."

"Do you have witnesses, Mr. Cornelius?"

"Let me leave and I won't tell a soul about any of this."

Rather than grin, Spike pressed his lips together and hauled Dante to Chauncey's door. He still held the man's hand.

Spike knocked.

"Lemme go," Dante hissed. He sounded desperate.

"I like holding your hand," Spike said.

"Hey, I ain't no faggot."

"No," Spike said without inflection. "Gays usually get born with brains in their heads."

Dante struggled. "Hold anything you like, just make sure Chauncey don't think I'm no wuss. That type of thing's bad for the image."

"You've got it." A handful of the back of Dante's pants raised him to his toes, and he squealed. Spike knocked again, harder this time. "Come on, come on."

"I remember now," Dante said. "He ain't here. He —"

From inside the hut, Chauncey asked, "Who the fuck's there?"

"Good friends," Spike said, and to Dante, "What part of New York are you from?"

Dante glared at him and didn't answer.

"Same place as Chauncey?"

"He ain't from New York, sucker. He's from Toussaint, and you know it."

"Funny, you both talk the same, and I could have sworn it was Brooklyn, or the Bronx, maybe. Tough-guy talk. Come on, where are you from?"

"Fort Wayne, Indiana."

Spike was nodding wisely when the door opened and Chauncey stood framed by the yellow light he'd had to switch on early because he had a need to shut out daylight.

"You're goin' to have to watch Dante," Spike said, helping his companion inside by the seat of his pants. Dante tripped along on his toes, adding a little jump from time to time. "He reckons he's from Fort Wayne, and I know that's not what you told me."

"Fuck," Chauncey said. "The perfect end to a perfect day. Where the fuck you been, Dante?"

"Here and there," Dante said, smiling. A disconcerting sight. With his eyes he gave what Spike presumed was a warning signal, and jerked his head in Spike's direction. "Got stranded hell and gone by a flat tire."

"You ain't got no tires," Chauncey said. "That's on account of you don't see so well. I make sure you get where you need to go."

Spike stuck out a forefinger and wiggled it. "Thank you, Chauncey. You solved my puzzle. You should have fessed up, Dante, and told me about your eyes. That explains why you were wanderin' in the woods. I surely am grateful we got the 911 call from the nice lady who thought she had a thug trespassing on her property."

The whole time he spoke, Spike watched Depew. He looked ill and as if he'd like to leap on Dante. He drummed the fingertips of his right hand on an expensive desk that looked ridiculous in the hut. "Thank you, Officer Devol," he said with the kind of smile that would make mothers cover their babies' eyes. "Might as well be honest. Dante wanders. Seems to be getting worse, but I'll take care of him."

Dante moaned.

"Good thing, too," Spike remarked with a straight face. "Must have gone thirty miles or more today. If he keeps that up he's going to show up missing one of these days — and with man-eating blisters on his feet."

Dante moaned again and Spike let go of his pants.

"Thanks for bringing him back," Chauncey said, edging toward the door. "I'll make a donation to the widows and offenders fund."

"That would be 'orphans'," Spike said. The way this man had kept himself out of prison was a testimony to the power of dumb luck. "Before we carry on with the small stuff, I got another point to clear up. Is it true Oiseau is living in one of your warehouses?"

"What's it to you?" Chauncey hauled on the waistband of his pants. "I believe in helpin' out the little people."

"It's nothing to me," Spike said. "Just like to be sure where to find folks if I need 'em. Would you mind if I asked a few other questions? There's been quite a lot going on around town lately, and since you're a man in the know, you might have something useful to share — without knowing it, of course."

"Thirty miles," Chauncey said, looking at Dante through narrowed eyes and as if he'd forgotten Spike was there. "How d'you get there? Take off the shoes and socks. I want to see your feet."

"*Chauncey,*" Dante said.

"Oh, yeah." Chauncey remembered Spike again.

"Can we get back to those questions?" He glanced at Chauncey's drumming fingers. "Have you been a participant in, or a witness to, any fights in the past few days?"

Dante's gape matched Chauncey's, who said, "What kind of question is that? The answer's *no*. I'm a respectable businessman. This town looks up to me. I ain't got time for that kind of irresponsible behavior."

"I didn't think you did." Spike kept on looking at the drumming fingers. "You better get your lovely wife to buy you some good garden gloves. You're ruining your nails — and I bet you don't use hand lotion before you go to bed."

Chauncey checked out the backs of his hands, then the palms. His Adam's apple rose and fell several times. "Precious takes one look at these and she's gonna be mad. I'd better get some dressings on." He did a Basset Hound imitation with his eyes. "How's a man supposed to curb his natural urges. I learned my trade from the ground up. I still like to get in with my men and do what I know best."

"I like a man who works with his hands," Spike said. "It's manly. By the way, I got a message from a woman. On the phone. I think it could have been Precious disguising her voice."

Chauncey found a metal file in a desk draw and went to work smoothing his nails.

"Hear what I said?" Spike asked.

"Women," Chauncey said. "Who understands the stuff they do?"

"I don't know, but this one could be a problem to you, so you might want to do something about what she's saying."

Dante, who stood in front of a small, distorted mirror hanging on a wall, had bent his splayed knees while he restored his hair to its usual pomaded elegance. He stopped pushing the front forward in a shelf and stared at Chauncey in the mirror.

The nail file spun through the air, hit Dante's back, and landed on the floor. Chauncey said, "Not hard enough. I'm losing my touch."

"Want to know what the lady said?" Spike said.

Chauncey shrugged. "Makes no difference to me."

"That's a good thing." Spike told him. "Easier on the nerves." He backed toward the door.

"On the other hand, I guess I'm sorta interested."

Spike made a dismissive gesture. "Had to be malicious. Couldn't have been anything to take seriously. She suggested that all the cars you get in here aren't on account of wrecks. She reckoned you do what she called *elective plastic surgery,* whatever that means. Some thing to do with new paint jobs and changing plates. But you wouldn't do things like that. Dealing in stolen cars is against the law."

Chauncey's mouth had dropped open, and Spike could hear him breathing.

"Nice to spend time with you two." And he had enjoyed the occasion. "Doesn't Chauncey ever put you to work for your supper, Dante? How come you didn't mess up your hands?"

"I wore gloves, Officer."

Chauncey thudded back and forth on the linoleum-covered floor. *"I wore gloves, Officer,"* he said, and switched to a mincing step. He flapped his hands. "I wore fucking gloves. You did what he wanted you to do — you admitted we did something together with our hands. Why didn't you just up and tell him we had a hell of a time getting the slab off that tomb with only two of us."

"I'm sorry, Chauncey."

"This is what I get for bein' good to my friends — and to my wife. You all turn against me. . . . Wait till I get my hands on that woman. I'll kill her."

"Don't do anything hasty," Dante said.

Chauncey took a good look at his so-called loyal friend. "Where is she? You were supposed to follow her and make sure you knew where she went. Every day you're supposed to follow her. You're doing a lousy job."

"How good would you do, following a mark in a Jag on foot? I gotta have wheels."

"And run 'em over some little old lady? You need that surgery."

"Nobody's touching my eyes. Forget it."

Chauncey's head felt like it would split in half. "She don't go far. She don't know any place but around here."

"Says you." Dante hitched at his own pants and exercised his neck. "You want to know what happened with her? You got it. I followed like you said. Suddenly she's walking beside me, mouthing off about you — and me. She goes to the Jag and I go with her. In she jumps and she's swinging past me when I manage to jerk open the door and throw myself inside. Coulda killed myself, but nothing's too much to do for my friend Chauncey."

An imagination wouldn't be something Chauncey would accuse Dante of having, but this heroic picture didn't fit the man. "Go on."

Dante pushed back his jacket, revealing his piece. "You aren't going to believe this."

Probably not.

"She drove so fast I couldn't believe some cop didn't stop us. Don't ask me where we went. You know I don't got no sense of direction. She drove and she started cryin'. Sheesh, she wouldn't stop. *Chauncey doesn't understand me. I love him more than my life, but I got to fight all the time just to make him notice me.*"

"Garbage."

Dante pushed out his chin and nodded. "Who knows what makes women tick? Anyway. It don't mean nothing. Forget the whole thing."

"She's drawn attention to my business. Devol's

going to be watching, which means I gotta cool it till he loses interest."

"Just let it go," Dante said. "It'll all pass over."

"Everything passes over in the end," Chauncey said, lowering his voice and taking pleasure in the clicking sound that came from Dante's throat. "Don't forget I'm as good as protecting you. You came here with a job to do."

"And I did it."

"It got done, more like it," Chauncey told him. "You just about fucked up before I looked after things. If your boss in New Orleans finds out about that, you're a dead man."

Dante looked belligerent. "He's never going to know."

"Not if your luck holds and I don't tell what I know. Now quit blowing smoke, and finish with Precious. She was driving around, bawling, and you were sitting there praying she didn't drive up a tree. What else? Did she call Devol in front of you?"

"No, she didn't. D'you think I wouldn't have stopped her? She drove till I didn't know what state we was in. Then we went off the road and way into all these trees. She seemed to know where she was going, but I can't swear to it."

"Then what?"

"Precious stopped the car."

"And?"

Dante blushing was an unnerving sight. "Aw, don't make me spell it out."

Chauncey's gut clenched. He took Dante by

the lapels of his jacket and slammed him against a wall. "Answer the question."

"It's embarrassin', that's all. She told me she thought one of her tires was going down and asked me to get out and check it."

Chauncey rested his forehead on Dante's chest. "You stupid shit. Let me finish this for you. Precious waited until you were out of the car and she drove off, didn't she?"

"Yeah. I ran after the car so I could try to see which way she went, but —"

"Shut up," Chauncey said. He was going to have to give up on delegating from now on. "Just — *shut* — up."

TWENTY-THREE

Marc stood behind Reb in front of the bathroom mirror and made it as tough as possible for her to apply first aid to her wet hair. But she didn't get mad, just kept on smiling and pretending she didn't feel a thing.

"If we can get out of here without anyone noticing we're damp, we're in the clear," he told her and kissed her neck.

She kept skewering pins into a topknot. "And if we *are* seen?"

"We behave as if nothing's happened."

Reb looked from her own ruined appearance to Marc's. "That should work. Especially if we run into Cyrus. If he notices at all, he isn't worldly or smart enough to figure out what we've been doing. He'll probably think we've been in the pool?"

"With our clothes on?"

She snorted. "That would make it harder to explain, that and there being no pool."

He wasn't going to visualize the scene. "What you're really saying is, you didn't like it. Not the way it was. It didn't feel right and it wasn't romantic. I feel bad about that."

An elbow landed in his unprepared solar plexus. "Oof." Marc pretended to be incapacitated. Then he grabbed her around the waist. "Your place or mine."

Reb turned in his arms and blew gently on his lips. "You are not original. Has anyone ever told you that?"

"Not until now. Do that again. The blowing thing."

She obliged.

Shivering, he told her, "You are so sexy."

"Let's go," she said. "Fast. First, be quiet and listen."

They stood nose to nose, each with an ear to the door. Reb shut her eyes and squinched up her face in concentration. Marc listened, too, but couldn't handle her expression. He lost it, and when she caught him by the ear and twisted, just a little, he laughed harder and she couldn't stay serious any longer.

The merriment subsided, leaving Reb with the hiccups.

He opened his mouth to speak, but she clapped a hand over it. "Not another word," she whispered. "You're enjoying this. Danger excites you." She hooked a thumb toward the door. "Out."

"You first."

"Uh uh." Her hands were on her hips. "We don't know what may be out there. You have to protect me. *You* first."

"Toussaint's most emancipated woman suddenly wants a big, strong man to protect her. If someone comes, you want to lock the door on me and leave me hanging out to dry."

She looked innocent, then smiled. "You've got it."

He opened the door. Reb's hand was in his by the time he led the way into the corridor — and confronted Cyrus and Madge outside the sitting room.

If only he hadn't knocked the shower on. There was no disguising the wet patches all over their clothes. "Hey, you two," he said to Cyrus and Madge. Reb hiccuped and eased her fingers from his. "Did you settle anything with Ozaire?"

Much too much time went by before Madge said, "I saw Cyrus leavin' and made him take me along. Ozaire's okay sometimes, but he can be a mean one."

Cyrus turned the corners of his mouth up. "Madge had to protect me. She's good at it. Maybe we should settle down for a chat . . . or probably not. You probably have to get on. Do other things." His voice faded away.

"We came because we've got a lot to go over," Marc said. Cyrus's discomfort added to his own. "That hasn't changed."

"That hasn't changed," Reb echoed. Trying to swallow her next hiccup didn't work.

Cyrus coughed. "Yes, well — Madge and I have been going over everything we know about Bonnie. Four heads are better than two, and you'd want to be involved anyway, Marc."

He'd been handed some hope that there might be support forming for his conviction that it had been Amy who died in the church. He stood back for Reb to enter the sitting room ahead of him. Cyrus and Madge would have to be deaf not to have heard the two of them laughing in the bathroom. Appearing the way they had told the story anyway.

"Would you like some water?" Madge asked Reb.

"Drink it backward," Cyrus said, apparently serious. "From the far side of the glass. And hold your nose."

Reb said, "The scientific approach."

"Gotcha!" Marc grabbed the back of Reb's neck. She jumped madly and spun around.

Marc's lips twitched. Cyrus and Madge watched Reb expectantly. She didn't tell Marc what she thought of him — and she didn't hiccup.

"See?" Marc said, feeling reckless. "Science gets the job done every time."

"Thanks for bringing in a little humor when things are so serious," Reb said. "I'll try to do the same for you sometime. Cyrus, did Ozaire come to his senses?"

"Lil's getting a raise," Cyrus said with a faint smile. "That seemed to make him happy. Just as well, because I couldn't have let him sell fish outside the church — not unless I let everyone in town set up a stall and sell their wares. But he didn't even mention *goings on* in the parish. It's hard for some folks to make a living around here."

"It is," Madge agreed. She looked good in jeans and a yellow shirt. "There isn't much left over, but we do a good job of keeping costs down and helping people, don't we?"

Cyrus frowned. "Maybe too good in some areas and not nearly good enough in others."

Marc didn't know what that meant and knew better than to ask. He realized they all stood stiffly in the center of the room. "It isn't my place to suggest it, Cyrus, but could we sit down?" His legs were still rubbery, but he doubted mentioning that would please anyone, least of all Reb.

"Sit, sit," Cyrus said and waited until Madge, Reb, and Marc had perched themselves on the comfortable furniture before planting himself on an ottoman. He smiled and slapped his knees.

"Um, what's happenin' in Toussaint is really weird," Madge said, not meeting anyone's eyes.

"Sure is," Reb agreed. She looked sideways at Marc, and he winked at her.

"Spike's spread too thin," Cyrus said. "He's got two part-time deputies who are wet behind the ears, and he doesn't earn enough to keep his family without having another business. He's industrious. Not being able to give every criminal case his full attention must kill him."

"I know it does," Reb said, leaning forward from the couch. "And he works with one hand tied behind his back. He has to answer to people he rarely sees, and ask permission for every move he makes."

Marc wiggled his toes inside his shoes. His socks were damp. "So he's in the same position most people are who work for someone else."

That comment won him the attention of the other three. They stared at him, and he figured what they were thinking wasn't complimentary where he was concerned. "Madge has to answer to Cyrus."

"That's really tough," she told him.

"And Cyrus has superiors. I don't know what you call 'em, but I bet he gets visits, and has to trot to wherever, when he's called."

Reb stirred. "We're straying. Spike's one man doing the jobs of several. That was the point. He could use all the help he can get — *without* being made to feel inadequate."

"Sorry," he said. "Didn't mean to knock the local sacred cow."

"What's got into you?" Reb asked, and Marc felt ashamed and foolish in about equal measures. She managed to just about turn her back on him and say, "What are you thinking?" to Madge and Cyrus.

"Just a minute," Marc said. "I'll eat the humble pie and get it over with. I could make excuses but I won't. Spike's a good guy, okay?"

"Okay," Cyrus said while the two women gave Marc exasperated glances.

"Does anyone have any theories? About anything." Madge's intelligent eyes watched each of them.

"Just the basic but obvious ones," Marc said. "I don't think Pepper Leach is a killer — or not the killer we need. Why he isn't putting up a fight to get out is anybody's guess."

"Agreed," Reb said, and Cyrus nodded. "But whoever's responsible seems to be shooting from the hip. It's beginning to look as if Bonnie may have been murdered after all."

"Why?" Madge asked.

"Why else would her body be —" Reb looked at Marc. His mouth was pressed shut, and there was a white line around his lips. "Why would her body be removed from the tomb if she died accidentally?"

"Because murdered or not, the body in that grave didn't belong to any Bonnie Blue," Marc said. "And whoever stands to lose if that comes to light knows I can prove it."

Reb wished she could hold him. He kept on going, seeming okay, but she feared for him.

"If that's true," Cyrus said, "we've got to make sure you stay safe."

Madge sucked in a noisy breath. Reb gripped the edge of the couch and felt sick. Why hadn't she thought of that? Marc was worried about her, so were Cyrus and Spike — so was she — but Marc was just as vulnerable to getting hurt as she was. And unlike her, he had the masculine misfortune of needing to prove how brave and strong he was.

She was grateful when Madge said, "Cyrus agrees that Bonnie's missing purse could be the lead we need. How about you two?"

"We search for it," Marc said.

"There was a search," Cyrus said. "Volunteers turned out. Must have been a hundred people."

"Yes," Madge said at once.

Reb added, "They searched for days and days, Marc. Even brought in a couple of dogs. But it was — there wasn't anything to suggest foul play."

"So everyone heaved a happy sigh and quit asking questions of any kind." Marc stood up and shook his head. "Forget I said that. That's what must have seemed appropriate at the time. We know differently now. We're going to find that purse, and I'm going to see Amy's possessions. What was there? One of you must remember something."

"A few clothes," Madge said. "One beaten-up suitcase. Toiletries."

"Her Bible," Cyrus added. "A gold crucifix on a chain — she was wearing it."

Reb watched Marc's face, but he wasn't showing his feelings.

"A set of jacks," she said. "She actually still played with those things. And a string cross on a leather thong. She also had a crystal ornament of a dove. Anyone remember something else?"

Cyrus and Madge didn't offer anything new.

The picture of the man and the baby had been on Bonnie's body. Reb could not speak of it, it had seemed so poignant and private. Spike knew about it, and he could make the decision about whether or not knowledge of it should be shared.

"Okay," Marc said. "I think you're right, and we have to make every effort to find the purse."

"Spike —"

Marc cut Reb off, "I'll tell him what I'm going to do."

"I'm with you," Cyrus said.

"Me also." Madge didn't sound optimistic that her efforts would be useful.

"And me." She would, Reb thought, do it to support Marc. "I'll also let Spike know and see if he's got any thoughts. We'll get plenty of help from the folks around if we ask for it."

"Yeah," Marc said. "I haven't forgotten the obvious. The purse could have been stolen for money and credit cards."

"She had no credit cards," Madge said. "I know that for sure, or I think I do. Nothing's come up about someone using cards with Bonnie's name on them. And I don't suppose she had much cash."

Reb's pager vibrated. She didn't recognize the number but used her cell phone to call back. Peggy Lalonde had gone into premature labor, she was told, and the girl was begging Reb to come. She frowned and said, "Go on." More information than "things are going fast" would have been useful, but she wouldn't waste more time. "I'll be there." She got up and hurried toward the door. "Peggy's delivering her baby early — too early."

Marc watched her leave with a sense of loss. What the hell did he think he was doing with her? He couldn't pretend he wasn't starting to need her about as much as the air he breathed, but he didn't have a good history with relationships — witness the fact that he'd never been in one that lasted. Was it fair to get in so deep when he might have to get out? He wasn't forcing her to get involved. Missing her because she'd gone to work was out of line. She had her own life, and what she did was important. A lot of life-and-death stuff.

"Her keys," Madge said, holding them up. "They fell out on the couch. I'll catch up with her and save some time."

"Marc," Cyrus said when the sound of Madge's footsteps thudded on the stairs. He cleared his throat and fidgeted. "I've seen wonderful results from our marriage-preparation classes."

"That's nice." If this were happening to any other man, Marc would find it funny.

"Yes. My brother-in-law — Jack Charbonnet — he swears by a jeweller he knows in New Orleans. Got Celina's, she's my sister, he got her rings from this man, and other stuff. Good prices, Jack says."

"Thanks for the suggestion. I'll get the name

in case I need it. Which hospital would Peggy go to?"

"Hospital? She's at home."

"You sure?"

"Of course I'm sure. They're the kind of family who get born, and die, at home."

"Where is it?" Marc sidestepped toward the corridor.

"North. Bayou side of Cemetery Highway, you can —"

"Thanks." He had to stop her from going out there alone.

TWENTY-FOUR

"I'm sorry, hon," Amy Girard said. "I know you're doing the best you can to help me, in the only way you know how, but I'm scared."

Precious almost wished she could like the woman. If she talked to Father Cyrus about what she was doing, he'd tell her to forgive her enemies. But this woman wasn't just any enemy — she'd been hurting Precious for years, only she hadn't known Amy existed until April, when she'd got a call from the crazy bird lady in New Orleans. Amy Girard had been making a fool of Precious even as Chauncey proposed marriage. She'd committed adultery with Precious's husband while he was on his honeymoon, and the adultery hadn't stopped until Precious found out about it — too late to save her self-respect, or to wipe away the pitying looks in the eyes of all those who had always known.

At the end of April she'd threatened to leave him, and meant it, but he'd begged forgiveness and promised it was all over. But he lied, just like always, and his last-ditch effort to keep Precious — because of Mama's money — had brought Amy to Toussaint looking for him.

Amy stood on a bath mat, shivering, her body too thin, too flaccid, even though it wasn't hard to see what a fabulous figure she'd had. She caught Precious looking at her and wrapped herself in a towel. "The chain got wrapped around that." She nodded to the toilet pedestal. "I couldn't reach the shower."

Among other things, Amy had also been unable to get to the canned food piled in the corner behind the door in the tiny room. They both knew Precious had messed up. One end of the chain was attached to a manacle on Amy's raw right ankle — Precious had clamped the other end to a pipe and rushed away without checking it out properly. She couldn't stand hearing Amy begging not to be left alone. Even when Precious was in the boat and rowing away, she would hear when the pleading turned to wailing and crying.

That's why she hadn't been back for a week. She shivered and took the top off a can of tuna. Forks were out of the question since they made usable weapons. "Here," she said, offering the fish to Amy. "Go slow, or you'll throw it up."

Amy shook her head. "I can't."

Precious left her and returned with a clean dress. She didn't get underwear because of the chain. "Get dry and put this on. I'll take you into the other room so you can rest easy for an hour."

Amy's tears bothered Precious, and she went outside the bathroom. She pushed her fingers into her ears to shut out the sobbing, only it didn't work. Thank god the faucet was close enough in there. She thought you died pretty fast without water.

"I'm ready," Amy said.

With her gun drawn, Precious undid the chain again. She'd already moved it free of the toilet. "Walk ahead of me," Precious said, gesturing with the gun barrel. Amy limped, whimpering each time the manacle dragged on her damaged flesh. "Sit there. Right there on that chair. Lift the chain and put your feet on the stool."

"Yes," Amy said. Her dark eyes had no luster. She sat down on the edge of the seat and leaned forward, making no attempt to touch the chain.

Precious lifted the woman's free foot onto the antiqued green stool, then held up the chain and helped maneuver the right leg up.

Amy said, "Thank you." Her long, gray-shot black hair hung about her face in matted clumps. "I don't deserve any kindness from you."

You're not getting any, babe. The damnable thing was that Precious felt something like hysteria clawing inside her throat, gripping her chest.

"If you want to finish it now, that's okay by me," Amy said.

"Shut up," Precious said. "I've got my own thoughts, me. My own decisions to make. You were lucky I came home when I did that day.

Don't forget that. Chauncey was planning to kill you. He still is if he can find you."

Amy pushed at her hair. Her sallow skin had a yellow cast, and purple pockets bulged beneath her eyes. "I wish I'd known you before," she said. "You're so good I think you would have given me the strength to do the right thing."

"You got to eat," Precious said, breaking a sweat. She backed to the kitchen counter where she'd heaped supplies from the boat. The box of crackers she wanted was in front. She opened it and returned to Amy. "Work on some of these."

Amy let her put the crackers in her hands.

"Eat," Precious ordered. "You don't want to die. Say it. You don't want to die."

A shake of the head was all she got from Amy.

"*Say* it."

Amy raised a cracker to dry lips and took a bite. "I don't have anything to live for."

"Well, then." What did it matter to her if the has-been didn't care about staying alive? "If that's the way you want it."

The scars of old needle tracks mottled Amy's arms. She ate all of the cracker, and another and another. Precious got her a glass of milk, and Amy sipped from it.

"Look," Precious said. "Don't go thinking I'm some sort of saint. But I *want* you to trust me. I *need* you to trust me, so I'm using you. Do you understand?"

Amy's laugh grated. "Everyone else uses me, why wouldn't you?"

Losers irritated Precious. "That's your fault. You know the old saying? You gotta lie down to be a doormat. Maybe you really hit the ground this time and there isn't any place lower to go. That means you've got two choices, you. I'm going to offer you a way out." *If she didn't change her mind.* "You can take it and move on. Get yourself healthy. Contact that rich brother of yours and ask him to help you start again."

"My brother?" Amy's head snapped up.

Precious ignored the reaction. "Or you can have the other. You can check out. It won't be like goin' to sleep forever on your own feather bed, but you'll be just as dead afterwards."

"Why did you mention Marc?" Amy asked. She actually had a little color in her face. "You haven't talked to him? You haven't tried to get money out of him?"

"Why would I do a thing like that?"

"Ransom. Don't hold your breath waiting to get it — he doesn't want to hear my name again, let alone *pay* to keep me around and bothering him."

It was so sad when families didn't have feelings for one another, Precious thought. She stood straight and wiped all expression from her face. "I don't need money — not from anyone. Your Chauncey keeps me in fat city."

"He isn't my Chauncey," Amy said quietly. "He never was."

Precious swallowed and blinked. Must be a lot of dust in the air.

She'd always been too soft, but she usually hid it better than she had today. "All men are depraved. They're corrupt, warped, self-centered, and perverted. They aren't nice."

"You're tougher than I am," Amy said, "Funny, 'cause you're about the best person I ever met."

What was that stuff they said about prisoners and their captors? The prisoner became dependent, then tried to please?

Enough of that. "Chauncey wanted to put you in another woman's grave. He was going to take her out of the tomb and give it to you."

"Nice of him," Amy said, with the first spark of spirit she'd shown since Precious found her. "Is that what he still intends to do?"

Precious considered. She felt daring. What did she have to lose by being honest with Amy anyway? "That idiot was supposed to let me know before he robbed the grave. I needed to be ready."

"What difference does it make. The result's the same. All he has to do is slide me in."

Precious laughed. Amy might not think her companion was so special if she knew what Precious had intended to do. "Nope. That's off. Your brother insisted on an exhumation — he thought it was you in there, see. Already in there, that is. He didn't believe there was anyone by the name . . ." She puffed up her cheeks and tried to order her thoughts. "Marc Girard thinks you were using an alias and you got killed and buried." And if Chauncey had treated her like a partner, worked with her, Amy's body would have been there to oblige Girard — only it would have looked the way Bonnie had — with the necessary changes — and they'd have interred it again.

"Uh huh," Amy said as if she were distracted. "Why would Marc care?"

"I don't have to know that. He does is all. He's turning Toussaint upside down, and everyone in town hates him. They all think he's going to interfere with their businesses because the Girards own the buildings. Getting an order to dig up bodies in the graveyard didn't help his popularity poll. People showed up for miles around. It was a spectacle."

Amy gulped. She scrubbed at her exhausted face. "I never gave that boy anythin' but grief. Better for him when this is over and he knows I'm gone. I can do that much for him. Precious, you never did say how you finally found out about me and Chauncey."

Again, what harm was there in telling it like it was. "I got a call from a weird woman who goes by the name of Oiseau de Nuit or something similar. She wanted a *reward* for giving me important information. When I told her to drop dead she gave me what she called 'a taste of my betrayal.' "

Amy dropped her hands to her knees. "Oiseau. Also known as Dirty Darlene — not because she's crooked, but because she's dirty.

She's also crooked. We had an apartment together. I wanted out, but the place was cheap."

"What did you do to make her hate you so much?"

"She doesn't hate people," Amy said. "She doesn't like them, either. She always needs money, and she saw a chance to make some out of me, that's all."

Precious pushed her hands into her pockets. She'd be driving home in the dark along poorly maintained roads. The dusky mist folded onto the swamp, gray into green. "She's in Toussaint. Oiseau's in Toussaint. She turned up at the exhumation, dressed in black drapes and whirling around like a witch of some sort."

"How come she knew about it enough in advance to get there, when you didn't find out until the day."

"Day before. She had plenty of time to get there."

"Not if someone didn't tell her," Amy said.

Precious considered. She paced the room, corner to corner, to corner, to corner. "She's got a contact in Toussaint, has to."

"She met Chauncey," Amy said. "Maybe he gave her a reason to hate him. He's the one who's most likely to get hurt by anything she decides to say."

"This is too much grief for me," Precious said and meant it. "Don't you want to rub Chauncey's nose in his own mud?"

Amy stared and twisted her hands together.

"Then maybe you could find a way to make your brother proud of you."

"How? Pose for scary posters to warn kids off drugs?"

"You're not on drugs now."

"Look at me." Amy pulled her hair behind her head and stretched out her free arm. "I might as well be using. I look as if I am. That stuff ruined me, but it's my fault. And when you do what I've done, the only good thing left to do is make sure you don't hurt anyone anymore."

Precious barely stopped herself from slapping Amy. She frowned at her, bent over her. "You and I got something in common," she said. "We both got worked over by the same lousy man. Only I'm not giving up. It's payback time for me."

"Good. It'll make you feel better. I should have said I'm sorry about the baby."

"Baby?"

"Back in March Chauncey told me you were expectin' and he owed it to you and the baby to break off with me. He's not so bad, see, not when he's got something to shape up for. I should have accepted what he said and not followed him back to Toussaint. He told me you lost the baby but that didn't change his feelings. He still owed you."

"Chauncey told you I was pregnant?" Precious thought her way through what she was hearing. "That's why he had to finish with you. Then, when you came out here he said I lost the baby. Cute. I wasn't pregnant. Chauncey, he doesn't want any children. He likes being an only child."

Amy took up the glass of milk and drained it. "He's a liar," she said. "But I knew that. Why wouldn't I expect him to lie about a baby? I know all about him, you know. All about his so-called business. As long as I did what he said, he trusted me to keep my mouth shut. Now he's afraid I'll turn him in to the law."

Precious wasn't learning anything new, apart from the pregnancy, miscarriage stuff. "You're right when you say he's afraid. I don't know how long I can keep you safe. He's going to know about this place in the end. The guy who's supposed to be finding it and offing you for him is a joke. Chauncey's sweating more over you every day. He'll decide to do his own dirty work and come after you himself."

"He hired a hit man?" Amy's voice was flat, but there was no missing the flicker of disbelief in her eyes. She raised her face. "Just now you said you were keeping me safe. That's not what you said before. You said you wanted me to suffer for what I did to you and you'd kill me when you were ready."

"That was — what do you call it? Words of passion. Or spoken in passion." Truth was she'd meant what she said to Amy in the first place, only Amy wasn't all bad. She was what Father Cyrus would call a product of circumstances. "Seems to me we've both got good reasons to make sure Chauncey never gets anything he really wants."

"You don't mean you want to . . ."

"I don't know." Precious felt different, she felt — *just*. "You knew him before I did. You've got cause to feel cheated, too."

Amy burst into tears. "You are the best, the very best. There can't be another soul with as much fairness and forgiveness in her heart as you. You're forgiving me, aren't you?"

Was she? "Yes. *Yes,* I am. I've been wronged. You've been wronged. By the same man. It's time to make him pay."

"I don't want you to do anything that'll make him hurt you."

"Thank you. I won't." Precious looked at the manacle and chain. "I'm going to take that thing off. I want you to stay here until I can find a better place — if we need one." She put her gun away and found the manacle key. "I'll leave in the rowboat like I do. Don't go into the water, like try to swim away from here. There's snakes —"

"And gators." Amy actually giggled. "I grew up here, remember? I'm going to try that tuna after all."

She started to get up, but Precious eased her back. "I'll get it for you. You rest up. There's lotion and some creams in the bedroom. Use them, and I'll leave you my makeup. I'm gonna buy as much time as I can for you to get plenty of sleep and pamper yourself. I need time to figure out a plan."

"We could think one up now and get right to it," Amy said.

Precious went for the tuna, got a fork from the kitchen, and handed both over to Amy. "I've already got parts of it," Precious said. "Chauncey's been real good, helping us out and all."

Amy looked blank. She put a forkful of tuna into her mouth and chewed slowly.

"He stole a body and put it somewhere. Now I'm going to find out where it is and drop some hints in the right places. Wrong places for Chauncey."

For several minutes Amy ate, concentrating on the food.

"I'll give Chauncey some advice," Precious said, getting so excited she bounced on her toes. "First I tell him the deputy sheriff and all have evidence to prove it was you in the tomb — including facts about you visiting our place and not being seen since."

Amy quit chewing.

"To save himself, Chauncey's got to make sure they *find* the body and discover it's not yours. See?"

"Not exactly."

Exasperated, Precious sighed. "I never was so good at explaining myself. Spike Devol will get a tip to stake out wherever the body is and wait. If anyone can hide something where it won't be found, it's Chauncey. Eventually Chauncey will show up to relocate the evidence where it'll be easier to find — I can convince him to do anything when he's scared — so he'll start moving the body. They'll catch him at it."

"How am I going to help?"

"Show up in court looking real good, and sit with me where Chauncey can see us."

Precious liked the way that sounded, but she couldn't afford to be a sentimental fool. If she showed up with Amy there would be too many dangerous questions. She'd like to set her free but didn't know how. In practice, the end of the story would have to be different — and time was running out.

TWENTY-FIVE

Marc's hands squeezing hers on the handlebars, his legs astride the front wheel, and his face bending over her in the glare of the Range Rover's headlights made Reb furious.

"You cut me off," she shouted at him. "You could have killed me."

The Rover's engine ran, and they had to raise their voices to be heard. "You were coming to a stop at the sign," Marc told her. "Yes, I cut you off, but I knew what I was doing. Get off that thing. I'll drive you."

"No, thank you. This is how I make home visits."

"Sure," he said. "And I'll bet everyone for miles around knows it. You are a sitting duck on that thing, cher. Please, Reb, don't fight me on this."

She couldn't believe he was doing this. "I have a patient in labor at a very critical stage in her pregnancy. Every minute may be crucial."

"Get in the Range Rover."

"I'm going to drive on. It would be a good idea for you to get out of my way."

"I'm not takin' the time to list all the reasons

why that isn't going to happen, but a reminder or two are called for. A tape recorder was put underneath your examining table. What do you suppose that was about?"

"Prurient interest in very private conversations. A Peeping Tom — or ear."

"Not with everything else we've been dealing with. You may be okay with the threats, I'm not. And they are threats."

Reb sighed. "I've already thanked you for your concern, but I think you're reaching too far on the tape recorder."

"Someone's trying to catch you talking about incriminating stuff — incriminating to them."

"That could be, but it's only a guess."

"You were the one who originally said you could be considered a threat. I think you're right. Get off the damn bike."

Nobody ever said she was a super-patient woman. "For the last time, kindly step out of my way."

"You are so polite," he said. "Too polite to run a man through with your motorcycle. Through the middle, in fact. Just imagine what you'd do to me."

"You are irresponsible." She gunned her engine. "My instruments are packed in back of me, and you're wasting my time. This is it."

The warning sounded good, but all she could do was keep revving the engine.

"Okay," he said, raising his hands in surrender. "We'll do it your way." And with that he managed a smooth move that landed him behind her on the bike. Into her ear he said, "Should have done this first. I never wanted to keep you away from a patient."

"Your car's running," she yelled.

"I'm calling Spike," he told her. "Ride."

She couldn't make out what he said to Spike on the phone, but they hadn't gone far when she heard the sound of a siren.

Marc held her around the waist, and she remembered he wasn't wearing a helmet. Applying the brakes, she drove onto the verge and twisted on her seat. "Helmet, dammit. In the Tourpak, and hurry."

He made a face resembling that of a wise-ass teenage boy who'd like to refuse, but he wrestled the helmet out and crammed it on. Reb took off again while he was lowering the face shield.

Gaston was probably at dog protection services by now, turning her in for neglect. She could be hours longer getting home. "Marc," she yelled over the intercom and was surprised when he answered. "You must have done this before. I need someone to check on Gaston. Madge would go."

"I'll call," he told her.

Toussaint wasn't even a dot on most maps. Clearing the straggling town boundaries to the north didn't take long, but immediately the road became a tree-tunnel, and Reb's headlight bored a hole through humid darkness. She wasn't too sorry to feel Marc's hands at her waist.

"I can't believe you do this," he said, his voice loud inside her helmet. "It would be dangerous even if you were a man and everyone loved you — or was scared to death of you."

Reb didn't answer. She had to concentrate on frequent curves in the narrow road. Moss became heavier and hung lower at night when dampness weighted it down. Mostly it flew away from the bike as it passed, but on occasion a length slapped Reb's face shield and she had to hold steady or risk swerving and sending the two of them into a swampy ditch.

Another fifteen minutes and they passed the turn to Pappy's Dancehall. A neon arrow flashed, pointing to the Lay By with its hourly rates. Reb was grateful for even that sign of life.

A vehicle approached from behind, and she checked in her mirrors. Some sort of wildly-painted van. She didn't recognize it. The burly driver was a dark shadow hunched over the wheel. He honked as if to make her go faster, but she was already exceeding the speed limit.

The van fell back, and Reb relaxed.

"You okay?" Marc asked.

"Dandy," she told him, and he squeezed her sides. The last thing she had time for tonight was dwelling on her feelings for him. They were too complex, and most of them were more than distracting.

"Watch out for the wise guy behind us," Marc said. "I think he could be playing games."

Driving on side beams that barely pricked the blackness in Reb's mirrors, the guy in the van had moved in close again, and closer. The lights moved to the outermost range of the bike mirrors, and Reb was looking at the front grill and bumper.

"Stay cool," Marc said as if he'd felt her tense up. "This one's nasty, but we should be out of his way soon. Shit!"

A glancing blow to the bike almost threw it aside. Reb hardly knew how she'd managed to keep them upright. She plowed into mushy gravel and opened her mouth to scream when she rushed at young tree trunks. But then she had control again and was back on the road, with the van dropping behind them again.

Marc leaned on her back.

"That was close," she said.

"That was a hit," he said, and sounded tight. "Hush," he told her when she started to react. "Barely a hit. He tapped my thigh is all, but another half inch and it would have been a different story."

Her stomach rolled. The turnoff to the Lalonde place wasn't more than a couple of miles now. All she had to do was keep her head until she could get out of the joker's way.

"Marc. The leg?"

"I told you it's nothing," he said, but wasn't convincing enough to please Reb.

"Bleeding?"

"Nah."

Once more the sidelights drew nearer. "I'm going to give you the number and have you call Peggy's place. Ask what's happening now. Ask for specifics."

Marc followed her instructions, then turned off the intercom at his end. He came back on as Reb, drawing her first full breath in minutes, made the turn onto the shallow hill down to the Lalondes'.

"We're going to be fine," he said. "But we've got trouble. Peggy's out playing bingo."

"Someone called from . . ." Why *wouldn't* she have believed the caller? "Are you sure you got the right number?"

"I'm sure." He didn't say that the van had followed them onto the slope, but Reb had seen it.

"This is a setup," she said.

Marc rubbed the middle of her back. "We're going to beat it by going where he can't."

The other vehicle bore down on them. "You've got it," Reb said. "Hold on tight."

She left the road for rutted land she remembered only for its lack of trees. The bike bounced, one wheel at a time, over dirt bars as big as man-eating speed bumps. Reb's teeth jarred together, and she heard Marc swear.

"He's coming after us. Get farther away from the road and pray he gets stuck."

Ahead, the earth was darker than the sky and separated from it by a fuzzy ridge. Reb recalled a razorback of land crowned with a Mohawk of scrubby vegetation. On one side there was standing water. Which side? Her low beam rocked madly, up, down, one side, then the other. It jiggled, and her bones felt like ice cubes being shaken in a mixer.

"Keep your eyes ahead," Marc said, his voice steady. "I'm right with you. He's still coming, Reb."

Without warning, the bike slid sideways. She wasn't wearing boots. If she slammed her foot down —

"Just keep us as stable as you can," Marc shouted. "I'll steady us." And Reb felt the instant when his shoe made contact with the mud. They kept on sliding, but gradually the wheels found traction.

"You've got it," Marc said, leaning forward over her. "He won't make it on this."

They shot ahead, and she grinned. Tears burned her eyes, and she laughed, and sniffed. She had ridden into a gully that grew a little deeper the farther they went.

"You knew this was here all along, didn't you?" Marc said. "You didn't want me to relax a muscle is all."

"How did you guess? I'm going to slow down a bit."

"Slower would be good now. Keep heading toward the bayou. I don't think we can be seen from the road at all."

The bike rattled less, and the engine settled into a quieter rhythm.

"Maybe we should stop," Marc said. "Let's see if he's still chasing us."

Reb wanted to keep moving. She wanted to be somewhere safe, inside with doors and windows locked. But she did as Marc suggested, came to a halt and switched off.

Breeze riffled grasses.

Beyond the rustling sounds, there was no sound. Reb closed her eyes and listened, and gradually heard crickets and frogs, the skitter of small animals. She concentrated harder, and felt Marc doing the same.

"Gone," Reb said, and all but collapsed over the handlebars.

Marc settled a hand on the back of her neck, and she knew he remained vigilant. "You were right," he said quietly. "Whether or not you know why, you spell a lot of trouble to someone, or more than one."

"I don't know anything," she said. "They may think I do, but I don't. I feel helpless — and dangerous to anyone who's near me. I'm worried about you —"

"Thanks." He interrupted her and didn't sound happy. "Let's get out of here. Time enough for postmortems later. Keep your feet up, I'll scoot us along until we come out of this valley or whatever it is. We're probably in the clear, but we're going to have a Chinese fire drill when we get to the road, and I'll be driving back just in case."

"Because . . ." Reb closed her mouth and

337

stopped herself from telling him he was no better at this than she was. "Okay, thanks. I could use the break."

Marc wheeled them through the soft earth. A lazy moon caught the suck and swell on the surface of the bayou. The air on her face felt cooler.

"A couple of hundred yards and we'll go back on the road and get the hell out of here."

"Sounds great."

Reb saw headlight beams before engine noise registered. Marc was right, they were close to a place where they could have returned to the road. Only their way was blocked by an oncoming vehicle, bearing down, gathering as much speed as the terrain would allow.

"He coasted so we couldn't hear him." Marc tried to jerk her from the bike but she hung on. "Get off and run. *Do* it, Reb."

"You get off first. It's coming straight for us. Marc!"

He tore her free and tossed her off. "Now run," he yelled. "I'll do fine."

She hovered between running away and running toward the bike. And the headlights bounced closer. Marc was on his feet, working his left leg over the seat.

"Marc," she screamed. He was injured. The hit that had been "nothing" had hurt him. Reb didn't have any decisions to make, she threw herself toward him and grabbed his shirt as his second foot slid free of the saddle — and the bike started to topple. "Run with me," she begged, dragging on him. "Don't think about the pain."

Glancing up, she was blinded by huge, glaring lights.

"Damn it," Marc shouted at her.

The front left wheel of the van hit the motorbike and Reb fell; she hit the ground with a force that drove out her breath.

Marc's body covered her. He plucked at her, lifted her head.

All around them the night screamed, metal on rock, brakes grabbing and sliding. Rubber burned.

"Be still," Marc murmured above her and she could have cried out with relief at the sound of his voice. "Don't move at all. Don't speak." He grew heavy on top of her.

The noise of the van changed, and Reb swallowed rather than throw up. An engine in reverse, whining, backing up fast. The headlights settled on them and stayed there.

"We are dead," Marc whispered. "If he doesn't think we are, we soon will be."

Smoothly, rapidly, the would-be killer continued backward, then the sound changed again, and in a roar, with scree flying, the van shot away.

TWENTY-SIX

"I'll call the doctor," Oribel Scully said. She hovered, her shaking hands outstretched, while Spike carried Reb into the rectory kitchen and Marc shambled in on Cyrus's arm. "You need taking care of."

"The doctor's already here," Reb said. "I don't need another one. Put me down please, Spike, I'm feeling better." That was a lie. Her nervous system might never recover. "I want you in Oribel's chair, Marc. Let's see if we can get your pants off without cutting them."

Oribel slapped a hand over her mouth, but everyone heard her squeal.

"The pants are shot," Marc said. "Do what you want to them. Like you said, it's just a flesh wound. If there was anything else, I wouldn't walk so well, would I?"

Reb had examined Marc perfunctorily while they'd waited for Spike, and what he said was correct. "You're right," Reb said and sat down hard on a wooden chair. "We lead charmed lives. We should be dead. We're going to be bruised all over, and I may have to suture that leg for you, but . . . gimme a minute, please. The pace of life has gotten too fast for me."

"You shouldn't forget you're a girl and not a man," Oribel said, with moisture in her eyes. "A motherless child. An orphan. Your father must be turnin' in his grave." She exuded pent-up agitation.

"Calm yourself," Cyrus said. "This is it, folks. Not another move gets made without making sure we've got backups. Nobody acts alone."

Spike tossed his hat on the table and pulled a chair between Marc and Reb. "Painful and dangerous as this was, I reckon we're going to get some breaks because it happened. The sheriff has put up roadblocks. Getting out of the area in a flashy van won't be easy."

"I should think so," Oribel said, and her voice broke. She tipped her head in the direction of William, who came into the kitchen from the garden. "Soon as I heard what happened, I called William in. We could need protection around here."

Cyrus nodded at William. "Good choice, Oribel. I don't think anyone's coming through you, William."

The man frowned and stood braced as if for an attack. "Things am goin' bad — more bad," he said. "There's evil in the town, and I ain't just talkin' rubber killers, me."

"Don't, William," Oribel begged, the color draining from her face. "You make it all worse."

As Reb knew well from an infamous altercation between Oribel and one of the instructors at the gym, Oribel was well able to take care of herself, but around men she became helpless. Reb wasn't sure if this annoyed or amused her.

The front doorbell chimed in the distance, and when Oribel moved to answer it, William waved her aside and went instead.

"You have a champion," Cyrus said to Oribel.

"Nothing said in this room is to go farther, understood?" Spike's tone made it known there would be no lighthearted diversions where he was concerned. "Understood?"

"Yes sir," Marc said, and Reb mumbled with Oribel.

Cyrus raised a well-defined black brow. "I shouldn't think that needs to be pointed out," he told Spike.

"I wasn't talking to you, Father Cyrus. But very few people are as good at keeping their mouths shut as you are."

Unbelievably, all Marc did was shake his head while he tore a bigger hole in a blood-soaked pants leg. Reb asked Spike to get her bag, which had been removed from her mangled bike and put in the cruiser. "Oribel? Do you have a first-aid kit? I need some sterile swabs to start cleaning this up with."

"I'll clean it up myself," Marc said, sounding wary. "Hold up, Spike . . . I've tried not to push you on this, but my sister's body is missing. What are you people doing about it?"

Coming from the hall, Wally slid just inside the kitchen and stood with his back to the wall.

"Later," Spike told Marc. "We're working on it. I'll go for that bag."

"Oh, Wally," Reb said while she took the kit Oribel gave her. "You should be at home in bed. We'd better call your folks right away."

"Don't. They'll get mad at me again. I've got to talk to you, Father Cyrus."

"In the morning will be soon enough." Cyrus approached the boy. "Let's get you home right now."

"I want to confess," Wally said in a rush. The incongruously long raincoat he wore was sizes too large, and his bare ankles showed beneath. His brown paper sack was beneath one arm.

Spike came in with Reb's bag in one hand and a phone clamped to his ear with the other. "Got it," he said, and hung up. He put the bag down beside Reb and stood with his hands on his hips. Reb had the thought that she couldn't imagine why his wife would find a bodybuilder more attractive. Unless Spike had some pretty terrible hidden faults, he ought to be a keeper.

"Wazoo's been lookin' for me," he said. "Mad as a wet hen, the dispatcher says. Pretty funny analogy."

Reb turned to Marc, whose expression was as blank as she felt.

"Wazoo?" Cyrus said.

"The bird lady. Mad as a wet hen. Get it?"

Marc and Cyrus chuckled, but Reb didn't see the big joke. "That's gotta be a guy thing. You mean Oiseau, or whatever she calls herself?"

"Yeah," Spike said, "Wazoo. Her vehicle's been stolen. Guess what it is?"

"A van with a cute paint job," Marc said promptly.

Reb couldn't keep from watching Wally, who looked more pained by the second. "Flying pigs," she said. "Stars and moons and one or two peace symbols — and a lot of stuff I didn't recognize."

"Why would someone use that to commit a crime?" Marc said. "Unless they wanted the vehicle to be easily traced. . . . Don't answer that. They wanted the vehicle traced. We're not dealing with rocket scientists here."

With access to her own supplies, Reb rapidly cleaned the wound on Marc's thigh. He didn't utter a single "ouch," and she figured she had Wally's presence to thank for that. She set out suture material and a syringe, and discarded one set of gloves for a fresh pair.

"What's the needle for?" he asked.

"Just a little stick and you won't feel a thing when I sew you up."

He held up a hand. "No sticks, no stitches. It's just a scratch. I'll take a Band-Aid."

He tried to pull his torn pants leg over the wound. Reb slapped his hands away. "Don't get in my way again. Look at that dirt, and I just cleaned the wound." Once more she snapped off her gloves and put on a fresh pair. "First I deal with this, then you can shower and we'll check you over. You're such a mess of mud — and blood. I need to be sure the only bleeding is from the leg."

"My body is in your hands, doctor," Marc said, smiling up at her. "Handle it with care."

Spike's eyes were blank. Cyrus didn't even try to hide his smile. "Excuse me," he said. "Wally and I have things to discuss."

Oribel stuck her head out like a turtle, and waited. When they all heard the sound of the door to Cyrus's study closing, she planted herself in front of Spike and said, "I have never, ever, been so worried. Not in my entire life. I've been wringin' my hands for so long, they feel raw. There is big trouble going on."

"We'd noticed," Spike said. He gave Oribel a reassuring smile. "Is there something else, something new we aren't already dealing with?"

"I'm just glad Cyrus was in the church and didn't notice." Oribel's eyes darted toward the hall frequently. "And there's so much goin' on he still hasn't caught on to. You called Madge, Mr. Girard. You asked her to go feed Gaston, bless his innocent heart."

Reb had given Marc a shot of Novocain and had already used forceps to thread the suture material and start pulling his wound shut. She couldn't do anything but carry on, and listen to Oribel.

"Ow," Marc said, although Reb knew he couldn't feel a thing.

"That was a couple of hours ago," Oribel said.

"She never came back. I tried to telephone her. She doesn't answer."

Cyrus waited for Wally to say something. He sat on the window seat, hunched over, his raincoat wrapped tightly about him. Nolan had been set aside.

"Confession became Reconciliation before you were born," Cyrus said. "Forgiveness. That's what we all want when we stray, and you can't have strayed so badly, Wally."

"I have," Wally whispered. "When Spike finds out he'll put me in jail."

"Hmm." Cyrus knew better than to laugh. "Whatever you say to me will go no further."

"Even if I've broken the law?"

"What was your crime?"

"Shouldn't we do the stuff?"

"Stuff?" Cyrus asked.

"You know," Wally said, wiping the back of a hand across his nose. "Bless me, Father, for —"

"On this occasion," Cyrus said, "we'll choose to dispense with all that in the interest of expediency — that means that since we're pressured right now, we'll keep things informal."

Wally got up. "Maybe you don't have time. Nah, you don't have time. I'll come back another day. It isn't so important."

"Sit down," Cyrus instructed. He didn't like the way Wally looked. "I always have time for you."

"I'm a thief."

Cyrus bowed his head and made sure he appeared suitably serious. "How many times have you stolen, my son?"

"Once."

"When?"

"Um, two days after Bonnie died."

Wally's tone, and the connection he made, raised the hairs on the back of Cyrus's neck. "You're pretty exact."

"I was scared."

"Of course you were, but now you're telling me about it."

"No," Wally said. "I mean I was scared *before* I stole it. I'd lost my bike, see, and I just wanted to get another one before Mama and Daddy found out, only I thought it would take too long to get the money."

"Your bike was stolen," Cyrus pointed out. "Not lost."

"Maybe it was borrowed. You could say I borrowed what I stole, only I can't put it back like the thief could put my bike back."

He stopped talking and hunkered down again.

"You still have what you stole?"

Wally nodded. "It was for the money, not that there was enough. Then I couldn't use it anyway, and I couldn't give it back."

"Why not?" Cyrus asked gently.

Wally's shoulders shook. "Because Bonnie was dead." He choked, and Cyrus gave him some tissues. From inside the raincoat he produced a cheap black plastic purse.

Cyrus stopped breathing. He sat beside Wally. "That's Bonnie's purse, isn't it? The one everyone was searching for that day?"

"I went where she left her car and started walking back, trying to think what she might think — being scared and all. I don't know why I cut into the trees, but I did. I wasn't even looking, not really. The sun shone on this, see?" He touched the silver-colored clasp on the purse. "I knew it was Bonnie's 'cause I seen it before. All I did was look inside, and there was her wallet. There was money in there. Bills. They're still there."

Wally should have given the purse up at once, but there was nothing to be gained by saying so. "We'd better decide how to deal with this," Cyrus said. "What do you think should be done?"

"I want you to decide." He pulled Nolan's bag beside him and rested a hand on top. "Poor Bonnie. She isn't even in her tomb. That's not right. They shouldn't do anythin' till they find her."

The phone rang, and Cyrus frowned. Who would call at this time of night. He wanted to ignore it, but considering what was going on, he answered.

"It's Reb. Cyrus, forgive me for interrupting but —"

"I understand. Just a moment." He covered the receiver and said, "Wally, how would you feel about having Reb, and maybe Marc in on this?"

Wally's eyes got huge. "Spike's out there," he whispered.

"We won't invite Spike until you want to."

"I don't want to." Wally thought about it. "Unless you say so."

"Reb," Cyrus said into the phone, "come and join us. Wally would like you and Marc here. Hey, what about his leg?"

"It's closed. Nothing too terrible."

He cleared his throat. "Not Spike right now, okay?"

"Spike had to leave. We'll be right in."

Cyrus replaced the receiver. "Did you look through the wallet?"

"Yep. Thirty-one dollars. Sixteen cents in coins. A lipstick —"

A knock preceded Reb's entrance. Limping, Marc was behind her.

Reb saw the purse at once and stood still. She turned around quickly and closed the door behind Marc. "Bonnie's purse. Where did you get that?" she asked Cyrus.

"I stole it," Wally said and pressed his lips tightly together.

"He found it." Cyrus corrected him. "Then he got scared and didn't know how to return it." At least he wasn't lying — yet.

"May I see?" Marc asked, taking the purse and scouring inside before handing it back.

"I found it, then I didn't tell anyone I had,"

Wally said. "There's money in the wallet and I was going to use it toward getting a new bike, only I didn't. But I did steal it; then I didn't know how to give it to someone."

Marc Girard smiled at Wally and said, "We all get into tough corners sometimes," but, as Cyrus observed, his attention quickly returned to Reb. Cyrus wasn't over worrying about these two getting involved — intimately involved and too quickly — but he was relieved to see Marc's slavish preoccupation with Reb.

"What's in it?" Reb asked, and Cyrus listed the contents as Wally had described them.

"No driver's license and no credit cards," Reb said, thinking about the photo, the one of the man with a baby. "Who knows what happened to the license. Not much to go on, but what there is needs to be with Bonnie's effects."

Oribel walked in without knocking, and Cyrus came close to getting angry with her. Instead he kept his voice steady and said, "You know better than to walk into my study when the door's closed."

"I'm in such a muddle," she said, and began to cry. "Spike didn't make it out of Bonanza Alley before one of those part-time deputies of his showed up. They've found Madge, and they're bringing her back."

"Madge?" Cyrus frowned. "What are you talking about?"

"She went to see to Reb's dog and didn't come back."

Cyrus sprang to his feet. "And you didn't say anything to me?"

"I didn't want to upset you."

"You didn't want —"

"*Cyrus.*" Marc stood in front of Oribel. "This is all one goddamn mess. Let the woman explain."

He didn't feel like letting her explain.

"She's all right now," Oribel said, peeking around Marc. "But she'd had a horrible time. They found that woman's van, and Madge was in back."

"She was what?" He broke a sweat. "What are you talking about?"

"There was a bag over her head, and she was tied up — and gagged. She got taken from Reb's place — out front. Never did see who did it. She's worried 'cause she didn't get to feed Gaston."

"Do you notice something these events have in common?" Reb said.

"Yeah, no one ever really sees anyone," Marc said. "This joker knows how to sneak around."

Cyrus wasn't in the mood to analyze the criminal. "You didn't *tell* me, Oribel." He had an unaccustomed need to get violent with someone.

"I didn't know anythin' had happened," Oribel said, her voice shrill. "I thought she would come back and I shouldn't give you more worry than you'd already got. That's where your trouble is" — she pointed at Reb — "that one. Whoever done it to Madge must have thought she was the doctor getting home. What haven't you told us?" she asked Reb. "That's what I'd like to know."

"That's enough," Marc said. "It's fine for you to be a fool as long as you don't upset good folks along the way. Why don't you get back to the kitchen. We'll go talk to Spike."

"I want to get Madge," Cyrus told him, and he didn't care if someone wanted to make something out of his concern for her. She was more than an assistant to him, but he knew how to handle any stray thoughts or feelings.

"Oh!" Oribel rushed from behind Marc, pointing as she rushed Cyrus. "Oh, that poor dear girl. Where did you get that? Tell me now." She screamed and tried to grab Bonnie's purse.

"Calm down," Reb said. "It was just found."

Oribel was chalky. She wore no lipstick, and her mouth matched her face. "What's in it?" She made another attempt to take it from Cyrus. "Is there something to help find out why she was out there like that? Why she went to the church? Oh, everyone I care for leaves me. If things keep going the way they are, you'll all leave me, too. That's if they don't get me first."

"She's hysterical," Marc said. "Can you help her, Reb?"

Reb had no chance to respond before Wally said, "This was in there, too." He held out a clip for a small handgun.

TWENTY-SEVEN

Not one word had been said about efforts to find Amy's body. Marc wouldn't have expected to be so cut up about something like respect for the dead, and the sister who had been lost to him before he ever really knew her.

If he didn't have Reb to think about, he might start ripping this molasses-paced village — who could call it a town? — apart.

Did he have Reb?

She and Attack Poodle were settling into the one guest room that was habitable again. The Conch Street house wasn't safe. Cyrus had offered her a room at the rectory, but both Madge and Oribel were staying there, and Marc had pointed out that Reb was without wheels and he was in a position to get her to the clinic first thing in the morning.

He hadn't missed the sharp disapproval in Cyrus's eyes.

Thanks to the people he'd hired to spend their lives working at Clouds End for the foreseeable future, Reb — and AP — would be comfortable. Just about anything Reb might want to eat was in the much improved kitchen, and major areas of damage had been shored up. Minor avalanches from the ceilings no longer occurred. Cletus's spruced-up quarters had impressed him so much that now he rarely appeared. He did enjoy secretive, apparently humorous conversations with the work people.

Marc had poured himself a Scotch and decided to try out one of the new tufted green velvet chairs in his mother's sitting room. He hoped his parent would decide to visit before too long and wanted her to be comfortable. The interior designer who was helping him said she just knew Mrs. Girard would be *thrilled* with the old-world opulence she'd obviously enjoyed when she lived at the house.

The furniture was too damn small.

For what it cost, the silk rug should be fabulous, and it probably was to someone with different taste. Peacocks and purple plums weren't his thing. Green silk on the walls might be okay, he supposed.

There were plans to be made. Unfortunately, attempting a cozy chat in Reb's room — or, better yet, in his own — probably didn't have a great success potential.

He didn't hear her approach until she was in the sitting room — with AP under her arm. She wore a white cotton jumpsuit, and Gaston sported a red bow on top of his head.

"Oh, to be your dog," Marc said.

Gaston smiled.

"I came to apologize for being a pill," Reb

said. "You're opening your home to me because you're concerned for my safety, and you've agreed to the irritation of my answering service ringing at any hour — and to driving me where I need to go. I should have shown more gratitude. Thank you."

He indicated a green velvet couch and said, "I think I should come clean about something I did in one of the bathrooms at the rectory."

She blinked, and blushed, but he felt no guilt.

"I was there with a lady, and . . . well, to be blunt, we got it on in the tub."

Reb held Gaston so tightly he yelped. "Don't talk like that."

"I only tell the truth, and I have to, because the lady and I got as close as a man and woman can get, but now she's treating me like a kindly stranger."

"Sorry." Reb looked at the floor.

"I might think you wished what happened never happened."

"Like hell." Her green eyes skewered him. "I loved every second. But we've got business going on here, and you know what they say about business and pleasure."

He shook his head, got up, and backed her to sit on the couch. Gaston made what sounded like a growling noise through his teeth. Marc held his muzzle in one hand and kissed his nose soundly. Then he let go and waited to be demolished. Gaston looked at him quizzically, turned several circles on Reb's lap, and flopped down — keeping his eyes on Marc.

"You're going to regret that," Reb said. "And don't ask me why. You'll find out."

"I'm terrified." Marc returned to his own seat. "I loved every second in that bathroom, too, and I think business goes a whole lot better if there's something personal mixed in to make the parties care about each other."

She ignored his comments. "You said we have moves to make and fast. I think I know what they are, and I'm volunteering for one operation. I'm going to May Lynn's beauty shop. She likes me, and I think she'll talk to me."

"That was number one on my list, but don't kid yourself she'll spill her guts about anything she thinks might get her into trouble."

She leaned back. "You disappoint me. And I thought she'd want to do a Wally and confess her sins to me."

"You're prickly," he told her.

"And you're insulting." The front of her jumpsuit was unzipped to a pleasingly low point. Unfortunately, she caught him concentrating on the middle of her chest and raised the zip with a snap. "Ow, ow," she said through her teeth.

Marc was on his feet and advancing. "What is it, Reb?"

She smiled a little. "Caught some sensitive skin in the zip," she said.

He made a sympathetic noise. "Boy, I know

how that can hurt." A poker face could come in handy. "Let me get you something to drink."

"No thanks."

"Okay. But you don't look relaxed. How can I help you with that."

She scowled. "Some things a woman has to do for herself."

"Cyrus might have something to say about that."

Reb leaned forward over a complaining Gaston and wagged a finger. "Have I ever told you how disgusting you can be, Marc Girard."

He tipped up his glass and smiled while he drank.

"Why don't you go to bed?" she said. "You had a nasty fall, and you've got a wound. Get some good sleep."

"I will — later. You had a bad shock, Reb. You may think you're invincible, but you're not."

"I don't think I'm invincible. At the moment I feel like an abused rag doll. I'm stiff all over, and I've already got spectacular bruises."

"Is a sauna good for that?" he asked. For his nonchalance, she thought, he should get an Oscar.

Reb considered. "Yes, very good. Should loosen up the joints and relax the muscles. Afterward you'd sleep better. Why don't you do that?"

Marc waved a hand. "Not for me. I'm too tired. But I make sure the thing's kept fired up and ready to go. It's right where it used to be, only it's been cleaned up. It's good in there. You go ahead."

"I might do that. Pepper Leach has to be talked to as well. Will that be hard to pull off, d'you think?"

He was as anxious to get at Leach as Reb was. "I'm not sure. I don't think there'll be a problem if he agrees to see us. We never went to the same schools, but I did know him a bit. I'm hoping he'll talk to me."

"I knew him," Reb said. "One of the nicest, quietest boys I ever met. And he can paint."

Marc got up. "You don't look so hot. Go take that sauna. There are all kinds of towels down there, and anything else you need."

She looked at him long and hard, got up, and left the room with Gaston under her arm.

He was, Marc thought, a reliable, mature man. Never, ever would he look for a way to sneak up on a woman in a sauna. Nope, he'd finish his Scotch and wait for Reb to come back up, just to make sure she was okay. He'd only go near the sauna if she was gone longer than he thought she should be.

Marble steps to the basement had stood the test of time. Creamy and veined with coffee color, they shone. Marc got to matching tiles that covered most of the basement and stood, listening. The house was built on a slope. At the back, French doors opened onto lush vegetation and a terrace surrounding a pool. A problem with the pipes would have to be corrected before it could be filled with water again. On the far side of the pool stood a long cabana, also in need of repair. Necessities came first — like the sauna, steam room, and showers. Marc turned up the corners of his mouth, but as quickly turned them down. Too much self-confidence wouldn't win any popularity contests with Reb.

He called, "Reb," before walking toward a pattern of light through the sauna doors and across the floor outside. She wouldn't hear him. Curled up in a soft white towel, Gaston heard, but went right back to sleep.

Standing beside the door, Marc stretched out a hand and knocked on the glass. Then he opened the room a fraction and said, "Reb? You okay? You've been in there ages."

She didn't answer him.

He let the door close, but his stomach did jumping jacks. Some people passed out in saunas. Once more he rapped on the glass and waited for a response — in vain.

She could be in the steam room or the shower. He averted his head and strode past to see if he could find her elsewhere. She wasn't elsewhere.

Enough pussyfooting around. He returned to the sauna and threw open the door. In the gloom inside, Reb lay, full length, on one of the wood benches that ran along two walls.

"Changed your mind about this?" she said, sounding dreamy. "You can't come in with your clothes on. Unless you want to."

"No," he said. "I don't want to do that."

Naked, she rolled onto one side and propped her head on a hand. "I think it would be good for you. Relax you, and soften up your muscles."

Some things might never soften up again, he thought. Beads of perspiration stood out on her skin. She ran her fingers over a rounded hip and flipped off the water. Her belly and breasts shone wetly.

"The heat's gone to my head," she told him softly. "I've got these feelings I can't even explain."

His erection was beautifully painful. He pulled his shirt off over his head. "Try to explain," he told her, and ladled more water over the stones. They spat and hissed. "Explain your feelings." He was already in too deep to crawl out. She was . . . he couldn't take his eyes off her.

Her eyes drifted shut. "Excited," she said, pressing long fingers into her against the part of her she was probably feeling most. "A little puzzled. We're in a crazy, dangerous nightmare, but I can look at you and I don't care about anything else."

Marc dragged in a hot, airless breath. "Me, too, cher. From where I'm lookin' at you right now I can't imagine ever wantin' to move out of this sauna." He stripped off the rest of his clothes and threw them all outside the door, together with his shoes. White towels were on a cabinet, and he took one, only he didn't wrap it around him. His wounded leg felt stiff but not painful.

"Telling a man too much is supposed to be dumb, but I don't have to look at you — or be with you — to feel the biggest charge. Okay, straight talk. Thinking about you makes me ache. I get wet. For the first time in my life I've had . . ."

"Yeah?" This was too damn serious to be a grinning manner.

"Spontaneous orgasms."

"Oh, baby. I wish I'd been there."

"I touched myself, my breasts, and here —" She pushed her fingers between her legs. "It happened again down here while I thought of you upstairs sipping Scotch."

She studied his face as if she intended to paint him, then moved on to his body. She could call that canvas "Study of a Ready Man." Her eyes reached his penis and stayed there. She ran her tongue over her lips, and his already beleaguered legs turned rubbery.

The thought of her getting off on him — all on her own — drove him wild. He tossed another ladle of water onto the stones and listened to them sizzle.

"You got the sexiest rear I ever saw," Reb said from behind him.

He looked at her over his shoulder and was mesmerized. With her free hand, she pushed her curly red hair back. Moisture had turned it dark auburn. Marc faced her.

She closed her eyes and rubbed circles over her belly.

Marc saw one detail, sweat beaded at the tips of her nipples, beaded and slowly getting ready to fall. He knelt beside her and licked away each drop. Reb shuddered and fell to her back with both hands in her hair.

Almost imperceptible was the rise of hips, the sucking in of her belly. Marc stroked her, as gently as he could. Kissing her was a salty trip. Her chin rose, and her mouth opened beneath his. She played the tips of their tongues together and panted when he caressed her. Her face and shoulders, her arms, legs, and feet. Then he settled his mouth on hers again and kissed her hard this time. He kissed her and paid attention to the parts of her he'd missed on the first pass.

Doing something important really well took time. This was important and Marc took his time. Several times he thought he'd climax alone, but he pulled back from the brink and concentrated on his lady.

"Enough," she said finally. "Please, Marc, I'm begging you, don't keep me on the edge like this."

Settling his chest on hers, he kissed her to silence while he massaged her thighs all the way to that happy place where he brought his thumbs together and in two light moves had her bucking off the bench.

She sank back and he left her, stretched himself out on the other bench with their feet touching.

"Marc?"

He jumped. She was staring at him, eating him up with her eyes again, holding the tip of her tongue between her teeth. "Love the view," she said. "I wish I had a great excuse to make you come down here and lie there naked — often."

"You surely don't think I'd need an excuse as long as you were going to be here, too?"

They tapped their toes together, then concentrated on lacing them. The result was shared laughter. Marc's turned to a howl when she ran an apricot-colored toenail along the bottom of his right foot.

She was too fast for him. Before he could leap up, she was upon him and probably thought she was holding him down. This time he closed his eyes. She rubbed her hands over him from head to toe and picked favored parts to kiss, lick, or blow upon.

"You're sensual," he murmured. "Or just plain sexy."

Rather than answer, her mouth slipped swiftly over him, and he grabbed for her, but just as quickly she withdrew, grinning, and moved out of his reach. "I'm going to take a quick shower and walk outside. I haven't done that in forever."

He was *dying* but managed to nod. She took off and left the sauna, too. Shivering, he waited outside the shower for her to finish. To go in would be to take away the control she seemed to be enjoying — not that he hated it.

Reb emerged, dripping, and paused to make sure nothing about him had changed in the past five minutes. It hadn't.

"Want to come with me?" She pointed outside. "If you do, be quick in the shower."

He didn't waste time arguing. In minutes he walked through the French doors and onto wet grass.

The outdoor lights weren't working, but the moon was, and it splattered shards of silver light through the trees and onto Reb's body. He knew he'd never get tired of seeing the way her breasts turned up at their tips.

She began to hum and clap her hands; she moved in time to the jazz she heard in her head, and when she went into an exaggerated stomp, she offered him her hand. "Ya-ya, the grass is cool, but the earth is warm."

They danced, side by side, whirling together in something that was half Cajun two-step, half polka. That was before they fell together and went into the swing. Her feet hardly touched the grass. Marc didn't care if his leg throbbed. Opportunities to dance naked under the moon — with Reb — might not come around too often.

"We've got our own strobe ball," she said, twirling. "Look at you. You should always have white highlights. You have no idea what it does for shoulders like yours. And your buns. You work out, don't you?"

"Yep," he said. "Enough to stop myself from falling apart. What's your excuse for being Princess Turn-on?"

"Hard work," she told him, coming to a standstill with her hands at his waist.

"You've got a fixation," he said, talking to the top of her head. "I'd say it was penis envy, only I've already told you it's yours if you want it."

"I enjoy looking at it," she told him. "If you can't cope with that, say so; otherwise keep your opinions to yourself."

Layering herself to him, she started them on a slow dance. Breasts to chest, her belly pressing another place, they revolved, and revolved, and when he raised her face he kissed her, long, long kisses that churned up his insides.

The doubts tried to force a way in. Marc pushed them away. He loved the woman, and she might just love him, too. If she didn't, he'd have to see if he could persuade her she did after all.

"Your leg," she said sharply, and stopped. "What is the matter with me? Inside at once. You should have reminded me."

He stopped her from rushing toward the house, put an arm around her, and walked with measured steps. "I should have reminded you? I didn't know you really thought I was stupid."

Once inside, she faced him again and studied him critically. "Are you weak?"

He tried, unsuccessfully, to camouflage a grin. "No, I'm not weak."

"That's good, then. I know better than to allow a person who could be in shock to over-exert. I'm being selfish. We should say good-night."

Marc whistled "Keep Your Hands off My Tout Tout" with his hands laced behind his back.

"Yes, well, I'll see you for breakfast — unless I'm called out."

"Where did you plan on going now, Dr. Tease?"

She shrugged. Marc thought she had the most beautiful shrugs he'd ever seen. "I'm going to try out the steam room — if that's okay with you. Don't worry, I've always loved all this. I never get light-headed. And I'm not a tease."

"Yeah, sure," he said, and she walked away, her sweet bottom doing its thing with each step.

She went into the showers, and he heard the door to the steam room open and close on the other side.

"Now run along," he said, catching Gaston's eye. "And you quit peeping, boy."

He couldn't go. Couldn't just leave her down here and walk away to what? A night of twisting himself up in his sheets and getting no sleep while he made love to her all on his own?

Okay, he'd be straight, just as she'd been. If she sent him away, so be it.

The steam room and showers had a common wall made of etched glass. Fish swimming under water, bubbles rising, weeds waving — he'd drawn the design himself and liked the way it made him feel.

Once more he tried knocking on doors.

Reb slid the heavy slab of glass open and waved him inside. He shut them in, and she said, "What?"

"You straight-talked. Now it's my turn."

"We've got to get them before they get us, haven't we?"

He nodded slowly. "Uh huh. And I don't think we've got much time left. Scared people do impulsive things, and we're tangling with some real scared folks." This wasn't the straight talk he'd had in mind.

"Oiseau should be talked to as well." She stood with her weight on one leg, apparently very comfortable being with him like this. "Spike will have a lot to say to her. The van business is too weird."

Reb stared up at him, and, slowly, she slipped a hand around his neck and pulled his face down to hers. Their kisses might be gentle, but they were also urgent. Her nipples felt like smooth rocks against him and when she stepped in real close, it was with her legs spread so she could straddle his good thigh.

Every move was slow. Steam billowed, they slipped together, deliberately rubbed skin to skin.

"Was that what you meant by straight talk?" she asked him. "The things we've got to do."

"The things we've got to do, yes. But nothing

to do with killers, or concentrating, or being responsible. I want to make love to you again."

With one arm she hugged him close; the other hand she slid down to hold him. "No more," Marc said. "I can't take it."

"Neither can I."

"I love you, Reb."

Steam blurred her features. She didn't answer him, but she did grip his neck and lift her legs around his waist.

Marc gasped. There were things the doc could learn about a man's restraint, or lack of it. Or maybe she already knew them all. . . .

He staggered, and she rubbed her fingertips across his lips. "You're too tired for this."

"I . . . no, I'm not too tired. I'm too tired *not* to do this. Hold on, cher."

TWENTY-EIGHT

"I miss you, Chauncey," Precious said.

He sat on the edge of the bed with his back to her, stretching. "It's six in the mornin'. Use very small words and keep your voice down."

One or two of the feelings she'd had for him lived on. "Don't get up yet." Give the boy a little more time and he'd kill those, too.

"What for?"

"Maybe I'm cold."

"It's already fuckin' eighty."

The words were the usual tough-guy stuff, but he hadn't moved from the bed. "It's cool in here," she told him. "Nice. Could be nice if you're under the covers with someone . . . you love."

He turned to look at her. "Did Amy get away?"

"No."

"You crashed that damn yellow moneymobile you had to have."

Just as she started to get angry, stupid tears filled her eyes. Why would he be sucked in by sweet talk from her? And why did she actually want him? She couldn't, not after all he'd done. She did want him.

"That's it, isn't it?" Chauncey said. "The Jag."

Precious looked away from him. They were so messed up. Not one thing about their lives was going good.

The mattress shifted. Chauncey lifted the covers and got in. He gathered her up in his arms the way he used to, and it was like something broke apart inside her.

"It don't matter," he said. "What's one more car to fix up? You don't never have to be afraid of me. What you want, you got. Hey, no cryin', okay?"

"There's nothin' wrong with my car," she told him. "I meant what I said about missing you. You're here with me, only you're not."

"You pushed me away. I never wanted it." He kissed her. "Only I earned it. I may be a dumb fuck when it comes to the feelings stuff, but not *that* dumb. I love you, too, baby."

She wasn't handling this the way she'd planned. Must be some sort of woman thing — hormones out of whack or something. She ran her fingertips down his spine. Memories, especially bad memories, couldn't be wished away, if that was what she wanted.

What she wanted was to wrap things up with Amy Girard. The thought of killing people didn't excite her. She shut her eyes to hold back the tears. The idea made her sick. That woman was ruined, scary ruined, and the unbelievable part was that Precious couldn't really hate her anymore, not knowing what her life had been —

and that it might as well be over.

"It's been two months," Chauncey said. "That don't matter as long as you'll give us another chance. We need each other more than we ever did."

She should tell him it had never been her he'd wanted, but the money she'd get one day. "I know I need you," she said and rubbed an instep up and down one of his calves. "Hold me."

He did it; he held her without instantly making the move on her.

Too late. Anyway, he was scared, and that's why he was being nice to her. He'd taken a fall and dragged her with him. No way would she get clean away after what she'd done.

Chauncey nuzzled her neck. The old feelings stirred, but not strongly enough to distract her from her purpose.

"I shouldn't have used sex to get back at you," she said, and maneuvered herself beneath him. "I guess it was the obvious thing to do."

Twenty-four hours of beard growth darkened his cheeks and jaw. The pomade had mostly rubbed away in the night, and his hair fell forward, wavy, with curls at his neck. The lines of his face and body might be blurred, his muscles not so hard, but her breathing shortened the way it had the first time they made love — on their honeymoon. Chauncey Depew had got himself a Catholic virgin, and he hadn't pushed for sex until after the ceremony. She'd believed he was mad about her.

His hands covered her breasts. "Don't worry your pretty head about all that old stuff."

She wriggled out of her shorty silk nightie. "Leave the black boxers on, they feel good between my legs."

He said, "Oh, baby," and sealed their mouths together.

There were questions to ask, and any way she did it he was going to think this was one more time she'd used sex to manipulate him. There was nothing soft about what she pulled free of the boxers. "*Oh baby* to you," she said, playing with him and listening to him moan.

"You ready?" he said, feeling her down there. Sweat beaded on his brow and upper lip, and wherever their skin touched was hot and slippery. "Yep, ready as you need to be." He chuckled against her ear.

Some of the excitement began to fade.

"You been to see our friend lately?" he said.

Precious felt sick. She could hit him and shout about him coming on to her because he wanted to soften her up, but she'd been the first one to do that. Could she blame him if he saw an opportunity for himself? "Mmm," she said. She didn't have to give him any information he could use, but she could lead him on and find out what she had to know in the process.

"She's a liability," Chauncey said. "Oh, baby, never mind her now."

"You're right. She's a liability, but we've got to be careful where we go from here." The setup

372

was perfect. "It must have been horrible having to open that tomb."

"Yeah."

"With just the two of you, I don't know how you did it. I wish you'd warned me it was happenin', we could have coordinated everything beautifully."

"We could have." He rubbed her, and she wanted him the way she had a few minutes before. Chauncey speeded up, and Precious panted. She had to struggle to keep a hold on him.

"Let yourself go," he said, while his ass practiced for the main event.

Obliging him came naturally. "Oh, Chauncey," she murmured.

"You call and I come runnin'," he said, entering her slowly. He'd always had finesse, which was probably what kept him in willing women whenever he felt like some variety.

"We have to figure out what to do with — you know — after I've finished. It could still work to pull off the switch. Put Amy in Bonnie's casket and figure out a clever way to make sure she's found — when we're ready."

He held her shoulders and worked hard, too hard.

"Where did you put her?" Precious pushed her hands inside his shorts and over his buns. "You feel so good."

"So do you. Oh, so do you."

"Give me the word and I'll do what I've got to

do. I need a few days to do a good job on her."

"Then Bonnie would be missing and they'd be lookin' for her," he said. "Keep quiet, baby. Let's enjoy this."

"I can't keep Amy locked up forever. She doesn't look so good. She might die on me."

"Would that be a problem?"

She was stupid, Precious thought, stupid, stupid to give him an opening like that. "If it happens before certain other stuff, yes. Everything's got to be just right. Chauncey, you don't want her death traced back to me."

"I don't want it traced back to either of us."

"Maybe we should let her go." Precious held her breath. "She'd be so grateful she'd never bother us again."

He laughed and increased his tempo. "She'd be more vindictive than when she got here. She'd ruin everything. No, sugar, just tell me where she is and I'll take over from here."

Precious needed what he was providing right now. She shut her mouth and gave it her all. Then, when it was over, Chauncey fell on top of her and lay there like a slick dead weight.

Her damp skin started to cool off.

Chauncey snored softly and clicked his tongue loudly against the roof of his mouth.

He'd betrayed her from the beginning. He didn't love her, never had, but he didn't want a woman's warm body around if he couldn't use it.

She shook him, and he rolled onto his back,

blinking at her. "Hey, sleeping beauty," she said, smiling at him. "I swear you get better and better."

Chauncey grinned and scratched his skin through the hair on his chest. "That's something I like about you. You recognize quality."

"Seriously." She tapped his nose. "Should I go ahead?"

He frowned at her.

"You take Bonnie into the swamps. They'll never find anything afterwards."

"We think with one mind," he said. "Only I had Amy in mind. A whole lot simpler."

"Sooner or later, Bonnie and her casket will show up. You weren't to know exactly when they'd do the exhumation, but you shouldn't have moved ahead until Amy was ready to go. Our only hope now is to put Amy wherever Bonnie is."

"Shut your mouth," Chauncey said. "You're confusin' me."

"What's confusing to you? You messed up. I'm going to help you out of a tight spot — because I love you." *Because you're a selfish prick and it's my turn. I'm going to set you up.*

"You can help me out by leaving this alone. I've got everything under control. Where's Amy? Don't mess me around anymore. Today's as good as any day."

Now she felt cold and sweaty. "No. It's going to be my way this time. I'll do it, and then I'll help you and Dante make sure everything's perfect for when Spike gets an anonymous tip." The tip he'd get so he could be there when Chauncey and Dante started digging. "Where did you bury her?"

"What makes you think we buried her?" He got out of bed and walked around to rip open the drapes.

"You put her in a crypt? How did you manage that? Did you just borrow a space, or what?"

"No."

"Oh my god, you got rid of the body? Completely got rid of it — the casket, too?" If he had, everything would change. "How?"

"I didn't."

"Damn you, Chauncey." She got to her knees on the mattress. "Play games with me and I can really fuck you."

"You just did."

She sighed. "So now you develop a clever mouth. I can arrange it so I come out smelling like roses and you end up in a penitentiary forever."

"I don't think so," Chauncey said. "You're my accomplice."

Getting mad was too much of a luxury when she was fighting for life as she knew it. "Finally you admit it. Good. Let's get the job done — together."

"It's not going to work the way you've got it figured. I don't know where Bonnie's body is, or her casket."

"That's not funny."

"No, it's surely not funny. Why would I move ahead with what we talked about and not tell you? I didn't. I was still thinking about it. The whole idea seemed crazy to me. I had Dante help me take the slab off the tomb just to see if we could do it. That was late the night before the exhumation. The casket was already gone."

TWENTY-NINE

May Lynn Charpentier's parents ran a trailer park. A double-wide at the entrance to the park housed her beauty parlor.

"How long?" Marc asked Reb, keeping the Range Rover idling out front. "I'll be back for you. Or I'll wait here, if you like."

"I'll be too long for that." She unbuckled her seat belt.

Marc caught her left hand and held it on top of his thigh. "Thank you for letting me into your life."

"I like being with you." A lump in her throat didn't help her attempt at sounding a little distant — in the interest of making sure he didn't end up feeling trapped, and that she came through with a chance for recovery if things didn't work out. That morning he'd driven her home to do her clinic, and on to make her rounds. Afterward they'd returned to Clouds End to check on Gaston. And they'd gone back to bed.

They looked directly ahead at the perfect oblong of emerald green artificial turf in front of May Lynn's. Marc's sudden shift in his seat startled Reb. He stared at her until she had to turn to him.

"Do you remember some of the things I said to you last night?" he asked. "And today?"

She looked into his somber eyes, and at the mouth she'd come to know so well. His hair was still wet from the shower they'd just taken, and there were spots of moisture on his denim shirt. He smelled clean, like the plain soap they'd used.

"Hey." He leaned closer. "What's up? Was it something I did — or didn't do?"

"No. We're moving — have moved real fast. Too fast."

His expression hardened, then he breathed through his mouth and said, "We've been working our way toward this for years."

She laughed uncomfortably. "In a way, I suppose — A to Z with most of the other letters missing in between. I'd better get in there and see if I can shake anything loose."

Marc kissed her. With his hands in her hair, he held her still and used his thumbs to frame her face. His eyes slid shut, and he kissed her until she pulled her mouth away. "It'll be a while," she said, smiling faintly at him. "I'll call you on your cell."

"Yeah."

He put the kind of hurt and disappointment in that "yeah" that was supposed to pull out whatever he wanted to hear from her. Or it could be he was in the mood again and wanted to take her back to Clouds End.

She opened the door. "Thank you for being kind to me. I've got to do something about getting a vehicle when I'm through here — and decide what to do about living arrangements."

"Call me," was all he said.

Reb slid from the car and slammed the door — just in time to catch three pairs of eyes watching her from a window. Which meant they'd seen Marc kissing her.

Without looking back, she walked along a red brick path that divided the phony grass, passed by precisely placed white tubs filled with plastic flowers, and took a step up to a covered porch where the trailer door stood open. A turquoise neon sign on the outside of the glass spelled "NEPO" from her perspective. A blues reggae number, and scents of perfumed hair products, wafted through a screen door.

She went in, and May Lynn, in floral nylon smock and black tights, rushed to dispense a hug. "You are *so* beautiful when you're happy, Doctor Reb. You are positively glowin'." She winked a blue eye. "Why, I might almost think you were in love."

"I think that's because you're in love and you imagine everyone you see is in love, too. Shall I go to the shampoo basin?"

May Lynn, naturally blond, too pale and too thin, said, "Uh huh," and felt Reb's hair. "Damp. Did you just get out of the shower?" She glanced at a cat clock with tail clicking back and forth on the wall, and Reb could almost hear her putting the kiss in the car, the time of day, and the wet hair together.

"Sure did," Reb said. Evasiveness fueled any fire. "Busy morning. It felt good to cool off."

The two girls who were May Lynn's employees sat one on either side of a nail cart. Each examined the other's hands and nails and talked loudly about having to keep up with the payments on their breast implants.

"Is the water too hot? No? Good." May Lynn used a liberal amount of shampoo that smelled like oregano and pineapple.

At first Reb kept her eyes closed, but she soon opened them and looked up at blue veins showing subtly through white skin on May Lynn's neck. A too-small, down-turned mouth made an otherwise pleasant face suggest peevishness. May Lynn caught her staring.

"When's the big day?" Reb asked quickly.

A wide smile transformed petulance. "December. I always wanted a Christmas wedding."

"You haven't had your blood work done lately. Let's do that."

May Lynn mumbled, "Yes," but without conviction. "I'm having feathers around the neck of my dress, and around the bottom of the sleeves and hem. It'll look so cute."

"You bet it will. How are you feeling about everything these days?"

"Fine," May Lynn said, too quickly. "My, you've got so much hair."

Reb had developed a sketchy idea about

trying to poke a hole in May Lynn's story about Pepper Leach. "It must have been terrifying when Pepper sneaked up on you like that. I bet you don't cross the park at night now — not on your own."

"I wasn't crossing it. He pulled me in there from the sidewalk outside."

And that was exactly the way she'd told it in court. "You've done so well, considering," Reb said. "A lot of women wouldn't have your strength. They'd go to pieces afterward. Many rape — and attempted rape — victims don't want men near them for a long time. Which is more than understandable."

"When someone loves you as much as my Jim, why, they heal all wounds. There we go. Let's put you at my station, and we'll get you a nice glass of tea."

Reb's protests that she didn't want any tea were swept aside, and May Lynn hurried into a small kitchen with swinging doors.

"We could go into Lafayette tonight, Rita," the darker haired of the two girls said. She finished removing Rita's nail polish and tossed the cotton in the trash. "We could get dressed up. Maybe we could take in a movie."

"How dressed up?" Rita asked.

"Oh —" Hands with nails almost as long as the fingers made sketchy patterns in the air. "So-so, y'know? Casual dressy. Jeans, but sequins on top."

"Yeah," Rita said. "Hey, Anne, here comes

that cute delivery guy — Craig?"

"Yum yum, he's good coming and going." Anne hopped up to peek through the window and rushed to sit again. "Check out his pecs."

The screen swung open, and a well-built man came in with a pile of boxes. He set them on the floor and checked them against his shipping documents. "I need a signature, please," he said, glancing around, apparently looking for May Lynn.

"Hi, Craig," Rita and Anne said in nasal voices, twinkling their partially painted fingernails at the man.

"Hi," he said, and May Lynn appeared to write her signature.

Craig left without a backward glance, and the screen slammed shut. May Lynn said, "The tea wasn't cold enough. I'm adding ice," and returned to the kitchen.

Reb closed her eyes and tried to put her thoughts in order. How could the world be so upside down on a beautiful day like today.

"Did you see that?" Rita said. "He didn't even look impressed we noticed him."

"Yeah. Scum. He doesn't even know we just made his day."

Reb grinned and wondered if she'd ever been *that* young.

"Get on the phone and make reminder calls, Anne," May Lynn said, arriving with the tea. "Rita, get those boxes unpacked, please, before the rush starts."

It struck Reb that May Lynn was businesslike and efficient. If she had personality anomalies, they didn't show.

"This is great. Cools the throat." The tea was too sweet.

May Lynn smiled and started combing Reb's hair through. "You have so much of this, and it's *so* curly. I think you should give a quarter of it to me. You'd still have more than enough."

This wasn't going to be easy, Reb thought. "It needs a trim but not too much off the length — you know the drill."

"I surely do. Something going on between you and Marc Girard?"

Reb couldn't stop herself from smiling. "Maybe."

"I know what that means," May Lynn said, raising a fine, almost white eyebrow.

"I'm sure you think you do. I've been having all kinds of thoughts about Bonnie Blue's death lately."

After too many seconds, May Lynn said, "Like what?"

"The whole thing about Pepper being the Rubber Killer — even though they couldn't prove he was."

"I don't follow you."

"You were blessed — you weren't killed, or raped. You got away. But you saw Pepper's face and that's how you identified him."

"Yes." May Lynn's small mouth pinched and turned way down at the corners.

"Does talking about this upset you too much?"

May Lynn shrugged. "It isn't my favorite subject, but it doesn't bother me that much. I'm strong."

"You surely are." Apparently uncannily strong physically for a woman who was underweight, anemic, and who in the past had broken bones in both feet — on different occasions — while stepping off a curb. "How did you see his face — did you say?"

"I did say. I struggled with him and pulled off the mask."

"And he ran away?"

"Yes." May Lynn took an absentminded swallow from Reb's glass. "My lawyer said he knew his crimes would come out, and that's why he tried to get away."

"But he was found at his home later that night. I admit I've been struggling with that. You know, from an academic point of view. Why would a man who had killed two women and attacked you —"

"He intended to rape and kill me."

"Or kill and rape you," Reb said, "the order isn't always the same."

May Lynn shuddered, and her eyes filled with tears. "I don't want to talk about it."

"I understand, I really do, but I've been thinking of starting a study, and Pepper might be a perfect subject for a control group."

"What kind of study."

Reb shook her head. "You don't want to

know. What kind of mask was he wearing?"

"A rubber one."

"Yes, but —" Reb took a calming breath. "What kind of mask? I guess I can't visualize it. Was it a gas-mask type of thing? That would be real scary with all that wheezy breathing."

"It was kind of like that," May Lynn said. "He breathed real loud. Everything happened so fast I didn't take notice of much but his face."

"I bet you didn't. Who would expect a thing like that to happen — and with someone you trusted. . . . So he wore a gas mask with a diving suit. Yuck. I didn't hear that. I know this is a stretch, but would there be any way Pepper could have got out and killed Bonnie?"

May Lynn gave a little shriek and sat down hard on a stool. "Doctor Reb," she said with a hand slapped over her heart, "what would make you come up with a dreadful idea like that? Bonnie wasn't murdered, she had an accident."

"I wonder if she did," Reb said. "I wonder if there were two rubber killers. But we'll never know now."

"Have they found Bonnie's body?" May Lynn said weakly.

Reb took visual inventory of the flights-of-ducks decor. She counted twelve sets tacked to pale blue walls. Each set was made of a different medium, from decoupage to painted plywood cutouts.

"Could be they won't find it. Don't you think?" May Lynn went on.

"Maybe. There's no news at all yet. Terrible thing." Reb barely stopped herself from saying it was a terrible thing for a man not to know where his sister's body was, even though she was sure it was Bonnie, not Amy who was out there, somewhere.

"We'd better move faster," May Lynn said. "That hunk of yours is still waiting out front. That's dedication for you."

THIRTY

With each pull on the oars, Precious's heart cranked up a notch. It beat in her throat and temples. She didn't have a soul she could ask for advice, so she just had to go it alone.

If she set Amy free, she couldn't trust her not to go straight to the law. Her only hope of staying out of jail — and hanging on to some respect in Toussaint — was to kill Amy and get rid of her.

Precious stopped rowing. She used a single oar to bring the rowboat about and give her a view of the house. Forlorn, that was the word for it. Left behind while the world, even in the slow bayou lands, moved on.

Amy hadn't had any luck — not once Chauncey got his hands on her. She wasn't strong like Precious, couldn't be.

She picked up the second oar and continued rowing. It was breathless again today — at least down here among trees that clawed the water and the clouds of bugs that swarmed on the surface. Even the water hyacinth needed more light than the canopy of vegetation allowed. Their flowers remained shut tight.

The stern bumped against rubber tires, cut in half and nailed to the bottom of the ladder. Precious tied up and climbed the stairs. This time she didn't bother to take the oars and lock them away. Instead she made sure the gun was loaded, and that the latex gloves were in her purse. She had a lightweight plastic coverall to make sure she wasn't splattered with blood.

Not the Rubber Killer this time, but the Plastic Killer. She didn't find her own little joke funny. She sat on the bench outside the house, thinking how she would do it and what she would do afterward. Not that she hadn't been over her plan a dozen times.

Papa would never believe she could do this. He'd taught her to respect the living and the dead. Along the way he'd taught a lot of inside stuff, some by just talking and some by working over a corpse with her handing him whatever he needed. Papa was a kind man, not that they spoke often with the way things were. He shouldn't have left Mama. She was a hard-headed woman, but she'd put him, and whatever he wanted, first.

People said her mother was tough, that she was too filled with anger against her ex-husband to have cared for him. She would have shown unhappiness if he'd meant anything to her, they said.

They saw Mama's dedication to health and fitness, and to her work for Cyrus, her absorption with helping run St. Cécil's, as a sign she might be glad her Harold was gone.

Precious looked at the gun in her hand. She could use it, oh my yes. Chauncey had taught her how for self-defense. There was plenty of room to drop the gun into the purse, too.

She unlocked the door and went inside. The windows were open. That surprised her because she'd kept them locked. But that was before she'd unshackled Amy and given her the run of the house. The place had been cleaned up, the groceries put away, and a glass jug held twigs and branches Amy must have torn from over-hanging branches. The door to the bedroom was slightly open. Precious walked quietly to look through the crack. Amy was in bed, curled on her side and facing the wall.

"Let her sleep," Precious murmured and made a soft-footed tour of the small place. Even the bathroom had been thoroughly cleaned and smelled of bleach.

Amy had believed her. She had worked away here and waited for Precious to come and set her free.

When she'd had her tabby cat — "Tickles," for his long whiskers that tickled — Precious had protected him from any danger. She'd treated Tickles as if he had been a person and when he died, at nineteen and in his sleep, she'd mourned his loss. Why, she'd cried until she couldn't open her eyes because she couldn't bear to see that little body not moving.

She locked herself into the bathroom and

took what she needed from her purse. Should she take off her clothes, just for extra insurance? Not that Amy was going to be found.

There was no way to hide blood from anything but the naked eye, and even making sure it couldn't be seen without police methods would take too long. She had to expect this place to be found, and it mustn't be connected to her. The sale had been cash in hand, but even though they'd never known her name and no legal papers had been filed, if luck went against her, the couple could pick her out. Finding them might not be easy, but she'd have to do it.

No. No, she couldn't do it. She was a God-fearing woman who believed a person could be saved, even if they'd done some bad things — but not the kind of bad things she was thinking about.

She turned cold, but sweat ran down her back. Her arms and legs ached, and her head. Crying wouldn't be useful, but she'd surely like to bawl.

Quickly, she packed the gun inside the plastic coverall and stowed it in the bottom of her bag with the gloves. The problem of the tape recorder still bugged her. She hadn't known why she was told to tape it in Reb's office, but she'd made an appointment and done it while she was getting dressed. Now she was supposed to retrieve it. What was that all about? She had too much on her mind.

When she went to Amy, control would be everything. She would make helping the other woman a way to atone. Father Cyrus would like that when she told him, even though he'd be so shocked behind his handsome, impassive Reconciliation face. How many Hail Marys would she get for this one? She was lucky it wasn't Christmas. He'd probably tell her to decorate the church.

It was time. She was ready, and warmth seeped back into her limbs. Tears sprang into her eyes, but they were relieved tears, maybe even happy ones, because she had broken free of her own hatefulness.

Carrying her purse because she wanted to make sure Amy never knew what might have happened, she went to the bedroom and pushed the door slowly open. "Amy?" The covers were pulled up so only her hair showed. "Amy, wake up. We've got to go."

No response. Precious felt a new charge of wariness. It took all the courage she had to go closer. Amy wasn't breathing.

"Oh my god." Precious put a hand on the woman's shoulder and pulled.

Her own scream shook Precious's brains and sent her falling into a chair. "No, no, no." She buried her face in her hands and shook her head over and over again.

When she could stand, she rushed from the room and out onto the gallery with tears streaming now.

She'd finally decided to do something good,

but she'd been too late. Amy had lost her nerve. She'd cut her own hair and tucked it under the covers to help turn the hidden pillows into a real enough "body." She hadn't trusted Precious, and the gators or whatever else likely got her had seemed like better friends.

Precious sat on the bench again, holding her purse to her chest and looking out through blurred eyes.

A rowboat, her rowboat, rested at the far shore. A lone figure stood beside it, waving at Precious. *Amy.*

THIRTY-ONE

Gaston lay between them in Marc's bed. After a couple of hours, during which he'd stared at shadows on the ceiling, Marc had given up on being cool with Reb choosing the guest room for the night and had gone to find out if she was asleep.

She wasn't. Gaston was.

Marc had picked up the dog, who awoke too dazed to do more than give a sloppy grin, and thrown the covers off Reb. When she tried to turn away from him, he hauled her out, too, and wrapped an arm around her. She didn't complain, just let him take her to his bed — where wily old AP had planted himself as a barrier to passion. Not that any passion had been in the offing as far as Marc could see.

He was still awake, and now Reb was asleep. Now there was justice. He'd told her he loved her, tried to show it the best way he knew how — and how was she taking all this? By getting mad when he said he'd buy her a safe car and that her home was with him until she could safely return to Conch Street. What had been wrong with any of that?

Once more he left the bed and wandered down the hall to the bare room where he'd had his computers installed. All he had to do was tap the mouse and he was looking at a multidimensional graphic of a room beneath a basement, reached by way of a door to a wine cellar and a sliding panel on the back wall. The clients would be storing furs down there, which meant there was to be a cooling unit. Marc enjoyed the quirky bits. The safe would be elsewhere.

He moved to another screen. Why did people always want the safe in their bedroom? They just had to be close to the jewels, he guessed.

"Marc."

Reb's voice broke in like a gunshot, and he straightened up fast. "I thought you were asleep."

"Whether or not I'm asleep isn't the issue. You need to go back to New Orleans. Back to work. I can tell that's what you're aching to do. Don't hang around here because you think you owe it to me."

He sniffed, and rubbed the space between his brows. And he screwed up his eyes. "Come again."

"You heard. And you need your rest; you've got a lot on your mind. There's stuff happening, and we both need to be alert."

Marc didn't point out that each thing she said was contradictory. Her sleep wasn't the issue, yet *they* needed to be alert. He should go back to New Orleans, to work, but she went on to talk about everything that was going down in Toussaint. "I told you I can deal with company issues from anywhere, and it sure as hell doesn't matter a hill o' beans where I park myself to do this stuff." He flicked a hand toward a computer. "I didn't make that up. My most important unfinished business is right here, and it's serious."

"You didn't really say if you thought there was anything significant in what May Lynn said."

He leaned against a desk and crossed his ankles. Breeze from the fans felt good on his bare skin. He'd like to take off his shorts but thought better of it.

"Marc?" Reb wore a utilitarian, brushed-looking nightshirt and managed to look like the sexiest thing he'd ever seen.

She crossed her arms under her breasts and glared at him. "Concentrate."

"I am." He was, indeed. "What I think is that we have to see Pepper Leach. Sure, you heard a few contradictory words, but if he's innocent and just sitting there and taking it, the big question is why? It's also time to bring Cyrus up to date. He knows Pepper, doesn't he?"

Reb eyed him suspiciously. "You want to bring Cyrus up to date — or you want to grill him about a parishioner? Pepper went to Mass regularly."

"Both. He's got the kind of insight into people that's beyond most of us." He got another evil eye and hastily added, "Although in your profession you've got to be in tune with the person as well as the body."

"We meet with Cyrus," she said and turned on her heel, arms still crossed. "And whether you like it or not, we should pull Spike in — when the time is right. He may seem quiet. He doesn't show much emotion, but he's smart. Anyway, we could need him to help us see Pepper. We bought his support by turning over Bonnie's purse. Now he owes us one. I hope Wally won't suffer for taking so long to hand that bag over."

She left the room, and Marc scratched his head. He was thinking of using Cyrus and should be reprimanded. But Reb planning to use Spike was just fine.

Back into the room she came, the big frown still in place. She took him by the wrist, and he let her drag him toward his bed. After all, sometimes a man had to give the little woman her own way.

Somewhere along the hall progress paused and he lost his shorts. That funny-looking nightshirt didn't feel so funny. The inside was silk and slipped over her skin like a hot, wet knife over frosting.

"My turn," she said, and took him. He had a vague notion to mention that this wasn't the first time she'd taken the lead — but vague notions didn't stick around.

THIRTY-TWO

On the way to Robertsville, Cyrus didn't utter a word. He'd said his piece when Reb and Marc told him what they intended to do — with Spike's help and blessing — and he told them, without inflection, that a man had to take the course he chose. If Pepper had wanted to say anything useful — useful to his own case — he'd have said it in court. His lawyer had given up because Pepper hadn't disputed any accusation May Lynn aimed at him. He'd neither admitted nor denied the two murders, and they hadn't been able to pin them on him, but he got the stiffest sentence his crime allowed. If he wasn't the Rubber Killer, the real culprit had taken a hike — maybe.

At the prison a guard told them where to park. It was dark, and they'd been informed that the governor was only doing this for Cyrus, who ministered to the prisoners at Robertsville, and it would be easier to allow the visit at night, when things were quieter.

Marc pulled into the slot and switched off the engine. Reb settled her sneakers on the dashboard and picked at signs of wear in her jeans.

"Spike doesn't think there's any harm in this," she said, for Cyrus's ears. "Mostly because he believes Pepper won't say anything different from what he's said all along. Pepper is settled into a routine, and he isn't complaining. He works in the kitchen and doesn't make any trouble. He's every prison guard's dream inmate."

Nothing from Cyrus.

"She's right," Marc said. "He reads, doesn't watch television, and writes to his grandmother every week."

"She brought him up," Cyrus said quietly. "A wonderful woman carrying a heavy burden. Hasn't left her house since her grandson was convicted, not even to visit him. She sends him cards — inspirational cards and books — but she can't bear to see him here."

Reb met Marc's glance, not so easy to do in Cyrus's presence. Every look told the story of what was happening between them, but this one showed something else: neither of them held out much hope of getting anything new from Pepper Leach.

Darkness in swampy places, with mist fingering its way around any obstacle in its path, had no beginning and no end. There wasn't a frame, a border, not even looking out through a window — just a slowly incessant shifting, sultry and unfriendly.

How many times had she almost called

Chauncey? Precious had lost count. She was afraid of him. He hadn't killed Amy — yet — but he might as well have. Now he was really desperate to keep his ex-lover from revealing all she knew about him. This time he wouldn't tell Precious not to worry about the damage she'd done because Chauncey would take care of everything for her. She knew how violent he could be.

There wasn't anyone else.

She couldn't friggin' well believe it. Amy, sick, weak Amy, had made a fool of the bleeding heart. Well, no more Mrs. Nice Depew. Payback time would roll around, and when she got the woman again, there'd be no backing off from what had to be done.

Shit, she had to get to shore before the bitch sent someone to find her, or worse, not just to find her but to kill her.

Swimming was the only choice, but she wasn't trying it at night. Thinking of what was in and under that lime green sludge turned her stomach. At least she had real good eyes. She'd need them to watch for whatever moved. She'd wait until early afternoon, when critters became less anxious to fill and refill their bellies and more interested in finding a cool spot to take a nap.

The sound that reached her announced either salvation or a death knell. Oars cranking in rowlocks and the soft slip of water around a rowboat hull. She stood to one side of a window and peered out. There was her boat, getting close. Whoever was rowing hadn't had much experience, if any, and pathetic splashes sent choppy spray into the air. A light in the boat shone toward the far shore — like that was the way it was supposed to be heading.

Finally the agonizing progress stopped, and she heard thumps on rubber.

"Precious, where are ya?"

She stared and didn't know whether to respond or pretend not to be there.

"Hey, it's me, Dante. I'm comin' up and in, sweets."

Sweets? This was unbelievable. Even if he didn't know Amy had got away, with Precious stranded in the cabin it was obvious someone had stolen her boat. She drew her gun, turned her bamboo chair to face the door, and waited.

Pepper Leach faced the three of them through heavy glass. He kept his eyes downcast and took a long time to pick up the phone on his side.

"Hi, Pepper," Cyrus said. "Doctor Reb wanted to come with me tonight and this is —"

"Marc Girard," Pepper said, glancing up and smiling slightly. "It's been a long time. You look great." He spoke in a soft voice.

Reb waited for Marc to respond. Finally he said, "You don't look too bad considering."

Pepper focused the full force of slate gray eyes on Marc. "Considering what? This isn't such a bad place to be."

"Better than painting in your studio?" Reb asked. "Are you painting here at all?"

Another silence went on long enough to have them all shuffling their feet.

"If you need paints," Cyrus said, "I'll ask the warden if I can bring them in. Madge paints occasionally; she'd like to get you some supplies."

Pepper shook his head. "Thanks, but I've got what I'm allowed to have. Charcoal and paper — it's good, I'm getting a lot done. Learning a lot."

The man was startling to look at. He was a little more than average height and well-conditioned, with a face that was all angles, eyes and brows sweeping up some, a cleft in his sharp jaw, and high cheekbones. Reb knew there was no particular way for a killer to look, but Pepper seemed a most unlikely candidate. Quiet, handsome, articulate, and artistic. Surely that didn't add up to him setting out to molest May Lynn.

"We're here to see if you can help us," Marc said. "No pressure, though. Just say the word and we're out of here."

"It's good to have company, but there won't be anything I can do to help you."

The answer came too quickly, Reb thought. She deliberately avoided looking at Cyrus or Marc. Pepper leaned his ear on the phone and studied the counter in front of him.

"Pepper," Cyrus said. "You know I'll be glad to talk to you on your own, don't you?"

"I was going to send word to ask you to come," the man said. He turned up the corners of his mouth. "You beat me to it. Soon you'll come back, will you?"

"Yes," Cyrus agreed at once.

A guard shifted his weight from leg to leg. He leaned on the wall behind Pepper, not far enough away for it to be impossible to hear if he wanted to.

"I saw May Lynn yesterday," Reb said. Trying to creep up on the subject wouldn't achieve a thing. Pepper was too smart.

For the briefest instant his nostrils flared and muscles in his jaw flickered. But the reaction was over quickly enough for Reb to wonder if she'd been the only one to notice.

"She's getting married in December," Reb said, knowing she was pushing her luck.

Pepper looked into her eyes. The man talked a good line, but he was miserable, desperate even. Badly shaken, she stared back but was the first to glance away. Marc watched Reb speculatively. He was too in sync with her now, as if he felt what she was feeling at the same time.

"I visited your grandmother," Cyrus said. "What a lady."

"How is she?" Pepper moved forward in his chair. "Did she say anythin'?"

A silence followed. Reb figured if she could see her own face as well as Cyrus's and Marc's, they'd all show how unexpected the latter question was.

"I didn't go in," Cyrus told the man. "She was busy."

Pepper made a fist with his free hand.

"She looks just fine," Cyrus added hurriedly.

"I was out to see her, too," Reb said, filling her expression with reassurance.

"Why?" Pepper broke a sweat on his upper lip. "She's sick, isn't she? Her heart . . . That's why you came to —"

"*No*, no, as far as I know her heart condition is stable. I went out to visit, that's all."

"Because she doesn't get out anymore," Pepper said. "And you wanted to make sure she hadn't died in her own house. Maybe some neighbor she won't see or talk to called you because they were worried. Was that it?"

"No it wasn't."

"Did she let you in?"

Mentioning seeing Joanie Leach hadn't been a good idea. "I couldn't stop, because —"

"Don't lie. Lyin' doesn't come easy to you, Reb, never did. Gramma wouldn't have you in because . . ." He sat back in his chair and raised his face to the ceiling.

"Because?" Cyrus asked gently.

"She doesn't even go to Mass, does she?"

A shake of the head from Father Cyrus was an unlikely response to such a question. He took a breath and said, "It isn't my place to talk about one of my parishioner's habits."

"I'm her only relative."

Cyrus jingled keys in his pocket. The guard came to attention and moved forward. Once he saw what had caused the noise he went back to lounging against the wall.

"Maybe we can talk more about all this when I come on my own."

"I didn't save her," Pepper muttered.

The air grew absolutely still. Reb wanted, so badly, to ask Pepper what he'd been trying to save his grandmother from. The others had to be longing to do the same thing.

"She's not taking Communion," Pepper said. "I never did have a way to ask her myself. On her cards — she sends one each week — but she doesn't mention getting any mail from me. I write regularly but don't think she reads it." He bowed his face. "I shamed her, anyway. I couldn't shame her again, could I?"

Marc said, "You'd never deliberately hurt Mrs. Leach."

"She thinks you're the best grandson a woman ever had," Cyrus added. He appeared to consider before saying, "In a way she's grieving. That's because she loves you so much."

Reb knew the questions she wanted to ask, if only she could do so without causing more damage.

To her surprise, Marc said, "I think you should paint again. You took too much heat for not wanting to do anything else — when you were a teenager. Why stop now?"

Pepper shook his head.

"The guys picked on you because you were quiet, especially the jocks. You just walked right through 'em. I admired you for that."

"You weren't around with the rest of the

rabble," Pepper said, but there was no bitterness in him. "There was a lot you didn't see. Forget it, please."

Cyrus scraped his metal chair closer to the glass. "If Marc agrees, I'd like to have him go with me to talk about the painting supplies —"

"Don't."

"Sure," Marc said, already on his feet. "If you don't want them, Pepper, don't use them, but we'll ask permission anyway."

"Keep him company till we get back," Cyrus said to Reb with a smile that was too innocent.

"I don't want to attract any attention," Pepper muttered. "If a man like me has any sense, he tries not to stand out around here."

Cyrus and Marc didn't hear. They were at the door, and when they'd been let out of the room, Pepper said, "I think you just got set up."

Reb raised her eyebrows. "Looks that way, only I don't know why. Could be they really think I shouldn't be there while they do this."

"There's nothing I can say to you that I can't say to them," Pepper told her. "It's nice of you to come, though. Why did you? Come?"

He had an honest face.

What kind of thought was that? Not scientific, that was for sure. "I'm not sure," she told him. "You've been on my mind."

The ceiling was high, high enough to put two floors in there. Everything white. What was that for? Pipes running everywhere, also painted white. If she looked at the place through slitted eyes it would be surreal. Albino and angular, with the only colors being in the breathing things: one guard, one prisoner, one doctor who didn't lie well.

"Cyrus and Marc? I've been on their minds, too?"

"Yes."

"So the three of you decided you'd get together for a humanitarian outreach." He sighed. "I'd take that and be happy, but I don't think it's the truth, do you?"

"No. I don't and it isn't." She indicated the guard behind him. "Does he listen to what we say?"

"I don't know. Probably."

"How do we check it out?"

Pepper blinked repeatedly. "We don't have to worry tonight," he said. "The guard — the one behind me — he's on 'H' deals inside. Everyone knows. He knows he has to stay on our good sides so we don't say anything."

She checked the man. He showed no sign of hearing a word. "Okay, so he can't hear. What about the telephone? Is it bugged?"

"Who knows? You plannin' to break me out, you?" Pepper laughed. "What do we have to say that the whole world can't hear?"

"You never did confess to killing the first two women," she said. "And they found no absolute proof it was you. Was it?"

"I'm here, aren't I?"

"For attempting to rape and murder May

Lynn, not for murder. They couldn't prove —"

"Leave this alone," Pepper said. "You can only cause trouble."

"I don't understand that attitude. Why didn't you do everything . . . no, why didn't you do *anything* to defend yourself?"

He took the phone from his ear. The only power he had was over whether or not he chose to talk to her, or to anyone on the outside.

Reb pointed at him and tapped her ear. Reluctantly he lifted the receiver again. "Will you hear me out, please? Let me talk. If you don't want to respond, that's your choice."

Pepper nodded.

"I don't believe May Lynn. I don't believe you dragged her into the park and tried to rape her, or that you intended to kill her."

His expression became fixed.

"Her story's so simple, but there are little things. Why would you go home afterward — to your grandmother's house — and wait for them to come for you? What did you do with the wetsuit?" She took a deep breath.

"Rubber can be burned," he pointed out.

"So they said. It stinks and makes a big mess. Where did you burn it? You didn't, did you?"

"No."

She thought about Bonnie's purse before she said, "Do you know how hard it is to get rid of something without trace? There was never a lead on what you did with it. Did you give it to someone else? To your grandmother?"

"No, dammit. You know my gramma, she'd never . . . I'm listenin' because I was brought up to be polite."

"Thank you. But you won't tell me what you did with the suit and the gas mask?"

"Dive mask. No."

"May Lynn called it a gas mask. If it wasn't you, it was someone else, and he's still out there. Eventually he'll kill again. It'll exonerate you, but it won't help his victims."

"We've talked enough." With the phone still to his ear, he stood up.

She was losing him. "Pepper, this is between you and me. If you don't want me to say anything, I won't. You didn't do what May Lynn said, did you?"

He closed his eyes.

"You didn't even see her that night."

"I saw her." Pepper looked straight at her.

"But it wasn't the way she said."

His eyes lost focus, and his throat moved sharply when he swallowed. "It doesn't matter. Not anymore. I've used up any courage I had."

Dante's shoes squeaked on the gallery boards. "Precious? Hey, Precious? You here?"

She raised the gun. "I'm here," she called. He knew she was, why else would he be here? Chauncey had given him the money to get his glasses prescription updated and had loosened up enough to let Dante drive one of his own cars, a pickup with a canopy. And he'd found her. That had to be beginner's luck accident.

So what was taking him so long? "What's keepin' you? You fall in or somethin'?"

He knocked on the door. "I don't want you mad at me, sugar. I only did what I was told to do."

"Get in here."

He came, opened the door, and poked his head inside — saw her gun and made to withdraw, only he shut the door before he was all the way out and slammed his head into the jamb. The large, black-framed glasses fell to the floor.

"For god's sake, Dante. I'm just bein' cautious, like I've been taught. Come *on*."

"I've hurt my head."

Why was it her lot to be surrounded by fools? "I'm sorry. Get in here and sit down." This was the man who held her future in his hands.

Dante picked up his glasses, repeatedly looking at her gun while he did so. "Chauncey ain't gonna be a happy man," he said.

"It wasn't my fault," Precious snapped, and closed her mouth. They might not be talking about the same thing, and she'd learned the evils of loose lips a long time ago.

"It ain't mine, neither." Dante sat in a chair facing Precious. He turned his head one way and the other, checking the cabin out. "You scratch my back and I'll scratch yours. Ain't that the way it goes? With two of us telling the same story, we're in the clear."

Precious shifted uncomfortably. So he could

tell Amy wasn't here and felt scared in case Chauncey blamed him for letting her get away. "You were too late is all," she told him, averting her eyes from the owl glasses that no longer sat straight on his nose. "How could you know what she'd do, any more than I did?"

Dante had found a handkerchief to mop his brow. "Thanks, Precious. You are one straight-up person."

"Thank you." Amy would be wandering now, trying to find a safe place to hide. A new and horrifying thought struck. "Did you check in the boathouse? Was my Honda still there?"

"Yeah. I followed you as far as that place where you leave the Jag. Almost missed you when you left in the Honda. It's still there — with the keys in it."

She would not be defensive of her actions. "Yessir, I believe in being ready to roll. So you just got here?"

"Hour and a half ago." He pushed his glasses back up his nose.

That was before . . . "You couldn't have."

"Did. That's what Chauncey said I should do. Wait in the boathouse and give you a chance to get over there. I hid my wheels and sat in your Honda."

"Chauncey doesn't know . . . You called and told him you'd found this place? You told him?" Of course he had. "I don't hold it against you. I'd have done the same in your shoes."

"Wish I hadn't," Dante said. "The way I

411

figure it, we gotta move fast, and talk fast. We need a story."

Precious stared at him. "What do you think Amy did?"

"Got away from you," he said promptly. "Fooled you and made it to the boat without you knowing. She must have got to the other side before you knew you'd lost her or you'd have tried to shoot her. I didn't hear no shots."

"Oh my. Oh lordy." She had to try to think straight. "You were in the boathouse when Amy got over there?"

"Yeah. Thought it was you coming. Kept on calling, and when you didn't answer, I thought you'd decided to give me a nice surprise. Jump me, maybe."

"Jump you?"

"Wouldn't be the first time." He leered at her. "Why else wouldn't you say nothing? I got ready and waited in the car where you wouldn't see me. I was going to give you a surprise, sweets. Heard you come in and, boy, was I ready for you. Only it wasn't you, it was Amy."

"You've killed her." A stony hardness blocked her throat. "Just like I keep on reminding myself, that woman never did have any luck. Chauncey won't be mad. He'll pin medals on you."

"I couldn't get to my gun," Dante said, turning a dull shade of puce. "It was under my clothes and I was lying on them. She grabbed the Honda keys and whipped out of there."

The picture he painted would be real funny if her life wasn't on the line. "But you caught her." Mad replaced sad. "After all I did for her, she tried to take advantage of me."

"I didn't have no clothes on."

"Uh huh." She wasn't going to like any of this. "So?"

"By the time I got my clothes on — thanks be I didn't take my shoes off — well, by the time I was out of there, I couldn't see a thing 'cause it was dark."

Precious held up a single finger. "Shush, you. You said my Honda *was* there. She tricked you and got it after all, didn't she? Shee-it, she's got too big a lead on us. She could be anywhere by now. Come *on*, Dante. We'll think of what we'll say to Chauncey while we drive."

"Can't do that," he said, drawing himself up. "The Honda's still there — without the keys. She stole my truck. I left my keys in it so I'd be ready to roll. Guess we think alike."

THIRTY-THREE

Cyrus pushed open the Pepto-Bismol pink door at All Tarted Up and walked into the crowded, almost silent shop. What he felt in the warm, fragrant bakery was anger and suspicion. Even Jilly Gable's cheerful patter wasn't relaxing the atmosphere.

The problem was Marc, who sat at a table with Madge. Cyrus decided he'd better take the other man aside and explain how the folks in Toussaint didn't change their minds easily and that his glowering presence would only make them more convinced he was the enemy.

"Madge," Jilly called. "You two only want the coffees? Nothing to eat? A poppyseed and date muffin? How about you, Marc? You had breakfast?"

"No," Marc said. He had already gotten to his feet. "Two of those as well, please."

Marc was too busy simmering — apparently at closed-faced customers waiting to be served — to notice it was Cyrus who had made the shop bell jangle. From her seat at the table, Madge saw Cyrus and smiled, and the next deep breath Cyrus took relaxed him. Madge was sanity in the midst of madness. Kidnapped and treated roughly enough to leave scratches on her neck, arms, and hands, she'd been in shock for several hours but made very little fuss and brushed any concern aside. He was a lucky man to know her and have her as his right hand.

"Don't you work for me?" Marc demanded of a man who got to the head of the line and picked up a bag with what must be his name written on it.

"I'm with LeadWorks, me," the fellow said, flushing all the way through his fine sandy-colored hair. "Working on the conservatory at Clouds End, Mr. Girard."

Marc frowned, and Cyrus waited for him to explode. Instead he said, "I thought so. Good morning to you."

The man muttered, "Good morning," and scuttled from the shop.

"All right," Jilly Gable said. Her coffee-gold skin glowed, and her clever, light hazel eyes filled with amusement. "This is a lovely morning. I'm glad to be alive; how about all of you?"

A low wave of assenting noises came from the dozen or so customers in line.

"Good," Jilly said. "How many of you have met Marc Girard? Clouds End belongs to his family. So does this shop — or the property it's on — and a lot of shops and businesses in Toussaint. Marc's come home to do up the old house and to check on the Girard holdings. Now I think it's just wonderful of him to deal with that in person, and I want to thank him right now. Thank you, Marc."

Marc picked up two coffee mugs with one hand and a plate of muffins with the other. He said, "Thank *you*," and went to the table he was sharing with Madge.

At 7:30 on a weekday morning Jilly's customers were mostly on their way to work. Heavy-eyed and not moving too fast, they responded to Jilly's cheery grin with sullen faces. Marc and Madge got frequent hostile glances.

Zeb Dalcour, who managed the ice plant, walked toward the door, saw Cyrus, and stopped. He was built like a small bull, and his big neck turned red above the open neck of his check shirt. "We goin' to the dogs, Father Cyrus," he said. "It's all over town that Doctor Reb is staying out at that house with Girard. He's a bad man, him. People around here don't forget. When he was a boy he was a troublemaker."

"I don't think so," Cyrus said, disturbed that the gossip mill had turned to complete fabrication. "I've never heard anything about that before."

Zeb squashed a bag of pastries into one of the pockets in his loose overalls. "Cletus knows."

Cyrus looked past Zeb at the slightly steamed-up glass cases of baked goodies. The bright yellow walls inside the shop were shiny, filmed with warm moisture. "Cletus?" Cyrus said when he trusted himself to be careful of what he said. "Cletus who's worked for the

416

Girards for years and who lives at Clouds End? I didn't know the two of you were close friends."

Zeb shook his big head. "He don't tell me, but he talks to all them workmen out there, and they talk to everyone else. Whole town knows those two are as good as shacking up. And Reb the town doc. Carryin' on around that place 'cause they think Cletus is nothin' and they all on their own."

"That'll do," Cyrus said, doing up the top button on the black suit jacket that already felt like a straightjacket and would soon be too hot.

"It's a rightful thing to see the priest in his collar," Zeb said, apparently deciding to cover whatever displeased him all at once. "There's not enough respect for tradition anymore."

Cyrus looked the man in the eye and said, "About Marc. I'm sure you forgot you were talking about things you don't know for sure, things that you wouldn't want to spread around in any case."

"That man's a bad influence on Doctor Reb. Before he arrived she never had a wicked thought."

"And what sort of wicked thoughts is she having now?"

Zeb puckered up plump lips and frowned. He wouldn't meet Cyrus's eyes. "You know," he said. "Carnal stuff. That girl didn't know about any of that. It's him curruptin' her."

"Zeb," Cyrus said. "Reb is not being corrupted by anyone. She's also a medical doctor and she knows *all* of that stuff. That reminds me. I don't think I've seen you at Mass for a few weeks. Wouldn't want you to miss the posters in the hall about this being prostate health month. Make sure you get yourself to Reb for an exam. Hey, Madge and Marc," he said with a nod to Zeb before he left him to sputter alone.

He sat beside Madge. "Stirring up trouble again," he said to Marc. "You are one mean man. Pickin' on all the nice people of Toussaint. How much are you raising the rents, anyway?"

"An early-morning clown," Marc said, grimacing. "Just what we need around here."

"You need something around here," Cyrus said. "How many tenants have you evicted so far?"

"Stop it," Madge said, sticking an elbow into his side. "Sometimes you aren't very priestly."

"It's my job to look after my flock, and that includes making sure they're in good spirits."

"I don't recall seeing you in here," Marc said. "Not that I've been in more than a couple of times."

"Madge and I arranged to meet here," he said, raising a brow at her. "I come in from time to time. Wally likes it if we visit Jilly and Joe."

"She's something," Marc said, indicating Jilly. "I don't remember her from before, but she's younger. She looks . . . I don't know."

"Quadroon," Cyrus told him. "Exotic. She and Joe have the same white father, but Jilly's mom was part white and part African American. Joe complains because he says Jilly gets all the admiring stares."

"Yeah." Marc lost interest. "What was the guy from the ice plant saying to you?"

"Nothing I can share," Cyrus told him.

"Coffee for you, Cyrus?" Jilly shouted from behind the counter.

"Yes, please. And one of these muffins." He pointed to the ones Madge and Marc had. "How come you're in town so early, Marc? Does Reb have early clinic?"

Marc picked up his mug and slopped coffee. "Shit," he said. "I mean, darn. Reb's got her own wheels. For the moment."

Cyrus looked at Madge, who raised her eyes toward a star-shaped paper lantern hanging over the table.

"Chauncey Depew showed up with one of those Beetles, or Bugs. Like Jilly's, only red. Said Reb's bike was brought to him and while it was being fixed she should use the car. That bike can't be fixed. It needs to be scrapped."

"Nice of Chauncey, though," Cyrus said. Marc had every reason to despise Precious's husband, but some things were better relegated to the past.

"He made sure to say how public-spirited he was being," Marc said. "Reb's the local doctor, so lending her a car is doing something good for the town."

"Well, it is." Cyrus smiled at Jilly when she brought the coffee and muffin.

"She doesn't need anything from him," Marc said, catching Cyrus's knowing eye. "Mainly I don't want her driving around on her own. Not until —" He glanced at Madge and down into his coffee.

Cyrus dropped his voice. "Madge doesn't want to be babied. And she already knows what's going on — don't forget what she's just been though. You were going to say you don't want Reb driving around on her own until we're sure we don't have a murderer on the loose."

"But we do," Madge said, her face giving nothing of her feelings away. "You know it. I know it. Spike knows it, and so does Reb. Most of the people in this town are on edge. I wasn't grabbed outside Reb's house for nothing."

Cyrus caught hold of her hand.

"Don't say it," Marc said softly. "I know what you're thinking, Cyrus. The only explanation I can come up with for his not going through with it is that when he found out he had the wrong woman, he decided killing and disposing of her was too much trouble."

"But I wasn't to say that, hm?" Cyrus said. The thought that Madge might have been killed sickened him. So did the idea that if it had been Reb who was snatched outside her house that night, she would be dead. "Madge, you wanted to talk to me? Do we need privacy?"

"No. I didn't think we should do it at the rectory is all. I'm worried about Oribel. I think she knows the Fuglies aren't bringing everyone

quite the joy she expected. She's unhappy —
probably depressed. You said that thing wasn't
cheap, Marc. She must have saved for it for
years."

Cyrus took a knife to his muffin and carefully
dissected it into soft squares. "I told her I appreciated the gift."

"She's sensitive," Madge told him.

"And she's got horrible taste," Marc said.

Cyrus shot him a reproachful look. "Sometimes we have to tolerate things we don't like.
I'll be subtle, but I'll find a way to make her
happy about it."

Madge sighed. "Of course you will, but that's
only part of it. Oribel and William are spending
time together."

Cyrus felt disoriented. "Oribel and William?
Our William?"

"I should have said William hangs around
Oribel, and she doesn't tell him to go back to
work. He watches her all the time, and she goes
all flustery. I think he's fallen for her and she
may be falling for him."

"That's not possible," Cyrus said. He pointed
to Madge's coffee. "Drink some more of that.
You're not fully awake."

"Unusual match," Marc said. "But she did
send for him the night Reb and I had our brush
with the mad driver. Seemed as if he was the
first one she thought of."

"William's reliable," Madge said. "Whatever
he does, he does well. But what worries me is

that Oribel may be turning to him because she's lonely. I know I shouldn't make judgments, but it couldn't work, could it?"

There were times, many of them, when carrying the burden of expectations others placed upon a priest became too heavy. "We don't know everything about either of them. Oribel has a lot to give — even if she does like to pretend she doesn't need anyone. And William, well, William is strong."

Marc chuckled. "Yeah, maybe Oribel's responding to the animal magnetism."

"That's not funny," Madge told him. "Oribel's spent her life looking after other people. And some of them let her down badly. Maybe now she wants someone to look after her, and she's turning to the first person who comes along."

"Change the subject," Cyrus murmured. Oribel coasted her bike to a stop outside and leaned it against the shop window.

Wearing a sweatsuit, she bustled in, her face glowing.

"Must have been at the gym again," Madge said. "She makes me feel guilty."

Oribel saw them and smiled. "I've come for the rectory order," she told Jilly, and marched over to stand beside Cyrus. "This is good for you, Father. I've been telling you for years to get out in the morning and breathe the good air before it gets too warm. It'll do wonders for you." She nodded cheerfully at Madge, and even at

Marc. "Guess we're expecting a roasting for a couple of days."

"You're right," Cyrus told her. Why did he feel anxious because Oribel didn't seem herself? Love made people different, everyone knew that. But William lived in a decrepit house on stilts in a swampy area of the bayou and had two lazy brothers and a wild daughter — and they all ate whatever they caught, in the water or elsewhere.

Cyrus cleared his throat and said, "We were just talking about your generous gift to the parish. I must thank you again. It's becoming an institution already."

He caught sight of Reb getting out of a red car and walking toward All Tarted Up and was glad to change the subject quickly. "This is a popular place this morning," he said.

Marc turned around and saw Reb, and the transformation of his expression to frank pleasure wasn't subtle. The man had a bad case. When she came in, she walked directly to him as if he were alone in the shop, pausing only to plant a kiss on Cyrus's cheek in passing.

"Your order," Jilly said, plopping a large pastry box on the table in front of Oribel. "Joe's going to be furious he missed being here with all of you."

"We are pretty irresistible," Madge commented.

Oribel checked the goodies inside her box and asked Jilly for tape to seal it down again. "Better get back," she said.

"Won't you have some coffee?" Jilly asked.

Oribel allowed herself to be persuaded, and Marc helped Cyrus push two tables together.

"What's the matter with you, Doctor Reb?" Oribel asked when she was settled. "You don't look so hot."

"I'm fine."

"No, you're not. How would you like it if I came to see you with a long face and told you I was fine?"

Reb smiled faintly. "That would be different." She looked from face to face. "Okay, it wouldn't be that different. I'll tell you why I'm not my usual chirpy self. I'm starting to wonder if we'll ever get to the bottom of what's going on in this town. And I worry something awful will happen again if we don't."

Marc put an arm around her shoulders, and she didn't resist when he pulled her head against his shoulder.

"Do you think if we tried to forget the whole thing it would go away?" Madge asked.

"It might seem to," Marc said. "But it wouldn't really. And it wouldn't be fair, anyway."

"Why?" Oribel asked.

Cyrus looked around the circle of people he liked and trusted and said, "Because it could be that someone is suffering for something they didn't do."

All eyes were upon him, and he quickly added, "We shouldn't say anything more. It could be dangerous." The shop was almost empty, but cu-

424

riosity was an art form in Toussaint.

Reb straightened away from Marc. "We need a break. We need someone to open up and be honest with us."

She meant Pepper Leach, Cyrus decided, and he agreed with her. Then there was May Lynn, who was not saying everything she knew.

From a side pocket in her bag, Reb removed a folded sheet and flattened it on the table. "I'm not supposed to have this, but for some reason I wanted to make it — and keep it."

A photocopy, not good quality, showed what appeared to be a man facing away from a camera with a baby in his arms and peeking over his shoulder. The picture was too dark, and there was a grid of jagged white lines on it, as if the original photograph had been torn up and taped together again. Cyrus turned the paper so he could see the picture. He ran a fingernail along one of the tear lines. He felt the shadow of violence, and it chilled him. There was something familiar about the shot, yet he didn't recall seeing it before.

"Bonnie had the photo in her pocket when she died," Reb said. "She'd stuck it back into one piece with tape. Or someone had. I felt it was very important to her. I wish it gave a clue to her story."

Marc leaned over the table to look, but shook his head.

Oribel made a choking sound and hid her face.

"It just wasn't fair," Madge said. "What happened to Bonnie. She was getting on her feet and then that. Not fair."

"You took a copy of the photo," Marc said to Reb. "Not something I'd do, but I'm not senti-mental." If he saw Reb's annoyed glance, he ignored it.

Cyrus had the thought that Reb ought to figure a man who had to deny feelings was protesting too much.

"Where's the real photo?" Oribel said through tears. "Is it with her?"

"Wherever she may be," Marc said, staring as if at nothing.

Cyrus read his thoughts. Each time Bonnie was mentioned, Marc would wonder about his sister. As much as he insisted he believed it was Amy's body that was missing, he must long to be proved wrong.

"It's with her things," Reb said. "The ones the investigators took. I'm glad I kept this. I think . . . this man could be someone special to her, and the child. The child could be hers."

"Stop it," Oribel said, her voice muffled. "Some of us are too soft to deal with these things."

The atmosphere got heavier.

Another jingle at the door broke their thoughtful stillness.

"Come one, come all," Jilly said, walking into the shop from the kitchens. "I might have known you wouldn't be far behind, Wally. Where's Nolan?"

426

Wally, his hair on end as if he hadn't combed it yet this morning, said, "He's not feeling so good. I'm keeping him quiet." And he sidled closer until he could stand near Cyrus.

"Morning, Wally," Reb said. She had a way of putting people at ease. "Can you help me out with this muffin. It's too much for me."

Wally shook his head, then remembered himself. "No, thank you. I had breakfast." He rolled onto the sides of his sneakers.

"There's always something to worry about," Oribel said. "What's the matter with you, Wally. Don't mumble, either. Spit it out."

Wally gave Cyrus a desperate look. Spike walked in, and Wally jumped. He fell over his sneakers, and Cyrus caught him by the arm.

"Such silliness," Oribel said, pulling the boy's head down so she could attempt to tame his hair. "You're a bundle of nerves, and it's not right for a boy to be like that."

Spike tipped his Stetson to the gathering and went to the counter where he took the hat off to exchange comments with Jilly in low tones. She smiled at him and tilted her head. Spike spread his hands wide on the edge of the glass cases, and there was no doubt that they were absorbed in each other.

Cyrus barely restrained a groan. Either he had a fixation and saw romantic attachments wherever he looked, or this town had been dusted with pheromones.

"Where do you think you're going?"

Oribel spoke so sharply to Wally that they all jumped. The boy had taken a step toward the door. He reddened and had nothing to say.

"The deputy," Oribel said, still not keeping her voice down. "That's what did it. He came in, and now you look like a scared rabbit. What's the matter with you? Just because your folks have no sense it doesn't mean you have to be afraid of everyone, least of all the law. As long as you don't do anything wrong."

Wally shuffled his feet. "I did something wrong. I found Bonnie's purse and didn't give it back."

"You've given it back now," Oribel reminded him.

"But something's going to happen to me," Wally said. "I keep waiting for it to happen. And I've been scared ever since I found the purse. Bonnie wouldn't have bullets if she didn't have a gun, would she?"

"You don't have to concern yourself with that," Marc said. "You aren't going to be hurt."

"That's right," Madge agreed. "Now we want you to sit down and be quiet for a bit. Just till you stop being upset."

"We won't let anything happen to you," Reb told him.

Oribel got another chair and guided Wally into it. "Hot milk, please, Jilly," she said.

Wally wrinkled his nose but kept the peace.

"Spike Devol," Oribel said. "Don't you have anything to say to the people you're supposed to keep safe? Not a word from you, as far as I can tell. You still workin' on that recording machine? Disgrace how long it takes, I say."

Spike leaned on an elbow and crossed one booted foot over the other. "I haven't been sleeping, Oribel. We've got a print, but it's takin' time to find a match."

"Better than nothing," Oribel told him.

Yet again the shop door opened, this time to admit William. Cyrus didn't remember ever seeing him in town before, much less in a shop like All Tarted Up.

He stood a few feet away and said, "I'm goin' to the church, me. You come, too, Miz Oribel."

Oribel didn't meet anyone's eyes. To Cyrus's confusion, she got up with her pastry box in her hands, mumbled a good-bye, and let William usher her to the sidewalk. He took the box from her and put it in her bicycle basket. Oribel walked beside him while he pushed her bike.

"Pheromones," Cyrus said, and drank down his now cold coffee. He set the mug on the table and found all eyes on him. "What?" He felt annoyed.

"Pheromones?" Reb said.

"Got to be. They're in the air. Why else would complete opposites like that fall for one another."

There were no arguments against Oribel and William as a couple. Cyrus would have found them comforting if there had been.

Wally said, "William and Miz Scully are nice. They're nice to me."

Madge gave Cyrus a "watch what you say" look.

"They aren't just opposites," Marc said. "They're two different life-forms."

Spike was the first to laugh, with Jilly a close second before they all joined in.

THIRTY-FOUR

Gaston was accomplishing the impossible. Marc must have tucked the dog under his arm to carry him into Reb's house. The instant pet sighted owner, he contrived to rotate until he hung, his belly and legs up, his flaccid neck and closed eyes down, across Marc's elbow.

"Look at this," Marc said. "This is the gratitude I get for bringing him with me. He's pretending I've murdered him."

"He likes being upside down," Reb said, closing the door behind Marc. "But he probably needs water. We're all used to hot around here, but this is a killer day. I swear I haven't felt a puff of breeze in hours."

"Are you ready to leave?" Marc asked, and she shook her head faintly. He was still fuming about Chauncey showing up with the car. Marc didn't realize that if he'd made his feelings less obvious, she would have politely declined Chauncey's offer and explained she intended to go into Lafayette over the weekend and buy another bike.

"The pool was filled today," he said. "I didn't think you'd say no to a swim before dinner."

She couldn't look at him, or even think about him without losing her concentration.

"Leave Depew's car here. You don't need it."

When he said something like that Reb wanted to pull his ears. She lifted floppy Gaston out of his arms and set him down. "Go ahead without me. I'm still waiting for lab results." She started toward the study, changed her mind, and went to her consulting room instead.

Marc was a step behind all the way. "It's after four. I know you. If I leave you here you'll forget the time."

And she wasn't allowed in her own home once it started to get dark. She pulled tissues from a box and blotted her forehead and the back of her neck. "This is getting old," she said. "A person has a right to be safe in her own home."

"Yes, she does," Marc said promptly. "But you aren't."

It was too hot to argue. "Don't worry about me. Go ahead and take your swim. And have dinner. You don't need to entertain me. I'll eat here and be out there before the light goes."

Marc put his hands in his pants pockets and braced his feet slightly. He narrowed his dark, dark eyes, and she had to look away.

Someone rang the front doorbell, and she had never been more grateful to hear it. "Excuse me," she said, intending to slip past him, only to be stopped by a gentle but firm hand on her arm.

"You there, Reb?"

Marc's grip tightened. "You didn't lock the door."

"Reb? It's me, Cyrus."

"*You* were the last one through that door," Reb said. "Come on in, Cyrus. We're in the consulting room."

Marc released her arm and hoisted himself to sit on the examining table. He said, "Hi, Cyrus. Good to see you," and sounded as if he meant it.

When Cyrus didn't immediately appear, Reb and Marc frowned at each other.

Cyrus didn't speak or make any noise at all.

"What do you think's up?" Reb whispered.

"Nothing would surprise me," Marc mouthed back. "Hey, Cyrus. Get in here. I want your opinion on something."

"Surely," Cyrus said. "Coming right now." He appeared in the doorway to the consulting room. His hair was soaked, and so were the shoulders of his jacket. Water trickled down his neck and under his collar. "Downpour," he said. "Tropical downpour. The rain bouncing off the sidewalks, but it'll be over as fast as it began. Too bad we can't hope it'll cool things down."

Reb knew Cyrus too well to be fooled by chatter that was no more than a substitute for whatever he really came to say.

"Must have just started," Marc said. He looked as puzzled by Cyrus as Reb felt.

If a contest were held for most mesmerizing male eyes, Cyrus would win hands down. Reb didn't think she'd ever seen his particular mix of blue and green, or that kind of mysterious depth. He could also look at a person and make life real uncomfortable — which was what he was doing at that moment.

"Will you tell Reb it's a bad idea to accept a gift from Chauncey Depew, especially an expensive gift," Marc said.

She turned on him. "Watch your mouth, Marc Girard. I don't like the way you make that sound, which is just what you intended. That car isn't a gift, it's a loan, and I accepted it because everyone needs second chances." Maybe it wasn't the real reason, but she wouldn't let this man know he could goad her into going against her instincts. "Couldn't it be that Chauncey's trying to turn over a new leaf?"

Marc gave her a sideways and measured look. "No."

Cyrus, smacking his palms together and walking back and forth, distracted them.

"Now what?" Marc said. "Hell, Cyrus, quit pacing."

"You're really into telling people what to do and think, aren't you?" Cyrus said.

Those few words muzzled all of them.

Reb picked up Gaston and hugged him, ignoring his outraged complaints.

"Must be nice to be perfect," Marc told Cyrus, his tight lips pale. "Was that the pull of the priesthood for you — the idea that you'd be able to push people around?"

"*Marc.*" The two men faced each other and both flexed their hands as if spoiling for a fight. "Oh, stop it, both of you. Where do you think you are, on the playground?"

"Don't hold anything back," Cyrus said to Marc. "Why not say what you really think about me?"

This was awful, unspeakable. "Grown men don't behave like this — not if they've got a brain cell between them."

"Not if they're as *reasonable* and intelligent as you are, you mean?" Cyrus said. "I . . ." He stopped with his mouth still open, and horror slowly brought a glitter to his eyes.

"That's not what Reb meant," Marc said, but the anger wasn't as strong. "She wouldn't deliberately do anything to hurt anyone — least of all you, Cyrus. She thinks the world of you." He drew himself up and let breath out slowly. "So do I, for that matter. Don't ask me why, when our history is so short."

Reb felt her chin quiver. She would not cry.

"You're good for Toussaint, Marc," Cyrus said. He sat down abruptly. "And I like you. Maybe that's because Reb thinks you're really something and she's got good taste."

"Enough," Reb said, holding her stomach and pretending to feel sick. "I can't take any more of this. We think we're all great. This is a good thing because it helps the peace. But we are not relaxed. Cyrus, you came —"

"To confess," he said, leaping to his feet

again. "Oh, grant me patience. Every word out of my mouth is the wrong one these days. I came because I believe I'm a piece of the puzzle. A *real* piece of the puzzle."

He made a good job of silencing his companions. For a scary moment Reb thought Marc was going to whistle in the name of nonchalance and resolved to make him suffer if he did.

He didn't.

They caught each other's glances and quickly looked away.

"Aren't you going to say anything?" Cyrus asked.

"You'd probably prefer it if Reb weren't here for this," Marc said. "Do it man-to-man."

Reb heard Cyrus swallow. "There's nothing man-to-man about this," he said. "Reb — could we look at that photocopy in a good light? The one of the photo Bonnie had?"

"You talk as if there wasn't a good possibility 'Bonnie' never existed." Marc said. His face was hard. "It's just as likely the photo belonged to Amy, not that there was anything familiar about it."

She wished she'd never made the copy, and even more so, she wished she hadn't felt compelled to display it at All Tarted Up.

"Is it still in here?" Cyrus asked, lifting her bag onto the desk. "I feel your pain, Marc. I don't have the answers you're looking for, but we aren't giving up on the truth. We will know everything in the end."

Marc stood beside Cyrus and said, "You bet we will."

Reb hoped they were both right. She slid out the photocopy and set the bag on the floor again. "It's really bad quality. If we asked, I'm sure we could get to see the original."

"Let's take a look." Marc unfolded the paper and smoothed it out. He turned on her desk lamp and trained it on the black-and-white photo. "I wonder how long ago it was taken. A bald baby has always been a bald baby. The guy could be any man in a dark suit."

Reb bent closer and almost bumped heads with Cyrus. "I don't know," she said. "Something's familiar, but —"

"The baby's name is Dwayne Errol Cyrus Charbonnet. Nickname's Deck. That started because he hit the floor a lot at one point, and it stuck. He's my nephew, my sister and brother-in-law's son. The shot's from his baptism a couple of years ago. I'm the man holding him."

THIRTY-FIVE

They hadn't come up with a single explanation for the photo. Marc was glad to finally be at home and to have Reb with him — and Depew's car still parked out back of the Conch Street house.

At Cyrus's insistence, dinner had been back at the rectory, with Oribel still in the subdued mood she'd reached by the time she left Jilly and Joe's place that morning. She served fried chicken and mashed potatoes with corn, followed by a peach cobbler. Oribel refused to join them and set off for home with a pinched appearance about her.

From every direction, Reb and Marc had approached the puzzle of the photo that had been in Bonnie's pocket. Why had she had it in the first place? Why had it been torn up and stuck back together? What would make the thing so important to Bonnie? Where had she found it — Cyrus didn't remember seeing it before.

Eventually Reb and Marc left, after agreeing to get together again tomorrow — and to ask Spike if he would join them.

This evening Marc had other issues on his

mind. He wasn't naive enough to imagine Reb would be ecstatic about one particular thing he'd done today. Not at first, anyway.

"Oribel mentioned some pretty personal comments being made about the two of us," he said when they were in the foyer and Reb showed signs of going directly to her room. "She wasn't completely candid. I think she was embarrassed to tell me, but thought she ought to. Protecting you was on her mind." The heat wasn't lessening, and inside a house that depended on fans hanging from twelve-foot-high ceilings, although it was slightly cooler, the air remained muggy.

Reb put Gaston down. "What sort of comments?"

"Silly stuff about our liking the sauna, that type of thing."

She blushed as only a redhead could. "How would anyone know about that? Darn their nosy hides; I hate it when folks waste energy interfering in other people's business."

He was grateful she was more angry than humiliated. This was the Reb he'd always known, the one who took him on at tennis when she was about seven and he was already on the junior high tennis team. And even after losing game after game, she wouldn't quit until Marc arranged himself on his face, on the court, and wailed that she'd worn him out.

"I asked you a question, Marc. How does anyone know what we have or haven't done?"

"We've done everything," he said with an angelic grin. "That's an exaggeration; there's a lot for us to get to yet."

Reb didn't look amused.

"There are workers all over the place," he said. Stacks of materials in the foyer supported his statement. "Someone makes a suggestion, and by the time it's repeated a few times, it gets blown out of proportion and embellished."

"You haven't mentioned anything that was embellished. We did — have enjoyed the sauna."

He wasn't about to snitch on poor, bored Cletus, who couldn't have felt important very often in his life. The old man had enjoyed the attention his revelations brought him and must have lapped up the way the workers hung on his words. "Gossip just is. Sometimes it's accurate by accident. It is now, about us. I wouldn't have mentioned it if I hadn't wanted you to be prepared in case someone says something."

She shook her head. "Come on, Gaston. Bedtime."

She couldn't be more ready for bed than he was, but he didn't expect to get much rest unless they went there together. And there was another issue to deal with first.

Rather than obey his mistress, Gaston sat in front of Marc and stared up at him. The dog had been bathed and clipped short all over in what Reb told him was a lamb clip — because it kept him cooler and helped stop him from picking up burrs from outside. The grinning

440

horror had a rainbow ribbon at the top of each softly puffy ear. Sickening. No self-respecting man would be caught with such a wimpy-looking dog.

"Gaston," Reb said again.

The dog placed his front paws on his enemy's shoes while he grinned up at him.

"You can't blame him for recognizing a man of character," Marc said and lifted Gaston into his arms. Who could blame him for using whatever advantage presented itself? "He's hungry, Reb. There's some white chicken meat in the refrigerator. I'll cut some up for him." Feeling smug could be a precursor to disappointment, but he'd take the chance.

Just as he intended, Reb followed him into the kitchen, where he gritted his teeth and stood Gaston on the table before cutting up some of the breast of chicken and adding a little leftover rice to the dish. Early that afternoon, while he'd been working, he'd gone on the Net and researched good stuff to feed dogs. The way Gaston all but danced while Marc finished mixing in the rice suggested the dog approved.

"That's really nice of you," Reb said.

Marc waved her thanks aside. "I doubt if I'll ever win him over, but that doesn't mean I don't like him and want him to be fit" — he smiled at her — "for your sake as well as his."

He pushed the dish toward Gaston, who immediately buried his nose in the food. Seconds passed to the accompaniment of loud chomping, then Gaston raised his head, stood on his hind legs with his front paws on Marc's chest and landed a sloppy chicken-and-rice-flavored lick on his benefactor's mouth.

"Oh," Reb said. "Look at that. How sweet. He does like you, Marc. And he's grateful. He hardly likes anyone but me, you know."

"That's nice." Marc broke the clinch and placed his new buddy back at his dish. "I've got something to show you." His stomach practiced pretzel twisting, but he made sure he showed no emotion.

"Can't it wait for tomorrow?" Reb said. "I've already got too much on my mind — like whether or not I should mention something I've been thinking about."

"Okay, you've got my attention and I'm asking: what have you been thinking about?"

"Meat pies."

Meat pies? "Uh huh."

"The ones from Jilly and Joe's. I guess they're really good."

"I wouldn't know."

"I expect lots of people get them, don't you?"

"Get to the point, Reb."

"The night someone hid in my closet and Gaston didn't raise any alarm, he was lured off with one of those meat pies."

"Did I know that?"

"I don't know. Anyway, seems to me we could ask Jilly to look up all the people who had orders for them that day."

Her motive didn't need explaining, but it had one or two holes in it. "We could do that. But that wouldn't account for people who walked in and bought one out of the display case."

She jutted her chin. "We could still think about the standing orders. It was the rectory order that made me think about it. I guess Cyrus really loves those things. He had six of them."

Marc studied her downcast eyes. "You counted them? Yeah, you counted them. Are you trying to decide if Cyrus has taken up hiding in closets and bashing his friends with coconut shells carved like monkeys?"

"Of course not." Her response was overly sharp. "I was telling you what gave me the idea to check the orders, that's all. I thought we could get Spike to ask Jilly."

"Be my guest." Some things should be done by those who dreamed them up. "I want to take you outside."

Reb gave him a speculative look.

"To introduce you to something new," he said and quickly added, "Something you haven't seen before." Tonight he was too smooth for his own good.

"Okay. Marc, we didn't have a chance to talk about that photo of Cyrus and the baby. I've got all the same questions he said he had."

"*Said* he had? Don't you believe him?" The notion of Reb being suspicious of Cyrus seemed fantastic.

"Of course I believe him. Oh, forget it. Show me whatever it is you want me to see so I can get some sleep. You're a kind man to have me here and watch over me, but I feel as if I'm pushing my welcome. I promise I'll do something about that."

He didn't say what he wanted to say, which was that she made him simmer by talking like that. She knew as well as he did that he wasn't just being "kind."

The outside door from the kitchen led to a neglected vegetable garden on the uppermost level of the grounds. Marc let Reb walk out ahead of him into the still evening and closed the door to keep Gaston from following.

The original coach house and stables still stood to the side of the house and set well back. No horses nickered behind closed stall doors anymore, but Marc planned to change that one day, even if only in a small way.

"Watch your step," he told Reb. "It's easy to twist an ankle on the cobbles." He took hold of her hand, and they walked to the coach house.

"You're making me curious," she said.

He swung open one of the wide doors. Every inch of the way the hinges squealed, and the door had dropped just enough to scrape the cobbles. A musty but not unpleasant odor came from inside, together with a blast of pent-up heat. Empty apple barrels lent a pungent scent, and warm dust mixed with the smell of old leather. Some of the family buggies and carts, and even a carriage, remained crowded together on one side.

"I remember this," Reb said, sounding delighted. "I remember when you used to take me to the plantation in the trap. If we passed any guys who knew you, they'd laugh, but you didn't care."

He'd cared, but not enough to bloody noses in front of a young girl.

The interior of the building was gloomy and the lighting a poor effort, but he switched on what lights there were and edged past the crowded equipment. He heard Reb moving behind him. He'd deliberately planned to come in this way.

He stepped into a cleared expanse and said, "What do you think?"

Reb looked at the light bronze BMW that stood there and said, "Nice car." She went to open a door and look inside, showing the polite enthusiasm expected when a proud owner showed off a new vehicle.

"Don't you love that smell, cher?" he said. "Sit behind the wheel. This baby's loaded."

Dutifully, Reb walked around and slid into the driver's seat. "It's really wonderful," she told him, and he got in beside her. "I like the camel leather. It's got a cool look, not that it matters with air conditioning."

His heart began to make occasional uncomfortable bumps. He hopped out and opened the second door to the coach house before getting in again. "Drive it. See how it feels."

She shook her head.

"The keys are in the ignition. Please, I want your reaction."

Hesitantly, she turned the key and the engine sprang smoothly and quietly to life. Reb glanced at him again before driving cautiously out of the coach house. "It moves like silk," she commented, settling more comfortably. "I'll go to the end of the driveway, then back. Driving this makes me nervous. I don't blame you for falling in love with it. What a thrill to own something like this."

Reb-the-honest. You usually knew pretty much what she was thinking and feeling. "Well, now you *know* how that feels."

She laughed. "Only vicariously, but I like thinking of you getting jazzed about it."

"I get jazzed about you, Reb. Jazzed enough not to need new cars. The Range Rover is practical for me. This is perfect for you. It's yours."

At least she didn't do what he'd expected and slam on the brakes. But she slowed to a crawl, or maybe she took her foot off the gas and the car coasted. She didn't say anything while they gradually came to a stop almost at the end of the drive.

A U-turn started them back the way they'd come. Marc held his breath, but the lady wasn't talking. Outside the coach house she stopped once more. "Would you like me to reverse it in the way it was?"

"Up to you," he said. "Your name's on the papers. From here on you won't have to worry about being as safe as you can be in a vehicle."

Reb drove into the coach house, nose first, switched off the engine, and applied the emergency brake. Then she sat there with her hands in her lap.

"You're mad at me," he said, remembering to breathe. "I knew you would be. Go on, get it all off your chest. Tell me what you think of me and my gift — and my presumptuous behavior. I can take it."

"What I want to do is give you a big kiss and tell you I've never been so surprised or thrilled in my entire life, only we both know I can't do that."

"Why?"

"Because a gift like this is totally inappropriate. If there are people around Toussaint talking about us now, imagine what they'd read into you giving me a BMW."

She was so darn logical. "Why *are* you so logical, dammit? And why do you care what people say or think?"

"Mostly, I don't." She moved his fist from the dashboard to her lap and held it with both of her hands. "But this is over the top. Oh, I love it, Marc. I want it, just like I wanted stuff at Christmas when I was a kid, but I've got to be strong. Thank you, but I can't accept it."

"You can and you will. Think about someone else first. Think about *me*. Stress could cause me to have a heart attack, and I stress over your safety all the time."

"It won't work. No thank you."

He fell back against the seat. "I am so pissed at you I could spit."

"That's nice."

"Don't mess with me, little girl."

She turned toward him and shoved his hand away at the same time. "I'm not a little girl. I'm a green-eyed monster who wants this car so badly she can taste it. You might want to be grateful I'm strong — for both our sakes. I'm sure you can take it back. There's some sort of grace period on these things."

"Green-eyed monster?" He showed her his teeth. "Green-eyed, you are, but you're no monster. This car stays. It'll sit in here until you use it, or it rots, whichever comes first. You can kiss me, though."

"Next weekend I'm going into Lafayette to buy a new motorbike."

"No you're not."

"I hate it when you try that masterful stuff on me. It doesn't work."

"The idea of you risking your neck on one of those things — again — is absurd." *Wrong approach.* "But you're right, I have no power over what you do or don't do. You can still kiss me."

"Oh, thank you." She turned a watery smile on him, leaned over, and pecked his cheek. He made a grab for her, but she was out of the car and running toward the house before he could extricate himself to go after her.

He jogged into the kitchen in time to see Reb make off with Gaston, and he bowed his head, praying for enough sense to leave her alone, at least for now. She hadn't behaved as expected, not at all. She wanted that car badly. He smiled, and as quickly frowned. Reb O'Brien was a stubborn woman, always had been. What would it take to make her accept the gift?

Marc thought about that while he slowly climbed the stairs.

Sleep wasn't only a good idea, it was a necessity. In the morning he'd be driving Reb into town again. He was glad to do it, and more glad she wouldn't be in Depew's handout. There were strings attached to anything the bastard did, they just didn't show yet.

How great it would be to see Reb driving the BMW. If he was honest with himself, he hadn't expected that to happen immediately.

He showered, and in the interests of trying to stay cool, went to bed damp.

An hour must have passed before he dozed. Dreams hovered in the limbo between sleep and being awake. Reb was in all of them, and they didn't help him slip into real sleep.

Pies, pies as big as babies and heaped beside his drafting table, started sliding when Reb laughed and gave them a push. Not pies. They were babies after all, and they crawled around the legs of his stool. He told Reb they needed their mothers, but she only laughed at him.

Cyrus was there too, holding a baby, until Marc saw it was really a big pie.

He tossed and threw off the sheets.

Lightning cracked, but it wasn't close. Quiet fell again, and Marc floated, his limbs heavy on the hot bottom sheet. He couldn't keep his feet still.

The next lightning strike brightened the sky beyond the windows he hadn't bothered to cover. A dull boom of thunder came soon enough. He prayed for rain. The tension in this night might suffocate him. Sweat ran from his temples back into his hair, and his eyes stung.

His door cracked open a few inches and he almost choked on his own excitement. Closing his eyes, he forced himself to lie absolutely still. Reb was warm and lovely, and sexy. She was also a woman who could take the initiative. Marc loved it when Reb showed she wanted him.

A snuffle followed a light thump on the bed.

Mark opened his eyes and glowered at the ceiling. Either he'd made more of a buddy than planned with his doggy delight cuisine, or he was about to get his throat ripped out.

Gaston flopped down close to his side and yawned, then made sounds like a cow chewing her cud.

Gently, Marc pushed the dog to the edge of the bed. The animal didn't get up even when he was propelled into space. He landed on the carpet with a sound like a melon rolling from a stall.

Gaston didn't cry.

Marc waited, listening hard. Geez, what if AP had fallen on his fuzzy topknot and cracked his teeny scull?

The intruder landed on the mattress again and crawled on his belly to rest his head on Marc's chest. That meant his sharp little front claws and pointy leg joints were digging into Marc's ribs.

Almost immediately Gaston's breathing settled into a peaceful rhythm, interrupted from time to time by a tiny whimper. He snuggled closer and gave Marc one small, loving lick.

Darn it, anyway. If the critter didn't look like an orange floozy, Marc might even like him.

Gaston would made a good hot-water bottle. His body was a miniature furnace, his wool unbearably irritating to overheated skin.

What could you do? Kick out a helpless, pint-size creature who trusted you?

Lightning came closer and closer and rolled in long, spitting sheets. The thunder that followed was never fast enough to ease the stifling atmosphere.

Raindrops hit the windows. Fat drops coming at an angle that threw them like pebbles against the glass. Faster and faster they came, and thicker. The rain hammered at the panes.

Marc sighed with relief but figured it wouldn't last long.

Gaston's body had reached boiling point.

He couldn't stand it. Holding the poodle against him, he slid from the bed and did his best to navigate the old hardwood floors outside his bedroom without making any noise. He was too heavy to get away with it and each step brought a creak.

Reb's door stood open a little. Keeping a hand on his collar, Marc put Gaston on the floor and gave him a careful push.

Gaston uttered one of his heart-wrenching whimpers and sat down. Evidently he didn't feel like pushing through a small space, so Marc shifted the door inward a couple more inches and patted Gaston's rear. He felt like the Grinch disposing of Cindy Lou Who on Christmas Eve.

He sighed with relief. The dog had continued inside.

Reb's light snapped on. "Don't you dare creep away without a word. What kind of a man are you, anyway?"

Marc realized he'd been hunched over and stood up straight. "Sorry. Thought you were asleep. I was just bringing Gaston back."

"Upsetting me," she muttered. "You know I'm lonely, but you're not doing anything about it. I'm so hot, and I don't like storms. Listen to it out there. Storms like this frighten me."

"May I come in, Reb?"

"Oh no, absolutely not. I don't force myself on people. Go back to bed. I'm going downstairs to watch television."

He glanced down at his faintly shiny skin and white boxer shorts. "You've got a television in your room if that's what you want."

"My room is too close to your room. I'm only human, darn it."

He was confused, and who could blame him. She suggested she wanted him with her, then said she didn't. Round in circles. And she couldn't watch TV in her room because her room was too close to his room?

She was only human?

What did she think he was — an alien? "Reb, listen to me."

"Go away."

"You want to make love, don't you?" He winced and waited for the onslaught. She didn't say a word.

"I'll take that as a yes. I'm coming in."

The door flew open hard enough to bang the wall inside the room. Reb, her long red curls looking as if they belonged on an electrocuted cartoon character, rushed past him and headed for the stairs. Her yellow silk sleepshirt barely covered her rear, and with each step she showed matching panties.

Down she went, pounding each step.

Marc thought briefly, then went in pursuit. He jumped down three stairs at the time, but Reb was moving like a woman powered by the best batteries. She took off across the foyer and into the dining room.

"Stop," he called. "You're going to fall over something and hurt yourself. That'll be my fault, too, I suppose, only you won't get any sympathy." But he was already excited and had the evidence to prove it.

Marc kept following but slowed down enough to make sure she could imagine she was keeping herself out of his reach. He heard her laugh and his body pulsed. She wanted the chase, but she also wanted to be caught. Reb had a wild side, and it drove him the kind of crazy that made him strong.

Reb had reached the conservatory and flitted along a pathway between the tall palms. A blue-black sheen penetrated the darkness enough to show the way. Her nightshirt became luminous in there. She paused, hiding behind a big ceramic urn. He heard her pant from exertion. He also heard rain buffeting a hundred panes of glass.

"C'mon," she said with laughter in her voice. "Or did I tire you out, old friend?"

"Keep on goading me, cher," he told her and set out walking the path with measured steps. "Better be careful where you step. You could damage yourself."

"That's okay. I'm a doctor."

He laughed aloud. "What's gotten into you?"

"You," she said. "Meet me on that lovely tiled bench of yours."

His gut contracted so tight he could hardly take a whole breath. He throbbed in all his parts, and his rigid thighs trembled.

"Come on, Marc."

He saw her moving through the shadows, saw

the nightshirt float to the ground when she took it off. If this was going to be anything but a thirty-second wonder, he had to slow down. Rather than take the shortcut to meet her, he continued on around the loop, and jumped when he saw her.

Reb stood on the bench, her feet spread, hands on hips, her breasts on his eye level.

Everything within him broke loose. He wanted her. Now.

Arriving in front of her, he grasped her waist and made to lift her down. Reb resisted. She braced her weight on his shoulders and brought her breasts to his face. And when he did what he had to and used his tongue and lips on her nipples, she wriggled and swayed and clutched at him.

His shorts went the way of her nightshirt, but he didn't bother to remove the panties. They came together when he knelt on the bench and pulled her feet from beneath her.

It was harsh and it was sweet — and too soon over.

"Did I break anything," she murmured against his neck.

"How would you do that when I have perfect aim?" He wanted to tell her he loved her, and he would, but not while they were panting and hanging together in the aftermath of sex.

"Oops," she said, and hustled from his lap. "The rain's too loud in here."

And off she ran again. He saw her go through

the door to the dining room and bent over to catch his breath. "You are going to regret this," he said softly, and followed her. He wished he felt as sure as he sounded. Reb was a powerhouse tonight.

He gave a fleeting thought to their discarded clothes, but didn't care enough to go back for them. Naked felt good in an atmosphere that ought to steam.

"Hurry up," Reb called out. "Or are you all tuckered out, sweets? Better get you to bed if you are."

She waited for him on the stairs. Halfway up the stairs, and as soon as she sighted him, she pretended to start mounting the bannister. "I always wondered what it would be like to make love sliding down one of these."

He groaned and pretended to stagger. "It might be painful, cher."

"Well decide. Quickly. I need your help."

With a mock howl, Marc leaped up the stairs until he could grab her and settle her knees on a stair. She braced her weight on a higher step and looked at him over her shoulder.

"Face forward — *way*," Marc said. "And trust me."

She giggled at that, but did as she was told.

He gripped one of her thighs in each hand and bent over her. She squealed, and he went where he wanted to be.

"Straighten up and sit on me."

She did, and he'd never felt anything like it.

He covered her breasts and pulled her against him. Reb screamed. He was too busy keeping everything together to say a word. Later he might have time to yell.

THIRTY-SIX

From Cyrus's windows, he and Madge saw Oribel coming. Swathed in a hooded yellow poncho with a bill above her eyes, she stood on the pedals of her bike as she often did when in a hurry, shot down Bonanza Alley, careened through the open gate to the rectory grounds, and screeched to a stop outside the front door.

Within seconds, the soles of her wet sneakers sucked at the hall floor and she arrived outside Cyrus's office breathing hard enough to be heard through the door.

"More trouble," Madge said. She looked tired. The past days had been hard on everyone.

Cyrus opened the door to admit Oribel, who darted in saying, "We don't have much time. May Lynn's coming."

A break, he thought. At last the break the four of them had expected but had no way to force. He went to the window. "Where is she?"

"It won't be long," Oribel said, unsnapping the skins that made her resemble a bathtub duck. "She talked to that Oiseau, or whatever her name is supposed to be, and when the woman told her she needed to *lighten her spirit,*

458

May Lynn said a lot of stuff and was told to see you."

Madge said, "How do you know? From May Lynn?"

"From Oiseau de Nuit, of course . . ." her voice trailed away and she turned pink. "I was over at Chauncey's. I dropped something off is all. Just happened to run into the medium."

"I see," Cyrus said, and he was afraid he saw too well. Oiseau de Nuit was the latest fad in Toussaint. He thought it unusual that the woman would tell someone to come to him.

"You don't want to see that May Lynn," Oribel said. "She's hysterical. I can't imagine what she wants with you. How much weight can a girl like that have on her spirit?" She turned to Madge. "We've got to look out for Father. He's always been too kind to these no-good women who hang around. He's too innocent to see he's a challenge to them. He needs saving from himself."

Stunned by her outburst, Cyrus said, "I'm sure you didn't mean that the way it sounded. I hope you didn't."

A shriek came from the direction of the kitchen where Lil Dupre had been banging pots and pans from the moment she arrived.

"I'll go," Madge said, sounding grateful for the diversion.

Oribel calmly sat herself down in one of Cyrus's chairs. "Good idea. I'll stay just in case that May Lynn needs quieting down."

"I think I'll call Reb," Madge said. "Just in case May Lynn's in a bad way." She winked to let Cyrus know she didn't take Oribel seriously.

Cyrus decided something might need to be taken very seriously today. "Please do that," he said, but Madge was already out of sight on her way to the kitchen.

"That Lil Dupre's a menace," Oribel said, whipping a tissue from the box on Cyrus's desk. She blew her nose roundly.

Madge returned at a trot. "Come out here. Now." She didn't wait for Cyrus to catch up. He walked swiftly after her with Oribel at his heels. "I had a quick word with Reb, and she'll be over," Madge told him.

Pots on the stove bubbled, sending up clouds of steam. The kitchen was an oven all on its own, and continuous rainfall didn't lighten the atmosphere. If anything, Cyrus thought he could see even more steam through the windows, rising from earth that was rapidly becoming waterlogged.

With her mouth gaping, Lil pointed outside.

Madge wouldn't meet his eyes, but Oribel hurried to stand beside Lil. "Ooh, ya-ya, Lil, you are so excitable. Calm down or you'll upset us all."

Lil shook a forefinger in Oribel's face. "You the one who upset us with your nonsense. If Father wasn't the good man he is, he'd have told you what he think about that thing out there for real."

Cyrus all but moaned. He didn't have to

stand near the window to figure out that something was amiss with the Fuglies.

"You are jealous," Oribel said. She raised her hand as if to slap Lil, but collected herself. "You're talking about a fine piece of primitive art. Father likes it, don't you? And Madge?"

Cyrus and Madge nodded emphatically.

"And just what are you screamin' about, anyways? You've been lookin' at those joyful creatures a time now. Why start screechin' about them today?"

"Look." Lil pointed again, and all four of them stood there, clearing circles on the sweating windows with their hands.

"Bit of a problem," Madge said.

After one look, Cyrus went to the door and out into the sopping morning. He enjoyed an excuse to get wet. At least it felt good for a few minutes. Oribel's "joyful creatures" had developed a list to starboard — or port — depending on what one decided was the front. Not a minor list, either. On the right side facing the bayou, the figures were ankle-deep in mud that already covered the concrete base at that point.

Madge — who had put on a raincoat — joined him. They surveyed the situation in silence.

"You can't trust anyone to do a good job," Oribel said when she reached them. She glanced to where the bayou was flooding its banks. "I told William to be careful on account of the water troubles, but he insisted there's no problem right here."

"There shouldn't be," Cyrus told her. "This spot's higher than most. But putting the sculpture in could leave a lot of softened soil behind, then the rain came — and who would figure for it to go on like this for so long and be so heavy?"

"I'm sorry, Father Cyrus," Oribel said.

"Don't be. William will be over at the church. Give him a call and ask him to take a look. He and those brothers of his can stabilize this until we decide what to do permanently." God worked in mysterious ways indeed. Each day more complaints about the sculpture arrived on his desk. Now he was getting a chance to move it without hurting Oribel's feelings.

Oribel trudged toward the house.

"Oh no," Madge said. "We're not going to be able to wait long."

While they watched, another half-inch of bronze legs sank from sight.

Oribel hadn't arrived at the kitchen yet. Madge whipped out her cell phone and dialed William's number. "It's ringing." She listened a long time. "Number not available," she said and dialed again, commenting, "Calling his place . . . Hi, Martha, is your daddy there?"

Cyrus watched her frown.

"Does he do that sometimes? . . . No, no, I'm not suggestin' anythin', just asking a question. Father's looking for him is all. How about your uncles?" She took the phone from her ear and looked at it. "I've offended Martha by suggesting her daddy could be in the habit of staying out all night. She hasn't seen him since he left to come here early yesterday. William's brothers are away. Sounds like she's worried but looking for trouble at the same time."

"Martha has a little problem with anger management."

Madge tutted and gave him a friendly punch. "I like you better when you forget you're a priest and say what you really think." She bit her lip. "Sorry, Cyrus, I shouldn't have said that."

She should be able to tell him anything she wanted to. He smiled at her, feeling rain drip off his chin as he did so. The truth was that they could never freely express personal feelings about each other.

He was grateful Wally chose that moment to push his bike through the mud and stand between them. "Oh, wow," the boy said. "Oh, wow." His voice was hushed.

"You've got that right," Cyrus said. "If it moves any more, we'll have to get a professional outfit in to lift it."

"That'll cost a lot," Wally said.

Cyrus didn't feel like discussing unexpected expenditures this morning.

"Something happened to my bike." Wally planted himself astride the front wheel and facing the handlebars. "Some paint's coming off."

"Is it?" Cyrus's plate was overflowing for one day.

"See this? The handlebar? All coming off, it

is. I'll get into trouble all over again." Sure enough, flakes of shiny black paint came away on his fingers. "There are scratches in the old paint underneath. Someone tried to fix it so I wouldn't know. Another thing. This isn't my headlight. Mine was a bit bigger and it had a rim of chrome around the glass."

"Someone repented for a sin and tried to make up for it," Cyrus said. "They borrowed your bike, and when they had an accident with it, they put it right. We should try to forgive. The paint can be done properly."

"Here comes Spike," Madge said. "Maybe you should tell him about this, Wally."

"Oh no," Wally said. "He's probably coming to arrest me." His serious face made Cyrus smile a little.

"Nothing bad will ever happen because of the purse. Now stop worrying about it."

"Thought we had a meeting here this mornin'," Spike said. He drew near to the bronze and closed his mouth.

Wally muttered that he had to go and bent to the task of propelling his bike through the mud again.

Spike turned up one corner of his mouth. "We can hope that boy keeps some respect for the law." He looked around, then at the sculpture. "Guess they overdid the dancing."

Laughter was beyond Cyrus, but he grinned, and Madge laughed enough for both of them.

"We're trying to track down William and see

if he and his brothers can do something. No luck yet. We'll have to hire equipment to lift it pretty soon."

"Almost makes me feel sorry for Oribel," Spike said. "She'll be mortified. I want you to listen to something, though. Now would be good as long as we're alone. Here come Reb and Marc," he added. "Those two seem joined at the hip."

An interesting thing about Spike Devol was that he rarely showed regret for anything he said. Already he was slipping a tape cassette into a bright yellow player. "The tape's a copy," he told them. "My daughter lent me her tape player."

Inquiries about young Wendy had never seemed welcome, so Cyrus didn't often mention her. "Is it a copy of the one from Reb's house?"

"Yeah." He waited for Marc and Reb to arrive and then told them what he was doing. "It's not much, but listen."

There was a click, and a woman's voice said, "You messed up. *Okay,* I'll do it for you." Another click, and then there were sounds, like the rustling of clothes, or just hands passing over the speaker or taping the machine under the examining table, maybe, then fading footsteps. Following two more clicks there were more footsteps, and Reb was heard talking on the phone. More background noise. Again two clicks. Gaston barking. The front doorbell, and eventually Cyrus's voice calling for Reb. From a distance Cyrus said, "I'll wait in the kitchen." The next click was followed by, "Yes, I'll do that. Wait in the kitchen, that's what I'll do. No, I'll sit on the stairs; that way I can say 'hi' the minute she comes in and I won't shock her."

Spike turned the machine off himself and said, "Why would you be in Reb's house shoutin' like that?"

"He just was," Marc said, and Reb looked pained.

Cyrus smiled and said, "That's right. I was waiting, and I tend to talk to myself sometimes. Comes from spending a lot of time alone."

Spike didn't even pretend to be convinced, but he turned the recorder back on. Clicks on and off followed and comments from Marc, Reb, and Cyrus that needed no explanation. Then it was over.

"That's creepy," Reb said. Cyrus noted that she didn't look rested. Neither did Marc.

"Let's hear the beginning again," Marc said, and Spike obliged — several times. "Not good quality," Marc commented. "But that's our clue, the woman's voice. Like we said at the time. Whatever's going on is amateurish."

"This is between the five of us," Spike said. "I'm stepping way over the line sharing it at all, but I'm hoping one of you will come up with a clue about the female." He replaced the recorder in an inside pocket.

From the kitchen doorway, Lil yelled, "May Lynn Charpentier wantin' to see you, Father."

"May Lynn called me, too," Spike said. "But she said she was sorry and hung up."

Cyrus met Reb's eyes, then Marc's. No interpretation was necessary. "I'll go up and see her now. Madge, go ahead and find someone to deal with this" — he indicated the bronze — "and figure out where we can put it."

"I can see to that," Marc said. "You're stickin' around a bit, Spike? We need that meeting."

"That's the main reason I'm here."

Cyrus closed out their voices and prayed quietly on his way to meet with May Lynn.

He scarcely made it through the kitchen before he heard Oribel's raised voice. "You think you've got such problems," she said. "You listen to a *heathen* talking nonsense and come rushing over here to bother Father. What you young people need to learn is that you don't have any troubles yet. They'll come along soon enough."

Cyrus increased his pace.

"When I start getting mail from the chancery in New Orleans, you mean?" For all May Lynn's brave words, her voice shook. "*Mr. Oran Scully.* You ought to be ashamed, pretending like that."

With complete calm, Oribel told her, "I'm studying for the deaconate by mail. They don't let women in yet, but they will, and I'm preparin' myself. Father Cyrus knows all about it."

He didn't know about Mr. Oran Scully.

"How did you find out my private business?" Oribel asked.

May Lynn giggled nervously. "I happen to be very close to your mailman, *very* close. He's my *fiancé,* and you can't get him into trouble for mentioning it to me because you don't want anyone to know what you're up to."

Cyrus just about ran the last few steps. "Hello, May Lynn, how are you? Thank you for keeping her company, Oribel. You might want to watch over the activity in the garden."

Oribel's face was masklike. She marched from the office without another word.

Cyrus closed the door. "You wanted to talk to me, May Lynn?"

If possible, she was even paler than usual. Her throat jerked with each hard swallow. She whispered, "Yes."

"Sit down." He pulled up his favorite chair for her and brought the chair from behind his desk for himself. "Would you like somethin'? Coffee?"

"Nothing, thank you. I've just come from Miz Leach's house. Pepper's grandmother."

He smiled encouragement at her while his stomach jumped around. "A nice lady. She's suffered a great deal."

"I know." May Lynn looked at her hands in her lap.

"It was nice of you to visit her."

Tears popped into the girl's eyes.

Oribel walked in without knocking and slid a tray on the desk. She poured coffee.

"What are you doing?" Cyrus asked, furious at her intrusion.

"May Lynn's upset, and I wasn't any help. The coffee cake's from Jilly's place."

He held his breath for fear of shouting at her, and when she caught his eye, she backed from the room at once.

"That was nice of Oribel," May Lynn said, and he supposed it was, but she knew better than to interrupt a private meeting.

Neither of them took the coffee or the cake.

"I've got to do this quickly, Father. I'm in so much trouble, and it's my own fault. I just pray my folks and my fiancé can come to understand. What I said Pepper did? He didn't. I made it up. Not entirely, but all the bad stuff."

He ought to be glad to hear her admission; he was glad, but he also felt sad for May Lynn, who was obviously suffering.

May Lynn cried openly, pressing her forefingers into the corners of her eyes. "Way back when we were in school, Pepper was one of the only people — guys — who were nice to me. And he was older, so he didn't have to even notice me. I've always been grateful for that. And I paid him back by accusing him of something horrible and letting him go to jail. There didn't seem to be a way out afterwards. All the time I expected to hear he was going to appeal, but he never did. He never defended himself at all. I thought he was doing that for me. That should have made me fess up, but all I could see was the shame I'd face."

Cyrus couldn't give her any comfort, not until

she'd told him everything. Then he'd have the task of persuading her to go to the authorities. "I'm listening," he said gently.

"It was Doctor Reb who made it impossible for me to go on. Just the way she talked. I could tell she didn't really believe my story — then I had to do something about it. I almost told Spike Devol today, but I lost my nerve as usual."

"Relax," he told her. "You're doing the right thing now."

"Pepper's a hunk. I never could figure out why he didn't have a girlfriend. He could have had anyone he wanted. They were all gaga over him. That night when I saw him going into the park he waved at me, and I got this thing in my head that he hadn't gone with anyone else because he liked me, but he was too shy to do anything about it.

"I followed him. He was sitting on a picnic table. Just sitting there with his eyes closed, and he looked so sad. I said, *boo,* and he almost fell off the table, but then we both laughed and I was happy. I was excited. And because he was shy, I came on to him." She pressed her lips tightly together, and tears slid down her face.

"Would you like some coffee now?"

"No thank you. We weren't kids anymore. I'm not forward, or I never was before, but I thought I was in love with him, and it was up to me to do something about it.

"He held me off. He didn't push me or say

anything nasty, he just held me off, and I don't know what came over me, but I didn't stop. I waited till he let me go and was sitting there looking embarrassed, and I climbed up to sit beside him. I kissed him before he could stop me, and he did push me a bit then. He looked shaken and kind of sick. He kept saying, 'No. I can't do this. Go away.' And I went mad. I was ashamed and angry. I told him he did want me. I said he'd deliberately made sure I followed him. And he didn't say anything else. Nothing.

"I . . ." She seemed ill. "I grabbed him and said I wanted him to make love to me. I don't know why I did it except I was lonely and I'd been thinking there'd never be anyone for me and everyone would make fun of me about it. We ended up on the ground and I fought with him. He tried not to hurt me, but I bit his neck and scratched his face. I tried to poke at his eyes. The marks were all there, the ones they talked about in court. There were photographs taken. Then Pepper didn't argue about it."

Cyrus didn't feel so good himself. He'd had his own brushes with infatuated women, but nothing like the horror May Lynn described.

"I know why he didn't argue," she said.

He held up a hand and listened to make sure no one was eavesdropping outside the door. He got up and opened it. No one was there. "Sorry," he told her and sat down again. "Why didn't he argue?"

"Because of old Miz Leach. She brought him

up, and he loves her so much. He was trying to save her feelings."

"By allowing himself to be convicted of attempted rape and intent to murder? And leaving himself wide open to be suspected of two murders? You even made up the diving suit?"

"Yes." She rubbed at her eyes like a child. "Everyone knew about the Rubber Killer and it just popped into my head. I think he thought his gramma was too old-fashioned to deal with the truth that could have saved him. You know, attacking me out of passion sounded horrible, and everything got worse when they talked about the murders, but I expect he thought she'd think the other was unnatural and she'd hate him for shaming her in her church."

Cyrus rested an elbow on one arm of his chair and scrubbed at his face. "I think I know what you're trying to tell me, but I can't put words in your mouth. Just say it."

"I didn't want to admit it to myself, but Pepper's gay. He told me that night. He'd been nice to me because he was nice to everyone — not that a lot of the guys were nice to him. Being gay's no big deal, but his gramma's old and she's got a real weak heart. He must have been afraid if she found out it could kill her. He'd know she could never understand."

"She's suffering anyway, so he didn't save her," Cyrus said aloud but to himself, remembering what Reb had said after they'd visited Pepper at the jail. "And he used up all his

472

courage during the trial, or he thinks he did. He's getting out of that place."

"I told Miz Leach I made it all up, but I didn't tell her Pepper's gay. The Church doesn't approve, Father."

"The Church is in a difficult position. Some things aren't up to the Church, though. His motives were the best, but they were stupid." *Thank God it would be over.* "Are you ready to go to the authorities? Today?"

She hesitated, and he feared she'd tell him she'd made her confession and wanted absolution. He wouldn't be able to keep her secret.

"When he didn't say I was lying, I began to believe what I'd said was true," she said, straightening up. "I'm ready to tell Spike now. I shouldn't ask, but would you come with me?"

He leaned to take her hands in his. "Yes, I will."

They sat there quietly. Cyrus felt an urgency to get Pepper set free, but knew he must go at May Lynn's pace.

Oribel's voice, raised in a kind of senseless wail, startled both of them.

"What is it?" May Lynn asked. He could feel her tremble.

"Wait for me here." Cyrus got up and left the room. Oribel grabbed him by the wrist. She pulled him through the house and out into the garden again where people surrounded the sinking sculpture. Several men Marc must have called in were there, and a pickup with a hoist on the back.

"Lower it," one man yelled.

Marc said, "Don't move a thing. Hold it steady."

Another man, whom Cyrus recognized as a local contractor, removed his baseball cap and swiped a forearm across his brow. He kept the hat off and let the rain beat on his head. "We got to get it high enough to slide boards underneath. Should be okay then."

"It won't be," Oribel said. "It's never going to be okay again."

Reb and Marc leaned forward, Madge swung toward Cyrus, and the distress on her face propelled him the rest of the way to join the group.

There had been a mishap. A chain attached to the winch encircled the figure at the left edge of the sculpture and a couple of inches of the deep concrete block beneath. That side had risen until the base just cleared the hole, while the other end had dropped even lower into the earth.

Cyrus saw Marc's grim expression, and the way Reb kept an arm around his waist. He disengaged Oribel's grip on his arm and went to stand with Reb and Marc. Spike was on his knees in liquefied sludge. A glance at Marc's pants suggested he'd done what Spike was doing now, got down to get a closer look at what they were dealing with — just how wet the earth was.

"Nothing moves," Spike said abruptly. "Including anyone here. Stay put. I'm putting in a call to Lafayette."

Marc got down on his knees, and Cyrus joined him. He heard something splinter and saw what the others had been looking at.

This place had been made into a grave, and whoever did this thing hadn't thought to make sure the concrete they poured was all around the cheap casket. A foot, what was left of it, hung through a gap in rotting wood.

THIRTY-SEVEN

This had been a day better forgotten — mostly. Marc waited for Reb in the conservatory. He liked being there and thinking about being there with her. Even Gaston's presence, curled up on the bench beside him, felt good.

He was in bad shape and knew it. He also liked it.

In independent mode, Reb had insisted he return to Clouds End without her, promising she'd be there well before dark. That didn't give her too much more time.

The police from Lafayette had descended on the rectory in a swarm and by the time he and Reb had been allowed to leave it was late afternoon. They'd walked out past a television crew and turned aside the microphone that was pushed in their faces while they went.

First thing in the morning, Reb would be observing an examination of the body that had been buried in its casket under concrete on the back lawn of the rectory. There had been talk of the possibility that Bonnie's stealthy and illegal removal from her original resting place threw the diagnosis of accidental death into serious question.

The coroner respected Reb's opinions and had requested her assistance. He'd told her he hoped that in looking at the evidence in a different light she might help him observe something small but important that had slipped by under the former assumptions. Marc hadn't given up on being there with Reb, but so far there had been no go-ahead.

A search was on for William and his brothers. Oribel was inconsolable — worried about William and battling guilt because she felt responsible for what had happened with the sculpture.

A yellow Jag convertible traveled toward the house going way too fast. He had a bad moment while he thought Reb might be the driver and trying to prove she could make her own choices when it came to cars, thank you.

It was Oribel's daughter, Precious, who got out of the vehicle, and Marc felt relieved. Relieved but irritated at the intrusion. There was one woman he wanted to see, and Precious wasn't the one.

He opened the front door before she could ring the bell.

"Hi," she said. "I hope you'll talk to me. I'm Precious Depew, Chauncey's wife. I'm sure you hate me, but I'm still askin' you to hear me out."

"Hate's a big word," he said, folding his arms. "What do you want?"

She tossed her shiny black hair, and searched in all directions. "It might not be a good idea to talk here."

"Why not?"

"Because what I've got to say is real personal, and I don't think either of us wants the world to hear it."

He thought before saying, "Come in. I don't have long, so you'll have to hurry."

Marc didn't attempt to take her beyond the foyer or to offer her a seat or any hospitality at all.

Dressed in black pants and a black cotton turtleneck with rhinestones at the hem, Precious appeared almost demure. "I know how you feel about my husband."

"No, you don't. But that has nothing to do with my feelings for you. I don't have any. Not good or bad. You aren't guilty of anything except real bad taste in men."

"Real bad," she echoed. "I saw Reb a while ago. She doesn't turn people away, no matter the hour."

Marc simmered. Reb should be giving a lot of thought to the hour, and she ought to be here by now.

"Could I sit down, please?" Precious asked.

He almost refused, but habit wouldn't allow it, and the woman appeared shaken and unsteady on her feet. "In here." He took her to his father's study, his study now, and pointed to the couch.

"I lost a baby a few days ago."

I'm sorry, would have sounded too harsh. "That's a sad thing."

"The baby didn't deserve it, but I did. I never

told Chauncey I was pregnant because I hated him. When I had to I was goin' to say the baby wasn't his and name his buddy as the father. I wanted to hurt that man so bad."

"Shouldn't you be at home, in bed?" Marc felt inadequate. He didn't know what to think of her choosing him as a confessor.

"I won't be going home," she said. "I'll stay with Mama till I know what to do. Amy's alive."

Marc glared at her. If he'd heard her right, she couldn't mean what she said. But only a monster would play such a joke.

"I don't know where she is," Precious said. "But she isn't dead, and I just know she'll find a way to get in touch with you, but you've gotta make sure Chauncey doesn't find out before she's safe. He wants her dead because she knows all about his so-called business, and he thinks she'll tell the law. She did come here to Toussaint. Chauncey got her, and he was goin' to kill her, only I saved her — kind of — to hurt him some more."

Someone came into the house, and Marc recognized Reb's footsteps. He found his voice. "In the study, Reb," he said, and to Precious, "What you can say to me, you can say to Reb, but I think you know that."

"Hey," Reb said, walking in. She saw Precious and raised her eyebrows at Marc.

"Precious is telling me a lot of things. I think she's a ways from finishing yet."

Reb sat beside Precious while the woman told

479

a fantastic story. When she'd finished they remained quiet for some time.

Finally Reb said, "We've got to find Amy."

"And get Chauncey Depew before he can do more damage. I'll try to get Spike to bring him in."

"His friend, Dante Cornelius, will back up my word," Precious said, avoiding any eye contact. "I know how to get hold of him."

Marc didn't wait, he put in a call to Spike, who said he was on his way to "have a chat" with Depew.

"When I told her you were looking for her, Marc," Precious said, her face puffy from the tears she'd shed, "she told me she didn't know why you'd care because she'd never brought you anything but trouble. I said she'd messed up but you'd forgive her."

"He will," Reb said, sounding far away. She frowned at Marc.

He didn't know what was on her mind, at least he didn't think he did.

"I'm going to Spike next," Precious said. "It won't be easy, but I'm gonna tell him everything, too."

Lucky Spike, Marc thought. This was the deputy's day for hearing confessions from badly misguided women. "You'd better get a lawyer lined up," Marc said.

"That's right," Reb said, inclining her head as if listening hard, and watching Precious closely.

"Okay. I'll do it."

That was it. That was why Reb looked the way she did.

Reb said to Precious, "Who told you to put a tape recorder underneath my examining table?"

THIRTY-EIGHT

If Cyrus got mad and sent him away, Wally would still do some investigating of his own. Since he'd gotten his bike back, he'd kept it chained to a fence post at the hotel. So far his mama and daddy hadn't noticed how paint came off in the rain, but they would unless he could get it fixed quickly.

The rectory was mostly dark, but a light shone out back, from the kitchen, and Wally avoided the squelchy ground by keeping his bike to the path around the house.

It wasn't really raining anymore, but his skin felt wet and chilled. The bayou bubbled and popped in the marshy ground where it had over-flowed. Even the lantern over the front door of the church was out. Wally felt creepy and hurried to tap on one of the kitchen windows. If Cyrus was in there, he could be concentrating real hard on a book, but he usually heard knuckles on the window right away.

Wally carried on to the back door, but Cyrus hadn't come to open it. Through the window, Wally saw papers on the table, so Cyrus must be around. Wally rapped the door, and a face appeared at the window. Wally jumped, then felt dumb. It was Oribel. She quickly opened the door and hurried him inside.

"What are you doin' here at this hour?" she said. She was already dressed to go home. "I suppose you want to bother Father. Well, some bad things happened here today, and he's needed somewhere else."

In spite of wearing only a T-shirt and shorts, Wally was too hot in the kitchen. "Well, I'd better go then." Guilt over planning to do more secretive things stopped him from leaving at once. "I will just go over to the church — to the shed where my bike was. I want to see if someone left a can of black paint there — the kind you put on bikes."

"Not in the dark, you won't. Get along home."

"I'll be just dandy," he told her. "And I won't make any mess over there. You know how it is when you've got somethin' itchin' your mind? You gotta do somthin' about it."

"With black paint?" She looked like grown-ups always did when they thought a kid wasn't making sense.

"I'll be in and out of there in no time. Don't you worry about me."

Oribel looked over her shoulder at a wall clock. "I can see there's no changing your mind. Headstrong, just like all children. I'll come with you."

"You don't need to do that."

"I don't need to do anything, but if a boy is

going over there, I won't rest if I let him go alone."

He smiled at her, secretly grateful he'd have her with him. No one messed with Oribel.

With Wally pushing his bike, they walked together from the rectory, across Bonanza Alley to the churchyard. The shed was on the far side, behind St. Cécil's and right across from William's custodial room.

Oribel paused there, and he peered at her. She looked funny. "Something wrong, ma'am?"

She sighed. "We're all worried about William. He hasn't been seen since yesterday. I might even have been the last one to see him, and we had words. I don't like to think it, but maybe I upset him and he took off. He hasn't even been home."

Wally touched her arm. "He'll be okay. You couldn't have said anythin' to make him go away."

"Prob'ly not. Now, it's black paint you're after." She opened up the shed and went in. Wally rested his bike on the siding and followed her.

Oribel's own bike was in there, and Wally felt sorry for her because although it wasn't old, it didn't look as cool as his. He began to look around, moving boxes to check behind and lifting two-by-fours, first one end then the other.

"What are you doin'?" Oribel asked, and she sounded cross. "Those things are nothing to do with you."

"I'm seein' if there's any broken glass been swept away, or fallen somewhere in here is all," he told her. "It would tell me something."

"Like what?" She wrapped her cardigan around her and pinched her mouth. It made her look mean.

Wally told Oribel all his recent and new troubles with his bike, and her face got kind again. "I've been thinking," he said. "It went missing right around when poor Bonnie had her accident in the church. Could have been the exact same day. I wondered if she could have borrowed my bike because her car ran out of gas."

"What kind of sense does that make?" Oribel said. She got close to him. "She went from the car to the church. How would you figure she had anything to do with your bike?"

He heard himself stammer when he said, "She could have come to get it, then used it to carry gas back to the car. Only she wasn't good at riding it and she fell off and scratched it all up. And broke my headlight. Maybe then she got scared and went to the church to pray."

"Rubbish," Oribel said. "I'll explain why, but first you come to my place and I'll help you fix that paint. My husband left everythin' imaginable out in his workshop. There's got to be the right stuff there. We'll use a sander to take the old paint down."

Oribel lived a ways out of town. Wally didn't even know anyone who said they'd been to her house. He didn't want to go out there with her.

"Father said he'd see to it that it got fixed."

Oribel brought her face close to his. "So why are you out here like this?"

He made himself look her in the eyes. "Because I wanted to see if the lamp got broken here. I don't think it did. But it could be that Bonnie took it. Just because we don't know what happened, and exactly when, doesn't mean it couldn't have been somethin' completely different than people believe. I'm gonna take a look out where her car was found. There might be bits of glass around there. No one was looking for that, so they didn't notice any."

"They didn't notice any because there wasn't any."

"I expect you're right. Anyways, I should get along home."

"Just like you always go home when you're supposed to?"

He tilted his head and said nothing.

"I can't let you go out there on that miserable road on your own, Wally. Surely you understand that."

He nodded.

She took her bike outside and waited for him to catch up. "You'll feel a whole lot better when that paint's fixed. Father doesn't have time to mess with things like that, but I do. Taking off some of his burden is my job."

Wally felt a bit sick. "You're kind. Could I come out there tomorrow?"

Oribel looked away. "I'd appreciate it if you'd

come now. I bet you didn't have your dinner, did you?"

"No."

"Neither did I. I've got something good for you — and I sure would be grateful for the company. We'll eat and attend to business. How's that?"

She was a lonely lady. Wally wasn't real good with grownups, but he could try to be helpful.

"Go wait for me at the top of the road," she said. "I'll get my things and be right with you after I lock up. If you like, I can call your folks and let them know you're eating with me."

"No," Wally said. "Let's just go."

THIRTY-NINE

An urgent call from Spike had put Marc and Reb back in the Range Rover and heading for town. He'd assured Marc that Chauncey was being brought in even though he couldn't do it himself. Worried about Precious's physical condition, Reb had insisted on making her stretch out on the couch and get some rest, at least until she and Marc returned.

She knew he was working hard to keep the peace about his feelings on the subject. They'd ridden in tense silence for twenty minutes when Marc couldn't control his tongue any longer. "I don't like leaving that woman in my house."

"What do you think she's going to do? Steal the silver?"

"You heard what she did." He didn't sound amused. "All the things she did. She intended to kill my sister, and she would have if Amy hadn't outsmarted her."

"She had plenty of opportunity to do it," Reb said. "She didn't. And she wouldn't have. She thought she could, but she doesn't have that kind of violence in her."

"No, just enough violence to chain Amy up in

a bathroom and leave her there for days."

"I can't believe it," Reb said. "But neither can I believe she put that tape thing in my consulting room. Even if she won't tell us who asked her to do it, we nailed her on that. Spike will be pleased."

"If she doesn't take off before he can question her."

Reb held up two sets of keys. "I learned something from her." She nodded her head at one set of keys, then the other. "The keys to her car, and to the one I've been driving. Which I won't drive again except to return it."

"She can walk out," Marc said. If she had hoped to soften him up, it wasn't working.

"I gave her something." She leaned her head against his shoulder. "That and her being so exhausted will make sure she sleeps. Get your mind off her, sweetheart. I'm more concerned about Spike being anxious to see us."

Marc put his cheek on top of her hair. "Anxious to see you. I'm an afterthought. Something must be going down and he needs you professionally."

"If I didn't feel like I've been in a wreck, I'd do indecent things to you, Marc Girard."

He didn't answer, but neither did he lift his head away.

"Did you hear what I said?" she asked. "Have I offended you?"

"Nothing we do together is indecent — cute as you make that sound. When you say something like that I don't think you know the power you have over me. If you did, you'd expect to be in that wreck you mentioned."

"Oh." She felt jumpy, excited — and uncertain. "I'd better watch what I say in the future. If you're driving."

"Never do that. Never change. Reb?"

She twisted to look at him.

"I don't want to go back to New Orleans. The setup at Clouds End is good for me. I think well there."

"I see."

"How do you feel about that?"

"I wasn't looking forward to you telling me it was time to leave Toussaint." The answer sounded inadequate, but she wouldn't risk making a fool of herself.

"Why is that?"

"Oh no," she said. "This isn't where you get to throw out harmless bait — harmless to you — and see if I go after it."

"Nothing I'm saying is harmless to me, cher. I'm the one on the line here."

So say what I think you're trying to say, if that is what you're trying to say. "Aren't we both on the line?"

"Yes," he said, glancing at her. "I guess we are. I know what I want to do about it. How about you?"

She felt tension ease and even a rush of happiness and hope, but he was going to have to work harder. "Let's talk about this when we aren't looking at a wall of flashing emergency lights," Reb said, reaching to rest her hands on the dashboard. "Spike called in backup. He wouldn't do that if there wasn't something big."

"Seems to me *everything's* big around here these days. It surely isn't the sleepy little burg I remember."

Spike had called from the ice plant. Police and emergency vehicles were crowded into the yard out front. Marc was stopped at the gates. He told a policeman who they were and whom they wanted to see before being allowed to continue.

"If I could afford the luxury," Reb said, "I'd be scared."

"I give you permission. I need the company."

No one else could make her smile like Marc could.

They parked as far out of the way as possible and walked to the building entrance. A medical emergency vehicle had been drawn up there, and the rear doors stood open. Inside the deeply cold plant noises echoed off fabricated metal walls and a high roof. Pipes ran wherever the eye turned.

One of Spike's junior deputies came toward them, the woman, and she didn't look happy, or well. "Deputy Devol's expecting you," she said. "He's back there." She pointed, then shivered and looked at the ground.

They thanked her and carried on, soon walking into an area where floodlights had been set up.

"Don't go in there like that," a man said. The plant manager, Zeb Dalcour, his round face even redder than usual, approached them carrying heavy, hooded coats and gauntlets.

Once they'd put them on, Zeb said, "Now these," and boots were the finishing touch. "Don't stay longer than you have to. You're not used to it."

The vast area they entered wasn't at all what Reb had expected of an ice plant. Steel containers of various sizes stood in rows, a bit like oversized library stacks.

"Somebody's hurt in here," Marc said, putting an arm around Reb's shoulders. "And it's bad. Got to be, with all the official manpower around. That's why Spike called you, because . . . I guess because you're a doctor."

"But you're thinking it doesn't look as if I'm needed here," she said, and she agreed with him.

Voices were loud now, but garbled because of the strange acoustics. Spike emerged, dressed much as they were, only wearing a hat with flaps that covered his ears. "I called you in too soon," he told Reb and gave Marc an abbreviated salute. "I thought you might pick up on a clue because you've been around some sticky cases. And, to speak the truth, I thought you might want to be here. But the ice is melting fast. Now we can see what we couldn't see before." Spike looked to Marc again. "Depew's in custody."

He turned on his heel and made his way along an aisle between containers. Water dripped from overhead where coils snaked in every direction. Even if it hadn't been so cold, Reb doubted she'd be breathing too easily.

"Reb." Marc stopped her. "If you aren't really needed, why go through something that sounds gruesome? You've dealt with too many things lately. Any one of them should be enough. Why add another?"

"This is my job," she told him. "To come to the site of a medical emergency when I'm called. And even if I'm not really needed, Spike said he thought I'd want to be here."

"Of course."

On the left side of the aisle, a door to one of the containers had been slid open. Police photographers congregated outside, talking together. Medics, their equipment on top of a gurney, stood silently by, watching whatever was going on inside.

"The blocks are up to three hundred fifty pounds," Zeb said from behind them. "They're made in freezing sections inside each container. Usually the containers are loaded onto our delivery trucks. Sometimes a customer picks up some blocks here, but not often. This one is all big stuff, and it could be that someone thought because it was way back here it might not be gotten to as often as some of the others. They thought wrong. Go on in."

The lead up wasn't encouraging. Marc stepped in front of Reb, but she hurried and walked beside him to where another man and two women stood — with Spike listening to what they said and glancing in Reb and Marc's direction.

"This is Marc Girard, and Doctor Reb O'Brien."

The man was older, with light eyes that hadn't seen something that surprised him in a long time. He greeted them civilly enough, then said, "I thought you said a priest was coming."

"He'll be here soon," Spike said. He turned to Reb and Marc. "This isn't pretty, but you've seen worse today. A backup I.D. from you would be helpful, Reb."

He took them a few yards to the left, past several sections. Reb hadn't noticed there was water standing at least an inch deep on the floor and spreading rapidly. It ran from an opening where a metal flap had been hooked back.

In un-Spikelike fashion, the deputy stood on the opposite side of Reb from Marc and put a hand at her waist. "Just say who it is and anything else that comes to mind. Anything that strikes you as familiar."

She broke free of them and stepped forward alone. For far too long she couldn't make herself say anything. Crying wasn't in her job description, but she cried anyway — at the sadness and enormity of it all.

"Reb," Marc said, taking her in his arms as best he could. "Just do what you have to do and let's get out of here."

"It's William," she said in a clear voice,

looking into the open, but dead and blood-encrusted eyes of the big man. He was still covered with ice, but enough had melted to turn it transparent so that he appeared to be behind a thick and dripping wall of irregular glass. "Shot in the head."

"That's what I couldn't see at first," Spike told her. "I recognized him from his size. And he's distinctive anyway."

"Smashed face," Reb said. "Another one. It's as if the killer thinks that by destroying a face, the person no longer has an identity."

William stood upright, his hands raised as if in a plea.

"Why didn't he fall?" Marc asked.

"He was already freezing when the shot was fired," Spike said. "Zeb explained how that could happen. We can't pinpoint the time, but according to Zeb it probably happened yesterday afternoon."

"You don't need me here," Reb said, turning away. "There's nothing anyone can do for him."

"Except find his killer," Marc said.

Cyrus walked toward them, his worried face visible inside his hooded coat. "I know what's happened here," he said and pulled the two of them aside. "Do me a favor, you two. I have to go from here to William's family. Take a run out to Oribel's and stay with her until I can get there. Regardless of the way they riled each other up, she thought the world of him. She'll take this hard."

FORTY

"You've never been out here?" Marc said. "Not even on one of your Florence Nightingale trips? I thought you visited everyone."

Reb trudged ahead of him on the wet gravel path that led through dense trees toward what they hoped would be Oribel's house. Finding the place had been a challenge, particularly since there wasn't even a sign at the entrance to the overgrown trail. They had left the Range Rover beside the road because the vehicle was too wide to take in.

"You don't make house calls for people who are never sick," Reb told him. "Oribel has the constitution of a very healthy horse."

"She likes her privacy," Marc said. "I can't believe she rides back and forth to town — the rectory — on a *bicycle*."

"It could be one of the reasons she's so fit."

Marc walked and thought. Then he said, "She's an odd duck. Or I think she is."

"Obsessive," Reb said. "And possessive where Cyrus is concerned. I'm sure it bothers him, but he's too kind to get rid of her. He probably wouldn't know how, anyway."

"Bingo." Marc caught Reb's hand and they stood still. "There it is. Bigger than I expected."

Oribel's home, single-storied and set in a large clearing, was built on short, thick, cinder-block pillars. A warm yellow glow shone from windows across half of the front and some of the right side of the building. The exterior appeared to be of split cedar, but it was hard to tell. A gallery ran along the front, and a white swing and rocking chair glowed in the dark.

"Pretty," Reb said. "I'd heard it was. Let's get on. I'm not looking forward to this."

They stepped into the clearing, and white lights, shining outward from the roofline of the house, momentarily blinded them.

"Yow," Marc said. "The lady is security minded. That's a good thing, I guess." He shaded his eyes and said, "Weird. The flood-lights came on and the interior lights went out."

"Now the floods are off again. What a relief." Reb held his hand tightly. "It's not weird really. It's sensible. If you're inside, you want to be able to see anyone or anything that moves out here, but you don't want to be seen yourself."

The floodlights flashed. Every minute or so they came on, then went out again. The interior lights remained off.

"She may not even be here," Reb said, sounding uneasy. "If she were, she'd see it was us and let us in."

"Not if this is something automatic and mostly designed to keep animals away. Let's find out." Side by side they covered the rest of the distance to the house, climbed steps to the gallery, and pulled the chain on an antique bell hanging beside the door.

The jangle sounded deafening and sang on too long.

Reb tugged Marc's arm and pointed. Oribel's bike lay on the gallery floor as if she'd simply dropped it on her way in . . . Wally's was there, too.

The outside lights cut out and didn't come back on.

Marc couldn't have explained why the hair on the back of his neck rose. Even in the gloom he saw Reb's eyes grow huge. "Why would Wally be out here?" she whispered.

He knew she didn't expect an answer. Evergreens around the house stood, shoulder to shoulder and black against a gunmetal sky. The bone chill of the ice plant remained with him and he shivered, and felt Reb's responding shudder.

"We'd better make a call," he told Reb. "I don't want to make a wrong move if it could put them both at risk."

"What do you mean?"

"I don't feel good about this. Like you said, why wouldn't Oribel come to the door as soon as she saw it was us?"

"I didn't feel like it." From the steps they'd just used, Oribel shone a flashlight in their faces. "I don't like uninvited company."

Reb jumped so violently, Marc steadied her.

"It's a good idea to take precautions," he said, but the hair on his neck didn't stop bristling. "I wish you'd persuade Reb to follow your example."

"Why are you here?"

"To visit you," Reb told her. "We wanted to see how you're making out. Cyrus is worried about you."

"Not really," she said, amazing Marc. "He's got his interests, and older women aren't one of them."

Reb squeezed his fingers tightly enough to hurt. "You know that's not true," she said, and laughed. "Cyrus treats everyone the same and cares about everyone the same. Where's Wally? I think he gets lonely a lot. It's nice of you to bring him out."

Oribel didn't reply at once. Then she said, "You shouldn't have come. Now it's too late. You've ruined everything."

"It's cold out here," Reb said. "I'd love to see your place, if that's okay."

"It's not."

What Marc felt was danger. It was raw and it was real, and he could tell Reb felt it, too. The most important job they had was getting Wally out of here.

"I apologize," he told Oribel. Her face was indistinguishable behind the flashlight beam, but her solid body seemed tensed. "I'm not too fond of visitors myself."

"You never should have come back to Toussaint. Your kind don't belong here any more than a lot of others do." She laughed, a humorless laugh on a single note.

"We'll put Wally's bike in the back of Marc's vehicle and take them both back. Wally should be in bed by now."

"His folks never know where he is. They'll think he's taken off. Just one more runaway."

Marc's mouth dried out. "Aren't you cold, Oribel? Reb and I are. I could use some of your hot tea."

"I don't make hot tea. Don't believe in it. You think you're being clever, but you're not foolin' me. You've figured stuff out — maybe. People didn't do as they were told, that's why. They can't keep secrets. Why do folks have to turn against the one who knows best? Causes nothin' but problems and extra work."

For the first time in his life, Marc wished he were carrying a weapon.

Oribel sniffed. "I haven't done anything wrong, only tried to look after the ones I love because they can't look after themselves.

"What am I thinking of?" she added. "I forgot for a minute. Wally's gone home. You go home, too."

Sweat had formed between Marc's palm and Reb's. "We'll do that. And you get a good night's sleep. How did Wally get home?"

"He walked. The light on his bike wasn't working. I went with him out to the road. That was a time ago. He's probably in his bed by now."

How long would it take Wally to walk twelve miles in the dark? Marc itched to test the bike lamp.

"You're bothering me." Oribel's voice rose. "Run. I want you to run."

"Not without Wally," Reb said.

Marc wished she'd held her tongue. "We should call Doll and Gator to see if he's there, in case we ought to be looking out for him on our way back."

A shot, fired into the air, silenced him.

"Got your attention?" Oribel said. "Start runnin'."

And wait for a bullet in the back?

"Run," she shouted. "I won't be wastin' any more bullets. The next one's for you, Doctor Reb."

"Separate," Reb whispered fiercely. "Confuse her."

He knew the potential wisdom of the idea, but he wasn't letting her go. "I can do more if I know where you are."

"Shut up!" Oribel said.

"On three, hit the deck and do what I do," he told Reb. "One, two, three." Down they went and wriggled on their stomachs to the edge of the gallery. They were rolling off when the next bullet skimmed close. "Under the house," he said, crawling rapidly in that direction. "She'll have to use the flashlight and that will tell us where she

501

is. We'll hide behind the cinder pillars."

"And we'll pray," Reb told him.

He was grateful the house was as close to the ground as it was. It should stop Oribel from following, since she'd have more difficulty firing at them. If they got to the other side — and Oribel didn't meet them there — they might be lucky enough to make it out alive. They couldn't do a thing to help Wally in their present situation — if he was still alive to be helped.

Reb scooted as fast as Marc over ruckled black paper covered with heaps of wet mud and animal droppings. He shoved her behind a big mud heap and flattened her, resting an arm across her back.

Their heads were side by side, and Reb pressed her cheek to his and murmured, "Where is she, Marc?"

"Don't know. She's crazy, isn't she?" he said.

"Yes," was all Reb said.

Marc heard a scuffle and squeezed Reb's shoulder. She muttered, "Oh lordy," and huddled close. "I love you, Marc. I wanted you to know that."

"Don't try to get out of that later. I'll hold you to it."

Not a regular giant rat, but a big white nutria, its pointy fangs glinting, squatted a couple of feet from their faces.

"Yuck," Reb said. "Let's move."

"Not till we see that flashlight. We don't want to go toward her."

Reb muttered and said something that sounded suspiciously like, "Shush," to the transfixed critter. "Go. Shoo."

Marc put his mouth next to her ear and said, "Shut up, cher. He's not botherin' us."

"He's bothering me."

"There." The flashlight beam did what it shouldn't be able to do if Oribel had been where Marc expected. It passed over their length. "Hustle."

He rolled over and over, making sure Reb copied him. He heard her harsh breathing and the way small sobs broke in her throat. Sweat soaked his body.

"Now scoot on your belly," he told Reb. "Fast. She's lost us for now."

Crunching together, they arrived behind another pillar, but facing the same way as before. "Guess we think alike," Reb said. "Too bad she's likely to figure we'd try this."

The beam traveled, swept the confined space.

A shot ricocheted off cinder blocks several pillars to their left.

Reb's breathing grew harsh. She dragged air in and panted.

"Hold on," Marc told her. He blinked repeatedly to clear his eyes of stinging sweat.

"She thought we'd expect her to come at us from the opposite direction," Reb whispered. "The pile of mud over there could be us from where she is. The shadows look right. That's what she shot at, but she isn't going to quit. We aren't going to get out of here."

"You believe that?"

"I'll say no if that's what you want to hear."

"That's what I want. Now keep your face down and push slowly backward."

She did as he told her.

"Damn it all." Oribel said, and they heard objects cracking together. She switched on her light but not to shine it under the house.

"She tripped," Reb said. "I think she's lost us."

"For now," Marc told her. They continued to shimmy backward. "Maybe she's hurt."

"Too bad the doctor's not in," Reb said.

The beam was still on and wavered. From the noises Oribel made, Marc decided he was right about her being hurt.

Reb squirmed and looked in the direction they were going. "A few feet more is all," she said. "Make a rush for it. *Now.*"

That was an order, and he followed the command, slithering with her into fresh air there was no time to appreciate. They didn't talk. Holding hands again, running wildly with no attempt to avoid obstacles, they dashed, bent over, around an outbuilding that might have been intended as a garage and into the cover of the closest trees.

"I'm calling Spike," Marc said.

Reb told him, "Be sure you don't draw her to us. We've got to get Wally."

Marc hit a button on his phone and covered

it, and his head, with his jacket. Spike answered at once, "Devol."

"Oribel Scully is trying to kill us. She may already have killed Wally. We're holed up in the trees at the northeast corner of the property — not far from the house. We can't leave the boy, and we don't know where he is."

Spike was a man who didn't waste time being shocked. "Don't move from where you are until evasive action becomes necessary. Dang it, Cyrus finished with William's family — the brothers were at the house all the time — and he's coming your way. With Madge. I'm already rolling. I'll make contact with Cyrus."

"He doesn't like cell phones," Marc said. "He doesn't usually turn it on."

Spike said something unintelligible, but Marc got the drift. "How about Madge?"

"Don't know her number. Just a second." Marc asked Reb, who shook her head no. "No help here."

"I'll try to track it down. I take it Oribel's got a gun?"

"Uh huh."

"Did you see it? What is it?"

"I didn't see it, why?"

"It would be nice to know how many rounds she's got in the clip."

A twig snapped, and it wasn't far away. Marc stabbed off his phone without any good-byes. Leaving it on would be nice if he had a vibrating feature instead of a ringer. "That was to the right," he said. "Spike doesn't want us to move unless we have to."

Reb backed into him, put a hand behind her and into his stomach, and silently pushed him. Step by careful step they moved away from the direction of the sound.

"I've got you, y'know." Oribel's voice rang out from another direction entirely. "You won't leave without Wally. He's a nice boy. Told me all kinds of things tonight. I almost felt like letting him go."

"Bitch," Marc said under his breath. The woman seemed to be near to them, but not in the trees.

"We can't shout back," Reb said. "That's what she wants so she knows where we are. I think she's guessing now."

"Know that nasty spider of his?" Oribel called. "The one he carried around in the open till Father told him it frightened people and he had to cover it? He put it in the grocery sack — in a box — or so he said. Seems he'd do anything to get attention. Well, it was his little joke. There wasn't no spider in that bag, he just carried it around and pretended. Anythin' to get attention. Devious. Even the children are devious."

Marc held the back of Reb's neck and squeezed. "I meant to say I love you, too."

"I know," she murmured. "I'm a lucky woman. Wally needs a real family. If I have my way, his folks will shape up."

He didn't mention how certain he felt that

Wally wasn't an issue anymore. "We can't just stay here."

"Spike said we stay, so we stay. Unless she sticks her miserable gun in one of our mouths."

Still to their right, the snapping and swishing of more undergrowth moved toward the clearing. Marc hoped to hell it wasn't Cyrus and Madge crashing around in there.

"You a bad woman," a husky female voice announced. "But I don't care what you do. I just want the money you promised my daddy and uncles for what they did."

"Shut your mouth, Martha," Oribel said. "I'll deal with you later. Come on out and go in the house till I'm finished here."

"Don't go, Martha," Reb murmured.

"I ain't goin' nowhere you say," Martha announced. "My daddy did anythin' you wanted. He was sweet on you. Now he's gone, but he did your work. He moved that body like you asked. Now we got money comin'. You give it to me, or I tell Spike how you used the kid's bike to follow that Bonnie — just in case someone got smart and found the tire tracks. You didn't want 'em to match yours. My daddy tried to hide the bike at our place while he was fixin' up the scratches for you, but I seen and he told me. And he told me about driving that bird woman's van for you 'cause he was too scared not to do what you said. I come with a gun of my own now. What you think I am, anyway? Stupid?"

"Great," Marc said. "Civil war, with us in the crossfire."

A shot whistled by much too close.

"You are stupid, Martha," Oribel said. "Come on out and we'll talk now."

"I can see you but you can't see me," Martha said. "My uncles give me some of them special glasses. You go get the money, bring it back, and then I'll tell you where to leave it."

"Your daddy turned on me. I didn't want to do anythin' to him, but he had to talk about tellin' everything to Father Cyrus. I couldn't let him do that."

"Just you do what I said." Martha sounded as if she was crying.

Oribel didn't answer, but after a few seconds they heard her footsteps cross gravel, then stomp on wood. A door slammed.

"What about Martha?" Reb said.

"Loose cannon," Marc told her.

"I don't know who you is," Martha shouted. "You what Oribel was talkin' to. I don't want no part of you. Just let me do my business and I'll be on my way."

No way would they be communicating with Martha.

Minutes went by, and they felt like hours. "Reb," Marc said, putting his lips against her ear. "Oribel asked Spike about the tape recorder. The morning we were all at Jilly and Joe's place. How would she know about it?"

"Marc!" Reb clutched at him. "Oh, Marc."

Oribel laughed from behind him, close behind him. "This is cozy," she said. "You gotta remember I know every inch of this place and you don't know it at all. I've got my little gun in your lover's back, Mr. Girard. Now we're on the same side." She pushed him hard toward the clearing. "You're gonna help me."

He and Reb shuffled forward as slowly as they dared.

"See who I got here, Martha?" Oribel said, laughing. "It's Doctor Reb and that handsome Mr. Girard. You know how all you young things drool over him. You drool over any man with a pretty face and a good body. Sluts is what you are. You want Father Cyrus, only you're never going to get him. The other ones tried . . ." Abruptly, she stopped talking.

Martha didn't say a word.

"Only way for you to get to me is through these two," Oribel crooned. "Which wouldn't necessarily be a bother to me. The doctor's another one with an eye for Father. Walk, you two," she said. "To the workshop. I don't like a mess in my house."

"Why didn't you want me to see Bonnie's body again?" Reb asked, and Marc held his breath, waiting for the shot that would finish the best thing he'd ever had in his life. Reb just kept on going, "You are one smart cookie, Oribel. I knew you wrote homilies for that no-good husband of yours, and they were good. But I didn't figure you for a real brain. I should have."

"I was always underestimated," Oribel said. "But don't you butter me up. I'm too smart for that, too."

Reb held her tongue.

"How did you figure it was me trying to shut you up?" Oribel said. "Was it in your closet? Or that dumb poodle and the pie. Some faithful friend to man, that is. Wave the food and he's gone."

"All I knew was that someone figured I was a threat — that I could have something damning on them."

"Don't swear in front of a lady," Oribel said. "If Bonnie hadn't come along, I'd have been okay. But she did, and she wanted him. I knew it when she picked that photo out of my garbage and kept the pieces. She never figured I'd seen her do it. That isn't no nephew he's holdin'. I knew by the eyes it was his baby. And it was hers, that Bonnie. That's why she wanted the thing."

It was all enough for Marc. He didn't need more proof of Oribel's guilt, just a little break to allow him to get out with Reb.

Reb said, "That doesn't explain where I figure in," and Marc gritted his teeth.

"Keep walkin'," Oribel said, keeping them between her and the vicinity from which Martha had spoken. "I've had it with talking."

In the distance, on the road, a vehicle approached, and Marc's spirits rose, only to sink again when the noise died away.

The three of them reached the workshop, and Oribel fumbled with a padlock until it opened. She pushed Marc inside first, then shut the door with Reb still outside. "Try anything and she gets it first, Girard," Oribel said.

Fear had done its worst to Reb. She'd arrived at being still terrified but numb, and much more afraid for Marc than herself.

"I only want to tell you," Oribel whispered. "You aren't half bad, or you wouldn't be if you could have quit trying to get between a good man's legs. You've been after Cyrus for years, and him with what they call *arrested development* — with sex, that is. You were just like Louise and Carla, though."

"You *were* the Rubber Killer," Reb said softly. "That's possible enough, I guess. You're a strong woman, and you had surprise on your side. But the first two victims were raped."

Oribel chortled. "In a way. Too bad they died before they could enjoy it. Put a dildo in a rubber and fire away. Easy. I saved Father from them."

"What about Bonnie?"

"Too bad, that. The business with May Lynn and Pepper gave me a way out, and I would have stopped for good." Oribel drove the gun harder into Reb's back. "But Bonnie was the worst of all. I saw her game. She wanted him to leave the priesthood, and the child was her excuse. Still, if she hadn't run into the church like she did that night, I might just have scared her off. I'd already dropped the bike, and I would have played the warning message I had William record. But she ran. Then she saw my face."

Heavy to her bones, Reb said, "You could have helped your daughter if you'd loved her like she loves you. What did you hope to get from a tape recorder in my consulting rooms? A soundtrack of Cyrus being seduced?"

"*Filthy* mind," Oribel said. "Precious is a good girl, but she's too much like her daddy."

Reb heard distinct movements coming from several directions and braced for Oribel to start shouting warnings for people to stay away. Eventually, if there wasn't a miracle, she'd squeeze the trigger.

"First two," Oribel said softly, her lips almost touching Reb's neck, "I thought that coroner might have figured out about the dildo and told you, but you were keeping quiet, not letting on what you and him really thought, to see if it happened again. I didn't see how anyone would figure it out, but it still seemed too easy. After Bonnie I figured you weren't really buying the accident story, but I was settling down again when that Girard arrived with his *exhumation*. He ruined everything. If you all had another chance at the body, you might have been too careful, and maybe there was something to pull me into it."

"That wasn't likely after all those weeks," Reb said and earned herself a whack across the side of the face with the gun.

She took the only chance she expected to get and caught Oribel's gun-toting wrist in a hard grip. It took only a second to figure out that the older woman was unnaturally strong. She swung Reb around her body and slammed her on the ground, knocking all her wind out and leaving her grasping her diaphragm.

Reb remained where she was, pretending she'd hit her head.

"You'd never have made it on the stage," Oribel said, chuckling.

Motion stirred the damp air. Reb opened her eyes to the impression of whirling figures, flying, kung-foo like, feet off the ground.

"Martha," Marc's voice cried. "Don't walk off. You'll get lost or injured."

"Sit on the ground," Spike shouted. "You're going to be okay."

Oribel was flattened, facedown, on gravel and uneven ground. She struggled enough for Marc to put more effort into restraining her. He pulled her arms up behind her back, and Spike snapped on handcuffs.

Sniffling, Martha joined the gathering, and Reb's eyes stretched wide open when she realized Cyrus had the girl in a hammerlock and had confiscated her weapon. The night glasses Martha had bragged about were pushed up on his forehead.

Reb wondered how much he'd heard of what Oribel said about killing to save him.

Madge stood on the other side of Martha, but

looked only at her boss; and for Reb, sadness pierced the madness of it all.

"Wally?" she said quietly. The door to the workshop was still closed, but she pulled it open. "How did you get out, Marc? Is . . . is he in there?"

"In there and okay," he told her. "I told him not to come out here yet. She made him get inside a burlap bag and tied it shut. Reckoned she'd feed him to the gators if he made a sound. There's a window on the other side. I climbed out and ran slap bang into Officer Friendly."

A ripple of laughter quickly faded.

"Stop her!" Reb started toward Oribel, but Marc fell on Oribel first. The woman had already sucked a shard of broken glass into her mouth and began to crush it between her teeth. Marc held her cheek on the ground. On her knees, Reb jammed a piece of wood between her jaws and went to work cleaning out debris.

Madge, with a sharp edge in her voice, said, "Don't you dare do a thing like that, Oribel Scully. Why, you'll never get into heaven if you do."

Engrossed, Reb made a note to tell Madge what usually happened with glass ingested by a human — very little.

Marc shifted, and Spike hauled Oribel, coughing and spitting, to her feet.

Looking past the woman at Reb, Marc smiled at her and tossed Oribel's gun to Spike, who said, "A .32 caliber Guardian ACP. Takes those bullets Bonnie had in her purse. Guess this could turn out to be one less thing to look for."

"Hick," Oribel said clearly. "Pumped-up, no-account apology for a law man. Careful where you keep the pistol, sonny. You wouldn't want to shoot your tiny little treasure off."

"That's it," Spike said; then he yelled, "I want some peace, y'all. Y'hear?"

AD
7/03
9H

ʃ∂
2/05

MG
5/03

ML   W   N⁴⁄₀₃